We'll Have the Summer

the Summer

A heartwarming novel about
Love, Life and Horses

Dutch Henry

2nd edition, revised

For my wife and daughter, with love.

Acknowledgements

This is the second edition of this my first published novel. Then as now I am filled with gratitude. The contributions, help and encouragement of family and friends keep me going then as now. I thank them for their loving guidance, helpful advice and feedback.

I love the new cover designed by Troy Locker Palmer but I have to tell you the incredible story of the original cover. When I wrote I did not yet know MaryAnn Kennedy, Brave or Helen and Jerry Cary. The string of 'coincidences' I'm about to relate will be hard to believe. While covering a story for the American Competitive Trail Horse Association and *Trail Blazer* magazine I met Helen Cary, the unbelievably talented photographer who took this cover photo. A few weeks later she sent me pictures of wild horses she had photographed in New Mexico. In fact they are the background on the cover. When it came time to create the cover photo I knew no one else could capture my story as well as she. It was Helen who suggested that MaryAnn and Brave be our models. MaryAnn Kennedy is a long time friend of Helen and Jerry. We needed a black and white paint for the horse, and MaryAnn's horse, Brave, is black and white. While my horse in the story is named Comanche as opposed to Brave, both are Native American names. Brave was also a rescue. Comanche and Brave both have one blue eye—the right one. The central character in my story is named Mary. MaryAnn also has a rescue horse named Callie; Sam and Mary Holt's daughter's name. The male model with MaryAnn is Helen's husband Jerry, who is a Vietnam vet like Sam Holt. Incredible coincidences, for sure. We feel our lives' paths crossed for a reason. It was meant to be.

MaryAnn Kennedy is a Grammy nominated singer/songwriter of songs for horse lovers. You can get to know her at MaryAnnKennedy.com. Her songs are fun, inspiring and touching.

Helen Cary is a professional photographer and you can contact her at HelenCary@bellsouth.net

Chapter One

L ast night's call had not been a complete surprise. In fact, when the phone rang at half past eight, she'd had an uneasy feeling it would be Dr. Stein. She was thankful Sam had fallen asleep and hadn't heard the ring. No need to worry him, yet. Taking another sip of coffee, Mary tried to push the call out of her mind, tried to plan some sort of activity that might clear her head. She managed a halfhearted smile as she studied the neat rows of flowerpots on the porch windowsills. First, she'd tend to her violets. Arizona's early June heat demanded she water the violets nearly every day. A small chore she looked forward to, and it was just about the only gardening she could do anymore. Not that she had ever been such a great gardener, but she'd enjoyed tending flowers of all kinds— potted, bedded, or wild.

Her morning routine had become, routine. Or, as her dear Sam liked to tell her, "as dependable as the sunrise." Every morning she gave herself a few minutes on their screened porch to sip a cup of coffee and watch the goings-on in the corrals. Then, depending on her energy level, she would either mount her golf cart and motor off to *supervise* Sam, or retreat to the cool comfort of the house. Lately she'd been doing a lot more retreating than supervising. She smiled to herself when she thought about the first time, he'd called her his "supervisor." Sweet Sam. He'd known she'd been too sick from chemo to do anything more than sit in the shade and watch him train a three-year- old mare. She'd caught him keeping watch over her one morning four years ago. He explained he was grateful for an

1

extra pair of eyes because the young mare was a bit sassy. Mary's role was "to serve in a supervisory capacity and make sure I don't miss any small details that might help the filly." Sam had a way of making everyone feel useful.

This morning she pondered the milky brown liquid, stirring it longer than usual and breathing in its rich aroma. *Dr. Stein will probably say I should give up coffee, too.* Ah well, she'd keep the coffee. Not much else left to give up.

She didn't cry, but her eyes stung as she watched Sam drive the old green truck and trailer around the house and on toward the barn and corrals. She loved him so. She loved the life they'd lived together. And she wanted more of it. More than it seemed they would be allowed to have.

As lately it had been wont to do with increasing regularity, her mind drifted back over that wonderful life. She touched a fingertip to the tiny diamond on her finger. Thirty-five years ago they'd been newlyweds. Thirty years ago, they'd bought this ranch together. Ten years ago they didn't owe a penny for the twenty-eight-thousand acres they had named, "Mar-Sa"— their names put together. A lot of folks had done that sort of thing in the seventies. For thirty years she'd worked next to Sam, spending almost as many hours in the saddle as him, doing whatever a working cattle ranch demanded. They raised beef to pay the bills, and a few years ago they had begun hosting paying guests who wanted to experience ranch life, but Sam's heart, like hers, was with the horses.

They'd raised a daughter, too ... There had been a time when the three of them could take on the world.

Mary wiped her eyes, moved around her violets, and, with her thumbnail, pinched off dead leaves. While she fussed over them, she kept one eye on the big corral next to the barn.

Twenty-five horses milled around in the big corral. Rusty, the only hand they could now afford to keep, sat on the top rail and waited for the truck to stop. Mary thought he and Sam had planned to trim hooves today, but seeing the trailer, she got the feeling Sam had changed his mind.

ठ»ᢌठ»ᢌठ»ᢌ

Rusty swung down from the rail and yanked on the Chevy's stubborn door handle. "Got no lights in the barn."

Sam nodded, then started for the trailer. "Reckon we won't for a little while."

"That means no electric in the lodge. Got to get it back before all the food goes to waste. Probably top a hundred again today. It'll be right hot in the house for Mary."

Sam paused at the rear of the trailer and looked toward the house. He could see Mary through the screen. She blew a kiss. He sent one back.

"Thought you were goin' to town to pay on the power bill. Got folks comin' Saturday. They're gonna want the air conditioners workin' in those cabins."

Sam swung open the trailer door. "We got to get him out of there ... Maybe we can give the folks a taste of real ranch life. Show 'em what it's like to rough it. Those pod things all these young kids got stuck in their ears work off batteries anyway, don't they?"

Rusty studied the poor horse standing in the hot trailer, leaning against the partition. Fifteen hands of bones with a hairy hide draped over them. Sam was sure Rusty knew where the power bill money had gone. Half the horses in the corral behind them had arrived in the same condition.

"Just had to swing by the horse auction while you were in town."

"Had some time before West Side Electric opened." Sam scratched the skinny horse's rump. "Killer buyer had him at one hundred fifty;

I put up our one sixty. Look in his eyes, Rusty. He ain't ready to die yet."

Together they backed the wobbly paint down the trailer ramp, then guided him into the first box stall on the left. The poor fella's hooves were so long, he nearly walked on his pasterns. He did have a spark in his eyes, though. They leaned on the stall door, watching the emaciated gelding pick at the soft hay in the corner, and almost didn't notice the sound of Mary's golf cart as it pulled into the aisle behind them.

"Sam, Sam, Sam." She smiled while she said it. No matter his own worries, she knew it would be an odd day indeed when Sam didn't give his last dollar, or breath, if he saw a need.

Sam turned, helped Mary from her cart, and walked her to the stall door. "What do you see?"

"No electric, paying guests coming in three days, food spoiling in the freezer, vet bills, and a missed mortgage payment."

"I have a plan for all that." He ran a hand down her arm and gently squeezed her hand. "Look at this poor fella again."

The paint bent his neck to look toward the stall door. His eyes, though sunken, were beautiful. One icy blue, the other a rich brown, but both shone with the same gripping intensity.

For a second, he looked about to nicker, but with a feeble head shake he turned back to the hay. Mary studied him a minute longer, then let out a soft gasp. "Comanche! Why, it can't be!" The skeletal horse standing before them had only been gone three years.

Weak as she was, she found strength enough to force her way between the two men and into the stall.

Only Sam noticed the lights come on.

The stall fan started with a puff of dust.

Then a dually pickup dragging a gooseneck stock trailer swung around the barnyard and came to a rattling stop in front of the corral.

Rusty looked at Sam, puzzled.

"Ran into Fred Jones in town this mornin'," Sam said. Mary turned to Sam, but her hands never stopped stroking the paint's back. "You're not selling horses. You can't bring Comanche back to me and in the same day, the same moment, sell more horses."

Sam pulled off his hat and stared at it as he turned it around in his hands. "Not selling any horses."

"Cows then?" Rusty asked.

"Sixty. Five hundred dollars a head."

Rusty took a long breath and a slow step back, looked at the ground between them and then said, almost in a whisper, "Start selling your breedin' cows and it leads to a mighty rough road."

Sam bit his lip and stood a second watching Mary fuss over Comanche before starting for the door. "I need a word with Fred."

Mary hugged Comanche's neck. She knew she was the reason for the rough road they'd been traveling. She let go, slid down into the soft straw, and just sat there, legs crossed, hands folded in her lap. Dying right now would be okay. Here in this clean straw. Reunited with the finest horse she'd ever known. She felt so much guilt. Poor Comanche, look at him.

Poor Sam, look at him. Her handsome cowboy. The years had really begun to show after she'd become ill. He still had the kindest eyes she'd ever seen. He still had those square, proud shoulders, too.

Sam had argued, almost violently, when she insisted three years ago they sell Comanche to pay on those mounting hospital bills. Mary tried to keep in touch with the Hardens. But as the pressures intensified here at home, and her stays in Conner County General became longer and more frequent, the correspondence eventually ended. They had seemed like such nice people, and their daughter was a skilled rider. If they didn't want Comanche anymore, why not simply return him? No, angry as she was at the moment, she couldn't blame the Hardens. They must have sold Comanche to someone else. Horses got sold every day.

"You going to be all right, Mrs. Holt?" Rusty asked. "I should give Sam a hand."

"I don't know." She'd cried so many times the past few years—never for herself, but for Sam and for their daughter, Callie. But she really wanted to cry now. Just be left alone to sit in the straw and cry. "Why don't you hand me my cane, and I'll sit here with Comanche. You go on, help Sam."

"I'm not sure about that. He's so weak he's likely to fall on you."

"Please hand me my cane, and go help Sam." The sternness in her voice was out of character and surprised her.

Chapter Two

Barbara sat on the kitchen counter, purposefully avoiding her mother and Philip, offering no assistance as they readied the car for the trip to the airport. Nothing she ever thought or said mattered to them anyway. She found this stupid idea of Philip's to spend the summer on some filthy ranch in the middle of nowhere disgusting. Just because their marriage was screwed up, why should she be forced to shovel horse crap for three months? Her mother made her sick, bouncing around the house like a newlywed the last few weeks, all excited about this ridiculous trip. She glared through the kitchen doorway at Philip as he wandered around the living room adjusting timers on the lights. What a pig he was. Maybe he'll fall off a horse and choke on his lying tongue. She could hope at least.

Philip finished with the timers, did a last check on all the window locks, then came to the kitchen and offered his hand. "Come on, Barbara."

"When I'm ready. I'll get in the car when Mother comes down." She knew he hated it when she talked back, which was why she did it all the time.

"Okay," Linda appeared in the living room, "I think we're ready to travel. Barbara, dear, how do I look?" She spun a graceful pirouette in the doorway, then finished with a dainty curtsy.

She had to admit, her mother looked pretty good in those tight jeans and that red cotton blouse. "You look fine."

"You look delicious." Philip put his hands on his wife's hips and drew her close.

"Let's get in the car." Barbara slid from the countertop and made certain to bump them as she passed by on her way to the front door.

She crawled into the backseat and watched Philip through the windshield as he strolled hand-in-hand with her mother toward the car.

What a pig. She glared at Philip.

Chapter Three

Sam, Fred, and Rusty leaned against Fred's dually in the barnyard while Sam drew pictures in the dust on the truck's hood. The air hung heavy with tension. No one had anything to say for a while.

"Fred, reckon you and Rusty can load those cows all right?" Sam tipped his hat back, staring straight into the bright midmorning sun, then refocused on his hand. "Mary will most likely want to spend the day in the stall with Comanche. I figured I'd stay with her, maybe work on his feet." Sam finished drawing a perfectly trimmed hoof in the dust then stared blankly down the lane.

"We'll get the cows. You go on in there. Mary needs you a dang sight more than we do."

"What cows are you sellin', boss?" Rusty asked.

"Anything wearing a yellow ear tag you boys can coax into the crowdin' pens on the north pasture." Sam started toward the barn.

"You ain't got but sixty of those two-year-olds left."

Sam stopped walking. "Load the heifers." He turned to Fred. "I appreciate this, neighbor."

"Been neighbors a long time. I'm just grateful I'm in a position to help out."

Rusty smacked his hat against his thigh, then fanned it in the little dust cloud he'd made. He nodded to Sam and climbed in the passenger side without another word.

Fred started his truck and leaned out the window. "If you don't mind me hanging onto Rusty for the day, I'll haul two loads today and two tomorrow."

Sam nodded and waved them on.

Standing just outside the barn door, Sam watched the gooseneck kick up a swirling dust cloud as it disappeared over the first rise. It was hard selling those two-year-old heifers. Selling off his future worried him as much as it did Rusty, but he could keep that to himself all right. With Fred's money and the money coming from the families arriving in the next couple of days, he could catch up on the new mortgage, pay a little on the hospital bill, and hold back enough to operate right up 'til December.

Seemed the money always wanted to run out over Christmas.

When the truck was gone from sight, he went inside the barn and stood quietly watching Mary dote over Comanche. "Needs a fair amount of attention, doesn't he?"

Comanche picked at the hay in the corner while Mary brushed him, singing softly. As Sam watched, his mind was playing tricks on him. His eyes saw a horse being raised back to life by a woman who was struggling to hang onto life herself. His mind's eye saw a stunning paint mustang being ridden by a beautiful and vibrant Mary. In that moment he heard the cheers from the crowd as Mary and Comanche finished their musical freestyle riding competition to win the state championship. It had taken the announcer nearly five minutes to quiet the crowd after Mary and Comanche had finished their bows. Sam wondered if the old boy still remembered how to bow.

What a day that had been. Mary and Comanche had captured first place in adult freestyle, and then Callie and Comanche had won the junior division. Two blue ribbons in one day, to one family—one horse.

Now that magnificent mustang had come back into their lives. This time he needed their help. It troubled Sam immensely, how close this wonderful horse had come to death. Had he not gone to town to pay the power bill; Comanche would be on his way to Mexico—to be slaughtered—instead of standing here with Mary. He couldn't help but wonder what had caused him to hook the trailer on the truck this morning before he'd left for town. He hadn't pulled that trailer for months. Hang, the brakes hadn't worked for more than a year.

"Oh, Sam, I hate that you need to sell your heifers." Mary looked to Sam with red, wet eyes. "I don't know how I could have ever sold Comanche."

Sam saw it coming. Mary was about to break down again. He flung the door open and hurried to her side. With his right arm on Comanche's back and his left arm around Mary's waist, he held them both close. Mary dropped her head on the horse's back, her tears dripping down the valleys of Comanche's ribs.

He stroked his wife's hair and allowed the thin gray and white strands to pass through his fingers. Not a trace of the thick chestnut brown remained. "We still have the older cows and thirty-two yearlin' heifers and the start of a fine batch of spring calves. Why, Rusty went out two days ago and counted thirty-seven calves."

Mary looked up and wiped her eyes on the back of her hand. "I'm sorry."

"Sorry for what?"

"Acting like a child."

"Nothing more precious than a child who can cry when they're supposed to. Or a grown woman, for that matter." He kissed her forehead.

"Oh, Sam! I did this to him."

"Here, here." Sam whispered and wrapped his arms around Mary's tiny waist, holding her close. Her eyes found his. "We don't know who did this to him. Hopefully we never will, because likely I'd kill the lout. What's important now is by some miracle Comanche has found us, and by God, we're going to do all we can for him."

As if following some unheard command, Comanche turned and nuzzled Mary so eagerly she nearly fell from Sam's embrace.

"What do you think? It appears he's ready for me to have a look at those feet." He had to laugh. That horse always could make Sam chuckle.

She wiped her eyes again and flashed a crooked smile. "I think he's stronger than he looks. That's what I think."

"I'll be right back." Sam left a bewildered Mary standing by her horse, sprinted to the golf cart, then drove at top speed to the house.

He raced the small white cart across the driveway, bouncing and swaying all the way to the house. Then, his antics funny enough for a comedic routine, Sam pitched a lawn chair onto the back of the cart and disappeared into the house. He ran back down the steps and held up a pitcher of iced tea as if carrying the Olympic Torch. With a boy-like spring in his step, Sam mounted the cart and drove only slightly less recklessly back to the barn, steering with one hand and holding the iced tea pitcher high in the other. He let go a happy laugh as he skidded to a stop just inside the doors. He knew he was putting on a first-rate show for his gal. That had been his plan.

Mary greeted him in the aisle with a shake of her head, a frown he knew wasn't real, and a waggling finger. "I'd better find a piece of plywood, so I can paint a speed limit sign and have Rusty mount it on a fence post."

Sam handed her the nearly empty pitcher, "Great idea. Then I won't have to drive all the way to Route ninety-six to get my speedin' tickets!"

"You haven't had a speeding ticket in twenty-five years!"

"Do you figure that's because they don't allow golf carts on Route ninety-six?" He snatched the chair from the cart and set it against the stall wall.

"Have a seat, beautiful." He took her hand and guided her to the chair, then gave a bow as if the white plastic chair were a throne and she a queen. Next, he hustled to the far end of the barn, grabbed a bale of straw from the stack, sprinted back to Mary, and set the bale next to her chair. Turning to the cart, he snatched a red and white checked tablecloth, waved it Matador fashion, spread it over the bale, and placed two coffee cups next to the pitcher of tea.

"Anything else the most beautiful gal this side of the Mississippi desires?"

"Nothing I can think of, other than a sweet kiss from the handsomest cowboy to ever drive a golf cart."

He swooped his hat from his head, dropped to one knee, pulled her tight, and pressed his lips to hers.

"That, Cowboy, is how a woman likes to be kissed." Fanning her face and flirting with her eyes, she reached for the pitcher and poured what little tea had survived the trip, equally into the two cups.

Sam raised his cup and offered a toast. "To Comanche!" Mary raised hers. "To Comanche!"

Comanche poked his head over the door. Sam had always suspected that the horse understood English. With a grin to Mary, Sam downed his tea, jumped up, took Comanche by the forelock, and walked him to the center of the aisle. "Whoa," he commanded with a proud smile. Comanche stood as he had been schooled to stand years ago and waited patiently while Sam crossed the aisle to the tack room and grabbed his bucket of hoof-trimming tools.

With the palms of his hands, Sam rubbed Comanche's cheeks to loosen the dead skin from where a halter had been left on, probably until it had rotted away and fallen off. Next, he examined the rotten skin under the horse's chin. Comanche jerked his head away when Sam dug at the stinking flesh with his thumbnail.

"Sorry, fella, but I'll need to clean up this nasty thing." He examined the old wound, then went back to the tack room for supplies. When he returned, Mary was standing beside Comanche, stroking his ears.

"I'll take one of those wipes, please." She held out her hand, giving Sam a look that told him she was having the first go at Comanche's physical therapy and rehabilitation. Mary wrapped the small wet towel around her finger and wiped gobs of black crud from inside Comanche's ears. As she nursed the horse, her eyes gleamed. Her movements, for the first time in too long, were decisive and strong. There was an aura about Mary that seemed to cloak her and the weak horse. Sam sat on the straw bale to bask in her tenderness and wait his turn at Comanche. Mary became completely involved with the task at hand and, gently and patiently, used wipe after wipe until, finally, the cooperative horse's ears were clean as a newborn foal's.

"Sit here and rest while I take a look at that sore under his chin."

"Hand me a few more towels. I'll clean this wound, then you can start on his feet."

"Maybe you should take a break," he argued.

"I will in a few moments, but I would like to dress this wound first."

Thirty-five years had taught Sam when his sweet Mary held firm, it was best to go along. He smiled, handed her the container of wipes, and placed a steadying hand on Comanche's forehead. In no time she had the sore cleaned and coated with a pink healing salve.

"Now, Cowboy, he's all yours." She returned the smile and retired to the chair.

Sam stroked Comanche along his neck and over his back. Mary had done a great job brushing him, and even though his hair was brittle and coarse, it was dirt free. He studied Comanche's feet while he petted him, then bent down, picked up the left front foot, placed it on the hoof stand, snared his hoof nippers from the bucket, and skillfully shaped a hoof nearly as perfect as the one he had drawn in the dust on Fred's truck hood an hour earlier. Without a break, he moved to Comanche's right front and trimmed it just as deftly.

"Might be best to leave 'em a little long for a week or so, fella. Give your tendons and pasterns some time to adjust to the new angle. In a week you can make another appointment. Then I'll give you a proper manicure."

He winked to Mary, but she'd fallen asleep. Carefully and quietly, so as not to wake her, Sam trimmed Comanche's hind feet. He was admiring his work when Fred's diesel came rumbling down the slope toward the barn.

"Oh my, I must've fallen asleep. I'm sorry." Mary pulled herself up in the chair.

"Just long enough for me to trim his hooves without you supervisin'," Sam teased.

"They look wonderful. Poor Comanche, he's absolutely exhausted."

"He's had a long day of it already, sure enough. Let's put him back in his stall and let him eat and rest awhile. It's time you get back to the house for a little rest yourself."

Together they put Comanche away, gathered the cups, and with Mary driving, headed for the house. She parked the cart next to the porch steps in the tin-roofed carport Sam had built a few years earlier when she made driving the golf cart part of her daily routine. The sign above read, "Golf Carts only." Today she didn't use the handrail he'd recently installed between the cart's assigned parking space and the steps. She did accept his offered arm, and leaned heavily on it as they negotiated the five steps leading to the front door. Before she entered the house, she looked back to the window in Comanche's stall. Sam followed her gaze. Comanche's head stuck out the window, and he was watching them with a long piece of hay dangling from his mouth. Sam knew he was smiling at them. He wondered if Comanche was remembering the time, so many years ago, when Callie had led him up those very steps and into the kitchen. That was years before he'd closed in the porch ... That was a lifetime ago

Chapter Four

Mary washed dishes while Sam relaxed at the tiny round table on the porch. As he dipped the last piece of his egg sandwich in his coffee, he spied Susan driving her Gator ATV in a direct line for the barn. He ran out onto the steps and waved for her to come to the house.

"Mornin', Susan," Sam said, swinging the screen door wide.

"I'm so excited! Rusty told me Comanche's home. How is he?"

"Mary's already given him the once over, and I started getting his feet in shape."

Mary joined them on the porch. "He must have had a terrible time. He never deserved this … He's in awful shape." She shook her head and took a long breath. "I wish …"

Susan offered a comforting smile. "He's home now."

Mary settled into the hanging porch swing and set it in motion with a push of her cane. "Home to stay." She patted the seat beside her. "Sit a while before you start … whatever you have planned for today."

Susan looked across the way to Comanche, who was hanging his head out the window again. "No, I'm going to say hello to Comanche first. You sit here and rest. I'll be right back. We do need to discuss supplies for this weekend."

Jumping to his feet, Sam swung the screen door open, then changed his mind. "Hang on a second." He shot them an ear-to-ear grin, let the door swing shut with a bang, and dashed to the kitchen. Knowing they were watching, he danced a bit of a cowboy jig as he washed and cut several apples and tossed the slices in a large bowl, all the while examining each slice as if preparing a fine meal. "Here you go." Sam proudly handed the bowl to Susan. "He's probably ready for a treat. Wouldn't you figure?"

"Yes, I *figure* he is." She gave him the pretend smirk she always gave him when correcting his grammar. He responded with the usual practiced look of befuddlement, pretending not to understand. And a wink. Susan snatched the bowl of apples, raised up on her tiptoes, and gave Sam a serious kiss on the cheek. Even though he knew she did it to make him blush, he blushed.

"Doggone you, Susan. Comanche's waitin' on them apples." He purposely put emphasis on *them*.

"I'm on my way." Susan shook a finger. "*Those* apples."

Sam winked again. "Uh-huh."

Mary motioned for Sam to sit beside her. Together they watched Susan cross the driveway and disappear into the barn. Comanche's head disappeared from the window. She took his hand and patted it gently. "She loves you for what you did, you know."

He shook his head. "I didn't do anything anybody else wouldn't've done."

"No one else would have Rusty when he was released from prison ... You were the only one."

"Well, heck, we needed the help at the time."

Mary cocked her head. "Uh-huh."

"He and Susan have been a great asset to our little outfit. And he's stayed sober since day one. That was the deal."

"You kept him sober." She kissed him.

"Didn't take all that much doin'. Just a little encouragement once in a while." Sam grinned, remembering one of the few times in sixteen years he'd had to ride herd on Rusty when he was going through a rough patch.

"You gave them a new start, self-respect, and a house they could call their own. She loves you for it ... And so do I!" She smothered him with a hug and kissed him again.

Sam struggled to free himself and shrugged, "I didn't give 'em their house. He built his own house, by golly."

"Yes he did, on your land, on your time, with your lumber, you big sweet, generous cowboy." She hugged him again.

He held the hug long enough to let her know how much he loved *her*. He knew he'd be nothing without her. He knew he'd never have been any good to anybody without his Mary.

"I reckon it's time I start trimmin' hooves. I've been stallin' long enough." He leaned forward, grinned, and rubbed his lower back. "This old back of mine isn't what it used to be, but it's gonna get real busy around here day after tomorrow so I'd best get crackin'." He gave her a firm smile. "When it gets too hot, you go inside."

"I intend to rest awhile, visit Comanche, then check on the cabins."

"I'm sure Susan has the cabins ready to go."

"Just the same, I'd like to go through them. I may even spend some time in the lodge kitchen."

He knew it had nothing to do with whether Mary trusted Susan to have the cabins and lodge ready for the guests. It had always been her way to do a final inspection before the guests arrived.

"Well, if you don't feel up to it today, you can check on the cabins tomorrow."

"I'd rather do it today, in case you decide to bring home another surprise."

Sam rose from the porch swing and turned to face her. "Not planning on any more surprises."

"I have always loved your surprises." Her eyes telegraphed that love.

He kissed her forehead and headed for the corral. Halfway there, he made a detour to Comanche's stall and stood quietly in the door while Susan offered the paint her last slice of apple.

"It's nice to see you haven't lost any of your manners, Comanche," Susan told the horse as he carefully used his lips to pick the thin slice of apple from the palm of her hand.

"Except for being two hundred pounds underweight, I believe he's the same horse who left us three years ago," Sam said.

"I don't know how anyone can do this to a horse." She brushed Comanche's rangy forelock from his eyes. "I sure hope there's a special place down below for that kind of person."

"The way I picture it, there's a place there where all the miserable louts can see everything they want, but they can't manage to get hold of it. For all eternity, just over the next hill, they can see, and even smell, all the food they want. But it's always just out of reach. They can see Heaven, way off in the distance. They walk and run, pushing, shoving, and fighting—but Heaven never gets any closer. Anyway, that's how I have it figured."

"I could second that idea. Maybe we should add the fires nipping at their heels."

Sam put his hand on Susan's shoulder and gave it a soft squeeze. "And a few bolts of lightning." He shook his head. "It's a mighty sad thing to see a horse in this condition." He turned to look toward the house. "Maybe you could go to the house in a little while. Mary was planning on a nap, and then she wanted to take a final run through the cabins. I'll be out here in the lean-to workin' on feet the rest of the afternoon."

He reached for the lead rope hanging from a peg on the wall, then went to the corral. As he swung the gate open, a good-looking sorrel quarter horse left the herd and trotted to him. Chester had been there fifteen years and knew the routine very well. Sam dropped the rope over Chester's neck and scratched his withers.

"Come on, Chester. You can be first." He led the horse to the lean-to, stood him squarely in the shade, reached up, and snapped on the fan. Most every horse in the corral could be ridden and handled by anyone. Chester, though, was their very best lesson horse. Over the years, dozens of folks had enjoyed their first ride on the quiet sorrel. For a few seconds, he leaned on Chester's back, remembering Callie's first ride. Remembering when Callie had been their little blond-haired girl, riding like the wind before her legs were even long enough to use the stirrups. Over the years, Callie and Chester had become inseparable. Sure, Comanche was more exciting, and Callie had loved to show off with him ... But Chester—he'd been her teacher.

When he finished with Chester's feet, he turned him out into the night pasture. Seventy acres that ran right up to the barn with plenty of water and grass. Even in a dry year like this one, the stream running through the night pasture never quit flowing.

An hour later, three more horses had been turned into the night pasture with Chester, their feet shaped to suit Sam. He was dropping the rope around the neck of the next horse when Fred Jones' rig rumbled up the lane. Sam didn't need another interruption, so he grabbed his hat and waved it. Fred tapped the horn as he drove by.

In the time since Mary and Susan had passed him in the golf cart on their way to the lodge, Sam had finished another five horses and turned them out into the big pasture. Deciding he'd earned a break;

he hung his hoof trimming chaps over the fence and started up the hill toward the lodge. His empty belly was making noises that would soon be loud enough to spook a horse.

The lodge sat atop a gentle rise behind the barn, about a quarter mile from the house. He and Mary had laid out the lodge site and the camp area for the guest cabins on the east side of the slope, so everything would be visible from the porch of the house. The lodge wasn't really a lodge at all. It was more of a roofed pavilion with a dirt floor and adobe walls three feet high on three sides. Large enough for the dozen picnic tables where the guests gathered for three meals a day, when they weren't on the range or an overnight trail ride. The kitchen area was completely closed in and included the washer and dryer for the guests.

The cabins were adobe as well. Three of them were only two years old. They had been built during the season with labor provided by guests who had asked to learn the art of adobe construction. Sam chuckled to himself when he thought about that summer. Without help, he and Rusty could build a cabin in three weeks from floor to roof, including doors, windows, plumbing, and electricity. That summer, with the benefit of two families' labor, they had barely managed to get the walls rafter-high before the season ended. Mary would point out, that the long construction period did include the four weeks it required for the adobe bricks to bake in the sun. An important fact that Sam conveniently failed to recall every time he told the story.

"I was sure hoping you ladies could fix a starving fellow a sandwich. I can feel my belly button ticklin' my backbone." Sam slid onto the bench at the table nearest the kitchen.

"You know the food in here is for the guests, but I suppose we could spare those two moldy pieces of bread, wouldn't you think, Mary?" Susan teased.

"We did find a piece of petrified bacon under the refrigerator," Mary joined in with a silly grin.

"I've had my eye on that piece of bacon jerky for some time now, and I was waiting for the right occasion. Go ahead, ladies, serve it up!"

Sam pointed to the dust cloud coming their way. "My guess is Fred and Rusty are gonna tote their empty bellies in here in about one minute. Better break out the bread and sugar-cured ham." He rubbed his hands together like a ten-year-old contemplating a Christmas present.

Susan simply smiled and swung open the big, double door refrigerator and retrieved a five-pound ham. Mary sat a pitcher of ice water and glasses on the table.

Just as Sam had predicted, the truck and trailer came to a noisy, dusty stop alongside the lodge, and Rusty and Fred joined Sam at the table.

"I guess we'll call it a day," Fred said. "I can leave Rusty here. My boys and I'll unload this bunch. I'll be back first thing in the morning for the next load."

Mary and Susan brought a plate full of sandwiches to the table and sat down with the men.

"I know what to do with this, sure enough." Fred snatched a sandwich before the plate settled on the table. "Thank you, Mary."

"You're welcome. Careful you don't bite your finger, now."

"Rusty tells me you've got folks arriving Saturday," Fred mumbled, chewing.

"Sure do. Four families. All but one will stay clear through Labor Day," Sam said.

"Well, that's good to hear. If me and the boys can help out in any way at all, you let us know."

"Could use Morgan's help wrangling again this summer. Problem is, even with all this," he waved toward Fred's rig, "we're still short of cash."

Mary reached across the table for Sam's hand.

"Tell you what we'll do. On the last trip out of here tomorrow, we'll load one of your two-year-old bulls on the trailer with the cows." Fred tapped the table with his fingers and grinned at Rusty. "That is, if Rusty can get one cornered."

"Oh, I can corral one for you." Rusty gave Sam a sly wink. "I know just the one."

"All right then, it's settled." Fred stuffed the last bite of sandwich in his mouth. "I'll take the bull, and you'll have a wrangler."

"I'll have his room ready in the morning," Susan said. "The same one he used last year. In the barn by the tack room?"

Sam gave her a nod and walked with Fred to his truck.

"Like I said before, you're a good neighbor."

"Like I said before, I'm glad I'm in a position I *can* help. I don't recall you giving it a second thought ten years ago when I needed your help. It's what we do out here. Lend each other a hand from time to time. You go on back to Mary, and I'll see you in the morning."

Sam stood, rigid and solemn, turning his hat over and over in his hand as he watched Fred drive away. He stood motionless until the dust raised by Fred's rig was a mile away, floating upward, unfolding like a storm cloud that was played out.

Chapter Five

As Sam walked through the barn doors, he could hear Mary telling Morgan that Comanche had opened his stall door latch overnight, one of the clever horse's old habits. Her soft chuckle as she spoke was like music to him. As his eyes adjusted to the dimmer inside light, he saw Morgan standing at Comanche's stall.

"Mornin', Morgan," he greeted the young man with a warm smile and firm handshake. "Good to have you back. Take your time settlin' in, but when you're ready to get at it, saddle the trail horses and take each of 'em for a short ride. We want to make sure they're all ready for our guests."

"Sure thing, and I'm ready right now. Spent the last hour setting up my room, and I was just about to come looking for you." He turned to Mary. "Anyway, Mrs. Holt, it's real good to see Comanche again. I know you'll have him in top shape in no time at all."

"That's my plan." She looked Sam dead in the eye, wiped her hands together and planted them on her hips. "I intend to ride him in this year's musical freestyle at the state fair. And gentlemen, I've promised Comanche a blue ribbon!"

Sam lost his balance and sucked in a short breath. Even if Comanche could be in shape in barely ninety days, a ridiculous thought in itself, Mary hadn't sat a horse in longer than three years. He hoped his shock and doubt hadn't been painted across his face. He'd support her in anything at all, even a crazy idea like this, if it gave her a dream to chase. Anything that could make her go on fighting. He knew he could live without a lot of things. He'd learned that. But Mary wasn't one of them. Right then, almost out loud, Sam thanked God for that poor, starved paint horse.

Pushing his way past Morgan, who stood slack-jawed in the stall door, Sam scooped Mary up, swung her in a circle any ho-downer would be proud of, and hugged her tight, planting a kiss right where it belonged. "By golly, Mary, we'll have him ready. That, my sassy little cowgirl, I promise you!"

Mary's face flushed, but her smile was wider than Sam had seen in years. "Well, Cowboy, I will have no choice but to hold you to your word."

Morgan stepped into the stall. "Mrs. Holt, I was a little fella when you won the state blue ribbon, but I remember it fine. I'd be honored to be your crew. That is, if Mr. Holt doesn't mind."

"If she'll have you, go right ahead, but remember I won't always be around to cover for you, and she can be intolerably demanding when she feels a competition closin' in."

"Don't frighten the boy away." Her eyes told him she thanked him for the compliment. "Morgan, would you mind inspecting the fence around the yard? I planned on putting Comanche in the yard at night. That way he can have some grass and get plenty of exercise. It does him no good to stand in this stall all night, and I wouldn't feel safe turning him out into the night pasture with the others in his present condition."

Mary gave the stall latch a knowing glance. Morgan smiled. Sam studied both their faces. Certain he'd missed a punch line.

"I'll take a walk around the yard right away. Then, Mr. Holt, I'll start working the trail horses and inspecting tack." Morgan tipped his hat and trotted from the barn.

Sam grinned and shook his head, "See what I mean? You have the poor boy running already."

"Sam, lift me up."

He had been about to argue, but decided it was worth the risk. He gathered Mary in his arms, stepped toward Comanche, and as gently as he knew how, lifted her onto his back. He felt Comanche tremble, then toughen up and accept the weight.

"Oh, Sam, how I've missed this." Even though she knew Comanche was horribly weakened, she could feel his energy passing to her. His bony back poked at her as she sat, but his warmth softened her and made her feel more alive than she'd felt for longer than she could remember. She was glad for Sam's arm still around her waist, but it was the sense of oneness with Comanche that overwhelmed her at the moment. She leaned forward, smothered her face in his mane, and wrapped her arms around his neck.

Still resting her cheek on Comanche's neck, Mary turned to smile at Sam. "Okay, help me down, please."

As gently as he'd lifted her up, Sam helped her from the horse.

"I think those sixty seconds have done more for me than all the chemotherapy in the world." She meant what she said. But now, she wished she hadn't said it. She didn't mean it the way Sam was most certainly going to take it. She hadn't even told him about the phone call from Dr. Stein's office. She'd been wrestling with her decision ever since she'd hung up the phone. Now was certainly no time to start treatments again. She couldn't spare the time. She wouldn't relinquish two days a week to drive sixty-five miles, one way, to be pumped full of toxins. Poisons that would leave her sick and flat on her back the other five days of the week.

His look, his touch, told her he knew exactly what she meant. "I'd better tend to business. I've got forty more hooves to trim."

"I'm taking Comanche to the yard, and I have every intention of sitting in the shade and watching him mow our lawn for the entire day." She tied Comanche's lead rope to the rear of her golf cart.

"I could have walked him for you."

"You've got things to do, and I'm certainly not helpless." She had a hint of cockiness in her voice, and a crooked smile on her lips.

As she stepped into the cart, she did take his arm for balance.

When Sam, Mary, and Comanche broke the shadow of the barn, they saw Morgan trotting their way. He probably would have made a silly comment regarding Mary, Comanche, and the cart, but a rising cloud of dust far out on the end of the lane caught his attention.

Barbara glared out the window when they turned off the hard road and headed down the dusty ranch lane. This can't be anywhere in the United States. The last three days her life (such as it was) had spiraled continually downward, beginning with leaving her friends behind. Next, sitting between her mother and Philip in the center aisle for six hours on a plane and having to spend a night in the same cheap motel room with them. Then yesterday's flight in an airborne museum piece to an airport that didn't even have a paved runway. It had a lovely restroom, though. Outside, around the back. Maybe one day they'd put plumbing in it. Now her cell phone didn't even work. Probably the only place on the face of the earth without cell service.

"Look up there, Barbara," Linda pointed. "That must be the ranch house."

Barbara leaned forward and peered between their heads toward the house.

"Oh, I see the barn. And look, there are the horses!"

Linda slid close to Philip and hugged his neck. "This is so exciting! Do you know I've never even touched a horse?"

Barbara slumped back. "Do you know I don't give a crap if I ever do?"

Philip made eye contact in the rearview mirror with Barbara. She shot daggers back. "Come on, we all agreed to give this a chance."

"I was freaking kidnapped! I didn't agree to anything."

The car slid to a stop, slamming Barbara into the back of the front seat.

"You're old enough to learn to watch your language, young lady," Philip warned.

Linda reached for her daughter, found her knee and squeezed hard. "I'm sure the people out here don't talk like that, dear."

"No. They grunt!" She shoved her mother's hand away. *What does she see in him?* Her mother sure could pick them. And this pig, number three, was the worst. Well maybe except for her own father. Barbara barely remembered him, thankfully.

Barbara and Philip exchanged glances through the rearview mirror again as he drove on—his controlling, hers defiant.

Between the house and barn, Philip brought the car to a stop a safe distance from the people, golf cart, and horse.

Linda was the first to bounce from the car. "Hi, we're the Cunninghams."

A tall man stepped up and shook her hand. "I'm Sam. This is my wife Mary. This young fella here is Morgan, our wrangler. We weren't expecting you until tomorrow. How was your trip?"

"It sucked." Barbara crawled out of the car.

"I'm sorry." Mary smiled at her. "We'll work extra hard to make certain your stay here at Mar-Sa is fun."

Barbara folded her arms and glared at her from a safe distance. "How are you going to do that?" She continued to back away one slow step at a time.

Philip offered Sam his hand. "I'm Philip, this is my wife Linda, and the pleasant one here is our daughter Barbara." The banging and rattling of a truck driving up the long lane interrupted the introductions.

"If you'll excuse me, I'd like to get Comanche in the yard before Fred pulls up." Mary started on her way, leading Comanche toward the house.

"Morgan will show you to your cabin." Sam's eyes bounced from Mary, to the truck, then back to Mary.

"Sure. Sure, I can ... I'll ride with you." Morgan said. "Which one, Mr. Holt?"

Sam was still watching Mary. "Seven." Then he started toward the house.

They piled into the car, Morgan in the back with Barbara, and drove away as the approaching truck and trailer stopped next to Sam in a cloud of dust.

"Just follow this road around the corral. Stay to the right of the lodge. You folks are in cabin seven," Morgan said.

Linda turned to face him. "How many families will be here this season?"

"You folks and three others."

"That's the lodge?" Barbara snapped as they drove by the long pavilion.

"We call it the lodge. It's where we eat when you're not on the trail."

"If you call that a 'lodge,' what do the cabins look like? Tents?"

Barbara got the answer to her question sooner than she liked when Philip stopped the car in the center of a ring of adobe cabins.

"They're not cabins! They're mud huts!"

"Oh, they're adorable." Linda scampered to cabin number seven. She was on the porch in an instant. "Look, Barbara, it has a delightful porch."

"Oh, goody. I bet it has its own dirt floor, too." Barbara groaned out the window, using just the right tone so no one could misunderstand her disgust at the situation she found herself in. She made a big deal of flicking the dust from her arm with her fingertips.

Philip sat behind the wheel and studied the cabins. Morgan opened the car door for Barbara.

She wasn't sure she was even going to get out, but Morgan held the door wide and offered his hand. She didn't know where it came from, but an uneasy feeling blasted her in the stomach. She accepted his hand, slid from the car, and mumbled, "Thank you." As she stepped by him, she caught herself looking him over, then let out a stifled moan and rolled her eyes.

Morgan smiled. "You're welcome, and they have plywood."

Philip pulled the car forward to the obvious parking spot alongside cabin number seven.

"What has plywood?" Barbara asked.

Morgan tossed her a grin, nodded toward the porch. "The cabins. They have plywood floors. No rugs, but plywood floors."

"Oh." She felt that stupid feeling in her stomach again then the teensiest bit of curiosity moved her toward the cabin.

Morgan reached up on the porch rafter and pulled down a key. "You can hang on to this." He unlocked the door, swung it inward and handed the key to Linda.

They stood in the doorway, staring into the cabin. Light streaming into the room through the small windows illuminated thousands of tiny dancing dust particles. Barbara noticed Morgan was at least an inch taller than Philip.

"You folks make yourself at home. If it gets too hot this afternoon, you can snap on the window air conditioner, but mostly these cabins stay pretty cool. It's the coolest place on the ranch with the tall trees and the big stream running just behind here." He turned and looked squarely at Barbara. "A few hundred yards down the stream, there's even a decent swimming hole."

She glared at him, not caring if the disgust showed on her face or not. Did this idiot think she would swim in some crappy mud hole? What a jerk.

Barbara's hard eyes followed Morgan's bouncing finger. "In the rear," he pointed, as he gave details in a pleasant voice, "is the bedroom. Behind that door is the bath. There's a coffeepot in the cupboard above the sink, and the box on the corner table by the window is a small refrigerator. Mostly, though, you'll have your meals in the lodge, around the campfire, or off the chuck wagon ... when you're on trail."

"There's only one bedroom? Mother!"

"Yeah, that's how we built them all. Most folks have their children sleep out here in the main room," Morgan explained. Linda danced to the built-in wood frame of a cot along the outside wall of the main room. "We'll lay your air mattress on here and then your sleeping bag on top. It's plenty big enough."

"That's what most folks do. Some of the cabins even have bunk cots," Morgan said.

"I'll bet the *children* love that." Barbara's voice dripped contempt.

Morgan backed toward the door. "You folks take your time settling in. You should probably stay here at the cabin. I'll see to it someone comes by with lunch. I'll be down around the corral if you need anything before then." He ran down the steps and up the gravel road past the pavilion, increasing speed as he turned the corner.

From her lawn chair under the shade of the massive live oak, Mary could see Sam trimming hooves in the lean-to. She'd carefully positioned her chair so she could watch her cowboy and her horse. Comanche was pulling grass with all the exuberance of a teenager entered in the state fair pie-eating contest.

Before settling into her chair, she'd unsnapped the lead rope from Comanche's halter and replaced it with a thirty-foot lunge line. Not that Comanche needed it, certainly not in the fenced yard.

No, the lunge line was for her benefit.

When she felt the need, the urge, the desire—the gentlest jiggle on the thirty-foot line and Comanche would march instantly to her side, proving he was still the fabulously responsive and willing horse he had always been.

She felt the urge. Gave an almost imperceptible jiggle on the line, and smiled as Comanche protested with a brief snort, snapped his head up, and marched to her. Mary dug her fingernails into the hair under his shaggy forelock and scratched his forehead. Her eyes stung a little when he leaned into it and almost dropped his head in her lap, the way he always had. Horses each had their favorite scratching place. Comanche's was on his forehead at the root of the forelock. He had another spot, too, just behind his withers.

Her eyes stung a little more when she wondered how many times he had longed for someone to scratch him over the past three years.

"That's my boy. I promise I'll always be here to scratch you." As soon as she said it, she realized the lie of it. She scratched and scratched until her fingers ached and she had a small pile of dead hair on her lap.

Comanche never backed away. Rather, his head grew heavier and heavier in her lap. She put her lips in the soft hair above his eye, kissed him gently, and lightly pushed his head up. Just before he stepped back, she unsnapped the line.

"Let's see what else you remember."

Realizing the scratching therapy was over, Comanche returned to his assault on the grass. She watched Sam release another horse into the night pasture. "Five," she counted out loud. Only five remaining horses required Sam's attention. At this rate, he could be done by lunch. She hoped so. She needed to sit with him.

Morgan rode from behind the barn on Chester, leading four saddled horses. He strayed from the lane and angled directly up the slope toward Mary. "I almost forgot how comfortable a ride Chester is." Morgan stopped alongside the fence, under the big oak.

"Is everyone behaving?" Mary asked.

"The horses are all doing fine." He lifted his hat from his head, wiped his brow on the cuff of his shirt, and gave Mary an ear-to-ear grin. "But I figure that girl Barbara ... well, I just figure, that's all."

Mary smiled. "Attractive, isn't she?"

Morgan settled his hat down on his head, picked up the reins, and gave a loud cluck to Chester. "Attractive as a hornet's nest!" He called over his shoulder as he rode away.

Mary smiled after Morgan as he rode over the high ridge behind the house. She watched until the last horse disappeared, then she looked back at the big corral by the barn. She could see Sam working in the lean-to. Only four horses waited in the corral.

Comanche had wandered to the far end of the yard and was very busy tearing and munching, his muzzle buried in the thick grass. She waited until he faced away from her.

"Let's see if you remember."

She raised from the chair on legs that were surprisingly solid. Pursing her lips, she made one short kissing sound, then watched.

The skinny paint jerked his head high, pricked his ears, and spun one right-hand circle with the speed of a five-year-old cutting horse, and then stood rock still. His one brown eye and one blue eye focused on Mary like laser beams.

Forcing herself to draw a deep breath, she pursed her lips, made two short kissing sounds, and watched.

She caught the excitement in his eyes the instant before Comanche exploded with energy. He spun two lightning fast turns to the right, stopped, dropped his head level, and shot that laser beam her way again.

Rivers ran from her eyes. Her legs melted, but as she collapsed to the ground, she snapped her fingers.

One snap.

Comanche flew to her.

Chapter Six

S am released the final horse into the night pasture, then paused a moment, leaning on the top rail. *Good looking herd and every one of them walking on perfectly trimmed hooves. Yes, sir.* A man could be proud of a job well done.

Fred's dually rattled up behind him.

Ambling to Fred's window, Sam leaned on the door and accepted the envelope Fred offered. "Appreciate it, neighbor."

"We have the final dozen heifers loaded, and one *rambunctious* bull. Tell Morgan I'll haul his mare in the morning."

"I'll do that. He's off shining leather somewhere. Warmin' up the trail horses. First family of guests arrived already."

"Drove by 'em on my way in this morning. Looked mighty city-fied."

Sam cracked a huge grin. "Most times they do. The first week."

"You'll toughen 'em up." Fred gave Sam a nod and a grin. "Got to go."

Susan drove around the rear of the truck and trailer on her Gator, waved to a departing Fred and stopped inches from Sam's toes. She enjoyed pretending to run him down, and he enjoyed holding his ground.

"Rusty left word we have a family here already. Thought I'd take them lunch. Want to join us?"

Sam looked toward the house. He'd caught some of the show Mary and Comanche had put on. "I don't think so. I'm mighty hot and tired. A day and a half of hoof trimmin' don't go as easy as it used to. Figured I'd have a shower, some lunch with Mary, then a short nap under the oak. Tell 'em we'll have dinner together in the lodge. Tell 'em ... six thirty."

Susan smiled. "Doesn't go."

"What doesn't go?"

"Hoof trimming *doesn't* go."

"With what?" Sam enjoyed pretending, too.

Susan revved the throttle. "Want a ride?"

Sam stepped in the rear bed of the Gator, gave her enough time to drive beyond the barn, then covered her eyes with his hat. It wasn't the first time, and like the other times, he was careful not to block her view—totally.

Susan let out an exaggerated scream of fear and tried, less than seriously, to push Sam's hat away.

An hour later Sam was feeling recharged after a shower, sandwich and brief nap. Pretty much, he guessed, the way Comanche had boosted Mary's energy. Recently he'd noticed how easily she would tire. Just like she used to, a few years ago. He'd begun to suspect, but would never ask.

Now, though, with Comanche back, she seemed revitalized. He resented the demands the guests would put on him now. He would gladly sell his soul to just sit, as he was doing this moment, under the shade of the ancient oak tree, and watch that gentle woman rehabilitate and retrain a grateful horse. There was just one problem. He was pretty sure he'd already sold or traded his soul a few years back.

For half an hour he had been relaxing in the shade of the mighty oak in the yard, watching Mary examine her old friend. Always the perfectionist, she inspected every inch, hair, tendon, and bone of the patient but pitiful-looking mustang.

Mary ran her hand along Comanche's spine. "I don't feel anything out of line."

If it weren't so sad, he might find that funny. He could see from where he sat, twenty yards away, that the horse's back was fine. It's really not hard to judge, when every bone along the topline is visible. *Look out, Comanche, she's coming at your teeth next.*

Mary put her hand under Comanche's chin and raised his head. She stood straight on, nose to nose, and slid her hand in under his cheeks.

Sam watched her face as she considered her patient. She'd want Doc Adams to come float his teeth. Tomorrow, he predicted.

"Sam, could you give Doc Adams a call? There are a few sharp edges that should be floated. Maybe he could come out tomorrow. Do you think Comanche's strong enough to worm? Or should we wait until he puts on a few pounds? I'll bet his teeth haven't been checked since he left us."

Sam smiled. "I'll give Doc a call right away."

࿐་ᄵ࿐་ᄵ࿐་ᄵ

Susan drove the Gator up to the porch of cabin number seven. She glanced at the red-and-white-checkered table cloth covering the picnic table. Apparently, the guests had already settled in. A not-so-tall, thin fellow wearing a brand-new hat stepped from around the corner of the cabin. Susan thought it funny how the guests always arrived with brand new straw hats. He looked good in his, though.

"I've brought tea and sandwiches."

The man came to the Gator and spent a second studying the machine and its driver. "The girls went for a walk, to find the stream." He tipped his hat. "Hello, I'm Philip Cunningham."

"Pleased to meet you. I'm Susan." She offered her hand.

Instead of shaking it, he helped her step down, then reached for the sack of food. "Allow me to carry those things for you. Come up to the porch and have a seat. We can get to know each other." She followed him to the porch. "I should really be going. I just wanted to bring your lunch and let you know we'll be serving dinner in the lodge at six thirty." She watched as Philip pulled a chair made of small logs from the table and gestured toward it.

"I'm sure you can spare a few moments to keep an east coast pilgrim company while he impatiently awaits the return of his women." Philip flashed a confident smile.

She sat and studied him as he slid into the chair across the table from her. Susan always noticed hands, how they changed over the summer. Like the hats. Brand new, shiny white hats, and hands. The hats weathered. The hands toughened. She tried to imagine what Phillip's hands would look like in a few months. The hat, she was sure, would become a little less stiff and dusty gray. His hands, though ... He might be one of those who always managed to keep clean fingernails. He looked the type.

Her eyes fell to her own fingernails and the dark dirt line under the tips. Self-consciously she made fists, palms down.

"Have you worked here long?"

Susan jumped. "What?"

"I was wondering how long you've worked here."

"My husband, Rusty, and I've been with the Holts for over fifteen years. If I may ask, what's your line of work?"

"Fifteen years, that's a long time ... I'm a high school principal."

"Really? How about that, I taught elementary school for a number of years. Yup, fifteen years, but it doesn't really feel like it's been that long. Nor does it feel like work. Feels like home. So, what brings you to Mar-Sa?"

Susan saw his eyes drop to his hands. She noticed, too, the way he drummed the tabletop with his fingers.

"It was Linda's, my wife's, idea."

"I see. You had other plans?" She wasn't sure she believed him.

"No, not really. Our marriage is going through a rough spot right now. Linda teaches at the same high school, tenth grade American history. Friends of ours had been here a couple of summers ago. Maybe you remember them. Paul and Lucy Keaton. They're coming again this summer."

"I do remember them. Two summers back. In fact, they helped build your cabin. Are they bringing their son—Todd, isn't it—with them?"

"No, Todd's put his education on hold, left the university, and joined the Navy."

Susan sat back at the news. "That comes as a surprise. I do remember Todd had a lot of energy. I hope the Navy can keep him busy. It'll be good to see Paul and Lucy again. Paul had plenty of energy, himself, now that I think about it. Is he still in politics?"

"He'll die there. He's a state senator now. Moved over from the House of Representatives."

"Next governor, then president?"

Philip leaned back in his chair, cracked a broad grin. "Wouldn't put it past him."

Susan pushed away from the table. "It's been a nice chat, but I should go back to work. Don't forget dinner. Six thirty in the lodge."

She was about to turn the key on the Gator when a dark green SUV rounded the corner behind the lodge and stopped by the cabins. "Looks like we'll have another family for dinner."

శ్రా~శ్రా~శ్రా~శ్రా

Standing ankle deep in the cool water, Barbara scanned her mother's pretty face. The stream was calm and quiet here, but she hadn't followed her across. Barbara lifted her eyes from her mother, up the grassy slope to the cabins in the background.

He was up there.

Her gaze drifted back to her mother. She's so sweet. And stupid. Why does she stay with him?

Her mother was acting like a high school cheerleader, trying to hang on to the star quarterback who was running around with the whole cheerleader squad.

"Barbara, are there little fish over there? There must be hundreds of them swimming around my feet."

She can't really care about little fish, can she?

"Barbara, hello?"

"No fish over here, Mother."

"Can't you find something to be happy about? Look around, child. It's beautiful here. Can't you pretend to like it? For my sake?"

Barbara let herself fall to the stream bank. "Why do you stay with him? You're young. You're pretty. Do you think coming out here to nowhere-land will change anything?"

"I love him."

Barbara jumped up, kicking the water, "How can you love him? Mother, he cheated on you. More than once! You've been married two years, and how many ... I can't believe you! Wake up! He's evil, filthy!"

Linda fell back on the grassy bank. "That hurt."

Barbara splashed her way across the stream and dropped to her knees beside her mother. "I'm sorry. It hurts me, too, when he ..."

Linda sat up and brushed the hair from Barbara's eyes. "Philip swore he'll never misbehave again. I want to believe him."

"He arranged this entire trip so he could be with Lucy Keaton. Don't you think it's odd to plan a three-month vacation with the same woman you had an affair with. Then promise your wife you'll be *good*? I'm fifteen and I can see through that crap! He's a pig!"

The blow to the side of her face nearly knocked Barbara over.

"I've listened to enough for one outing!"

Barbara backed away, rubbing her face. "Did he teach you how to hit, too? He's good at it! I guess it's easier to hit me than believe me." She turned away and started to run. She kept running, ignoring her mother's cries for her to stop.

Chapter Seven

Barbara's words stung Linda's ears as she trudged up the hill to the cabin. Still, she wouldn't give up on her marriage. Quitting was easy. She'd quit too many times already. Three husbands, two divorces. Why did men always behave this way? What was it about her that made men think so little of her?

She stopped behind their cabin, put her hands on her hips, looked skyward, and inhaled. She held that breath in just the way her yoga instructor had taught her, then exhaled slowly. Better. Now another breath: hold, hold, exhale.

Linda turned the corner. And choked.

On the porch of the cabin next to theirs, Philip sat very close to Lucy Keaton.

They're only talking. After all, we're going to talk to each other every day. For three months. Am I as stupid as Barbara thinks? No, no I'm not stupid. I'm a good wife. I'll be a good wife, and he'll be a good husband. We'll have a fantastic summer, learn to ride horses, learn to live on the trail ... Learn how to hold a marriage together.

"Why hello, Lucy, when did you get here?" Linda realized the surprise and disappointment underlying her words, and quickly marched directly to Lucy and hugged her.

"Just fifteen minutes ago. You look wonderful. I like your hair. You look younger with it short like that."

Linda took a step back. "Younger?"

"I'm sorry. What I meant is you look so darn cute." Lucy pushed her own hair back with an airy flick of her fingertips.

"Thank you. I like what you've done with yours." Linda's voice held a hint of sarcasm.

"Colored the gray is all."

"Well, it looks ..."

"Okay, okay, you two are both beautiful." Philip moved to Linda and reached out a hand. "Where's Barbara?"

Linda brushed his hand away. "She's still exploring the stream." She cast a glance toward the driveway. "I don't see Paul."

Lucy rolled her eyes. "He had to stay for a vote. He'll be here in a day or two."

Philip moved closer to Linda. "They've brought us sandwiches to hold us until dinner, which is at six thirty in the lodge."

Linda stood firm, hands on her hips, while her eyes traveled up and down Philip. She could feel how her gaze made him uncomfortable. She'd never garnered that reaction before, and she savored the feeling. Then, with a look that could almost be misunderstood as kind, she told Lucy, "We'll give you time to settle in, unpack." She offered Philip the same look. "I could do with a sandwich right now."

Without another word or glance, Linda marched to cabin number seven.

Philip was only a step behind her. After closing and locking the cabin door, he snapped, "What was that?"

"Ground rules."

He grabbed her shoulder, twisting her toward him. "What *exactly* do you mean—*ground rules*?"

She stared at his free hand, wondering if he'd hit her, then realized she didn't really care. "If this is going to work, there have got to be ground rules."

"For crying out loud! We were only talking about Paul. She's really pissed that he sent her ahead on her own while he plays senator."

Since he didn't hit her, she pushed on. "Talking's allowed. As long as it's chaperoned."

He mimicked Linda through tight lips. "*'If this is going to* work'— you're going to have to trust me."

She slid into the chair at the tiny round table, looked out the window, and bit into her ham sandwich. Around a mouthful, she whispered, "Earn it."

෧෨෧෨෧෨

Mary opened the double doors on the stainless-steel refrigerator in the lodge and grabbed a pack of hot dogs. "I feel like a campfire. Hot dogs on sticks, lemonade, and kettle cooked beans. And coffee, of course, for Rusty and Sam."

"Sounds wonderful." Susan went to the shelves where the canned goods were stacked then paused to look at Mary. "Have you ever wondered why so many people think a working guest ranch will solve marital problems?"

"What?"

"The family who arrived earlier today. When I took lunch to them, I had a chat with the husband. He told me their marriage was going over a rough spot."

"Seems every year there's one. They never last the season. Either they break up or can't wait to go on an impromptu second honeymoon in Las Vegas. Sometimes I wonder about the ones who find love again. Do you?"

Susan snared a can of beans from the shelf behind the counter. "I do, sometimes. We still get Christmas cards from the Millers."

"Feels good when things work out for them." Mary laid the package of hot dogs on the table and sat on the bench. "You should have seen Comanche this afternoon. He gave me two terrific spins! He looked so proud of himself. Doc Adams is coming in the morning to float his teeth and look him over." She hesitated. "Susan ... I'd like you to go to see Dr. Stein with me on Monday."

The can of beans fell to the floor.

"Mary, no. You've been doing so well. You look better than ever."

"He called two nights ago, said my counts were off. Not bad. He doubts I'll need to start chemo again, but they want to do more blood work. It's different now. I want to ... I don't want to be sick again ... I don't want Sam to know. Not until I know more. Okay?"

Susan sat on the bench and pulled Mary to her. She wouldn't let the tears start. Not in front of Mary. Rusty had told her about Mary's plan to compete at the state fair. Whatever it would take, she would be there for Mary. "Of course, I'll go with you. You shouldn't keep it from Sam, though. He should be the one to go with you."

Mary pushed away. "No! You know Sam. If ... if Dr. Stein thinks ... well, if anything is wrong, Sam won't allow me to do the things ... to work with Comanche. You know the routine, no sun, plenty of rest."

Indeed, she did. How many times had Mary been through it? How many times must she go through it again? "I'll do whatever you say. Even lie to your husband, and mine. If you don't compete this year, what's wrong with next year? You build yourself up, Comanche uses the year to get back in top form, and next year, as the kids say today, you 'kick some serious butt.' "

Mary looked away. "There won't be a next year."

Susan gasped, covering her face, then fought back a flood of emotions. How could she feel compassion and sorrow at the same instant she was so awful mad? But she did. She spun Mary so their eyes met. "Don't you ... don't you ever say that again! Ever!" She grabbed Mary and squeezed her hard, holding her while they rocked gently. "Promise me you'll never talk that way again." She tipped Mary back to look in her eyes.

Mary gave Susan an okay-I-won't smile, wiped her eyes, then pointed to the far end of the lodge. "Look, here comes Morgan."

The long, happy strides of youth carried Morgan toward the lodge. In the sun's glare behind Morgan there followed Sam's tall, long-legged figure. Off to their right strode Rusty. The three men converged just outside the lodge, like the Earps on their way to the O.K. Corral.

Sam marched right up to and over the table nearest Mary, sat on it with his boots on the bench and pulled her to him. "How about that! The two most beautiful women in Conner County, under one roof."

"And hard at work fixin' vittles, which sure makes 'em even more beautifuler," Rusty chimed in, dodging the wet rag Susan threw at him.

"I finished exercising all the horses, Mr. Holt. Every one of them is sound and ready to go," Morgan announced proudly.

Sam shook his head and chuckled, but his eyes stayed locked with Mary's. "That's great. They'll start earnin' their keep on Monday. What've you girls been up to?"

"Planning dinner and taking inventory," Mary said.

Susan caught the hint. "Yes, and we noticed we're in need of a few important items, so we scheduled a store run for Monday."

"We'll most likely be gone the better part of the day," Mary continued.

Sam's surprise showed in his voice. "Hold on, now. How can we start the season with both cooks gone?"

"I can cook."

Everybody turned to face the pleasant voice coming from behind.

Linda Cunningham stood half in, half out of the shadow cast by the lodge's overhang. "I can cook. The brochure says this is a working ranch and all the guests are expected to do their part."

Sam held onto Mary but turned to face Linda more squarely. "Well, howdy, Linda, but by Monday there'll be a dozen hungry mouths to feed. That's a lot of cooking."

Susan kept her eyes level with Sam's. "We won't be leaving until after breakfast, and we promise to be back for dinner."

"There, see? All settled. Some time on Sunday, you ladies can show me what you had in mind for lunch. My daughter and I will take it from there." Linda rubbed her hands together and joined them at the table.

Morgan searched all their faces. "What about tonight? I'm mighty hungry right now."

"We decided on hot dogs and beans, by the fire," Mary said.

"Summer's just begun and we're down to hot dogs and beans already?" Sam's smile belied his question.

Susan seized the opportunity. "It'll be better after we make that run to town on Monday."

"Guess I'll start a fire." Morgan hustled to the pile of firewood stacked neatly outside the lodge, gathered an armload, and started for the fire ring.

⩩⩩⩩⩩⩩⩩

Mary took Sam's hand, led him out to the fire ring and got comfortable on one of the long split-log benches that circled the fire pit. Sam busied himself helping Morgan stack what she considered an overly large supply of wood for tonight's cook fire. When they had what was in Mary's opinion enough wood to roast a steer, they stood up and grinned at each other. Like Sam, Mary knew what was coming next. Morgan had taken charge of the fire pit three summers earlier by declaring that, for all the cooking they did, they needed a cook fire pit that was up to the task. Working evenings for a week, he'd dug a pit a foot deep and eight feet around and lined it with rocks. On the end nearest the lodge, he'd installed a three-foot-tall iron pole and, with Sam's help, fashioned a swinging arm and a hook to hang the large black kettle on so that it could be moved closer or farther from the heat, depending on the needs of the beans. Morgan was ever diligent and respectful when handling the horses and assisting the guests, but fire-starting allowed the boy to pretend to ruffle Sam's feathers. She knew Sam loved to pretend to be annoyed by Morgan's prank.

She caught the wink Sam tossed her way when Morgan dowsed the overly large stack of wood with way too much kerosene—his standard and reliable method of starting a fire. As he'd explained to Sam one day, "Kindling takes too long when a fella's hungry." She knew both of them enjoyed the roar and smoke of a fire started this way. She leaned back when Morgan flipped the lit match toward the kerosene-soaked stack of wood.

Whoosh. The flames shot skyward, black smoke billowed, and instantly, the wood began to crackle and pop. The sudden heat backed Morgan away a few hurried steps, right into a chuckling Sam.

"Good fire there, Morgan."

"Sure is. Like I said, I'm darn hungry and ready for a couple of dogs."

Sam nodded toward the four-feet-high flames. "Might be a minute or two before we can get close enough to roast a dog."

Morgan grinned. "I'll fetch the roasting sticks while the fire takes hold."

Susan, Rusty, and Linda approached the flames cautiously. Susan set the tray of dogs and beans on a table next to the cooking arm.

Rusty fanned the flames with his hat and gave Sam a broad grin. "If I ever need a signal fire, I sure hope Morgan's with me."

"Best hope he's packin' plenty of kerosene."

With Linda's help, Mary and Susan hung the bean kettle on the hook of the outstretched cooking arm and emptied three cans of beans into it, just as Morgan returned with the roasting sticks.

Mary crossed the circle to Sam. "If you don't mind, I think I'll head to the house. I'm getting tired, and I'd like to say goodnight to Comanche." She read the worry on Sam's face. "You stay and visit. I'll be fine." Leaning down, she kissed his stubbly cheek. "Honestly, I'm not sure if I'm all that tired or just want an excuse to go play with him."

Hand in hand they walked to her cart. "Sure, you don't want my company? Maybe we can get in a little smoochin' under the oak tree while Comanche mows the lawn. You know, with the guests startin' to roll in, smoochin' time might get tougher to schedule."

"You tempt me, Cowboy." She laid her finger on his lips. "I'm anxious to get Comanche back out to the grass and I'll be waiting for you at our secret smooching hideaway a little later. Meanwhile, you stay and tell our guests a tall tale or two." She stepped into the cart and tipped his hat with her finger. "You've always got a tale or two."

He kissed her cheek and whispered, "I'll tell 'em about the time you were arrested in Amarillo."

She gasped. "Sam, I was never arrested in Amarillo! Or anywhere else for that matter."

Thoughtfully, he scratched his chin. "Maybe it was some other brunette I was rodeoin' with at the time? Hmmm, it's a good story, though. Maybe I'll just change the name. You know, to indict the innocent."

She gave her crooked smile, shook her head, and tread on the gas pedal.

Heading down the drive, Mary came upon Philip and Lucy on their way to the fire. "Why hello, Lucy. Susan told me you'd arrived. It is wonderful to have you back with us. Sorry to hear Paul has been delayed."

"You know Paul, the ever-devoted politician. He's afraid a bill might pass without his two cents. He'll be here in a day or two."

"Well, I look forward to seeing him again. I'm sorry, but I need to excuse myself. I'm a little worn out. You folks have a nice evening and enjoy the hot dogs."

"You know, I never eat hot dogs when we're at home, but here, I love them." Lucy moved Philip forward. "You've met Philip Cunningham?"

Mary smiled. "Yes, good evening, Philip. I hope your daughter has settled in."

Philip shook his head. "She's a little unhappy right now, but she'll come around."

"I'm sure Barbara will surprise us all. Well, good evening, enjoy the fire. It's a dandy, and I'll see you at breakfast."

Lucy leaned into the golf cart and gave Mary a quick peck on the cheek.

Comanche reached over the stall guard and nickered when Mary stopped her cart in the barn aisle. "Hello, handsome. Are you ready for some more grass?"

Another soft nicker.

She looked toward the tack room. "Maybe I should find the fly wipe and rub some on you before we go up to the yard. The mosquitoes have begun to be quite a bother, haven't they?"

Inside the tack room door, she paused while her eyes searched the shelves. At last she spied the little green plastic container on the second shelf. Crossing the room to fetch it, she gulped a breath when she saw the trunk in the corner.

The show trunk. It contained things she hadn't looked at in years. As her left hand reached for the little green bottle, her right hand brushed the trunk lid. She fell back, gripped the fly wipe in both hands, and gazed at the trunk. Should she open it? Memories. A trunk full of memories. The last time she'd closed the trunk lid, she'd slammed it with anger. No, with hate and anger. And frustration. Hate, anger, frustration, and—sorrow. And bitterness.

She backed to the tack room door; eyes fixed on the trunk. No hate now. No anger. Or was there? Mary didn't know. How could she? Was she supposed to know the difference between hate and bitterness? Between sorrow and anger?

Her eyes traced every line of the solid wooden trunk. Sam had made it for them. For her and Callie. He painted it that shiny red. Callie loved red. Red and silver. Mary always believed her daughter had inherited that preference from her because they were Mary's favorite colors, too. She had to smile when she remembered sewing their costumes together, the three of them—Callie, Susan, and herself. Oh, how Callie would fuss over each and every minute detail. Nothing could be less than perfect for that girl.

Oh, Callie looked beautiful in her costume. Through watery, stinging eyes, Mary stared at Callie. She was standing right there, in the tack room, fussing like she always did with the silver fringes on her vest. Then the vision evaporated.

Chapter Eight

"Good morning," Susan greeted Sam.

"Mornin', Susan. Mary will be right along as soon as she has Comanche settled. She's showing Morgan where to put up some temporary electric fence in the night pasture." Sam swiped a piece of toast. "He'll no doubt miss breakfast."

From behind the stove, Linda wagged a threatening finger Sam's way. "Wait your turn, boss. Or host, or boss-host."

Sam laughed then eyeballed the folks sitting at the picnic tables in the lodge. "They look hungry, too."

Susan gave Sam a playful shove. "Go. Sit. Mingle."

He looked through the lodge and out toward the upward-sloping ground beyond the last fence. His gaze trailed into the open expanse as far as his eyes could reach. He considered throwing a saddle on his horse and riding up the long hill. A mighty fine morning it was for a ride, not too hot, a few dark clouds in the distance. He longed for the mornings, not so many years ago, when he and Mary, and most days Callie, too, would do just that. Sometimes even on school days. Often, they would turn and race out the long lane, reaching the hard road just seconds ahead of her school bus.

He chuckled a little when he recalled Callie's early morning protests. Sure she was always ready for a good run, but that girl loved her comfy bed in the mornings, too.

"Mr. Holt?"

Jolted from thoughts of the past, Sam turned to face a stranger. "Yes. I'd sure feel more comfortable if you'd call me Sam."

"Join us at our table, won't you, Sam?" She smiled pleasantly.

He studied the woman standing before him. Dressed in a sleeveless white cotton blouse and faded blue jeans, with her hat shifted back just a tad, she looked very much as if she belonged there. "We pulled in well after dark last night." She offered her hand. "I'm Nicky Bartlett, and that hunk at the table sporting the new Stetson is my husband, John."

Sam held back a chuckle, because he could see two men sporting new straw Stetsons. The tables were usually arranged in two rows of six, all under the protective roof of the pavilion, but many times when only a few guests were eating—like this morning—someone would pull a few tables together to make a circle, so everybody could take part in the conversation. He recognized one new Stetson wearer as Philip Cunningham, who seemed to be involved in a conversation with Lucy Keaton, at a table to his left. He gave them a friendly nod and tip of his hat, then followed Nicky and sat beside her. "Sorry we missed your arrival, folks. I hope Susan and Rusty settled you in okay."

John reached across the table and shook Sam's hand. "I thought about calling on the house, but we noticed lights at the cabins and found all these good people sitting around the campfire. They made us feel right at home."

Nicky squeezed John's hand. "I'm so excited to be here. I haven't ridden a horse since I was a girl. When do we get to pick our horses?"

"You're welcome to go to the pasture and take a look over the fence anytime. Please don't go in without our wrangler or myself on hand. All our horses are well-trained and certainly safe, but they are horses."

"It's been more than twenty-five years since my butt's been in a saddle," John said.

"Most folks get right back into the swing of things within a few days. You never really forget how to ride. What have you been up to for twenty-five years that kept you off a horse?"

"The normal things. Raising a family, earning a living. Minding the wife."

Sam smiled. "How do you earn your living?"

"Well, I'm retired now. Was an electrical engineer." Sam thanked Linda and leaned to the left as she set his breakfast in front of him. "Electrical engineer. That's impressive. Takes a good bit of gray matter to master that occupation, I reckon."

John turned to Nicky with a grin. "Can't be that tough, or I'd have never made it."

She gave her husband a playful shove. "Don't listen to him. He built a fine business, a well-respected company now operated by our two sons and funding our retirement."

Retirement. That had been his and Mary's plan, too. Looking past John and Nicky, he spied Mary driving her cart up the road to the lodge. "Don't believe I'll ever retire. I wouldn't know what to do with myself." Of course, spending all his time, for the rest of time, with that sweet woman would work out just fine. Right then, Sam decided to loosen the reins this summer. Rusty, Morgan, and Susan could handle most everything day to day. He'd save his time to spend with Mary.

After navigating her cart between the rows of tables, Mary stopped next to Sam and greeted the newcomers with a warm smile. "Good morning. I'm Mary."

John helped Mary to the table while Sam made the introductions.

As she settled onto the bench, Mary leaned over to kiss Sam's cheek. "Morgan has a little to do yet, but when he's finished, Comanche will have a few acres to himself in the night pasture."

"He'd better hurry if he's gonna beat the rain." Sam pointed toward the western sky, which was filling fast with thick, dark clouds.

Rusty joined them at the table. "Rain's long overdue, boss. I hope it rains all day. Burnt grass don't fill a lot of cows' bellies."

Sam surveyed the fast-moving, threatening clouds, which only a few moments earlier had looked harmless. "Looks like an all-day pounding comin' in for sure."

Barbara moved around the table, topping off everyone's coffee. "What do we do if it rains all day?" She looked to the table at the far end of the circle where Philip, her mother, and Lucy sat chatting and finishing their breakfast.

Susan brought another plate of pancakes from the kitchen and set them between Philip and Lucy. "Sometimes we just stay here in the lodge and eat and talk all day and watch the rain. Out here, we're fond of rainy days."

Barbara straightened up and studied everyone's faces, "Sounds great for you old people, but I'm already going nuts."

"Barbara!" snapped Linda.

Mary was near enough to Barbara to reach her hand and give Barbara's a gentle pat. "That's okay. All of us old people remember the days of our youth and the energy that kept us restless."

Barbara yanked her hand away and backed up a step. "I'm not restless. I just hate being here!" She glared at Phillip through eyes narrowed to slits, then turned her gaze on Lucy. She smiled grimly when Lucy looked away.

Linda jumped up. "Barbara, I want you to ..."

"That's all right. I have days I'd rather be somewhere else myself." Sam laid his hat on the table and looked at Barbara. "Tell us where you'd rather be today."

Apparently caught off guard, Barbara could only shrug her shoulders. As she backed away from the table, she kept her eyes on Sam.

So did everyone else.

"I don't want to be *here*." Barbara spoke in a low voice, still glaring at Sam. "I want to go home. I want to be with my friends ... I'm not a stinking cowboy!"

Sam nodded slowly, meeting her hard stare with a warm smile. "I see." His voice barely above a whisper. Sam cupped his chin, struck a pose like a great thinker, and held it while he manufactured a pondering look. "Well now, I'm curious, what would you be doing at home?"

Barbara threw her arms in the air. "Hanging out with my friends. Going to the mall. I don't know. What the crap do you care?"

Linda stood up. "That's enough, Barbara! Go to our cabin." She turned to Sam. "I apologize for that."

"Don't apologize for me!"

Sam caught the look that passed from mother to daughter, and the one Barbara leveled at Philip. He gave a quick glance to Mary, and was about to assure Barbara things would liven up here when they got busy with the horses, but was interrupted by a thunderclap so loud it shook the rafters.

Barbara ran from the lodge. Linda was about to follow, but Philip held her arm.

"Let her steam a little. Alone," Philip said.

She pulled free. "Do you think we made a mistake?" Before he answered, Philip gave everyone his disarming smile. "No. She'll come around."

The clouds opened, dumping sheets of pounding rain on the metal lodge roof. The rain hit the roof with drops so large and furious, they drowned out all conversation.

Susan stood to offer more coffee, then pointed toward the lane. Far in the distance, barely visible in the dim light and pouring rain, a car was driving up the ranch road. Curiosity had no time to take root, however. Strong wind gusts began to blow rain under the lodge roof, so everyone hustled toward the kitchen wall. Sam, Rusty, and John hauled tables to the kitchen so everyone could crowd along the sheltered wall, safely out of the driving rain.

～⚖～⚖～⚖

Mary sat down first, then Linda joined her. Mary noticed the sadness in the other woman's eyes and felt her own heart constrict with sympathy. Knowing the rain would pound her words to silence, she simply made eye contact as a gesture of comfort, from one mother to another. She watched Linda open the snap on her left blouse-pocket, then, with trembling white fingers, reach in and pull out a tiny velvet pouch.

Mary leaned forward, very interested in the lavender pouch. She watched those unsteady fingers fumble with a yellow drawstring, slip into the pouch and retrieve an odd piece of jewelry. Mary tried to meet her gaze, but Linda seemed totally absorbed by the tiny purple crystal attached to the silver chain. Linda turned the crystal over and over in her hand, stroking it gently. Her fingers no longer trembled.

The rain lessened enough to permit speech.

"What a lovely crystal. May I see it?"

Linda looked at Mary and caught her breath. "Why yes. It's amethyst."

Mary held the crystal in her fingers and examined it.

On one end of the silver chain was a purple, thumb-sized, diamond-shaped crystal. The chain, about four inches long, ran up to another smaller, elongated clear crystal. "I've never seen anything like this. It's a beautiful piece of jewelry."

"Thank you. It's my pendulum. I carry it with me always. It was given to me a few years back by a very special friend."

"Pendulum? Do you hypnotize people?"

"I have, but I use it mostly when I help people with Reiki sessions. Or used to. Philip won't allow it anymore. He's worried about what people might say. Being a teacher, you understand."

Mary held the pendulum up and allowed it to sway gently. "What would they say?"

Linda looked Philip's way. Seemingly satisfied that he was thoroughly occupied in conversation with John and not interested in what she and Mary were doing, she folded her hands and leaned forward. "Some people don't understand or want to hear about anything that doesn't come from modern medicine," She darted another glance at Philip. "It's a shame, too."

"Why do you say that?"

"They want everything fixed with a pill or surgery. There's a place for that, but there's a place for holistic treatments, too. According to Philip if certain people found out I practiced Reiki … He's afraid my work would embarrass him."

"Really? So tell me about Reiki."

"It's a method of holistic healing." Linda pointed to the crystal, now spinning in a clockwise circle on the end of the silver chain. "The practitioner lays her hands on the person receiving the treatment and allows the universal life energy to flow through her hands and pass through the patient."

Mary handed the pendulum to Linda, who promptly dropped it in the velvet pouch. "What does the pendulum do?"

"Not everyone who practices Reiki uses one, but I believed in the healing powers of crystals before discovering Reiki. I use this pendulum to help me focus the energy and open energy blockages. Sometimes I use other crystals as well."

The rafters rattled with the force of a thunderclap, just before another downpour pelted the roof.

Barbara dashed under the roof and slid onto the bench next to her mother.

A soaked Morgan ducked inside, stomping his feet, slapping his hat against his leg, and shaking the water from his arms.

The white car Susan had spotted earlier stopped just outside the lodge. A man and woman braved the torrents and ran inside the lodge.

"Hi, we're the Collier's. We bring rain!"

Chapter Nine

Comanche leaned into the brush, savoring every stroke. The rain had lasted well into the afternoon, but the sun was blazing once again. Mary stood with Comanche under the massive live oak in the yard, waiting for the veterinarian's arrival.

Dr. Lester Adams should roll in any minute now, and she was anxious to hear what he'd have to say. Diagnostically, she was pretty sure she'd already covered it all well enough on her own. A lifetime of working with horses had given her an impressively complete knowledge of the mechanics of a horse. Comanche's legs, feet, and lungs all appeared strong and healthy. His gut sounds were good. He was a bit dehydrated, but the way he'd been eating and drinking, he'd have that fixed in a day or two. There was only that one little problem ...

Comanche's head shot up, and his eyes focused out the lane. Following his lead, Mary turned to look. "Ah, Dr. Adams. He's gotten a new truck since you've seen him, but I'll be willing to bet you know it's him."

She tied Comanche's rope to the bumper of her cart and drove, leading Comanche to the barn. She watched the truck speeding her way and marveled at the lack of dust. In fact, she was certain the fields flanking the long lane appeared to have regained a bit of a green tint. Field grass is so tough. Weeks of heat and sun can beat it down, then after one rainy morning, it's fighting to turn green again.

Mary turned to look at the skinny horse marching contentedly behind her cart. "A lot like you. A little rain and you'll bounce right back."

She parked in the wide aisle of the barn, untied Comanche, and sat on the rear of the cart. When she reached up and scratched him under the forelock, he dropped his head thankfully. "How about me, Comanche? Are you going to help me bounce back?"

The skinny paint pushed his head into Mary, nearly unseating her.

Dr. Adams trotted into the barn carrying his bag. "Afternoon, Mary. Sorry I'm running so late. Two sand colic's this morning. Hope this morning's rain helps."

He set his bag next to the cart and, holding his chin and mumbling to himself, walked a slow, thoughtful circle around the horse.

Comanche watched his every move with his ears pinned flat.

Mary scratched the horse's neck and laughed. "He remembers you, Lester."

"Sure seems that way. First thought, there doesn't appear to be anything a few months of proper diet won't handle. Except this blue eye of his. I don't like the way it's clouded."

Mary had noticed it that morning. She was hoping it was a temporary thing. She knew a horse could go blind in one or both eyes when it had been starved back this hard.

Dr. Adams ran his hand along Comanche's topline, all the way to his croup, then on to the dock, and finally fingered his way to the tip of his tail. Comanche kept his ears flat but turned his head to watch the doctor.

During the examination of his legs, chest, neck, and belly, Comanche gradually relaxed his ears. When Dr. Adams moved to examine Comanche's teeth, the ears went flat again. There was no question in either of their minds what lay ahead.

"He hates the dentist," Mary offered.

"I do, too."

After administering a sedative, Dr. Adams gathered his dentistry tools, a bucket of water, and a headlamp, then leaned against Mary's cart while they waited for the sedative to do its job.

"You doing all right, Mary?"

She slid her palms down her thighs. "Most days. He's gonna be a big help." She nodded toward the sleepy horse. "What do you think about Comanche's eye?"

"I'll examine it real close while he's sleepy. Could be a simple infection. Maybe even has something in it. We'll pull some blood, check for anything that's not obvious. I'll worm him, then give him a few vitamin shots and broad-spectrum antibiotics. You do what you always do with a horse. The rest is up to God, I suppose."

Up to God. How could he know she wasn't sure if she trusted God to handle everything anymore?

"Looks like he's willing to cooperate now. Let's take care of those teeth."

Within half an hour, Comanche's teeth were in top shape, and he was resting comfortably in his stall. Dr. Adams leaned on the stall guard and studied his patient. "He's in remarkable condition, considering the situation. Still the fighter he was the day Sam found him. I even believe his eye will be okay. You be sure to put the drops in three or four times a day, until they're all gone, and keep him on the supplemental vitamins."

Mary slipped into the stall and stroked Comanche's mane. "He doesn't know how to quit, that's for sure." She wondered about herself.

"Twenty years ago, this summer, wasn't it?"

"Callie was four years old. Boy, didn't she fall for him? Remember your first visit to the ranch? You had just taken the practice over from Dr. Beck after he retired. You helped me teach Callie how to bottle-feed an orphaned foal. Comanche took right to it." She gave him a few pats on the neck.

Dr. Adams went to Comanche and stroked his mane. "I remember. Sam had carried this poor little fella over the rump of his horse all the way from the BLM grassland after he'd found him standing by his dead mama."

Mary looked up and smiled into the air. "I had to keep a tight rein on Callie. She thought he needed a bottle every five minutes."

"That's the year you folks started leasing that chunk of land, as I recall."

Mary hugged Comanche's neck. "Sam knew we couldn't save them all, but he was sure we could save a few of the wild horses from slaughter. He loves those wild horses. Funny how it is, you know. They need him to survive, and he—well, you know Sam and his horses."

"Sure do." Dr. Adams took her hand, "There's a fine herd of wild horses running free out there, thanks to you and Sam. Close to thirty now as I recall from last year's roundup."

"I just don't know what'll come of it all. Lease payments for the grassland every year, taxes so high on the ranch, now with the mortgage ..." She stopped herself before she could say anything about the hospital bills. She'd burdened him with too much already. Lester was a good friend. He didn't need to stand there and listen to all her problems.

He met her eyes and held her gaze. "You can count on me for this year's check-up for the wild herd again. You just call the office and leave word when you and the guests have them ready to corral."

⁊⧽⁊⧽⁊⧽

Barbara knew as soon as she saw her mother curled up on the porch glider holding a soda can against her cheek that Philip had hit her again. She looked at the chair lying on the ground beside the cabin's porch. He'd probably thrown it at her.

"Mom?" She gently touched her mother's arm and sucked in a quick breath when she saw the fear in her mother's eyes. Like she always did. To protect *him*. Her mother recovered quickly and sat upright, forcing a fake, if broad smile.

"Silly me, I tripped on these steps in the dark and bashed my cheek against the darn porch post."

Barbara pulled the hand that held the soda can aside. "Philip hit you again. Don't lie for him. He's not worth it." She stared at the cabin door. "What set him off this time?"

"I'm not really sure. I was hard on him yesterday when I came back to the cabin and found him sitting with Lucy." She grinned at Barbara. "I told him I was gonna lay down some ground rules." She raised her eyes and sighed out loud. "It didn't go over well at all ... But I stuck to my guns!"

Barbara stared at her in shock. "Wow! Two days of this nowhereland air must be affecting you. Heck, you never stick to your guns. Unless it's about something I did!"

"Well, if I'm sticking to my guns, you weren't a lot of help in the pavilion this morning."

"Yeah, well, I still think this ranch idea sucks. You know Philip is gonna spend the summer showing off to Lucy, and anybody else he can fool, acting like some big man when all he is, is a first class lying piece of ... " Her voice trailed off.

"Barbara! Stop it! ... He's not! He's my husband." Linda opened the soda and stared out into the dark.

"Oh yeah, and the post hit you." Barbara started away but turned back at the bottom of the steps. "You know, for a minute I thought you might be waking up!" She ran down the hill.

Linda hurried down the steps after her, "Barbara, it's dark out. Come back here! Where are you going?"

She waved over her head without turning. "For a walk. Go in to your *husband*!

As Barbara ran, light shining through the barn's wide-open double doors lit her way. She stopped just inside the doors. All the lights were on, bright as day, but thankfully she didn't see anyone. Only the white golf cart parked in the center aisle. She climbed in the driver's seat and rested her head on the wheel. A second later a voice floated from the box-stall. "I'll get a lead rope and then we'll go up to the yard for the night." Barbara looked in the direction of the voice.

Mary started out of the stall to retrieve a rope and gasped. "Barbara, why ... Is anything wrong?"

"Nothing you can do anything about." Barbara mumbled without raising her head.

"You're all out of breath." Mary gave her a concerned look.

"I felt like running. So I ran. What do you care?" Nobody ever really cares about anybody anyway."

Mary raised her eyebrow. "You're right. It's your business, but as long as you're here, would you go into the tack room and fetch me a lead rope? The snap on this one seems to have broken."

Barbara sat firm and gave Mary a look she was sure made it clear she had no idea what the old woman wanted. What's more, why should she care?

"See the door with the green sign that says *Tack Room*, behind you? Next to the fire extinguisher." Then, it was as if she'd read her thoughts. "It'll save me a few steps, if you'd be so kind."

Barbara twisted in the seat and found the door. "Yeah. I see it."

"The light switch is by the door. The lead ropes hang on the left, in front of the saddles."

Reluctantly, Barbara slid from the cart and slowly shuffled to the door. She paused a second inside the open door, registered the darkness and the smell of leather, then found the light switch. The ropes hung exactly where the woman said. She stepped farther inside and grabbed the first rope, a white one with a brass snap on the end. Before leaving the room, she looked around at the neat rows of saddles waiting on their wooden stands. In the far corner stood a large rack overflowing with saddle blankets. Hanging on the wall next to her, above a wall-length bench, were leather halters and all sorts of other things she guessed were important to these idiot nowhere-land hicks.

Barbara switched off the light, closed the door, and carried the rope across the aisle to Mary. "Crap, you have a lot of stuff in there. What do you do with it all?"

"Thank you." Mary smiled and accepted the rope. "In a few days, you'll begin to become very familiar with all of it." She led Comanche to the rear of the cart, with Barbara following close, tied the rope to the bumper, then sat on a fender.

Barbara leaned against the wall and looked out into the darkness. "I don't want to be here, you know. They made me come."

"I heard you say that once before. I'm sorry you're not excited about your vacation."

"This isn't much of a vacation." Barbara huffed, then turned to face Mary. "You've been married a long time, right?"

"My goodness, where did that come from? Yes, Sam and I have been husband and wife for thirty-five glorious years." Mary held up her left hand, showing her engagement and wedding rings. "Sam wanted to buy me a bigger diamond once, but I wouldn't let him. It's not the size of the diamond that matters. It's what's inside a man's heart." She put her hand to her chest and gave an exaggerated sigh.

Barbara paced halfway to the open doors then turned and walked back to Comanche. "That jerk Philip is my mom's third husband."

With a start, Mary sat up straight. "I see. He seems like a nice man. Of course, I don't know him as well as you do, but he has good manners and he's rather handsome. You don't think much of him, I gather."

Barbara stroked Comanche's back, then shook the hair from her hand. "He's shedding."

"He sure is. There are some brushes in the bucket over there. Would you like to brush him?"

"Everybody always thinks Philip's so great." She stopped petting the horse and backed away, turning to investigate the white five-gallon bucket sitting next to the wall. "I never saw a horse in person before. Well, I rode a pony one time when I was four. At a fair. My real dad took me. It was right after my mom divorced him." Barbara timidly selected a stiff-bristled brush from the top of the bucket and held it up for Mary's approval. "This one?" She wasn't about to sort through all the stuff in there. A brush was a brush.

"Yes, that's the one I'm using on Comanche right now, to get through all his heavy shedding." Mary stood and moved to the horse's head and scratched his forehead. "Brush him gently in the direction his hair lies."

Barbara stared at her. "I know how to brush a dog! We have a Golden Retriever named Goldie. She sheds all the time, too ... She has to spend all summer at my uncle's because we came here. I wanted to bring her, but Jerk-head said *no*." She focused on brushing Comanche's back and ribs. The grateful horse leaned into her strokes. "Why is he so skinny? Is he sick or dying or something?"

Mary hugged Comanche's neck and kissed his cheek. "No, *he's* not sick." She hugged his neck again. "He'll bounce right back. You'll see."

Barbara stopped brushing to watch Mary. Was she crying? *Wow, what's wrong with her? She's acting like the stupid horse is her kid or something.* "Hey, are you all right? I mean, are you crying?"

Mary snapped up. "Yes, yes, I'm fine." She swiped her hand across her face. "I should get him out on the grass." Then she turned to Barbara and smiled. "I'll bet your mother is wondering where you slipped off to by now."

"I doubt it, but I'm tired, anyway." She started for the door, pitched the brush in the bucket, and pointed to Comanche. "I think he's a nice horse." Then she sprinted through the doors. After one last look toward Mary, Barbara ran up the hill to their cabin. As she raced past the first cabin, she saw the new arrivals, the Colliers, on their porch. She waved but didn't break stride.

Her mother was still on the porch, still sitting on the glider wrapped in a blanket. "I was beginning to worry. I've read stories about people wandering away and getting lost forever in nowhere-land."

"I was in the barn." Her mother gave her a quizzical look. "I just ended up there. Lights were on, and I went in to look around."

"You must have had a long look. As I said, I was beginning to worry."

"I was fine." Joining her mother on the glider, Barbara squirmed and wiggled until she was snuggled tight, then rested her head on her mother's shoulder.

"I suppose we should get to bed. I heard we'll get our introduction to the horses tomorrow."

"Beat ya. I brushed a horse tonight down there." She pointed to the barn.

"Really? The city girl who hated this whole idea spends her first night in the barn and cozies up to a horse while everybody else has to wait for the riding instructor."

"Do you think the old lady here is all right? I mean, do you think she's creepy?"

"Barbara! What on earth?"

"The horse I brushed is some old sick horse she was sitting with. You know what? She looks as old and skinny as the horse. She was nice and friendly and all, but wow, she's creepy. Hugging and crying all over that sick horse."

"Maybe it's a special horse. You know how much you love Goldie."

"Why'd you divorce Dad?"

Linda pulled the blanket up over her nose. "We've been all through that, too many times. Do you miss him?"

"I did at first, but he moved away and stopped calling and stuff. I don't know—it's not that I miss him, really, just, sometimes I wonder what it would be like if you'd stayed married."

Linda wrapped her blanket around the two of them, pulled it over their heads, and whispered, "Me too."

Chapter Ten

Before going to the lodge the next morning, Mary led Comanche to his newly fenced pasture. She drove her cart slowly. Her mind, though, was running at top speed as she strategized Comanche's and her return from retirement. Gaily whistling "Back in the Saddle Again," she inched the cart to within inches of Morgan's feet before stopping at the gate.

"Good morning, Morgan," she called in perfect cadence with the song she'd been whistling. He held up a long wooden-handled screwdriver. "This hinge needed a few screws. I noticed it yesterday but ran out of time. Stay seated. I'll untie Comanche."

"Hold on a second. We need to put in his eye drops first." She dug in her shirt pocket for the small plastic bottle.

"Eye drops?"

"When Dr. Adams examined him yesterday, he said these might help clear up his eye. Would you?" She handed the bottle to Morgan.

Steadying Comanche's head with his left hand, and using his right thumb to push back the eyelid, he dropped two drops into the cloudy blue eye.

"Good boy!" He praised Comanche, gave him a friendly pat, then untied him. "He sure is easy to doctor. Not like Ruth. I'd sure hate to put drops in her eye!"

They looked over the board fence into the adjoining pasture at Morgan's horse standing between them and the herd. She was a fine mare, a descendant of Mar-Sa breeding stock, part wild horse, part tough-blooded quarter horse. Born on the grassland five years ago, she'd blossomed into a fast, tough, smart horse. Befitting her nature, she stood with eyes and ears aimed their way, watching Morgan and Mary, ready to sound the alarm and rush every horse in the pasture to safety should the need arise. No matter the herd or pasture, Ruth always assumed the role of alpha mare.

Morgan whistled to Ruth. She stomped her hooves and shook her head. He whistled again, louder and shriller. Ruth came at a run.

Morgan scaled the fence, coaxed Ruth closer, and mussed her mane. She snorted, shook her head, spun, and galloped away.

Mary ran her fingers through her own thin white hair. "Ladies frown on fellas mussing their hair."

Ruth put on a show of running and bucking, then stopped and shot a hard-eyed stare in Morgan's direction. "She's ready for the Fourth of July race, that's for sure."

Mary smiled. "So is Sam. He's full of himself, so sure he'll hang on to the trophy for the third year. His stud, Bullet, is fast, but between you and me, I think Ruth has a pretty good shot."

Morgan jumped from the fence and slid into the seat beside her. "You think so? I mean, I think so, but … You think so?"

"I do. She has drive, competitiveness, spirit. She's tough in a way that reminds me of Comanche." Ruth arched her neck, squealed, and kicked up her back legs before driving the herd away. She charged them at a dead run, snaking her neck, ears flat. "Yeah, I'd say you two stand a good chance at winning the trophy this year."

"We were second last year by only half a length. Remember?"

She gave Morgan a congratulatory pat on the back. "I sure do."

During the short ride to the lodge for breakfast, Morgan's words rushed out of him as he detailed his plan to work Ruth every day for the next few weeks so she'd be in top shape and ready to take that coveted trophy.

As she listened, she felt a little jealous of his youthful enthusiasm and energy. Boy, a little of that could go a long way for her and Comanche. Just listening to him made her tired.

No. No, it didn't. It made her hungry. Hungry for her own trophy that she and Comanche would win at the state fair. The one they'd work toward all summer. She knew he was tough enough. Was she? She'd need to get on a horse again and get herself in shape before pushing a heavy workload on Comanche.

"Morgan, when you take the folks out on the trail, why don't you leave Chester here? Wouldn't it give you the perfect opportunity to condition Ruth for the big day?"

He laughed. "Sure, but do you reckon the guests are ready for a cross country race? I mean, Ruth can set a fast pace when she has a mind to."

"Maybe they'd love it." Mary laughed as she drove around the corral behind the barn. She slowed the cart at the sight of her husband waving his hat in the air to flag her down. As if she'd ever pass him by!

"How about givin' a hungry cowboy a lift to the lodge?" He jabbed his thumb out in hitchhiker fashion.

"Hop on, Cowboy. We're headed that way."

Morgan jumped to the ground. "You know what? I'll walk up the hill."

Mary pulled the cart into the lodge and glanced around to make sure everything was operating smoothly. Susan and Linda were serving the guests. Stacks of pancakes, Susan's specialty. Plates of crisp bacon, pots of coffee, pitchers of cold orange juice, and glasses of milk littered the tables. She and Sam found seats at the end of a nearby table and prepared to enjoy the early morning banter.

Paul Keaton had arrived overnight and jumped up to come greet them. "Morning, Mary, Sam." He nodded respectively as he slid onto the bench beside them. "It's great to be back in the open-air world of horses, cows, and sunshine. Lucy and I have decided we'll be moving to Arizona when I retire. Of course, we'd need to find a homestead near Mar-Sa so you can keep an eye on our livestock and such."

"Gonna take up ranchin' after politickin' are ya, Paul?" Sam asked with a grin.

"Ah, well, I suppose it might be wishful thinking, retiring I mean. You never know, though. The good people in my district back home might make that decision for me one day." He turned to Mary. "It's so good to see you, and in case this old bony cowboy didn't say it today yet, you look radiant." He kissed her hand.

Mary blushed and thanked him. *I do feel a little more chipper this morning. Perhaps there was nothing to worry about, after all. Perhaps she'd been letting the doctors keep her reined in more than she should have these past few years.* She watched Paul settle in again between Lucy and the Colliers and attack a stack of flapjacks. She picked at her pancakes, then decided to eat hearty. She would need to fuel the furnace if she was going to build herself up again into competitive form. Watching Sam answer the Colliers' stream of questions, and even one from Philip, who seemed pleasant enough despite his stepdaughter's assessment, Mary felt a wave of contentedness wash over her. What a beautiful morning it was. Bright sun, enthusiastic guests, and Susan's award-winning pancakes, which by now Mary had enjoyed two helpings of.

"Maybe I should help Susan clean up," Mary whispered in Sam's ear.

"They have it under control, and Linda needs to learn the ropes if she's gonna cover for you tomorrow. Besides, you don't want to miss my big speech."

Tomorrow, yes tomorrow. Mary twisted her hands together and smiled at Sam. She wasn't going to allow tomorrow to ruin today. Not completely, at least.

Sam stood and raised his hands for attention. "I would like to take a second now to thank you all for coming to our ranch for the summer. After breakfast we'll gather at the large corral. Rusty and Morgan will introduce you to a few horses. I'll be on hand to answer questions and cheer you on. As this is Lucy and Paul's second summer visit, I officially designate them house parents."

Paul hopped up on the table. "I'm here to serve you! If there is anything I or my office can do for you, please don't hesitate to call. I thank you for your support."

"We're not in the Capitol," Lucy whispered, loud enough for all to hear.

The lodge exploded with catcalls, laughter and orders for Paul to have a seat. Paul took it all in with a big smile and a deep bow, then blew kisses all around before sitting down and returning his attention to their host.

Sam grinned. "There's plenty of work on a ranch this size, but we'll make it fun, most of the time. In a few days, you'll be able to sit a horse. Of course, some of you may want pillows instead of saddle leather, but you'll get there. Our first activity, about a week from now, will be to move the wild horses from winter range to summer grass."

Zack Collier raised his hand. "You mean, in a week you expect us to learn to ride well enough to move a herd of wild horses? I'm a hockey player. I've never ridden a horse. Sure, I want to learn. That's why we're here. But in a week?

Mary grinned at Sam. Someone asked that question every year.

Sam answered it the same way every year. "The horses you'll be riding know their job, and they like most greenhorns. The wild horses we'll be moving may not be as keen on greenhorns, but they know the routine. Generally."

Debby Collier grasped her husband's hand. "See? It's just like I told you. The horses know what they're doing."

"They do, and one of the ways we try to help is to match you with horses who seem to take to you."

"Well, I'm sure gonna give it my best, but a week still seems mighty fast," Zack said.

Debby shook her head, smiled wide, and roughed his hair. "You're not afraid to hit the glass at fifty miles an hour, but you're worried about riding a horse?"

"When I hit the glass, I have pads on." Zack tossed Sam a still-worried look.

Sam gave him a friendly chuckle. "Wear your pads. We won't mind."

Zack faced his wife and shrugged. "I wanted to bring them."

"You'll do fine, Zack. When you all finish up breakfast, wander down to the corral. Morgan, Rusty, and I will have a few horses ready for you to try on."

Mary sat comfortably in the shade of her cart's roof, watching her cowboy do what he did best. He stood beneath the bright sun, in the middle of the big corral, surrounded by a circle of horses that were attached by leads to some very nervous people.

She loved and admired Sam for his remarkable ability to comfort man or beast. As he gave the same talk he gave each year, she watched the horses drop their heads, close their eyes, and relax into a dreamy, sleepy state of mind. She had invented a game over the years, selecting the guest whose shoulders would soften first and the one whose shoulders would remain stiff almost to the end.

This year she'd not count the Keatons. They'd been through the process already, so they knew the secrets. Philip Cunningham, she guessed, might never get it. He'd be the last to soften, if he let down his guard at all. Both the Colliers stood rigid, eyeing their horses with open fear. Zack kept a wary eye on his horse while Debby stood at her rope's end watching Sam and Rusty. Her cute, timid smile reminded Mary of a child expecting to be scolded.

Nicky and John Bartlett stood close together their horses behind them were already asleep. The Bartletts' past experience with horses gave them an edge.

Linda Cunningham held her horse with a loose, comfortable grasp that surprised Mary since the first time she'd touched a horse had been about seven minutes ago.

Refusing to participate, Barbara sat atop the fence at the far end of the corral.

"This is Woody." Sam patted the saddle fastened to a barrel next to him, standing on four wooden legs. "I call him that for two reasons. One, old-time cowboys would sometimes call their saddle, *wood*. Two, if you look close, you can see he's made of wood, except for the barrel part. I never got around to giving him a head, didn't want him to outsmart the pilgrims." The group chuckled, even Philip, Mary was pleased to note.

"In a minute, I'll have you walk around the circle one by one, ground-tie your horse over here by me, and step onto Woody. I'll balance you in the saddle so your first feel of leather is on a horse I know for sure won't get away from you." Here he stopped and walked a slow circle around Woody, patting the barrel in front of the saddle, as if to calm a nervous horse. "But let me caution you ... people have come off Woody. He gets downright annoyed at folks who ask for too much speed. He kinda likes to just mosey along."

Mary was impatient to go to Comanche, but she hadn't picked a winner in her soft shoulder contest yet. She settled deeper into her seat to study her contestants as they were introduced to Woody. Paul and Lucy went first. Good job, smooth mount, great posture, but, Mary reminded herself, they'd been to Mar-Sa before. Next, the Colliers stepped up to the treacherous, stationary horse. Wasn't it polite of Zack to allow his pretty blonde wife to go first? Mary chuckled softly to herself when it became obvious Debby Collier seemed more interested in the precise placement of her hat than how she settled into the saddle. Well now, look at Zack showing off. He just might turn into a rider if he could learn to follow Sam's instructions. The Bartletts, more Sam's and Mary's age, their confidence in each other shows. Their past experience with horses shows, too. Nice job, you two.

Philip approached Woody with the air of a conquering knight. He tossed the lead rope to the ground with such force, his horse snorted and bolted.

"That's all right. He can't go far." Sam held Philip's arm as the embarrassed fellow settled into the saddle on the wooden horse.

There's my stiff shoulder winner this year.

"He'll carry on all night about what a dumb horse he had," Barbara said. "Find a way to make it Mom's fault."

Surprised, Mary spun about to find Barbara standing behind her. "Oh, I didn't realize you'd come over here." She offered Barbara a seat in the shade. "How could it be your mother's fault?"

The young girl laced her fingers and looked across the corral to her mother. "It doesn't matter. He'll blame her. He's a stupid creep. I hate him! I want to go home. How do you stand it out here, in nowhere-land?"

"Well, I've been living here with Sam for thirty years, so I guess nowhere-land *is* my home." Mary purposely gave Barbara an exaggerated, inquisitive look. "Nowhere-land?"

"That's what it is." She shrugged. "I mean, how do you live without cable and cell phones?"

"We manage. I suppose you don't miss what you never had. I could ask you how you manage without horses."

"Weeeell," Barbara strung out the word sarcastically. "I suppose because they invented cars?"

"I'd heard about that."

Barbara smiled, then sobered. "You're really sick aren't you? I mean, you look ... sick."

Mary drew in a long breath. "I was ... Barbara, why do you dislike your father so?"

"Stepfather. And I don't *dislike* him. I hate him. He's a pig! They weren't married a year before he cheated on my mother. She thinks nowhere-land has some magical power to fix their marriage. Why does she bother?"

Mary thought a second as she watched the young girl hurl dagger eyes toward her stepfather. "Looks like your mother is next to try on old Woody." She tapped Barbara on the shoulder and pointed to the barrel-horse, purposely shifting the girl's attention from her stepfather. She noticed Barbara's eyes soften. They watched Linda lead her horse to Woody, drop her lead rope, and gracefully slide into the saddle on the barrel. "First place for the soft shoulder award," Mary announced.

"What?"

"Oh it's a silly game I play each summer. I try to guess who'll be the first to take to the horses. This year I declare your mother the winner!" Mary decided not to mention where the girl's stepfather placed.

Chapter Eleven

Mary stared at the hospital entrance through the windshield. She hated that building. It had become impossible for her to see it as anything but the enemy. Cold brick walls surrounded by a sea of menacing black asphalt. The main entrance with its covered walkway screamed at her, screamed a warning, "Come here, come to me. I'll devour you."

Susan opened Mary's door. "Do you need my hand?"

She looked up at her and forced a weak smile. "I think I do."

Susan helped her from the car and led her across the lot toward the main entrance. Mary never looked ahead, choosing instead to stare at the ground and follow Susan's lead.

The automatic door slid closed behind them. The smell hit Mary with all the force of a kick in the face. That horrible smell of medicine, ammonia, and stale air. Why did hospitals have stale air? That smell brought back the memory of lying in her hospital room, lying there for hours while the chemo dripped into her arm, making her sicker by the drip. Is that what her future held? More stale air, more chemo?

"Do you want me to go in with you?"

Mary hadn't noticed that they'd stopped at Dr. Stein's door. She raised her eyes to the solid, dark wood door, recognized the smudged brass plate in the middle, boasting his name. What was it like to be a doctor? To tell someone she had a horrible invader in her body? An invader that wanted to take everything she had and leave nothing for her loved ones.

What would happen when she died? Would she still see Sam? Feel his touch? What about Callie? Would she see Callie?

"Mary? Would you like me to go in with you?"

Oh Susan, dear Susan. "Yes, please, I ..."

Susan squeezed Mary's hand, took a deep breath, and opened the door.

They'd painted the office. It used to be a pale blue, but now the walls were yellow. Who would choose yellow? Such a cold, unfriendly color.

An unhappy-looking young woman came from behind the desk. "Mrs. Holt? Dr. Stein is running a few minutes behind, but I'll help get you settled in the exam room. He'll see you there."

Get settled? What did that mean, exactly? Why would she say, "Get settled?"

Holding Susan's hand, Mary followed the young woman into the examining room.

"Step on the scale please."

Mary barely heard her but did as she was told.

After scribbling in the file with her obnoxious red pen, the woman helped Mary onto the paper-covered table and turned to Susan. "Will you be staying here with Mrs. Holt?"

Without hesitation, "Yes."

"I suppose you can have a seat in the corner." Turning to Mary, "I'll be back in a second to get your temperature and blood pressure."

After she'd gone, Mary wanted to say something, anything, to Susan. She couldn't think of anything to say. Her mind raced with thoughts, but they flew so fast, she was unable to hold one long enough to share it. What was wrong! Was she going insane? That must be it. Right here, in this horrible, yellow room, she was about to lose her mind.

The door swung open and the same nurse came in. Why would Dr. Stein hire such a miserable-looking woman to work for him? "Dr. Stein is almost finished. He just wants to make a call, schedule a few tests, and then he'll be with you." Sitting on the stool next to Mary, she held out her hand. "Now, may I have your left arm, please?"

Even though it was merely moments, it seemed like an hour before Dr. Stein entered the room and sat on the stool by the paper-covered table. He looked older than Mary remembered. Not as much as she did to him, she imagined. She watched him look at her file, pretending to study the numbers and words. Why bother? He already knew what he was going to say. Did he need to work up the nerve to change her life? What a phrase, *change her life*. It was almost funny.

He gently dug his fingers in the flesh under her jawbone. She watched his eyes. He moved those tender hands to her shoulders, pressing his fingertips into her muscle. Next his soft hands slid down her spine, carefully palpating each vertebra. Mary couldn't stop a faint smile as she remembered examining Comanche exactly the same way.

"How have you been feeling lately?"

What if she lied? "Very well. In fact, I feel better today than I have in some time."

"That's interesting. As I told you on the phone, your latest blood work raised a red flag or two. There is no question your counts are off. Frankly, I would have expected you to feel a little tired. You do have nice color. Maybe a little sunburn?"

"For the past few days, I've been spending a bit more time outside. I've started a project."

Dr. Stein took both her hands, held her arms out in front of her, and turned them over. He studied the white underside, then slid his hand along first one arm then the other, and into her armpit. He paused, gave her a feeble smile, then dug his fingers into the flesh, causing her to flinch from the slight pain.

Finally, he released her. "I'd like to schedule a few tests."

Oh, boy. Mary cupped her face, took a deep breath, and looked up toward Susan. "How much will they cost?"

Dr. Stein gently pulled her hands away from her face and held them tightly. "You can't think about that now. First, we need to get you well, and to do that, I need some answers. This is serious."

Losing both breasts hadn't been serious? How did it get more serious?

"I don't know ... What kind of tests?"

"To be thorough, we should have an ultrasound, a CAT scan, and an MRI. I'd like to schedule them as soon as we can. This week, if possible."

"I thought I already had the surgery, and the chemo, and the radiation to be thorough. I don't know ... The blood tests ..." She looked at the floor, then dug the heels of her hands in her eyes. "They could mean more chemo?"

"I can't be certain without these tests and some more blood work. I'd like to make arrangements today. The longer we wait, the more difficult it becomes. I've made preliminary calls, and I think I can schedule the ultrasound and blood work for Thursday, the CAT scan and MRI for Friday and Monday."

The quiet that swallowed the room was deafening. Mary had had all of this she wanted. How could she explain what she felt, what she feared? Only Sam could help, but his answer would be the same as always: *Do whatever, Doc. Do whatever it takes.* She couldn't do that to him. How could she leave him with any more debt? How could she?

Mary slid off the table. "How much will it cost? I mean, after my insurance ... How much will we owe?"

"That's not important. What is ..."

She grabbed his hands and stared deep into his eyes. "Dr. Stein, it is *extremely* important. You may schedule, but I'll need to know, with certainty, what we'll owe after the insurance."

Dr. Stein slid his hands from her grip and then gently wrapped them over hers. "I'll personally make the calls to your insurance company." He stood, still holding her hands. "I'll call you tomorrow ... in the meantime, you should limit your exposure to the sun."

Mary and Susan sat in the car in the cool shade of the barn, holding hands. Shopping on the way home from the hospital for the few items they really did need had done little to improve Mary's mood. Susan, as always, was trying to cheer her up. The effort felt strained and obvious. To both of them.

Mary knew what she needed.

"Susan, could I ask you to fetch Chester for me?" Her gaze carried her far up the hillside behind the house. "I'd like to visit Callie."

"Are you sure? Dr. Stein told you to stay out of the sun. Why not take your cart? I could ride with you."

"No. I'll ride Chester. The trip to town has had a strange effect on me. I feel, I don't know ... energized. I know I should be exhausted, mad, maybe even hateful. But suddenly, now that we're back, I feel simply ... invigorated. I suppose it's the calm before the storm, but nevertheless, I'll ride Chester. Please fetch him, won't you?"

Good old Chester. Sam was fond of saying he'd never met a kinder horse. Chester was always willing to cooperate, and in no time,

Susan had him saddled and ready to go. She led him to the mounting block in the small corral where Mary stood.

"Susan, could you do me another small favor? Would you move Comanche to the yard? I'd like him to be able to watch me." As she settled into the saddle for the first time in nearly four years, she looked to Comanche, standing with his head over the gate of his personal pasture. Whenever possible, he would fix those mismatched eyes of his on Mary.

When Susan moved Comanche into the yard, however, those mismatched eyes were full of confusion.

Mary knew exactly why he was confused. He was expecting her to pony him behind, as she had often done when she'd ridden Chester. But things were different now.

"Maybe next week, Comanche. After Sam finishes your feet and you've gained a few pounds. For now, eat grass." She smiled to Susan and clucked to Chester, who stepped off smoothly and started for the trail leading around the house and up the hills behind. She knew she needed to be out of sight before Sam discovered her plan. At best, he would insist he come along. At worst, he would forbid her the ride.

Walking along at Chester's smooth, easy pace, Mary felt so very comfortable. Something about a horse.

Comanche followed along inside the fence as far as he could. When the trail led her and Chester away from the yard and straight up the hill behind the house, Comanche shook his head, reared, and screamed a loud, shrill scream that made her realize how badly she'd missed his silly antics. No matter the situation, he was always the biggest clown or finest showman. Or best partner.

Mary turned and yelled, "Ye-ha! Let it rip, Comanche! You'll be running up this hill in no time!" Then she touched her heels to

Chester and cantered smoothly up the long hill. Comanche screamed after them until they were a quarter mile away.

What a feeling! No medicine known to man could do this! A beautiful afternoon, the grass sporting a refreshed green color after yesterday's rain, the sky a sparkling blue. Not a cloud up there, not even a jet stream.

After a short run, Mary's legs warned her that her body was not in the same shape as her mind. She brought Chester down to an easy walk and followed the trail straight up to the peak of Callie's Summit. Sam and Mary had christened the area during a picnic celebration there on Callie's first birthday. From the crest, it seemed a person could see for hundreds of miles over the rolling hills and valleys.

Once over the highest point, the first sighting was always the top of the lone ancient dogwood tree. As Mary and Chester began their descent on the far side, the black iron fence surrounding the old cemetery came into view. Riding closer, the stone markers became visible. Finally Mary could see the bench Sam had so lovingly made and placed by Callie's grave.

꿍ꗛꗛꗛꗛ

Sam and Rusty had been working in the implement shed most of the afternoon, readying the canvas-covered chuck wagon for the trip to the wild horse range.

"I reckon she's ready for travel again."

"Sure glad we didn't need to replace that axle." Rusty gave the big wheel nut a final twist, stood up, and dragged a dirty shirt sleeve across his sweaty brow.

"Let's pack one along, just in case." Sam walked a lap around the wagon. "Yep, she's ready to go. What do you say to a cool drink in the lodge?"

"I'd say we earned one, boss." Rusty slid the extra wooden axle under the wagon frame atop the beams and then lashed it with rope on each end.

Halfway to the lodge, they were intercepted by Paul, Philip, and Morgan.

"You boys ready to hit the range in a few days?" Sam asked.

Philip spoke first. "I think I'm catching on. But Linda, I can hardly get her off a horse."

Paul laughed. "Unless it's to cook in the lodge. She sure likes that kitchen."

Sam gave Philip a half-grin but studied the man's eyes. "We'll give her a crack at cookin' out of the back of a covered wagon in a few days."

"That woman will cook anywhere, anytime." Philip said.

The five men entered the lodge side-by-side and, in strides of military precision, conquered the tables nearest the kitchen. Susan, Linda, and Barbara were busy behind the long counter that separated the tables from the kitchen area. The smell of fried chicken wafted out to greet the men.

Sam moved to the counter and leaned on it, grinning like a ten-year-old boy who wanted a special treat before suppertime. "I had in mind a long drink of cold tea, but by golly, half a chicken would fill the bill, I reckon."

Susan pushed back her hair, gave him her most reproving look followed by her most loving smile, and shook a finger his way. "Chicken's for supper, in about an hour. Tea we'll gladly serve you."

Sam straightened up and glanced from face to face. "Mary resting?"

Susan's face flushed. She never could keep much from Sam. "She went to see Callie."

Sam spun around to look out toward the house, saw Mary's cart in the carport, then fixed his gaze on Susan. "How'd she get there?"

Her face got redder. She whispered, "She rode ... Chester. Sam, she ..."

He whirled from the counter, leaped a table in his path, and hit the ground running. Gaining speed with every stride, he raced down the hill to the corral that held his personal horse. Unaccustomed to that kind of approach, Bullet snorted, spun away, then faced Sam from the far end of the corral. Sam snatched his halter from the post, swung on the tall horse's back, and kicked him into an immediate flat-out gallop.

They flew as one down the drive, around the house, and up the trail that led to Callie's Summit. As they rounded the turn by the yard fence, Comanche took up the chase. The skinny paint charged along until the fence stopped him. He reared and screamed in protest. Sam demanded top speed from Bullet, who obliged, sending dust and stones flying high in the air behind them with each powerful stride.

Over the top of Callie's Summit. Down the other side. Soon, Sam saw the top of the dogwood. Next, the leaning black fence. Then Chester grazing peacefully behind the graveyard. Finally he saw his wife sitting on the bench, next to their daughter.

She looked up at him, smiled her beautiful crooked smile, and opened her arms.

He was over the fence in an instant, cradling her. "Mary, you foolish girl. You know better! This is a steep trail. You could've come off Chester. What were you thinking?"

Eyes sparkling, she pushed him from her and whispered, "I've come off horses plenty of times." Then she kissed him.

He had to laugh. "Yes, you have. But, Mary ... things are different now."

"They are." She turned toward the grave at their side. "I miss her. I wanted to tell her about Comanche, not about the sad things. I told her I intend to win again this year and bring her the ribbon." She fondled the faded, tattered blue ribbon nailed to the back of the bench. "I told her I'd hang it right here ... with hers."

He pulled her tight, buried his face in her neck, and drank in her smell. The lavender powder she loved mixed with the sweat on her neck and the fresh smell of her cotton blouse.

When they'd finished their cry, Mary spoke, her voice soft and unsteady. "Sam, this is very important to me ... This may be our last summer."

His body went limp. He studied her face and found it very serious. "No. No, Mary. Don't say that! Don't think that! Mary! ... What? What?"

She looked away and slowly stroked Callie's headstone. "I saw Dr. Stein today."

The strangling feeling in his throat almost choked him. He had to fight to breathe, let alone speak. "I can't hear this. I don't ... I'm not ready to hear this."

He cussed himself for being weak when he knew he must be strong for her. How could he be the strong one? Mary had always been the one he leaned on. Her strength had carried him when they'd lost Callie. For thirty-five years she'd been his strength, his life, his very breath.

She took his hands. "Comanche and I are going to win that ribbon."

He leaned away, wiped his eyes on his shirt cuffs, and, as always, gathered strength from his wife's courage. No matter what horrors they'd had to face, they'd always faced them together. It had always been Mary's strength that pulled them through, together. But she needed *him* to be strong now. He couldn't show weakness. As much as her courage gave him strength to go on, he would dig deep inside himself, mix his love for her with her courage, and make the magic that would give him the power to help her now. This minute, this month, for however long she wanted. Whatever she wanted.

"Danged right, you are!" He kissed her cheek, walked over to Chester on unsteady legs, then came back with the saddle blanket and spread it on the grass. "Lie with me awhile. We'll watch the sunset while you tell me how you're gonna win that blue ribbon."

She pointed to the blanket, giggling a little. "That's an awfully small blanket for two."

"Reckon it is, isn't it? It sure seemed like a good idea when I hatched it. You take the blanket, and I'll take the grass."

He helped her to the blanket and then crawled next to her. The view from the old cemetery was endless. Rolling hills as far as the human eye could reach. Miles away to the west, the sky was turning red. Deeper, darker red with each passing moment. They didn't need to talk. They needed only to hold each other, seeking comfort, next to Callie.

When Sam felt the tears trail down his cheek, he moved his head. He didn't want Mary to notice.

Maybe she'd noticed just the same.

"Dr. Stein wants to start tests again. I wasn't going to tell you."

He jerked upright. "Why not? Why would you keep that from me?"

"Money." She hugged his waist and hung on.

She might as well have stabbed him. "Money? Money? ... Mary? What's money! ..." Sam held on hard, shaking, trying for strength. "When does he want to do them?" He tried to sound strong, but only managed a broken whisper.

"Thursday, Friday, and Monday." Her voice grew softer with each word, as if she were reading the closing words in a long novel she wished might last a few more Chapters.

"Fine! We'll go together! Rusty and Susan can handle the guests while we're gone."

"I haven't agreed, and I won't. Not until I know how much ..."

"That's not fair. I don't care how much it costs. We're going." Try as hard as he might, he couldn't yet understand this.

Mary sat up and brushed his hair from his eyes. For a long second she looked deep into his soft brown eyes. "It's hard to put into words. All this debt, all this money. I see the pain in your eyes, and I see the love there, too. I feel so selfish. Don't you understand? It's not fair to you, to leave you with all this debt. I mean, we've gone through this twice already. I was scared then."

He started to speak. She stopped him with a single finger to his lips. "Shhh, listen. I'm not scared now. But if I were to think these huge mountains of bills caused you to lose Mar-Sa ... well, I wouldn't want to die knowing that. Mar-Sa is us. You, me," she waved a hand toward the headstone, "and Callie. I'm counting on you to keep alive what we've built together."

Sam looked away. He couldn't bear to see that determination in her eyes, knowing what it meant. "Why are you so horribly sure you're going to die? ... Mary, this isn't like you. Are you just giving up? You've never been a quitter. You never let me quit. All the times over the years, you were the strong one ... When Callie died, you held this ranch together until I came to my senses. You're the strong one. Why are you acting like this?" He looked at her, his eyes begging. "Why are you giving up?"

She stood up, pulled a leaf from the dogwood tree, pretending to study it. "I'll go for the tests, alone. I'll make Dr. Stein schedule them for Monday and Tuesday, and I'll stay overnight. And you're going on the wild horse round-up."

"No! I'm going with you to the hospital. How can I go on a round-up with you in the hospital? How can I go without you? You're talking crazy ... "

That made her smile. "I haven't gone on a round-up in four years, silly. They won't know anything right away, anyway. You know how long it takes to hear anything. We're old pros at this testing business."

Barely able to control his breathing, he gazed at her. Thirty-five years of loving her had taught him one thing. It was easier to move a make it rain than to change Mary's mind once she'd made it up. "You've got me there ... How about if Susan goes with you?"

"Deal. Who'll cook on the trail?"

Dear Lord, why were they talking about this now? He sucked in a deep breath. Details, Sam. Focus on details. "I reckon Linda Cunningham and her daughter can help Rusty out with that."

They sat in silence, watching as the moon began its trek upward. In a little while, it shone brightly enough for them to pick their way home.

Chapter Twelve

Mary sat with Comanche and Chester under the live oak in the yard where she could watch all the activity in the corrals. This was a big day, the last day before they set out for the wild horse round-up. Folks were still getting to know their horses, learning to ride together, learning to follow Sam and Rusty's advice. She admired the guests' persistence almost as much as she admired the horses' patience.

She turned guilty eyes to Chester, who stood eagerly watching the goings on in the big corral. She should have taken him for a short ride this morning, as she had for the past three mornings. The morning had slipped away from her somehow, and now it was too hot. She'd have to wait for evening.

Why had she taken so long to water her violets this morning? By the time she'd finished tending to her plants on the porch, a job that hardly held her interest these days, the sun had already started building a high temperature for the day.

Maybe after three mornings in the saddle, her body had begun to drop hints that she wasn't up to her self-imposed challenge. She considered that fact as she fed Comanche his late morning snack. She considered it and brushed it aside.

"Of course, we're going to win!" She was certain Comanche heard her every thought. He plowed his nose deeper into his tub of beet pulp and apple slices, while Chester stretched his neck out and swiped with his tongue, trying hard to weasel in on Comanche's good fortune.

"Why can't he have any?"

Surprised, Mary turned to see Barbara coming through the gate into the yard. "Oh, hello, Barbara. The reason Chester can't have this is because he'll get fat. It's a high calorie meal, designed to help Comanche gain weight." She looked down at the corrals. The horses had been turned out to the pasture, and everyone was headed to the lodge. "Is it lunchtime already?"

"Yeah. I was watching you this morning." Barbara shuffled her feet as she spoke, then looked back toward the lodge. "You're like Mr. Holt. Good with horses, I mean."

"Why, thank you. I was watching you a fair amount, as well. I'm quite impressed." Mary had noticed the uneasiness in the girl. "I predict you'll become a fine rider." She smiled at Barbara and scratched Comanche's forehead. "You may even surprise yourself."

"I'm doing it because my mother wants me to. I don't care about horses." Barbara moved closer to Comanche and stroked his mane. "You sure spend a lot of time with him. He's the ugliest horse here." She turned to Chester. "I wanted to ride Chester."

Mary tugged on Comanche's forelock and pulled him close, then offered an apple slice to Barbara, "You may give this to Chester. He'll thank you for it ... Comanche needs a lot of time and attention. He's healthy enough and in a few more weeks, you'll hardy recognize him."

Barbara offered the apple slice to Chester, who happily licked it from her palm. "Well, they told me to tell you lunch will be ready in a few minutes." She backed away a few steps more, then turned and ran to the lodge.

Mary watched her leave and decided to fix herself a sandwich in her own kitchen when she was through here.

Comanche abandoned his empty feed tub to stroll to the water trough for his after-snack drink. This was Chester's big break. He moved in, dropped his nose into the tub, noisily slurping and licking the sides and bottom of the plastic tub, determined to extract every last morsel Comanche might have missed. While he slurped and licked, Mary leaned against the solid quarter horse and pulled a tangle from his mane. Finished with his drink, Comanche came to repossess the feed tub, his ears pinned flat. Chester retreated obediently. Mary smiled, realizing the cloudiness in Comanche's blue eye was nearly gone.

After a quick bite and a tall tumbler of cold tea, she reconsidered her plans for the day. It wasn't so hot, not really, and a short ride would be exactly what she needed. She stood at the gate, Chester in tow, scanning the lodge. Everyone seemed preoccupied with food and conversation. If Sam saw her, he'd most likely object. In fact, as she studied the thermometer that hung in the shade of the porch and saw the long red needle stuck between eighty-five and ninety degrees, she felt the first hint of a second guess herself.

I've ridden on hotter days. You were younger and healthier then.

"Chester, old friend," she hugged his neck, "you'll take good care of me, won't you? How about a walk in the stream to cool us both off?"

She looped Chester's lead through the hook on the rear of her cart and drove inside the barn to saddle up.

It was Comanche's loud protest at being left behind that gave her away.

Mary was reaching under Chester's belly for the cinch strap when Sam marched into the barn.

"Plenty warm, don't you reckon, Mary?" He leaned under Chester on the off side and passed her the cinch.

"Thank you. I'll stay in the trees all the way to the stream. Just a short ride there and back, with a little splashing mixed in."

"It'll be ninety or better by the time you get back. If you're set on goin', I'd better come along."

She stiffened. "I'll be fine. In fact, aside from a little soreness, which is to be expected when a person's gone this long without riding, I feel better than I have for some time." She secretly wondered if she were being honest with herself, but her look told him to hold his protests, and to hold the reins while she stepped into the saddle.

As she rode through the barn toward the double doors on the far end, she called to Sam, "Would you finish Comanche's feet today?"

"Sure thing.

She felt like giving him a show and clucked to Chester, who immediately broke into a quick lope.

Sam yelled after her, "Doggone you Mary! Be careful now, you shouldn't overdo it!"

❧❦❧❦❧❦❧

Since they had the afternoon free, Linda and Barbara decided to take a stroll along the stream. Philip had offered to help Rusty, Sam, and Morgan give Susan a hand loading the chuck wagon. The other guests were all in their cabins enjoying a final afternoon in air-conditioning before they set out in the morning for the wild horse range.

"Who needs air-conditioning?" Linda waded into the center of the stream. "This water is so cold." She glanced back at her daughter. "So what do you think about horses now? Morgan says I'm a natural."

"You do look good on a horse, and I like your cowgirl clothes." She pointed to Linda's fringed blouse. "I still hate it here." She sat on the bank, dangling her feet in the cold water.

Linda swirled her leg in a wide circle, making little waves in the calm, nearly waist-deep water. "Why do you hate it here? I think it's so beautiful. Fresh air, pretty horses, you can see for miles, and the Holts are nice people. Don't you think?"

"I'm a kid, Mom. I grew up in the city, *remember?* I like to shop, go to the movies. I'm the only kid here! And I miss my friends. What *not crazy person* goes away for a whole summer?"

Linda cracked a pretty smile, "Morgan's your age. He thinks you have the *makin's* of a fine rider."

Barbara smiled.

Linda noticed. "I see."

"No, you don't. He's a long-legged redneck whose idea of a good time is brushing a horse."

"I'll bet he could surprise you, if you gave him a chance."

"Mother, please. I'm only fifteen. Oh, I forgot … you were married by then."

Linda knew those words were meant to hurt. Funny thing was, they didn't. "I waited until I was nineteen to get married, the first time." She fell backwards in the water, completely submersing herself, and stayed under for a second. There's more than one way to change a subject. Popping up, she sucked in a long breath and wiped the water from her eyes. "Tomorrow we ride the real, honest-to-goodness trail. And I'm the *cookie*! That's what they call a chef out here, you know, Cookie."

Barbara looked at her mother, standing in the middle of a stream, wet from hair to toe, grinning her silly grin. "You're a *cookie*, all right. A giant sugar cookie. Always trying to sweeten the world … That, Mom, I meant as a compliment."

"I'll take it as one! How sweet!" Laughing, she slapped the water fast and hard, drenching her daughter.

Barbara charged through the assault and shoved her mother under the water, pinning her for a second, until her hand came up in surrender.

Gasping for air, Linda pushed her hair from her face. "I'll burn your eggs every morning!"

"Have you ever cooked over a campfire?" She grinned. "I'll bet you never even killed a buffalo."

"Not since the wagon train of sixty-eight. Eighteen sixty-eight!"

They laughed and hugged in the cold water. As they pulled themselves out of the water a while later, Linda was amazed to think that a week ago Barbara wouldn't have even dipped a toe in a country stream. They hadn't laughed this hard together for a long time either.

❧❧❧❧❧

"It's time we head back." Mary lifted Chester's rein, turned him toward the stream bank, and rode out of the water. At the top of the bank, she paused to look up the trail in the direction of the barn, then decided to follow the trail along the stream instead. "It's cool enough here under the trees, and on second thought, I'm not ready to go back just yet. We'll swing by the cabins and say hello to the guests."

Chester dropped his head and obediently, patiently, meandered along the stream's edge. Shaded by tall willows and cottonwoods, the trail by the stream was one of Mary's favorite places on the ranch. As she rode along, on a horse walking so slow she suspected he'd fallen asleep, she realized how badly she'd missed the trail, the stream, the trees. The saddle.

There was little, Mary decided, that could be as pleasurable as a slow, quiet ride on a comfortable horse, by a stream in the shade.

Well, except for a fast ride on a smart horse, in a ring with loud music and louder applause … and a blue ribbon. She missed that, too. That was coming.

Maybe the tender love of a man. That she had.

Maybe the joy of a child's love. That she would always have … in her memories. Mary reached forward to stroke Chester's neck. "Do you ever think of Callie? She loved to ride you. You and Comanche. But it was you who taught her all the right moves." She watched a tear splash on the horn. "You and Sam."

Chester stopped. Mary wiped her eyes, then patted his neck. "Yes, I hear them, too."

She urged Chester on at a quick trot and hurried along toward the sounds of laughter. Rounding a gentle bend in the trail, they came face to face with Barbara and Linda, laughing loudly and splashing each other. She stopped Chester a few feet from Barbara. "Why, hello. Isn't it simply a perfect day for a dip in the stream?"

Barbara huddled close to her mother.

Linda turned to Mary. "Appears your horse has been dipping, too."

"Chester likes a good swim." Mary gave the wet horse a friendly pat on the neck.

Barbara stood up, backed a few steps, and then stopped as Mary's words sank in. "Horses can swim?"

"Oh my, yes. Some horses are great swimmers. Cowboys often swam their horses across rivers by sliding off their rumps and holding onto the tail. In that way, they were towed across the river." Mary smiled and cocked her head. "A lot of cowboys couldn't swim."

Barbara cautiously moved a step closer toward Chester. "Why didn't they just ride the horses across the river?"

"Sometimes they'd do that, but those saddles and blankets get very heavy when they're wet. It's easier on the horse to tow them across."

Linda remained standing behind Barbara but smiled.

Barbara moved another tentative step closer to Chester. "Can he swim? Did you ever do that with him?"

"Well, no, I haven't, but my daughter has. Would you like to try?"

She retreated a step. "I don't know. The water isn't deep enough here for me to swim, and he's a lot bigger than I am. Besides, we were going back to the cabin." Barbara grabbed her mother's arm and tried to drag her away.

Linda gently pulled free, stood her ground and with a broad grin asked. "Didn't I hear Morgan say something about a swimming hole?"

"Mother!" Barbara stomped her foot.

Mary shifted in the saddle to point ahead. "Just down the trail about a half mile. If you like, Chester and I will lead the way."

Linda threw an arm over her daughter's shoulders. "Let's give it a try. We're already wet!"

Barbara leaned close, held a rigid pose, and whispered something to her mother.

After pondering the matter a moment, Linda turned solemn eyes to Mary. "Do you mean to sneak us away and drown us?"

"Mother!" Barbara shoved her away, nearly knocking her off her feet.

Mary caught the devilishness in Linda's eyes. "Have you paid your bill?"

Linda replied cleverly, "Not yet, but we promise to pay it soon."

Mary clucked to Chester and started down the trail, calling behind her, "In that case, you're safe to swim with Chester. Follow us to the swimming hole. Wouldn't make any sense to drown you before we had your money."

Barbara and Linda fell in line behind the quiet sorrel. Mary smiled to herself as she listened to Barbara's persistent protests about swimming with a horse and a woman who just might be crazy. She held Chester to a slow walk and led the way, straining her ears and trying to guess why Barbara thought she and Comanche—who she was certain she heard Barbara refer to as that skinny old horse—were scary enough to be in a Stephen King movie. Only able to catch every third word or so, Mary couldn't be sure, but it sounded as if Barbara was quite serious in her dislike for her and most unhappy with her own life in general. Mary's smile broadened when the trail widened at the swimming hole's edge. "Let's see if we can't show a young girl a good time today, old fella."

"Here we are," Mary called out in a singsong voice.

The trail opened into a meadow of lush grass, sloping down to an inviting pond circled by tall willows. A few feet from the water's edge, a row of picnic tables sat under a canopy of low-hanging branches. Under a nearby cottonwood tree, a pretty white gazebo waited to welcome visitors.

Linda ran ahead, splashing into the shallow water lapping up on the sandy beach. "This is a wonderfully beautiful place! It's like a scene in a movie!"

Mary slid from the saddle, disappointed to feel the stiffness settle over her legs. She took a second to gather herself before raising the stirrup to loosen the cinch.

"Here, let me help you with that." Linda hurried over, lifted the saddle from Chester, and set it on the ground. Then she slid the blanket off and laid it on the saddle. "Now I'm ready to swim with a horse."

"Okay, then." Mary smiled at Barbara and said in a stage whisper, "I guess you're going second." Ignoring the girl's wanna-bet? look, she led Chester to a bench. "Step on up, Linda, grab a fistful of mane and pull yourself up."

Linda hopped onto the bench and grinned timidly at Mary. "I haven't gotten on a horse without a saddle yet."

"Grip his mane, bend your knee, take a bounce and swing up." Mary gingerly acted out her own instructions with an imaginary horse.

Linda gripped Chester's mane, bent her knee, took a short jump, and made it halfway. Then she fell to the ground laughing.

Even Barbara started to laugh. "Here, let me boost you. Morgan showed me how to give a leg up." She supported her mother's leg and gave a slight push. Linda rose into the air, settling gracefully onto the horse.

"You're all set." Mary led Chester to the water's edge and handed the reins to Linda. "Just move him forward into the water and keep him walking. When you reach the deep water, you'll feel him start to swim. Then slide back over his rump, grab his tail, and hold on."

Linda gave a faint smile and held up the reins. "What about these?"

"Let them lie over his neck. He'll circle back to the beach on his own."

Linda signaled the horse with a cluck. Chester stepped into the water and walked toward the middle, where he stood chest deep. Then suddenly, he dropped lower in the water. Linda let out a yelp as she sank with the horse until the water was over her lap. Chester swam out farther, with only his head above water, his tail streaming out behind him. Linda clutched his mane and grappled for the reins.

Barbara cupped her hands around her mouth. "Mom, slide off!" Her mother didn't seem to hear her. Barbara turned to Mary. "Why won't she slide off? She's gonna drown him!"

Mary smiled. "No, he won't drown. She can ride him that way. She could even steer him with the reins if she wanted to, just like any other time."

Barbara ran knee-deep into the water. "Mom, use the reins! Turn him back!"

Linda sat perfectly still, rigid as a post. Chester continued swimming toward the far shore.

Barbara shot a frightened look to Mary. "Can he make it all the way across?"

"He can, but watch this." Mary put two fingers in her mouth and let go a loud, shrill whistle.

Chester instantly turned around, swimming hard, while Linda sat motionless, her eyes glued to his ears, her hands holding his mane in a death grip. He walked out of the water and came to a stop alongside Mary.

Barbara ran to her mother and helped her to the ground. "Mom, what happened?"

"I'm not sure. It felt so strange when he lost his footing and sank so quickly, then he started to swim ... I forgot to move."

"You're always such a scaredy-cat. It looked like fun!"

"You did just fine, and I'm sure Chester loved it." Mary turned to Barbara. "Your turn."

She studied the dripping horse. "Isn't he tired?"

"It'll take a lot more than a short walk and a two-minute swim to wear him out." She patted his neck with a shaky hand. "But I'm afraid I need to find a seat."

Linda was by Mary's side in an instant, taking her by the arm. "We should get you to the house. You do look a little pale."

"I'll be fine after I rest a little." With a smile and long breath, she moved slowly toward a bench. "Barbara, come with me to the tables. Bring Chester," she called over her shoulder.

Barbara tossed her arms in the air. "Mom, let's go. You swam a horse. I don't care even a little bit about doing it."

Linda grinned at Mary, "I guess she's afraid that she can't do as well as her mom."

Barbara sighed, grabbed the reins, and led Chester over to the tables. Before Mary could say anything, she stepped onto the table and slipped onto Chester's back with the ease and grace of a dancer. Throwing her arms wide like a gymnast who had just completed a difficult routine, she tossed her mother and Mary a smug look that shouted, *There.*

Mary leaned her elbows on the table and held her gaze, noting the confidence and arrogance in the tilt of the girl's chin. She watched as Barbara picked up the reins, turned from the table, and started for the water. Then she made her move.

"Barbara," she rose from her seat and went toward them, "bring him back my way, please."

She turned him Mary's way and stopped directly in front of her. "What?" her voice was a combination of impatience and boredom.

Without a word, Mary placed her hand on Chester's poll. He obediently dropped his head. Deftly she slipped the bridle from over his ears.

As the reins slipped through Barbara's hands, she protested, "Hey, what are you doing?"

Mary held back a grin but could do nothing to hide the gleam of challenge in her eyes. "I noticed that you looked a little bored with it all. As Sam would say, it may be time to step things up a notch."

"Mother, I knew it! She *is* crazy!" Barbara raised her right leg to slide off.

Mary clucked and touched Chester's right front shoulder. The timing was perfect. As Barbara moved left to slide down off his back, Chester stepped left, under her, keeping her squarely on his back.

Barbara grabbed a fistful of mane. "What was that?"

"A very smart horse giving you your first lesson in tackless riding. You told me this morning you wanted to ride Chester."

"Yeah, but I wanted to ride him in the corral with everybody else. Not out in the woods where you can do whatever you're planning to do to Mom and me." Mary studied the girl's face and registered the hardness of it. She placed a hand on the girl's thigh. Barbara pulled her leg away.

Mary allowed her hand to rest on Chester's withers and gave Barbara a motherly look. "I've known from the moment we met something about me upsets you. I'd like to fix that. I've enjoyed watching you ride this week, getting better each day. You're a natural. You're sensitive, aware, and gentle. Not with your words, of course," she winked at Linda, "but with your behavior. You feel the horse. I think you hear the horse. Now, before you swim, I'd like to show you something I'm reasonably certain you'll like."

She narrowed her eyes. "Are you going to put the bridle back?"

"No."

"Mother. Must I?"

Linda encouraged her. "I'm intrigued. Why not give it a try?"

Barbara scowled. "Let's get it over with."

"You see, you're not the least bit frightened, are you? A little angry with me and your mother, but not at all frightened. And you'd never touched a horse until a week ago."

"He's not much to be scared of," she huffed.

Some remarks were simply unacceptable. Mary checked Barbara's hands, making certain the girl had a firm grip on Chester's mane, then made a loud kissing sound and at the same time, touched Chester in the center of his chest. In a flash he reared up, just a little.

Barbara held on tight, but a nervous squeak escaped her clenched lips. As soon as she realized she was safe, Barbara glared at Mary, "What the crap was that? You are trying to kill me! I knew it, Mother! She's nuts!"

Yet she didn't dismount. Mary nodded with approval. "I wanted you to realize that like spooky old me, Chester has a few surprises."

Stunned, Barbara shot a look at her mother, who simply smiled and shrugged. She forced herself to look at Mary, who also smiled and shrugged. Chester, at least, stood patiently. Without smiling or shrugging.

Mary gave Barbara a knowing wink. "Now, settle deep into your seat, relax, and breathe normally."

She did as instructed. Chester softened and perked his ears.

"Think about what I tell you, wait for my cue, then do it."

"Do what?"

"Gently fill both hands with mane, drop the back of your seat deep, pick up on his mane just the least bit, and give him one cluck. Do that, and he'll take one step back."

"Really? We didn't learn how to back up yet."

"Chester will teach you. Ready?"

With a look of mild interest, Barbara picked up mane, dropped her seat, and clucked.

Chester backed up one step.

"Holly crap! It worked!" Barbara fell forward, hugging his neck. "Wow, that was freaking awesome! Mom, did you see that?"

Linda stood up and clapped. "I did. You did excellent. Isn't it exciting?"

Mary chuckled, then got serious again. "Now, relax, keep your right hand in his mane, and move him forward to the pond the same way you would if he were saddled."

"How do I steer him?"

"You can use his mane, or cue him with your knee."

"How?" Barbara touched her heels to Chester's sides, and moved him ahead, toward the water.

Breathing hard, Mary followed along. "Left turn, tap him lightly with your left leg. Right turn, do the opposite. He'll also respond if you simply move your hand in his mane left or right." Mary watched a second more, then, satisfied, turned away and started for the tables. "I'm going to sit."

Barbara walked Chester into the shallow water as Sam pulled up with Mary's cart.

Sam hopped from the cart and trotted to Mary at the tables. "I was getting worried. You've been gone all afternoon."

Mary patted the bench beside her. "Hush, have a seat and watch."

He slid in next to her, nodded a greeting to Linda. "I've been watching from up there behind the cabins. I figured that young'un was gonna make a mighty sharp rider."

"Great job, Barbara," Mary shouted. "Now head for deeper water." She stood up and moved back to the water's edge. "When he starts swimming, slide off his rump. I want you to swim for the other shore."

"How do I steer him?"

"With his tail."

Barbara twisted around to face Mary. "I was starting to believe you." Accusation hardened her voice.

Sam stood up. "You should," he called out to her and tossed a wink to Linda.

Barbara threw an arm in the air. "Okay ... how do I do *that?*"

Before answering, Mary blew Sam a kiss. Then she called, "Steer his tail like you would his mane, except opposite."

"Opposite?"

Linda ran to the water's edge. "Yes, baby, his mane is in the front and his tail is in the back, so it's opposite, of course."

"You're no help!"

Linda turned to Sam. "It is opposite, right?"

"Yes, ma'am." His ready smile soon faded as his gaze drifted over her face.

She raised her hand to cover the new bruise under her eye and looked away.

Mary reached for Sam's hand and led them knee deep into the water. "When you slide off, keep hold of his tail with your right hand. Swim along behind. When you want to turn right, give a tug toward the left. He'll move right. When you want him to turn left, tug right, and he'll move left. You're on your own now. I'm going back to the table."

Sam nodded to Linda. "She's gonna make it to the other side, all right."

Barbara slid back over Chester's rump, lost his tail, but quickly recaptured it. She turned and waved to her audience. Chester swam with powerful strokes, straight for the far shore. Soon he walked up the bank with Barbara following behind, holding his tail.

They stood side by side on the far shore, looking across the pond. "How do I get back?"

"Same way, only *opposite*." Sam gave Linda a quick wink.

"You're not my instructor anymore!" Barbara shouted.

Sam, Linda, and Mary looked at each other and burst into laughter.

Chapter Thirteen

"I'm glad you brought the cart." Mary slid into the driver's seat while Sam tied a soggy Chester to the rear.

"When I finished Comanche's feet and you were still gone, I figured I'd better come looking."

"I'm not sure if I should be grateful you worried, or angry that you were so certain I needed help."

Sam climbed in the passenger seat and made a big show of getting comfortable. "Go on and be mad if you like, but I'll never quit worryin' about my pretty gal."

She stepped on the gas, gave his hand a squeeze, and held onto it while she steered the cart along the path. He talked happily as they drove along, detailing precisely his plans for the following morning. He loved those wild horses. He loved sharing them with folks who'd remember the trip the rest of their lives.

She loved him because he loved so generously.

She watched his face; happy he could find a little relief from the burden she'd become. She listened to him tell her about the three-year-old mustangs he and the guests would trail home, and she thanked God for the years she'd had with this sweet, tender, tough man. She thanked Him but begged for a little more time. Not for herself so much, but for Sam. She needed more time, to give him one more happy, spectacular memory.

"Hey, hold on here, Mary. By golly, you're gonna run smack into the barn door." Sam lunged across her lap and spun the wheel. Mary slammed on the brake. The cart rammed into a stack of straw bales. Chester banged into the rear of the cart. Comanche squealed from the far end of the barn.

Mary swiped her free hand over her eyes.

"Mrs. Holt! Are you all right?" Morgan, wide-eyed and puffing, raced to the cart and reached for her hand. Embarrassed, she stepped from the cart and offered Sam a feeble smile. "I was daydreaming."

Sam tilted his hat back, hooked his thumbs in his belt, and cracked his silliest grin. " 'Bout me, I'll wager."

"Mr. Holt. She broke a headlight."

కా≼కా≼కా≼కా

Rounding the corner of their cabin, Linda saw Philip sitting on the porch. Her eyes darted to Barbara, then back to Philip. His posture alone revealed his mood.

She grabbed Barbara's arm. "Let's not do anything to make a fuss. Quick showers, clean clothes, then we're off to the lodge for dinner. Promise me."

Her chin jutted toward the porch. "It won't be up to us."

She was right, and Linda knew it. Holding Barbara's hand for courage, she climbed up the steps and marshaled her most pleasant voice. "We had a wonderful swim."

"Left me here alone all day."

"We did invite you. You said you wanted to help load the chuck wagon." Linda sat next to him and motioned for Barbara to go inside, "Go ahead, baby. I'll take a shower after you."

After she'd gone in, Philip said, "Yeah, well, that took all of half an hour, then everybody went back to their cabins and left me to twiddle my thumbs, alone."

"Oh, I'm sorry. Barbara and I were having so much fun, and we both rode a horse in the water! It was amazing. Well, I was a little scared, but Barbara really took to it."

"It's always Barbara, isn't it?" He rocked his chair back.

Not knowing how to respond, she said nothing, but her silence seemed to have been the wrong choice. She wrestled with trying to think of something to say, but as that familiar twist took over his mouth, her mind went blank.

He rocked forward and leaned close to her. "I get pretty stinking tired of always being second fiddle."

She tried a smile. "Oh, Philip, how could you say that?" The narrowing of his eyes told her that was the wrong response, too. When he grabbed her hand, panic choked her. "Don't." She tugged at her hand, but he squeezed tight.

"Okay, Mom, the shower's yours." Barbara called from inside.

She knew he was spoiling for an argument. When he raised his hand, she jumped up so fast she tipped her chair.

"Hey, folks, ready to go to dinner?" John Bartlett was standing at the bottom of the steps. "Nicky's gone on ahead with Debby and Zack. I hear you're going to be head cook on the trail, and figured I'd start buttering you up early. To get extra beans. So," he grinned, "I hustled over here to walk you to dinner. Philip and Barbara, too, of course."

Linda, seeing the color of Philip's face darken to a deep red, turned to John. "We'll accept your kind offer, but I need a minute to clean up. Been swimming."

Retreating into the cabin, she nearly knocked Barbara down. "I'll only be a minute," she whispered. "John has offered to escort us to dinner. Isn't that nice?"

Barbara rolled her eyes. "Mom, it's a hundred yards."

It would feel like miles, if she were alone with her husband when he was in a mood. Linda held her arm. "Please keep John here while I clean up." Secretly she hoped he'd have a calming effect on Philip. "I'll be quick."

Before she'd closed the bedroom door, her blouse and jeans were in a pile by the bed. She hurried into the shower, allowing herself only a moment to appreciate the warm water running down her face. Why did she always say things that made him so mad? Why did he seem to enjoy getting so mad?

She dried her hair, wrapped herself in a towel, then darted to the bedroom. And froze after two steps. "Philip!" "Let them go. You stay here with me." He sat on the bed staring out the only window in the room, not bothering to look her way as he spoke.

"Oh, but I couldn't let Barbara go alone. It wouldn't be right."

"It's all right to leave me here alone?" He turned away from the window to glare at her. His eyes could hit as hard as his hand. "Maybe this cowboy crap wasn't such a good idea." He turned back to the window.

The only thing outside that window was Paul and Lucy's cabin. My God, Barbara might be right about him and Lucy! "What's the matter? Is Paul running interference between you and Lucy?" Did she say that? She heard it, but did she say it?

Philip jumped up, smacked her cheek, and shoved her down on the bed. He stood a second to look at her, then huffed and turned toward the door.

Linda cupped her face with one hand, reached out with the other, and would have said she was sorry, but Philip didn't give her time.

"I'm going to town." He slammed the bedroom door behind him.

Almost. She almost had the courage to tell him to stay. Instead, she held her breath.

She heard John ask him what was wrong and heard Philip explain in a very pleasant voice, "Nothing. Just need a few things from town." She waited until she heard their car start and drive away, then she let out the breath she'd been holding.

She wiped her face with the towel, then pulled her favorite gray tee-shirt and patched jeans from the shelf. "I'm almost ready. You and John can go ahead. I'll be down in five minutes."

Tears and makeup didn't mix very well, but with some effort, she managed to hide the ugly.

She tied her hair back in a cute ponytail, grabbed her hat, and danced to the door. Whatever she felt inside was staying there. No outward clues allowed.

Having recovered from her day's activities, Mary insisted Sam allow her to join them in the lodge for supper. After all, she argued, they'd all be heading out in the morning, leaving her and Susan alone for two weeks while he and the guests rode the range. Once Sam acquiesced, she had Morgan and Rusty rearrange the tables so that everyone could sit together and enjoy the night air and lively conversation.

"So, Fourth of July is a big deal here," John Bartlett said.

Mary snuggled closer to Sam. "It is, and it grows every year. Last year we had five hundred guests."

"No kidding. How'd such a thing ever get started?" Zack asked.

Morgan slid his hat back. "Well, it's my birthday."

Everybody had a good laugh. Zack gave Morgan a solid slap on the back, nearly unseating the boy's hat. "That's great, kid, but really, how'd you come to host such a party?"

"It was our first year with the outfit." Rusty aimed a look in Susan's direction. "I'd been through a couple'a rough years and was feelin' pretty low. Sam hired me on around Christmas time, gave me a chance. And a house. Me and Susan knew he didn't really need the help ..."

"Come on now," Sam spoke up. "You're a fine hand, and I wouldn't want to be without you or Susan."

"Yeah, well, he says that now, but sixteen years ago ..." Rusty cleared his throat, "sixteen years ago, he took a mighty chance on a no-good drunk."

In the stunned silence, Mary studied Sam's face. He never liked being the topic of conversation. She was pretty sure she wasn't the only one to see him bite his lip and turn away.

"Anyway," Rusty continued, "one night we were finishing spring round-up, not far from where we're headed tomorrow. We were chewin' the fat 'round the fire, and ol' Sam starts tellin' us about his rodeo days. Seems before sweet Mary reined 'im in, he cut a wide swath and was a heck of a bull rider. 'Course he goes on about how much he loves his Mary and all, but he made a plain tale of it, how much he missed rodeoin'. Right that very night, I hatched a plan to throw a Fourth of July party for him. Me and Susan, and after a while Mary pitched in, too. We went full gallop into plannin' a humdinger of a show."

Sam shook his head, laughing, then swung an arm over Mary's shoulder and kissed her. "Kept the entire affair a total secret from me until the trucks started rolling in on the morning of the Fourth. Boy, howdy, was I surprised. They even managed to rustle up a few of my old rodeo buddies. Ol' boys I hadn't seen in years."

"Bull riders, all of 'em," Rusty hooted. "We had us an over-the-hill bull-ridin' event. Next to that pretty little gal doin' the trick riding, it was the hit of the day."

John angled to get a clear view of Sam. "How'd you do?"

"Well now, some of those boys had kept their boots in the game a sight longer than I had."

Mary ran a finger along his shoulder. "He broke his collarbone."

John squirmed and rubbed his own shoulder. "Ouch!"

"Only bone I ever broke in my life. Darn bull ran smack into Fred Jones' truck."

Rusty laughed and pointed up in the air. "Ol' Sam was sure enough going for the over-the-truck, high flyin' award that summer."

Zack stood up and felt his shoulder, making sure all the parts were in place. "See, folks, as I was saying in this very lodge just a few days ago, pads are a good thing." He gave Debby a weak, wishful smile, "Still wish I'd brought mine along."

Sam gave Zack a reassuring grin, "Young fella, there ain't nuthin' on this ranch as ornery as the bull I pulled that day."

Rusty let out a hoot. "Well, not since we sent that two-year-old Santa Gertrudis along with those cows to Fred's spread the other day, there ain't."

Sam shot a look of alarm and concern to Rusty. "You sent Monkey?"

Rusty nodded. "Sure enough, boss. You said to pick him a good, ornery one. I figured Monkey was as ornery as they come."

"Well, doggone it. Did you warn Fred, at least?"

"Naw. Didn't need to. Ol' Monkey went ta educatin' everybody right quick, first lick outta the trailer." Rusty shook his head and let loose a devilish chuckle. "Fred's still mighty proud ta have him, though."

Sam studied the questioning faces turned his way before he responded. "Monkey is a fine young foundation bull, but he has a lot of pep and attitude. More than most, I'd say."

Debby let out a muffled gasp. "Is he dangerous?"

"Only if you get between Monkey and his harem," Rusty said with a laugh.

Sam held up his hands. "Okay, folks, with Rusty's help, I'm sure we could go on all night about poor Fred and his new bull, but it's getting late, and we've got a big day ahead of us tomorrow. You folks are free to sit around these tables and visit all night. Keep in mind though, tomorrow's gonna start for all of us about two hours before sun-up." He took Mary by the hand, tipping his hat to the group. "Try to get between the blankets before too long," he said, then led Mary into the shadows.

Chapter Fourteen

S am sat on the edge of their bed, pulling his boots on in the dark. "How're you feeling this morning?"

It required effort, but she reached out to touch him. She thought about lying, but there would be plenty of time for that in the near future. "Stiff, tired and raring to go! Yesterday was fun. I had a great time last night talking and visiting with our guests." She dragged her hands up and down over her thighs. "I may pay for all that visiting this morning." She flashed him a timid grin.

"I can stay home. Rusty can ramrod everything all right."

"No, I want you to go. Susan will take fine care of me, and besides," she rolled close, pulled him down, and kissed his stubbly cheek, "I'm going to be busy with Comanche and Chester." She drew her fingers over his chin. "I wonder how long this white beard will be in two weeks."

He made a point of rubbing his stubble against her nose, then gave her a slow, hard kiss. "I reckon a good bit longer."

As he stood, she reached for him. "Sam, help me up."

"It'll take a while to get everything ready to roll out. Why don't you rest and come to the lodge in an hour or so?"

She gave him a look. He pulled her to her feet.

"Thank you."

They left the house in the early morning darkness. Cane in hand, Mary hardly acknowledged her violets as she hurried across the porch. But she did accept Sam's arm to navigate the steps. Comanche greeted them at the bottom step, bright-eyed and ready for his breakfast, even though it was two hours earlier than was routine.

She pulled a lead rope out of the cart and hooked him to the bumper. "His feed can on the porch is empty. I'll feed him in his stall."

Sam helped her into the seat, then sat in the cart next to her. He reached across the seat and slid his hand on her leg.

Mary rested her free hand on his, then gathered it up and squeezed. She didn't miss the look of discontent that washed over his face. She knew he was fighting to hold back more arguments as to why he should stay back off the roundup, that he was afraid to leave her for two weeks. That she was just being stubborn and strong-headed. Yes, she admitted to herself, she was nothing if not strong-headed. She drove the cart into the well-lit barn, jumped out before Sam could help her, and led Comanche to his stall. The cane stayed behind in the cart.

"Morning, Mary, Sam." Rusty tipped his hat. "I sent Morgan to fetch the mules. Figured we'd toss 'em in a stall while we have breakfast. Let 'em fill their bellies before we hitch 'em to the chuck wagon."

"Good idea," Sam affirmed. "He'll have an easier time catchin' 'em while they're still asleep."

Morgan appeared at the far end of the barn, leading the pair of tall, high-spirited, high-stepping mules. "Not quite, Mr. Holt. These fellows have plenty of get-up-and-go already this morning."

Once the mules were settled, the three men clambered after Mary into the cart.

On the way to the lodge, she drove with reckless abandon, spurred on by Rusty and Morgan's hooting and howling, who were clinging to the cart's roof and bracing themselves against the narrow platform in the rear. Were it not for Sam's extra weight in the seat beside her, she was reasonably certain she'd have flipped the cart, but she was in the mood for a little craziness.

"Mary, doggone it, slow down," Sam yelped.

She flashed him her crooked smile, her secret weapon, and guided the heavily-laden cart to an abrupt stop near the tables. Morgan and Rusty jumped down, straightened their hats, and headed for breakfast, pretending to complain to each other about the rough ride.

"How's the song go? 'Girls just want to have fun!' " Mary leaned on Sam's arm, stepped from the cart, and they walked hand in hand to the table.

"Fun? That was flat reckless." He tried to give her a stern look.

"Yeah, it was." She gave him a look that was positively devilish.

He knocked back her hat and ruffled her hair. "You're still my bad girl, aren't you?"

"Forever."

"Breakfast is served." Linda banged a black skillet with a wooden spoon.

Mary found a place near the end of the table. This morning, she was more interested in watching and listening than talking. She enjoyed the lively conversation and antics, everyone speaking at the same time, most of them with mouths full of breakfast. She listened to Sam assure Debby Collier they would indeed be taking tents with them and that they hardly ever saw big cats anymore. Inside, Mary longed to be part of the trip.

"Well, according to the Bureau of Land Management, both big cats and wolves are making quite a comeback," Debby countered.

"That's true, and frankly, I'm glad to see it, but we've never had much trouble."

"*Much* trouble?" She shot a wide-eyed look at Sam.

"Now, I didn't mean to say we had trouble. Nothin' of the sort. But we have lost a calf or two over the years."

"Yeah, but we never lost a guest," Rusty declared and stomped his boot, hard. The lights went out. "No sir," he finished in the dark. "Not a single guest. Ever."

Mary could see white teeth and white eyes all around the table. They all laughed when Susan let "dang it" slip from the darkness of the kitchen.

"Doggone wires, anyway," Sam mumbled. "Sit tight, folks. I'll flip the breaker and have the lights back on in no time."

"Let me give you a hand," John Bartlett offered. "Sounds like this happens every now and then."

"Appreciate it. Folks, you all finish your coffee. We'll have these cantankerous lights back on before you can say, 'A rat ran over the tin roof with a piece of fat in its mouth.' " Sam retrieved a flashlight from Mary's cart and led the way around the tables to the electrical panel in the rear of the kitchen.

ॐॐॐॐॐॐ

With his long-bladed pocket knife, Sam removed the one screw that held the rusty cover in place, shone the light along the breakers, and flipped the one that had tripped. The lights came back on. A cheer rose from the front of the lodge.

"Mighty old panel box," John noted.

"Sure is. Was old when we installed it. I guess you'd know about that sort of thing."

"You folks have a supply house around these parts? I could change this box for you, if I survive the wolves and big cats."

Sam studied the old contraption. "It's not right to bother you on your vacation, but we do have a situation here. I'd hate to lose the food in the freezer."

"Well, then, it's settled. You bring me back from the wilds of Arizona alive, and I'll take care of changing the box." "Alive? Yeah, I'll bring you back alive, and thanks, I appreciate it." His heart wasn't in the words. His heart was with Mary. Sure, she'd be fine with Susan to look out for her. What if Mary was right? What if this was to be their last summer? Shouldn't he spend each second of it next to her? He followed John back out to the dining room, barely noticing as Paul Keaton raised his coffee cup in a toast to them.

"Listen, I've been thinkin' ..." He sat close beside Mary. She turned to him and brushed a finger over his lips.

"No. You're taking the guests to the wild horses, and you're bringing home some fine three-year-olds. I look forward to seeing the young ones each year. This year even more. The wild, eager look in their eyes. Their strong, young bodies. I'm anxious to see who you choose this year. Maybe a stallion who looks like Comanche."

He slid his hand on her thigh and patted softly. "You're a challenge. Always have been. My sweet, tough challenge."

Her lips made that crooked grin that always melted him. "Can't change me now." She cocked her head.

He wanted to say something, but his throat was clogged. So he leaned against her and closed his eyes. He held her for a second, trying to memorize the feeling. Is it possible to make a memory of a feeling? If he could, would he have her forever? He kissed the tip of her ear. "Can't change your mind?" A little drop of wet slid down his cheek.

She slid her arms around his waist and held on tight. "Bring some pretty horses home."

"Ummm, Mr. Holt … want me to hitch the mules?" Morgan stood before them, slowly turning his hat in his hands, fingering the edge of the brim.

Sam looked up, surprised to see the lodge was empty except for the three of them. With his hat, Morgan pointed toward the big corral. "They were anxious to pick their horses. Rusty took 'em down. That's all right, isn't it?"

As Sam stood, he slyly dragged a hand across his eyes. "Well, son, let's go give 'em a hand." He leaned down to Mary. "You bring your cart when you're ready, give us a big sendoff."

"I'll stay here for now and help Susan finish loading the chuck wagon."

"Oh yeah, the chuck wagon. Well, okay then. But don't overdo it."

Morgan slapped his hat on his head. "I'll bring the mules around."

"Good idea." Mary gave him a motherly smile.

❧❧❧❧❧❧

After they'd gone, she sat watching everyone in the big corral while she made plans for her day. First, she'd help Susan pack the rest of the supplies for the trip, and then she'd take Chester out for a ride. Maybe she'd tow Comanche. He might be ready for a walk and a little exercise. That's it, take Comanche along today. Maybe Susan could ride along as well.

"Wagon's loaded." Susan plopped down at the table. "Wanna go down to the corral?"

"I was just getting ready to give you a hand." Mary was surprised Susan had already finished. That was Susan. Always efficient.

Morgan appeared around the corner, leading the mules to the chuck wagon waiting behind the lodge. "Looks like we'll get an early start."

Mary glanced at Susan, stood up, and started for him. "Let us help."

"Sure you can take this one." He handed one of the mules' leads to Mary.

She snatched the rope before Susan could intercept it, and they and their mule fell in step behind him. Watching him back the mules into the traces, Mary felt a tug in her gut. Didn't she really want to go with them? Of course she did, but it made no sense. Those awful tests were coming up, as was the competition.

She and Comanche had to get ready.

Eleven people and twenty-two horses clambered around to the rear of the lodge. Every person led two horses so the same horse would never be ridden two days in a row. The guests circled around the pile of gear stacked in the lean-to and picked up their bedrolls, which Morgan and Rusty had already assembled. Each bedroll contained a blanket, rain slicker, and a small, one-man tent.

Debby Collier cornered Morgan, "How far is it to the wild horse range?"

"If we follow the truck road," he pointed to the obvious path to their right, which ran up and over the treeless, almost barren hills, "it's about twelve miles, but we'll be taking the scenic route along the river and over the mountain. That way it's about thirty miles."

Her eyes widened. "Thirty miles? Are we ready to ride thirty miles?"

Morgan nodded. "Sure, but don't worry. We only go about three miles today, first day out and all."

Mary found a good seat on an overturned bucket just far enough away from of all the hustle and bustle to be out of the way but close enough to hear the excited chatter, while Susan helped the guests strap their bedrolls to their saddles. She wasn't really so tired In fact, she felt pretty darn good. But she was enjoying just watching and listening. Paul and Lucy Keaton knew the drill and were the first guests ready to hit the trail. They tied their mounts to the rail and helped the Cunninghams with their horses and equipment. Barbara led her horses away from the crowd. Mary wasn't surprised to see she had picked Cactus, a solid little red roan. For a wild horse, the little mare had become quite the people-pleaser. Mary had had her eyes on the filly four years ago when they'd brought her home from the wild herd. That had been the last time Mary had gone on the trek to the wild horse range. But things happened in life. Things happened—and plans changed.

"I wanted to tell you I like the horses now, Mrs. Holt." Barbara stopped alongside Mary, holding Cactus' rein. "I really like Cactus." She gave Cactus a healthy scratching on her neck.

"She's become quite the little teacher. She just might replace Chester as our best lesson horse one day."

"I would have picked Chester, but you know, he's like, your horse."

Mary smiled. "You'll do better with Cactus. Chester is not a big fan of long rides anymore. In fact, he always preferred to perform in the ring. He likes applause. He and Comanche."

"I decided on Leroy for my second horse. Morgan says he's a good swimmer, and there's a lake in the summer range where we're taking the wild horses. I'm gonna surprise everybody and swim him the way you taught me."

Mary searched Barbara's eyes. "You're bound to surprise them." She gave a happy chuckle. "Remember to listen to Sam and Morgan. You're about to have an experience that will be like nothing you've ever done." Mary could see that Barbara was eager to start, so she didn't finish her thought. The girl could figure it out by herself. "Just be sure to have fun!" She regretted she'd not be there to witness the transformative effect she knew the trip to the range would have on the girl.

"The wagon's headin' out! Time to mount up, folks," Sam hollered. Then he leveled Mary a long, solemn stare.

"I guess I'll see you in two weeks, Mrs. Holt." Barbara stepped gracefully into the saddle and started Cactus away. After a few steps, she turned back, leaned low, and spoke just above a whisper. "Philip's still a jerk and a creep."

Mary caught her breath and grinned as she watched the young girl trot her horse to Leroy, snag his lead, and fall in line first behind the chuck wagon. Then she mounted her cart and drove full speed straight at Sam, skidding to a stop inches from his toes. "I'll need a kiss hot enough to last two weeks, Cowboy."

"Well, I reckon I'm just the fella who can rustle up a tall order like that." Sam pitched Bullet's reins to Susan, dropped to one knee, pulled Mary close, and laid one on her. Morgan circled the guests around the cart, flapped his arms and strutted like a drunken eagle struggling to lift off, and started a ruckus. Within a second, everyone chimed in, hooting and hollering, Paul's booming voice ringing out above them all. The cheers outlasted the kiss by a full minute. Mary, never embarrassed by Sam's willing displays of affection, pulled him down for another go.

Rusty yanked his revolver and fired a shot in the air.

Stunned, the group fell silent, the horses danced, and Sam spun around to frown at Rusty.

Mary beamed.

"Sorry, boss, but like they say in the movies, we're burnin' daylight."

Zack Collier hadn't had enough. "Aw come on, Sam! Give her another!"

The kissing and cheering started all over again. Rusty holstered his gun, slapped the long reins smartly on the mules' backs, and drove the wagon away, shaking his head but sporting a huge grin. One by one, the guests began to fall in line behind the wagon and ride away.

"Here's lookin' at you, kid," Sam said in his best Bogie imitation.

"You know I can't do Bergman, but of all the ranch houses, in all the world, I know you'll come back to mine." She pulled him down for another sweet kiss.

Chapter Fifteen

Sam stopped his horse near the lean-to shelter at the first campsite along the trail. A quick glance around told him the site had suffered no real damage from the elements in the months since he'd last visited it. No more than a few downed branches and a single piece of tin blown loose from the lean-to roof littered the ground. He cocked his head to give the lean-to a closer look. A few nails will fix that loose corner. He rode Bullet around to the front of the wagon and nodded to Rusty. "This outfit made some pretty good time today." He pushed his hat back and wiped his brow with his leather glove. "Nice, small bunch of folks." He twisted in his saddle to check on the riders. The guests were strung out in a single file down the trail. Philip Cunningham rode directly behind the wagon. Barbara and Morgan brought up the rear. "Looks like the youngsters are startin' to hit it off."

"Morgan figures he's got a private student, I reckon." Rusty sent a wide grin to Sam.

"She looks all right on a horse, sure enough. Reminds me a lot of Callie."

Debby stopped her horse next to Sam, stepped down, and looked around. "This truly is an enchanting spot." She made an exaggerated gesture of rubbing her sore behind. "Are you sure we only rode three miles?"

Sam grinned. "Give or take a few hundred yards. Tomorrow we'll do closer to ten."

He gave everyone time to dismount and find their legs, then announced, "Folks, we always tend to our horses before we see to ourselves." The guests all gathered around Sam, holding their horses' reins, waiting further instructions.

"Unsaddle your horses and hang your equipment on the rails under the lean-to. You can turn your spare mounts into the corral yonder." He pointed with his hat to a combination split rail, rope, and board fence that weaved its way through the tall willows, oaks and aspens. "You'll need to walk the horse you rode today to cool 'em, then rub 'em down, the same way we showed you back at the house. See Morgan for your groceries, then stand with your horses till they clean it up. By then, Rusty and Linda should have beans and coffee ready."

Paul looked around, giving everybody a friendly smile and a lighthearted warning, "Beans and coffee." He shook his head as if apologizing. "He's serious, folks. I'd forgotten the staple on the range is boiled beans, salt pork, and ash cake." He gave a good-hearted chuckle, then started for the corral.

"Ah yes, but this year there may be a new twist. Range cooked beans seasoned with my secret chili powder." Linda's voice held obvious pride.

"I'll tend to your horses. You go ahead and start the beans," Morgan offered. "I don't like my beans too spicy, though."

"Thank you, Morgan. I bet you'll love my beans." With a wink, she handed her horses off and started for the wagon.

Sam always saw to his own horses. He liked to lead by example, and there was also the fact that Bullet was a bit ornery, and the young stallion he towed, Smoke, had a way to go before he'd be ready for a greenhorn. Walking Bullet in a wide arch, Sam studied all the horses, carefully inspecting their backs, legs, and feet as they followed their riders in a circle among the trees. He chuckled under his breath. The horses always fared better than the guests for the first few days. Barbara and her mother seemed to be in fine shape. The Bartletts and the Keatons were a little sore. As for Zack, he wouldn't let it show if he were about to drop over. His pretty young wife, now *she* was sore.

One by one, the guests led their horses to the corral and received a small scoop of "groceries" from Morgan. Everyone lined up along the inside of the fence and poured the grain into their feed tubs so the horses could munch away.

Sam enjoyed listening to horses chewing. It gave him a feeling of peace. He was leaning with his arms draped over Bullet's back, wondering what Mary was doing, when Barbara approached him from behind, Cactus and Leroy in tow.

"Is Cactus as smart as Chester?" she asked.

Turning, Sam grinned at the young girl who'd had no interest in horses such a short time ago. "Horses are a whole lot like folks. They all got their own blessings. Chester, he's a giver. He'll give all he's got. Likes to take care of his rider. Stays under him, if you know what I mean."

"Yeah. You mean he won't dump you."

"That's right. Smoke here," he pointed to his young stallion, "he ain't come along just yet. Most likely he'll stay a tad ornery, like Bullet." He gave Bullet a pat on the neck. "But ya know, that's how I like 'em. Means they stay sharp, don't miss much. Then the rider's gotta stay sharp, too. Sorta stay a step ahead of 'em."

Irritated, Barbara moved closer to Sam. "What about Cactus? *Is* she as smart as Chester?"

Sam rested his hand on her shoulder. "Well, ya know ol' Chester, he showed up ready to be a lesson horse. Found him at the auction a number of years back, in about the same shape as Comanche's in today. He came around quick, took to Callie right off. Why those two ..." He stopped himself, taking a second to remember. Then looking away, he scratched Bullet behind the ear. "Yeah, by golly, Chester's a thinker, that's for certain. He ain't thinkin' about getting' into trouble, you understand. No, ma'am, he's thinkin' about what his rider's doin'.'"

As the horses finished their grain, the guests released them and began to gather around Sam and Barbara to follow the talk about Chester and Cactus. Only Philip remained behind, struggling to unbuckle the halter on his horse. Everyone heard the cuss words fly, and saw his foot lash out at the horse's head, but the clever horse easily dodged the blow, gracefully swinging his head high as if to say, "Nice try." Losing his balance, Philip grabbed the empty air with flailing hands on his way down. He hit the ground with a solid thud.

As Sam bolted toward Philip, he fought the urge to give him a taste of his own medicine. Instead, he offered a hand and pulled Philip to his feet. As his ear passed Sam's mouth, he whispered, "Threaten one of my horses again—or your wife—and you and me, we're gonna do a little more than talk." With more vigor than necessary, Sam brushed the dirt from Philip's back then started for the frightened horse. In a pleasant voice, he announced, "I'll slip that halter off for you. Might be a good time for a quick refresher."

Sam snapped his fingers and the haltered horse trotted to him. When he draped his arm over its neck, the horse dropped its head, as it had been schooled to do. "See, folks, the horses all know the routine. Drop head, slip off halter, bridle, bit, whatever you're working with. But if you go at 'em like you're in a hurry, they'll pull up on you ... And nobody's tall enough to unbridle a high-headed horse."

Sam leveled narrowed eyes at Philip, who stepped up to take the halter but kept his eyes trained on the ground.

The tense moment passed when Nicky Bartlett asked, "Where, uh, where would one ..."

With a wide grin, Sam nodded to a rustic, slope-roofed shack. The door, sporting a carved crescent moon, hung by only a top hinge made of a leather strap.

Nicky touched her hand to her lips and smiled sheepishly, "Oh ... I see," and started for the little shack.

Suddenly a loud banging and rattling of pots and pans turned everybody's attention to the chuck wagon where Rusty stood waving a black skillet. "Come and get your beans while they're hot!"

Ready to spoon her beans, Linda stood behind the wagon's tailgate, which now served as a makeshift table.

Paul ushered Lucy to the chow line. "I know I'll soon grow weary of watery beans, dry bread, and burnt coffee, but this evening, I'm ready for a *cup of dark gargle* and a *plate o' beans*."

Lucy sent a reproving glance to her husband and dropped her eyes to the pile of multi-colored beans just deposited on her tin plate. "Thank you, Linda ... It looks ... delicious."

"Thank you for your vote of confidence." Linda said. "I tasted as I cooked, but the real test will come when I've fed you all and tackled a plate of my own."

"Pretty darn good, I think." Paul nodded and licked his finger. "As far as range beans go, I mean."

৯৯৯৯৯৯৯

By the time Linda and Rusty joined everyone by the fire ring, the guests had cleaned their plates. Linda glanced across the fire but offered no smile to Philip, who was leaning comfortably on a blanket-covered log, his leg inches from Lucy's. She chose a spot between Morgan and Barbara to pick at her own beans.

Just enough twilight was settling in so that the lively flames painted dancing images on the faces of the tired bunch. Linda watched Sam tell Debby how to set up her one-man tent. Her eyes wandered back to Philip, then to her daughter, who caught her mother's gaze in her own. For the first time since she'd wed him, Linda seriously questioned her situation.

As her gaze drifted back to Sam, who was speaking with a kindness and understanding she'd never received from Philip, she felt a sudden longing to be touched by a tender man. She studied Sam as his lips, hands, and eyes moved, gentle and strong at the same time, giving her a feeling of security. Then she knew. She realized what had always been missing in her life. None of her husbands had ever made her feel secure, safe, cared for. She'd always felt ... owned, controlled.

Now she studied Philip as he talked to Lucy. Although his words were too faint to hear, his body language told her all she needed to know. Philip wasn't strong or tender. He thought he was tough—as Barbara had often said. Bullies always thought they were tough. Why hadn't Sam let that horse kick the *attitude* out of Philip? Better yet, maybe Sam should've roughed Philip up, right there in front of everyone. With a quivering hand, she brushed the tips of her fingers over her most recent injury. She turned back to Sam. He was looking right at her. Linda flattened her hand over her cheek. Embarrassment washed over her like a wave.

ॐॐॐॐ

Barbara waited until Debby was putting her tent up before she approached Sam. "So, Mr. Holt, I don't think you answered my question."

"About tents?"

"No, not tents." Barbara jumped up, tossed her arms in the air, then looked Sam dead in the eye. "Is Cactus as smart as Chester?" She sat down and shuffled her feet in the dust. "I mean, you told me all about Chester, who, by the way, I wanted to ride this week, but Mrs. Holt needed him." She reached over and jabbed a finger in Sam's shoulder. "I want to know if Cactus is as smart as Chester."

Sam leaned back against his log, scratching his stubbly chin thoughtfully. "Now, Barbara ... Cactus, she's a range horse. Born wild, ya see. That's not a bad thing. Horses born wild make good partners, all right, but they tend to always stay a bit more independent. Smart as Chester? I think yeah, she most likely is, but Chester has a number of years on her. Chester has had a lot of experiences that Cactus ain't had yet. The girls, Mary and Callie, when they got interested in competing in freestyle riding, why by golly, Comanche and Chester got put through their paces. Over the years, they both won a bucketful of ribbons."

"Can Cactus do that? That freestyle stuff? Whatever it is?" She looked at her mother, her excitement evident. "I never won a ribbon. Not for anything."

"Well, young lady," he tapped her on the shoulder, "we may be able to change that in a few weeks. On the Fourth." He turned to Morgan. "When we get back, you can get her started on pole bending. Cactus should be pretty sharp at that."

Barbara looked from Sam to Morgan and back to Sam. "Pole bending? What's that? I want to win a ribbon with a horse, not arts and crafts crap. And I want to learn how from *you*." She pointed directly at Sam.

He sat up, scratched his chin, and cleared the ground between his boots with a stick. Using the stick like chalk on a chalkboard, he drew a line of six small circles in the dust. "Oh, young lady, this takes a horse all right, a smart, fast horse. And a sharp rider."

Before he went on, Sam locked onto Barbara's eyes. "I think *you* are a sharp rider. I'll be around if you need me, but Morgan's got the ribbons in pole bendin'." He returned his attention to the little circles in the dust between his boots, "These circles are poles, about six feet high, about twenty feet apart. Now," he dragged his pointer along and around the circles, "you start down at a flat-out run, turn after the last pole, and weave your way back, turn at the end, weave through them again, then gallop home. All in less than a minute."

"Wow," Barbara whispered. "I never galloped!" She snared her mother's hand and squeezed it.

Morgan laughed. "You will in a few days, on the mustang range."

Paul Keaton added, "That's for sure."

Debby Collier jumped up. "I don't think I'm ready to gallop just yet, Mr. Holt. Frankly, I'm a little scared."

Sam sent her a reassuring look. "No one needs to run a horse if they're not ready for it. In fact, I'd rather you each took it easy. As we told you during the lessons, when in doubt, slow your horse or stop. Don't worry, we've never had an injury here." He pitched a smile Rusty's way. "Well, no guests, anyway."

Debby gave a halfhearted nod, then searched the faces around the circle. "Anyone else need to go to the, uh, toilet?" Linda, Nicky, and Lucy joined her on the darkened path.

Paul ran a glance over the faces of the men. "Ever wonder why they do that?"

"Give us a chance to miss 'em." John Bartlett said with a grin.

Rusty, who had been quietly hacking away on a stick with his long-bladed hunting knife, paused and looked up. "Naw, it's so they can find their way back."

Chapter Sixteen

This wasn't the first night Mary had gone to bed alone. Heavens, when a marriage endured for over thirty-five years, there were many times when life got in the way of routine. She sat on the bed, looked out the window, and said goodnight to the half-moon. It was a game they'd started long ago. Sam had told her that whenever they went to bed apart from each other, they should say goodnight to the moon, and the moon would be happy to pass it along. She had to smile when she remembered the fuss Sam had raised in the hospital until they'd moved her bed closer to the window so she could watch the moon come up each night.

In a few days, she'd be back at that horrid hospital. That awful place. Couldn't she change her mind? Not go? She didn't need any tests to tell her what she already knew. And the money. The terrible money. Those hospitals loved to schedule tests and charge for all their high-priced equipment that couldn't help a person anyway.

She went to the window to gaze up at the moon. Even though it was only slightly more than a half-moon, it shone brilliantly enough to light the grounds around the buildings. She found comfort in the view from their bedroom window. The barn, lodge, and corrals all had the touch of Sam's hand on them.

From the window she could see the results of the wonderful lifetime she'd shared with her sweet, giving man. Sighting along the top ridge of the barn, she was able to pick out the sections in the roof that defined addition after addition. The barn had grown ever longer as their life together had grown ever fuller. When she was gone, that long barn would stand as a testament, a reminder of the precious years they'd spent loving each other.

She thought back to the day she and Sam had set the first pole for the first section of that long barn. It had been a very, very hot day, until the rain started. They'd run, laughing and dancing, into the house to wait out the storm. She looked around the room, remembering ... It had been the first time they'd made love in this room. Sam never even noticed the roof leaking. Poor old house, empty for a bunch of years before she and Sam bought the ranch. It had taken them years to overcome the neglect and restore the house, practically rebuilding it.

She turned away from the window, walked to the wall, and looked at her favorite picture of Callie sitting proudly on Comanche, holding their blue ribbon high. With trembling hands, she took it down and kissed it. Then she wiped a single tear from the glass. "That's what we did, Sam. Built a ranch, lost a daughter ... I'll not cause you to lose the ranch, too." Mary ran her fingertip along the outline of Callie's face, traced her smile, then kissed the glass again and returned it to its perch on the wall.

Vision blurred, she looked out the window again and searched the ground until she found Comanche, sleeping comfortably only a few feet from the front door. She drew back the blanket on her bed, slid in, and squirmed until she could see the moon. "Goodnight, Sam."

She pulled his pillow to her nose, took a deep breath. No, this wasn't the first night in thirty-five years she'd gone to bed alone. But it was the first night she *felt* alone.

Sam wasn't too surprised to find Rusty in the corral with the horses. He was surprised to find Morgan and Barbara with him.

"Evenin', boss," Rusty greeted.

"Nice night for a stroll." Sam pointed to the bright half-moon. "Thought I'd give the horses a final check before I turn in, but I see you three have that under control."

Rusty grinned. "Well, Barbara wanted to give Cactus a goodnight apple."

"Takin' to the horses, are you? Well, that's good. I hope you have a great summer. One to remember."

Barbara palmed her apple. "It's not like I thought it'd be, Mr. Holt."

"That's a good lesson to learn at a young age. Most things aren't."

Sam gave each horse a quick once-over while the four of them walked together between the sleepy horses in the moonlight. He was a little afraid to ask her what she'd expected. "I reckon leaving your friends behind for a whole summer can be a lot to ask of a young girl." He shot her a grin. "Might help some if we had cell phones out here, right?"

Morgan pulled back his hat. "Mine works fine at home and at most places ... just not here."

Rusty scoffed, "I never had one, don't need one."

Barbara surprised them all. "I can't believe I'm about to say this, and don't any of you tell my mother, but I'm already over it."

"Our secret." Sam laid an arm along her shoulders, looked down warmly into the eyes that met his, and guided her along. "Let's see if we can't find Cactus."

"She's layin' down yonder." Rusty pointed to their left.

The bright moonlight glistened on Cactus' white spots, a hundred feet ahead of them where she lay flat out on her side, sound asleep. And snoring.

Barbara's explosion of shrill laughter startled all the horses, but mostly Cactus, who bounced to her feet in one move. She stood blinking and swaying her head, as if trying to decide if she should bolt with the others or stand up to the threat. Whatever that threat might be.

"I didn't know horses snored!" Barbara coughed out a surprised laugh, shrugging her shoulders in apology. Her steps slow and gentle, she inched toward the watchful horse and reached out to offer her apple. Cactus, recovered from her scare and finding no immediate threat, raised her head, marched right up to Barbara's outstretched hand, and bit the apple in half. All of the horses in the corral knew the sound of teeth crunching into an apple. In an instant the group was surrounded by inquisitive noses, demanding snorts, and anxious hoof-stomping.

Before Cactus could snatch the remaining half of the apple, Morgan's horse, Ruth, barged through the crowd and confronted Barbara. Ruth stood a hand taller than Cactus, and her intimidating size backed Barbara up a step. Ruth followed. Her eyes locked on the remaining half-apple. Barbara's legs got tangled up and down she went. Ruth caught the apple midair. Morgan caught Barbara mid-fall.

"Holy crap! I thought that big horse was going to take my hand off!"

Morgan tipped Barbara back onto her own two feet. "She's a little forward, all right."

Rusty and Sam grinned at the warning on Barbara's face. A warning Morgan never caught.

"*Forward*? What the crap does that mean?" she shouted at him. Solemn-faced and silent, he backed away. She turned on Sam. "Aren't your horses supposed to be safe? Holy crap! I coulda lost a hand. Holy crap! What does *forward* mean even mean?"

Sam liked her spunk and found himself sorely tempted to tease her. He bit his lip, knowing that with this little firecracker, there'd likely be plenty of other opportunities for silliness. He could see, out of the corner of his eye, Rusty was enjoying the moment. A quick glance in the other direction revealed Morgan standing a safe distance away. He donned his very best "I'm serious now" look. " 'Forward' is a word we use sometimes to describe a strong-willed horse. Of course, we call a horse 'forward' if it gets along the trail at a good clip, too. Let this be a lesson, young lady. Always remember, no matter how *safe* a horse is, it's still a horse. Get too careless and you could get hurt."

Barbara gave Sam an apologetic look. "Was I careless?"

Sam held her eyes and smiled reassuringly. "No, I didn't mean to say you were careless, mighta just come out that way. But you see how quick things can change around a horse. Stuff happens too fast sometimes."

The horses had all given up on their apple quest and gone back to grazing by the time the four of them reached the corral gate. As they waited for Rusty to untie the rope holding the gate closed, Barbara surprised Sam with a question. "How'd you get Mrs. Holt to marry you?"

He eyeballed Rusty and Morgan and then turned a sheepish look on the girl. "What?"

She swung the gate open, motioned the frozen-in-place Sam through, and explained. "I was just thinking, and I wondered how you and Mrs. Holt met and got married and all."

Rusty offered no aid. "I never heard the story from you either, boss. Heard it from Susan and Mary plenty of times, but never from you."

"I thought we were talking about forward horses." Sam's look telegraphed his befuddlement.

"We were, and you said things can happen too fast, and that made me think about my mom marrying that creep-of-a-jerk Philip too fast, and that made me wonder about you and Mrs. Holt. You know, being married, like, forever and all."

So far, he'd done a pretty good job of getting through the day without worrying too much about Mary. He glanced up at the half-moon, tipped his hat, and then pointed to the dwindling campfire. "Looks like most everybody's gone to bed. We oughta think about it, too. Gonna be a longer day in the saddle tomorrow."

Rusty sprinted ahead a few yards, then called back. "Nope, they're all just sittin' around the fire, chattin'. Reckon they'd like to hear it, too?"

Sam stopped walking, pulled his hat off, and scratched his head. "Well, now, I'd rather ..."

"Please." Barbara tugged on his hand. She held on and swung herself like a grade school kid until she got him moving again. "Look, everybody's still awake." She pointed to the group huddled in the glow of a lively fire.

When they strolled into the campsite, Sam tried one more time. "It ain't much of a story. Once she saw me, the other fellas didn't have a chance."

"Fellas, as in more than one? How exciting!" Barbara snuggled in next to her mother and pulled the blanket over her knees. "Mr. Holt is going to tell us how he and Mrs. Holt got married."

All the guests sat up a little taller and studied Sam with expectant faces. Morgan tossed a few pieces of wood on the fire, then settled down on his blanket, apparently as ready for the tale as anyone.

"Folks, it ain't nothin' to tell, believe me. Why don't we roast a few marshmallows and call it a night?"

That wasn't going to satisfy anyone, now that the mood was set. They started up with rhythmic chants of "We won't go 'til we know!" led by Paul Keaton.

"Okay, okay, but you're gonna be disappointed," Sam conceded. He straddled his blanketed log and scratched his stubbly cheek, as if in deep thought. He worried, though, that he might not get through the telling without breaking down.

Debby Collier leaned forward. "Well?"

He sucked in a long breath, pulled off his hat, and slowly wiped the inside rim with a finger. "I reckon it was … nineteen sixty-nine. I was ridin' bulls and ropin' calves in Phoenix."

Rusty poked the fire with a long stick." Sixty-eight, boss, but the Phoenix part is right."

Sam counted on his fingers, shuffled his hat. "By golly, you're right. It was sixty-eight."

Rusty grinned. "Heard this a few times, from Susan."

"I'd had a good day ropin' calves and ridin' bulls the day before and was killin' time sittin' on the rail behind the chutes when this pretty little gal comes ridin' by, carryin' the flag for the National Anthem. Boy, howdy, was she a looker, all decked out in a tight fittin' outfit, red and silver. Never will forget that."

Debby clapped her hands. "Was that Mary?"

"Sure enough, but 'course I didn't know it at the time … She was ridin' a fine, high-stepping buckskin named Thunder … She went on to be state champion barrel racer later that very year."

"He didn't know she had a big brother then, either," Rusty volunteered.

"That's right. Found out pretty quick, though. I remember watching her carry the flag around the arena. She opened that ol' buckskin into a flat-out run, set that flag to wavin', and her hat to tuggin' on its strings behind her. Her long brown hair floatin' out on the wind. By golly, I thought I'd seen the most beautiful gal in the world." He tipped his hat and nodded to the ladies. "Beggin' your fine ladies' pardons, turns out I sure had."

"How did you get to meet her?" Barbara blurted, then looked sheepishly around the circle of faces lit by bouncing flames.

Philip walked over to Linda and whispered something that washed the color from her face, before walking into the darkness toward his tent.

To spare Linda embarrassment, Sam ignored the slight, even though he made a mental note of the shock painted on Linda's face and the way her hand trembled as she covered her mouth. "After she ran barrels that day, I went to search for her ..."

Rusty laughed. "Found her brother instead."

"Oh, that's so sad," Nicky said.

"Yeah, it is, 'cause he was a big fella who didn't take to guys like me chasing his little sister. But I had done real good on the bulls that afternoon and was feelin' big, so that evening I got cleaned up and went looking. I found their rig, sucked it up, and knocked on the door. Her brother, Robert, answered and told me to get lost. Seemed the family was hopin' she'd marry some other fella they were right fond of.

"I spooked around that night and found out they were going to Albuquerque next, so I hightailed it there myself. All I had to my name at the time was a pretty reliable sixty-two Chevy truck, an old horse trailer, my ropin' horse, Topper, my saddle, and a change or two of clothes. So, it was easy to pull up stakes and go whenever and wherever I wanted to. I'd spent two years traveling around following the rodeo circuit, hirin' on at a ranch here and there when I needed money, but I was a free spirit for a while there."

Sam thought of Mary, alone at the house, and pretended to have a little smoke in his eye.

Debby wanted more. "Well?"

He cleared his throat. "When I got to Albuquerque, I didn't park my rig until they'd pulled in, so I could set up within sight. My plan paid off. That night I noticed a small ruckus going on at Mary's outfit, so I wandered over. Mary was having a bad day. Her boyfriend of two years had broken it off, and her horse wasn't quite right.

"I'd always been pretty good with horses, so I figured I could lend a hand there." Sam looked around the fire-lit faces, shrugged his shoulders, and gave a chuckle. "But I'd never had a girlfriend, so I decided I wouldn't say anything about her breakup. Well, her brother comes right up to me and tells me to skedaddle, but Mary had seen me ride and she says howdy.

"I take a look at her horse, and sure enough, he was off his feed. I tell her he'll be right as rain in a day or three, but he ain't doin' barrels today or tomorrow. Robert says they might as well pack up and head out. But she won't hear of anything like it. She was already in the runnin' for the state championship. She'd find a horse, and she'd ride."

Linda leaned close to the fire and reached her hands out for warmth. "You lent her Topper."

"I did. Of course, it wasn't all that easy. Her brother, well, he saw right through me. And ol' Topper, he'd never done barrels."

Debby gasped. "What did you do?"

"First off, we went to see the judges and get permission for Mary to skip that day's ride and run barrels twice the next day. That settled, it was time for Topper to meet Mary. We set up barrels in the field behind the stadium." Sam wiped his face and drew a long breath. "Folks, I'd worked with horses all my life, and I'd met a lot of really talented people … When she started workin' with ol' Topper, I knew two things right off. Number one, I'd lost a horse … Number two, she was the gal I was gonna marry!"

The girls all cheered. Zack, always the competitor, had to know. "How'd she do?"

"You have to understand it's a tall order to take a calf-roping horse and turn him into a barrel horse in a day ..." Sam couldn't hold back the tears. "When Mary sets out to do a thing ..." He choked up, swiping his hand across his face. "My Mary—she's a scrapper. Nothing's gonna beat my Mary."

No one breathed while Sam ground the heels of his hands into his eyes. "She ran first, and second, best times the next day." His voice cracked and broke.

Rusty noisily tossed a log on the waning fire, sending sparks shooting high and giving his boss a break. "Go on, tell 'em what happened next."

Linda seemed to want to help. "It's obvious what happened next. They took Mary's winnings and raced to the church and got married."

While Rusty's log had settled down into a nice calm fire, Sam had regrouped some and figured he owed it to them to finish. He wanted to remember, too.

"We traveled together for two months, and we actually did all right. Winning money, I mean, and getting along. Ol' Topper was never the same, and I sure wasn't either. Uncle Sam was about to send me on an errand to Southeast Asia. I didn't get up the nerve to tell her until two weeks before I had to report.

"That was the first time I saw her cry ... We took Topper and Thunder out for a ride, camped out for a week, living off the land in the mountains of Wyoming. It was around a campfire like this that I asked her to marry me. By golly, you'd have thought I'd just given her the entire world. She jumped across the fire and knocked me plumb on my back and never let me up for air."

Sam sent another solemn look around the fire. "I don't mind tellin' you all ... it was her sweet-smellin' letters that brought this long-legged cowboy home in one piece. We were married two days after I got back."

Teary-eyed, Debby Collier let out an audible sigh. "Someone should make that into a movie."

Barbara laughed. "My mom's story could be a mini-series."

Linda gasped, shoved her daughter, then shrugged her shoulders.

Nicky and John Bartlett excused themselves and strolled hand in hand toward their tents. Paul and Lucy said goodnight next.

Sam felt worn out. "Folks, if you don't mind, I'm heading for my bedroll." He tipped his hat, picked up his blankets, and headed for the corral. He had a special place where he liked to spread his blanket, where the sounds of the grazing horses could whisper him to sleep. He settled into his bedroll, strained his ears to listen to the end of Debby and Zack's wedding day tale. Their voices gradually faded, the fire died out, and the moon smiled down at him. He smiled back. He wasn't cold, but he pulled the blanket up to his chin. "Goodnight, Mary."

Chapter Seventeen

They rode into the setting sun, the chuck wagon out in front, the guests trailing along behind on tired horses. For three days, the troops had trudged along a well-established trail that followed a strong, flowing river and wound its way through pleasant meadows and thick woodlots. Now they were finally cresting the grade they'd been climbing for too long and staring in wonder as the land opened before them, rolling and barren. Far off in the distance ahead of them, high mountains circled the range, standing in gray-green contrast to the brown-hued flatland in front of them.

Gradually, the riders lined up along the ridge, sitting their horses side by side as they stared out over the range. They had seen open grassland back at the homestead, but except for Lucy and Paul Keaton, none of them had seen anything like the vastness of what lay before them now.

Zack stepped from his horse. "Wow!"

Paul laughed. "That was pretty much my first impression, too."

Barbara rode up to Sam. "Where are the wild horses?"

He smiled at her. "Out there, somewhere." He nodded toward the open land. "They'll show up in the morning. Folks, we'll set up camp near the corrals." Sam twisted in his saddle to point the way.

Rusty started leading the mules toward the campsite, complete with a sheltering lean-to for their equipment, a long, tin-roofed pavilion, and another rough-looking privy. The smaller corrals behind the pavilion were at the tree line and offered plenty of shade and grass for their mounts.

Sam admired his guests as they assembled at the corral. Given three days on the trail, they'd become a decent team. Already, they needed far less coaching. He sat Bullet a short while longer, watching them dismount, un-tack, and tend their horses. Certain Rusty had things in hand, he passed Smoke's lead to Morgan, then put his heels to Bullet and shot off at a run toward the open range. The big stallion and he both could use a good run after spending three days plodding along at a mule-drawn-wagon's pace. Up one hill, down into the next valley, he let Bullet have his head. The willing horse thundered along, blowing and puffing, stretching his powerful legs for the longest stride he could give. After cutting a wide arc over the range, Sam finally turned and galloped back toward camp.

When they crested a sharp ridge seconds later, Bullet suddenly snorted and gave a quick crow-hop. Coming their way at an impressive speed were Morgan and Ruth. Sam was up to the challenge, eager for it, in fact. He turned Bullet to intercept. Beside the ridge, running parallel with the camp, Ruth pulled alongside Bullet, reached out her neck, and gnashed her teeth, threatening the stallion.

Sam guided Bullet safely away from those dangerous teeth. "To the camp!" He pointed with his free hand then settled in for the race.

The guests lined the crest by the pavilion, hooting and hollering. Sam could hear his and Morgan's names in the chorus of cheers. He looked to his left and grinned at the serious expression painted on Morgan's face as the youth pushed his mare for speed. Bullet had already run nearly flat-out for more than a mile, and even though he showed no sign of fading, Ruth held a slight advantage.

Stride for stride, she matched Sam's big stallion and, little by little, nosed ahead. Only a few hundred yards remained to the finish. The guests began to drift toward the obvious finish line, an opening between the two largest corrals, while they maintained a loud, crazy chorus of cheers.

Rusty leaped up on the top rail, hat in hand, ready to serve as the finish line official.

Sam knew Bullet had a little more to give but didn't ask for it. He kept his stallion going steady but allowed the teen and his mare the thrill of victory. Do 'em both good to win this one. Fourth of July is right around the corner.

At breakneck speed, they galloped down the lane and flew past Rusty, who waved his hat wildly and declared the winner to be, "Morgan on Ruth by half a length!"

Sam patted Bullet on the neck and gave a wide grin as the powerful horse slowed to a walk. He enjoyed a good run, too.

Mary asked Chester for more speed. He responded with a new burst of energy. When they flew around the last barrel and by the judges' booth, Susan hit the tiny button on the stopwatch. "Nineteen seconds flat!"

"Pretty darn good." Mary fell forward to hug Chester's sweaty neck. Well, not bad for a sick woman and a horse on the backside of a long career. She trotted Chester to the judges' booth, located along the corral's fence under a single tall oak, and stopped in the shade. "He's really helping me get my legs back in shape."

"How are those legs doing?" Susan's questioning smile looked forced.

"Hard to tell until I dismount," she lied, "and I'm not quite ready to yet."

"You're not running the barrels again?"

"No, twice is enough. But I do feel like a ride along the river. I think I'll take Comanche along for a walk. Care to join us?"

"You go on ahead. I should load the truck. After three days of Rusty's beans and salt-pork, the guests are bound to be craving a decent meal."

"How long til you need to leave for camp?"

Susan checked her watch. "Let's see, it takes half an hour to drive to camp. It's two now. I should leave by four, which would give Rusty, Linda, and me half an hour to set up for supper."

"Don't leave without me." Mary tapped her heels to Chester and trotted away, straight for Comanche's daytime pasture. She heard Susan call after her, "Wouldn't consider it!"

Her trip to Conner County General was only a day away, but tonight she'd join in the fun on the wild horse range and snuggle by a fire with the kindest, long-legged cowboy God had ever created.

For the past three days, Mary had taken short trail rides on Chester. Despite what the future might hold, she was determined to strengthen any parts of her body willing to accept the challenge. As for the parts that weren't willing to join in the fun, well, she'd handle them in another way.

Eager to play, Comanche ran to the fence alongside the barn and let go his loud scream. Trotting, stomping and snorting, he demanded to be included. Mary swung down from Chester, but as her feet touched the ground, she held a tight grip on the saddle horn while her unsteady legs insisted on a second to regroup. Her fury with those legs was tempered by her amusement over Comanche's antics.

"I wouldn't go without you," she soothed the over anxious horse. She looped Chester's reins over a fence rail, pushed open the gate, and snapped her fingers. Comanche trotted to her, quivering with excitement.

"You might be a little disappointed, boy. We're only going for a short walk to the stream." She slipped on his halter. Then she led him to the corner of the barn and gave him a thorough brushing. Starting to fill in between the ribs, she noted. Coat's a little glossier, too. She turned Comanche's head to examine his blue eye. "Well, this seems to have cleared up nicely." She gave him a hug around the neck then started back to the patiently waiting Chester.

They traveled down the hill toward the stream. Chester set the pace. Comfortable for her but too slow for Comanche, who signaled his displeasure with occasional head bobs and snorts.

"Feeling full of ourselves, are we? You'll just have to wait until next week, then I think you might be ready for a little work under saddle."

She twisted in the saddle in order to watch Comanche's stride. Good steady walk. Good square foot placement. Nice head balance, holding his tail relaxed. Yeah, a few more days off, then we can get started. Light work at first of course, but he'll be ready on time. Just look at those legs and how they've steadied up already. She slid her hand up and down her own thigh.

"It'll be whatever it'll be," she said aloud, then pointed a finger at Comanche. "You and me fella, we're going for the blue ribbon!"

She stopped Chester at the top of the stream bank, then coaxed him down. She'd chosen a fairly steep place to descend just for the fun of it. Chester stepped obediently forward, squatted on his haunches and slid down into the water. Comanche followed them to the center of the stream, and without a second's hesitation, he dropped to his belly and rolled in the water.

Mary laughed a loud, happy laugh. How wonderful to know that whatever had happened to this marvelous horse, nothing had robbed him of his devilish personality. He was as playful, prankish, and wonderfully spirited as ever. She watched him stand and shake like a dog, sending cool water droplets showering over her and Chester, who protested by splashing the water with his front hoof.

She gave Comanche a few seconds to regroup, then started Chester up the bank, wiped the water from her face, and told Comanche to follow. She smiled at the paint. *Yeah, that blue ribbon's as good as ours.*

Riding slowly on the trail back to the barn, Mary ran the movements of her last "freestyle to music" competition over and over in her head. What would she change? What would she keep the same? She still had a little more than two months to work on it. The state fair wasn't until the first week of September.

First, she would dig out those old tapes her brother had made and study them. Then she'd get Sam to rework the speakers in the corral. Or should she use the big arena after the rodeo on the Fourth of July? Might be better there. More room, better sound. Maybe John Bartlett could help out with the speakers this year. A real professional job. She'd ask him.

As they rounded the corner of the barn, she looked to the lodge. Susan had already parked the green Chevy truck by the kitchen door and loaded the coolers. Mary jerked her arm up, glancing at her watch. Three forty-five. She'd been gone for an hour and a half. Seemed like fifteen minutes. "Susan, I'll be ready in a jiff."

Susan waved acknowledgment but stayed steady on her task.

Mary slid from Chester, catching her breath as her feet touched down, shocked to realize how much weaker her right leg was than her left. After slipping the saddle from Chester, she took a moment to roll her shoulders. Both shoulders were a bit sore. These little aches and pains are to be expected. After all, she was pushing herself to get in shape. Wasn't she?

She rubbed down both horses, quicker and less attentively than usual, but she was in a hurry, and they could roll all night in the grass. After hanging the wet towel over the rail, she turned to gather the leads, stopping to study her open hands. She made tight fists. Huh, nothing new here.

Leading the horses to Comanche's private pasture, Mary considered a quick shower to freshen up but quickly rejected the impulse. She'd require another one after sitting around a smoky fire for an hour or two, anyway. She was anxious to see Sam and tell him how fast she was getting back in shape.

"Ready to go?" Susan had snuck the old truck right up behind her.

Mary glanced down at her wet, hairy, muddy shirt and jeans and had to laugh. "Yeah, I'm ready." She hopped into the passenger seat. "Sorry I bailed on you, but I had a delightful ride."

"No problem. Now we're off to the mustang range." Susan gave the old truck some gas and Mary a kind smile. "I'll bet those cowboys and cowgirls are ready for a decent meal. I know I always get awfully tired of beans and salt pork after a few days."

As they drove over the first rise, leaving the homestead behind, Mary gazed out her window and surveyed the grassland that stretched endlessly ahead. She hadn't gone to the wild horse range in four years. *Queer, isn't it, how dying makes you feel like living?*

෨෬෨෬෨෬෨

Mary was the first to spot the campfires. "There they are. I'm so excited! I feel like a teenager. Look, there's Sam."

Susan aimed the truck for the campfire, and Sam. Mary stretched out of the window farther than was sane or safe, and yelled. "I'm coming in for a man-sized hug, you tall, lean, hunk of cowboy!"

"Mary!" Sam bolted for the truck, yanking the stubborn door open. "Mary, by golly, if this ain't the best surprise ever." He scooped her off the truck seat, holding her high in the air, then twirled them both around in a grand circle.

"I was thinking about you all day, wishing I could see you before you went to the hospital. By golly, I'm sure glad you came out here." He lowered her to the ground and looked her over. "The trip wasn't too much for you, was it?"

She swung his arm, grinning wildly. "No. I feel perfectly fine. When I came in from my ride on Chester, Susan hadn't left yet, so I hitched a ride."

"You went for a ride, too?" He stepped back and studied her face. "Now, don't overdo it. Doggone it, don't push yourself. Okay?"

Susan was in the truck bed, sliding a cooler to the rear. "She ran barrels, too."

"Mary! On Chester? Now doggone it, you keep misbehavin' and I'll quit this round-up to babysit you ..." Sam took another step back and found a grin. "How'd you do?"

"Nineteen seconds flat!" The guests had gathered around the truck and wagon by now. Linda and Rusty finished sliding the coolers from the truck bed and set them on the nearest table.

Rusty grinned wide and tipped his hat. "Great time! Sounds like you're gettin' your old legs back."

Mary snatched Sam's hand and marched him to the table with a gait so light she wondered if she might be floating on air. "It felt wonderful. I don't know why I've waited so long. You should have seen Chester. He thought he was five years old again. We ran those barrels as if we'd never missed a season."

"By golly, Mary, I ... I don't know what to say." Sam settled in beside her and pulled her close. "Hot dog, it's good to see you tonight."

Rusty opened the first cooler. "Looky-here, folks. We got us roast beef and all the fixin's."

When everyone had heaped their plates with *real food*, they found comfortable seats around the main campfire. Mary snuggled up to Sam.

"That's a real good time on Chester, Mrs. Holt," Morgan said. "Do you think you'll run him on the Fourth?"

"Thank you." She squeezed Sam's hand. "I have a little something to attend to, but if that works out, then yes, I'll run barrels with Chester on the Fourth of July. Comanche needs some more time and conditioning. He has bounced back nicely already, though, and I hope to start working him lightly under saddle in a few days."

Barbara settled on the blanket between her mother and Sam. "I hope your doctor's visit goes all right tomorrow."

"Barbara!" Linda let out an embarrassed gasp.

Barbara stared at her mother, a confused look on her face. "What? I didn't know it was a secret."

Mary smiled at her, at them both. "It's not, and thank you." A hot feeling rushed up her back. "Forget about that boring old doctor's visit. Tell me what you all will be doing tomorrow."

Debby rubbed both hands up and down her sore thighs. "I hope we get a day off."

Paul laughed politely, then glanced at his wife. "We didn't get started yet. Let's see if I remember correctly. If the wild horses don't show up in the morning, we start looking for them. When we find them, we herd them into the big corrals. Then the real fun begins."

Nicky Bartlett leaned forward into the glow of the fire. "The real fun?" She shot a concerned glance at her husband.

With a nod, Paul passed the torch to Sam. "You're doin' dandy, Paul. Go ahead."

He scanned the circle of fellow campers. "Well, after we pen the horses, we need to run them through the working chutes, check them over one by one, and give them their needed vaccinations."

Debby gave Sam a worried look. "Vaccinations? You mean give the horses shots?"

"Yes, ma'am, but don't worry, Dr. Adams comes each year to do any doctorin' that needs doin'. He should roll in just about noon tomorrow," Sam explained.

Zack gave her a hug. "Now it sounds like we're gonna start real ranch work."

Debby pushed him away. "I'd like to volunteer to stay behind with the wagon, maybe help Linda cook."

Mary laid her head in Sam's lap. He stroked her cheek.

"That'll be fine. Anyone else who needs a day out of the leather can stay in camp. Most likely, the horses will be within eyesight by sunup, anyway. When they sense us here in camp, they often get too nosey to stay away."

Philip was the first to bid everyone goodnight. Then, bit by bit, other guests began drifting away from the fire toward their tents. Rusty and Morgan excused themselves to make a final check on the horses. By the time the moon shone high overhead, only Mary, Sam, Susan, Linda, and Barbara remained basking in the aging fire's glow.

Barbara angled toward Sam. "So can I run barrels, too?"

Sam pushed an errant strand of hair from Mary's eye and saw she was asleep. "I'm sure you can. First, find your balance and get comfortable with speed out here where you have plenty of room, then work with Morgan on the poles a little."

She gave him a disappointed look. "What about barrels?"

He looked down at Mary. She winked back. Sam stifled a grin. She wasn't asleep after all, just pretending.

He found a short stick and drew another diagram in the dust. Mary snuggled deeper into his lap. With the tip of his stick to the left of the first of three dots in the dust, Sam drew a line mapping the course around the dots. "You choose your first barrel, left or right, start inside, circle around to the outside, keeping your turn tight, run to the second, round it tight as can be, then go for the third barrel, ring it, turn your horse loose, and run for home. Champions do it in fifteen seconds, some less." He dropped his stick and mussed Mary's hair.

Barbara stood over the dust-drawing, her hand on his shoulder. "Wow! She can do that? Wow. Can she teach me?"

"Sure." He gave Mary a secret wink. She gave him one back. "You'll need to get some fundamentals down first. Get comfortable on a fast horse, learn the poles with Morgan, then we can tackle barrels."

"Hmmm," Barbara looked toward the corral, "I've got to talk to Morgan." She started away then turned back. "I won't be long, Mom."

Linda laughed. "Watch out for snakes."

Barbara tossed a careless wave over her shoulder but slowed her pace as she headed to the corral.

"She hasn't been this excited about anything for a long time." Linda marched right up to Sam, yanked off his hat, and kissed the top of his head. "Thank you!" She sprinted after her daughter, singing softly.

Susan stood. "Poor Morgan. He's afraid of her, you know." She smiled down on them. "If you two camp counselor-slash-lovebirds will excuse me, I'll go load the truck."

"I'll give you a hand." Sam shifted to get up.

"I'll take care of it. You two keep on doing what you're doing."

Mary giggled. "Happy to."

He pushed his fingers through her hair, looking deep into her eyes. "I've got to go with you tomorrow."

She twisted in his lap and traced his kind eyes with a quivering finger. "I desperately want you to be with me, to hold me while those horrid machines look inside me. But they wouldn't allow it anyway. You'd be stuck by yourself, pacing in some stupid waiting room, worrying about me. Making yourself sick. No, I don't want to lie in that tube-monster and think of you fretting in the waiting room, worrying about me. I want ... I need ... to be able to close my eyes and see you racing across the range on Bullet, running with the mustangs, waving your hat and shouting. It's the only way I can get through this. You understand, don't you? I need to see you being my big, strong cowboy. I need to ..."

She reached up, grabbed his hair, pulled him down again, mashing their lips together, and cuddled those scratchy stubbles. They weren't on the open range next to a dying campfire anymore; they were in the bedroom of the old house, with its leaky roof, giggling and laughing and making love.

ॐॐॐॐॐॐ

Sam stood on the road, watching the truck's taillights fade. With a hard fist, he pounded his thigh, walked a few steps forward, as if he would run after the truck, then dropped to his knees. Sucking in a long, raspy breath, he sat down, cross-legged, in the dust. The truck disappeared behind the first ridge, its headlights creating an orb of light in the dark sky. He watched it climb out of the hollow, smaller now, the headlights casting a wide yellow swath up the next hill. Two more times the lights changed from a stabbing yellow beam on a faraway hillside to radiance in the sky over a distant valley.

Loud voices from the direction of the chuck wagon turned him away from the distant and shrinking truck lights. The campfire had nearly burned itself out, but the glowing coals lit the side of the wagon, revealing the image of two dancing silhouettes against the wagon sheet. Sam looked back to the truck, now a tiny light not much bigger than a firefly, pulled himself to his feet, and blew a kiss toward the speck of light. Smiling at the dancing silhouettes, he started toward them.

After a few strides, he realized they were not happy voices, nor were they dancing. He kicked his speed up a notch, just as one silhouette raised its arm.

"Hold on there." Sam took in the scene before him, tensed his muscles, and jumped the fire pit. "Is everything all right?"

Philip lowered his arm and stepped away from Linda. "Yeah, yeah." He skulked away, muttering loudly and kicking the dirt.

Linda turned to Sam. "We were having a little tiff. It's fine now."

Sam examined her face, registered the split, bloody lip, the nervous eyes.

"Linda, what's going on?" He sat on the wagon tailgate and reached for her shaking hand. "Are you going to be okay?" He held her hand and stroked it gently. "Do you want me to talk to him?" They'd already talked to the bully once. This time, he wouldn't use words.

She sat next to him and drew a long quivering breath. "No ... I don't know ... Sam, I don't know why he gets so mad. I think I'm becoming afraid of him."

He let her rest her head on his shoulder while she cried.

Chapter Eighteen

The only thing left to do was water her violets. Her bag already packed and waiting by the door. She'd almost packed two, but with a little extra effort, managed to stuff everything into one. It was only overnight, after all. One change of clothes, two undergarments, a toothbrush, toothpaste, deodorant, a hairbrush, and a book she hadn't started. She'd packed her own pillow and pillowcase. Sam's picture and Callie's. No makeup, no nail polish.

"Well now," she smiled as she gave the last pink violet a drink. "That'll have to hold you a couple of days. Mommy's going away. I'll be back real soon."

She made one final pass downstairs to check the lights, stove, and windows, then picked up her bag and started down the porch steps. Comanche trotted right up to her, blocking her path to the gate.

"Goodness, Comanche, is it me or this apple?" She held out her hand, offering the apple. He pushed his nose into it, bit the apple in half, and chewed happily. As she offered the second half, Susan pulled up in her car. "Let's put you in the pasture with Chester, and then I've got to go." Mary bent over to tie him to the rear of her cart, then suddenly snapped straight up and jammed her fists on her hips. "No. I think today we'll walk."

Susan hurried from her car. "Are you sure?"

She sighted the distance to Comanche's pasture, where Chester stood at the gate waiting. "Yes." She handed her bag to Susan. "I'll be flat on my back long enough over the next two days."

Susan gave her an uncertain nod, then pitched the bag into the car and joined her on the walk. Comanche, certain it was time to play, had a bounce in his step that made Mary laugh. "He's sure going to be disappointed."

Susan swung the gate open and stepped out of the way. "You'll make it up to him in a few days." Her voice expressed both certainty and doubt.

Mary led him a few yards into the pasture, wrapped her arms around his neck, and hugged tight. "I've got to go away awhile. You be sure to listen to Susan, eat all your vitamins, and don't be too pushy with Chester." She slipped off his halter. "I promise we'll play in a day or two." Her voice cracked. Comanche paused a second, enjoying the brisk scratching Mary offered on his withers, then snorted and raced away.

The trip to the hospital passed too quickly. As Susan drove into the main parking lot, Mary's eyes arrowed straight to that imposing entrance. *"Back so soon?"* it taunted her.

They sat together in the parked car for a moment.

"We should go in."

"I suppose we should ... Did I tell you, for one night and three tests, we'll owe another five thousand dollars ... after the insurance pays its share?"

"I'm sorry. I wish it were me." Susan turned to face her but focused her eyes on Mary's hands. "You know, Rusty and I have put a little money away."

Mary sucked in a sudden breath. "Oh no, Susan! That's not why I said that." She studied her friend. Of course, that's not why she'd said it. Why had she said it? This hateful cancer. It takes from everybody, not just you, but your family, your friends. Everybody, anybody. It takes from everybody and spreads guilt everywhere. You feel the guilt because it's your cancer. Your friends and family feel the guilt because they aren't sick so they say things they hope will make you feel better. She shook her head. "I'm sorry ... I suppose we should get it over with." Mary opened the door, grabbed her bag, and marched with purpose toward the ominous, covered entryway.

They took the elevator to the second floor. The doors opened directly in front of the nurses' station. Mary felt like she was walking into a madhouse. Everyone looked so frantic. How could they know what they were doing? Phones ringing, people crowding the counter demanding attention, overhead pages blasting ... insanity. Maybe they did that on purpose. Maybe they figured if they looked busy enough, no one would have the nerve to complain about the cost.

She studied the three women working behind the counter. The one on the phone, telling a Dr. Milner he'd need to come in right away, looked old enough to be her own mother. A very pregnant, very well-dressed young woman rested both arms on the counter while she analyzed some poor unfortunate's file. She'd probably have her baby in a week or two. Start a new life.

"May I help you?" The third woman behind the counter had kind eyes, dark brown like her skin. Mary noticed a wedding band as she flipped the page on a huge appointment book sprawled on the counter between them. A wedding band and bright blue nail polish. "May I help you?' she repeated.

"Mrs. Mary Holt. Dr. Stein has scheduled some tests for her," Mary heard Susan say. She'd forgotten her friend was standing next to her. Dear Susan. Mary could always count on her. She should have had children. She would have made an excellent mother. Mary's eyes strayed back to the pregnant woman. But then, if you never have children ... you never lose them.

"Mary, I've arranged a private room for you." Dr. Stein seemed to suddenly appear next to her, offering his hand and a friendly smile.

She backed away one step, her eyes on the wheelchair. "Why, thank you. Doesn't a private room cost extra?"

He moved the wheelchair alongside her, signaling her to sit.

She obeyed.

He leaned in, close to her ear. "I pulled a string and your insurance company will pick up the bill for the room."

"Thank you." Mary said in a soft, unsteady whisper. She reached for Susan's hand as Dr. Stein gave the wheelchair a gentle push.

"I've cleared my day today, and I'll be observing your MRI. I was able to rearrange the schedule so it will be done first thing."

He wheeled her into room 211. This room was yellow, too! What had happened to the blue rooms? Soft, baby blue was much friendlier than this cold, offensive yellow. The pictures on the wall were a nice touch. They helped to offset the ugly brown sofa that consumed the wall under the window.

A single, thirsty violet sat on the window sill.

He said something to Susan then gave Mary's arm a soft pat. "Someone will come for you in about fifteen minutes. You can go ahead and change into the gown, and I'll see you a little later." And he was gone.

"A single room. That was nice of him." Susan looked uncomfortable, as if she couldn't think of anything else to say.

Mary stood, pushed the wheelchair aside, threw her bag on the bed, and took a long breath. "Susan, could you stay? I mean, would you wait here until I come back?"

"You know I will. Can I help you change?"

Mary stared at the pale, gray and white striped gown folded neatly on the foot of the bed. "I don't know." She struggled with trembling, uncooperative fingers to undo the top button on her blouse. After several fruitless attempts, she dropped on the bed and ripped her blouse open, sending the pearl-white buttons flying. "I hate this!" She tore off her prosthesis bra and flung it.

Susan fell on her knees, cradled Mary's legs and dropped her head onto Mary's lap. She held tight to her friend's legs, swaying gently, humming softly.

It felt good to have Susan hold her. Somehow reassuring ... comforting in a motherly kind of way. Mary dug her fingers into Susan's thick, brown hair and remembered when her own hair had been thick and brown. She knew sometimes a person's hair grew back in its natural color after chemo. Hers hadn't. Instead, it had come back white, thin, and brittle. Of course, having to endure chemo treatments every year for four years in a row most likely hadn't helped. She slid her fingers through Susan's hair, patted her back, and braced herself. "Okay now."

As soon as Susan stepped away to wipe her eyes, Mary swung the striped gown around her shoulders, tied the string, and wiggled out of her jeans.

Mary had folded her clothes and stacked them neatly on the corner of the bed and Susan had finished collecting the buttons by the time a young woman dressed in a red and white uniform was knocking timidly on the door she'd just stepped through. "I'm here to take a Mrs. Holt for her MRI."

Mary looked at Susan and opened her mouth, but no words came.

"I'll walk along." Susan held Mary's arm and guided her to the wheelchair.

"It's only down the hall to the left." The woman turned to Susan, "There's a waiting area in the corridor."

Yes, I suppose I'll need to go in there alone. I've done it before. I know what to expect. Lie in that cold noisy tube for an hour. At least Dr. Stein hadn't said anything about dye this time. The last time he'd used it I was sick for two days. Why didn't he need to use it this time?

Susan kissed her on the cheek. "I'll be right over there." She pointed to the sofa, chairs, and table arranged in the wide spot of the hall, directly across from the door Mary was about to enter.

Mary squeezed her hand and wished for Sam.

From atop Bullet, at the highest point of the rise, Sam searched the valley below. "Doggone 'em, they're hidin' good this morning, aren't they?" he asked Zack and Paul. A mile away, Rusty waved his hat high over his head. He hadn't sighted either of the two bands of mustangs.

Zack unwound the leather string holding his canteen to his saddle horn, popped the cork and took a long, satisfying swallow. "I guess they have home-court advantage."

"They sure do, and they know it. Sometimes both bands are close enough together that we can push 'em in one bunch. Sometimes not." Sam touched his heels to Bullet and led the trio into the next arroyo at a quick trot. Through mesquite, cactus, and bramble brush they trotted. By now, the three had blended into an effective search party, and they rode together, not in a fashion that would reveal the newness of the team, but rather like long time comrades.

They kept the pace steady but easy. The distant mountains grew ever larger on the horizon.

Paul moved his horse closer to Sam. "How far from camp are we?"

He signaled a halt, stood tall in his stirrups, and looked back to gauge the distance. "Ten, twelve miles, I reckon."

Suddenly Zack pointed to a brown cloud rising over the next valley. "Hey. What's that smoke?"

"Ya-hoo! That's not smoke, boys! That's dust! My guess is Morgan's bunch found both bands in that gully. Easier for us. You boys follow me. We'll ride this ridge, keep 'em from turning north. Rusty'll handle the south, and Morgan's group'll push 'em toward the corrals. They'll be running hard at first, stay with 'em. But don't hoot and holler. Don't crowd 'em too much. We want 'em to slow down to a nice easy walk before we get to camp." Sam clamped his hat on his head and shot Paul and Zack a ten-gallon grin. "Let's go, boys!" He gave Bullet a swat on the rump with his reins and turned the big horse loose.

Bullet tore away. Sam bent low, giving him plenty of free rein, and shook his hat in the air. "Are you watchin', Mary?"

Running well ahead of Zack and Paul, he found himself in a perfect position to turn the herd when they thundered over the crest. The lead stallion saw Sam and Bullet and tried to turn the herd north.

Morgan, Barbara, and Lucy were too far south to hold the herd. Sam cast a look over his shoulder. Zack had fallen behind, but Paul was moving up fast. Sam signaled for Paul to follow and Zack to hold his position.

Sam kicked Bullet up another gear and rode hard for the stallion. Waving his hat and yelling for the wild horse to turn, he narrowed the gap between them. He was close enough now to see the stallion's flattened ears and intense eyes. "Hey, hey, hey, big fella. Easy now." Sam yelled out to the stallion, who only ran harder. Sam asked Bullet for all he had left, and the powerful horse responded by switching into a still higher gear. The wild stallion had more, too, and he used it to turn the herd. Sam began to think the mustang would slip through, then out of nowhere, Morgan and Ruth exploded over the ridge, Barbara on Cactus close behind.

With his escape cut off, the stallion turned the herd back down the ridge they'd just raced up. Rusty, Philip, and John were already there, poised to cut off any escape. The herd tightened and began to slow.

Sam waved his hat. "Good job, everybody. Now let's ease 'em along to camp."

The riders circled the tired herd and rode along at a comfortable walk.

In the midst of the exuberant chatter, Barbara trotted Cactus next to Sam. "That was totally *awesome!*"

ॐॐॐॐ

They sat face to face, their knees nearly touching. She saw his lips move, but she heard no words. Just a low hum, like the melody to a very sad song. His hand on hers felt soft and warm. She hadn't realized how cold she'd become. She watched his hand stroke hers, and then shifted to look in his eyes, which were focused on her hand, their hands. He looked so sad. She felt sorry for him. How many times did the poor man need to go through this? Was it worse to tell someone, or was it worse to hear it? She'd soon find out, of course. She would need to tell Sam. But that wasn't the same, really. It would only be one time. Poor Dr. Stein, he did this ... God alone knew how many times.

She watched his lips. He was still talking, probably saying things she should hear, but all she heard was that steady hum. How could he have so much to say? He'd already told her the worst. Did anything else matter?

She wished Sam were here with her, holding her tight. She'd like to feel his arms around her, his beard tickling her. What was her big strong cowboy doing at the moment? Racing across the range on Bullet? Chasing the mustangs? She hoped so.

"How long will I be able to ride a horse?" she interrupted Dr. Stein's droning.

He jerked his gaze from their hands to her eyes. "What? Mary, weren't you listening? Your cancer has moved into your spine, your bones. We'll need to start treatment right away. I'm admitting you for a few days to do some blood work, begin radical chemotherapy, and schedule radiation treatments."

Mary glanced around the horrid yellow room. Why had he sent Susan out into the hall? She should be there. "If I don't do any of those things, how long will I be able to ride a horse?"

"Mary." He spoke her name sharply, as if trying to wake her from a nightmare. "If you don't take the treatment, you're going to die. Don't you understand?"

"Doctor, if I take the treatment, will I be cured?"

He reached out, put his hand on her shoulder, "No one can say for sure, but we haven't many options. This appears to be an aggressive form of cancer. We'll need to attack it with everything we have. I wouldn't think you'd feel much like riding a horse for a while. In fact, I'm surprised you look as strong as you do now."

"Well, here's another surprise. I think I'll opt to forgo *attacking with everything we have.*" She tipped her face back, found Sam's and Callie's pictures hanging on the yellow wall (bless Susan for the thought) and dried her eyes with the hem of the pale, gray and white hospital gown. "People die every day, Dr. Stein. I want to *live* ... right now."

He pushed his glasses aside. "That is precisely why we've got to start treatment."

She studied his worried eyes. He didn't understand. How could he? He'd devoted his life to treating sick people with all the marvels of modern medicine.

"Do you know I had gone for four years without riding a horse?"

"I didn't ..."

"For four years I thought I was too sick, too weak to live. I pitied myself. I pitied Sam. I did all the things I was supposed to, endured all those horrible treatments. Doctor, do you know how much money we owe now?"

"Mary, the money isn't important. We've got to get you through this."

"We fight with the insurance company every month, and where has it brought us? We owed two-hundred and fifty thousand dollars ... before today."

"There are ways to work that out."

She wouldn't be quieted. "For four years I ... lived like I was dead. My last treatment was eight months ago. I watched my dear Sam work himself beyond what a man should be asked to do. I grew numb watching him. Each day had a cloud over it. A cloud of guilt and shame.

"Dr. Stein, I've known for a little while now something was going on. I wasn't surprised when you called. The morning after your call, Sam brought home a very sick horse. A horse I'd sold three years ago. A horse I'd won a wall full of ribbons with, Callie, too. This sick, tired horse has made me feel more alive than all your treatments. Who knows why he came home when he did? Who knows why he was made to suffer the things he did? I made him a promise. We'll win one more blue ribbon. And you know what? He's recovering splendidly." She broke a smile. "Sam can't believe the progress. Comanche's and mine. I've been riding every day now for over a week. I ran barrels yesterday, and I went to the mustang range for a campfire last night. I'm living again, and I'd rather live for three months than die for two more years."

He rubbed his hands over his eyes and let out a sigh. "That's just about right."

She'd been powerful, in charge while she'd pled her case. But to hear Dr. Stein bluntly state the fact. "I'm going to die in three months?"

Absently he bit his lip. "It's hard to say with certainty but ... yes, without treatment you have very little time. I'm sorry to push this way, but you have no choice. You need to start treatments, possibly today."

She'd felt so brave all this past week, positive that no matter what the tests revealed, she would refuse the painful, expensive treatment. In the face of these facts, though, her conviction wavered.

"Mary."

She had to think of Sam. But she couldn't ask his opinion. He would never give up. It simply wasn't in his blood. "Do the treatments, Mary. We'll fight this. It's only money," he'd say. But it wasn't only money. It was everything they'd spent a marvelous life together building. She knew he'd sell Mar-Sa. Hadn't he already suggested it? Then what would he have left? This merciless, horrid cancer would kill her anyway, if not this year, then next. She'd be gone and Sam would have another two hundred thousand in bills ...

No, she'd fight her own way, the only way she could. She'd live till she died and give her sweet man one more summer. One more summer and one more, very special blue ribbon.

"Mary ..."

"Doctor," she interrupted him in a voice now edged with steel, "we seem to have come full circle, as they say. So, I'll ask again. How long will I be able to ride a horse?"

He shifted his gaze, looking her in the eyes. "I don't know. As I said, you look stronger than you should at this point. A month, two, three at the outside. You'll know. Do you have any idea what you're asking for?"

She worked up a smile. "I know very well what I'm asking for." She paused. "I guess I can go home now." She stood and started digging in her bag for the extra blouse.

He held her by the shoulders and turned her to face him. He spoke softly, his eyes sweeping across her face. "It's not in my power to force you to stay, but please, call me anytime, day or night. If you change your mind. Or even if you don't, I'll be here for you."

She left him sitting on the bed, picked up her bag, and went into the bathroom to dress. He was still sitting on the bed when she came out with a glass of water in her hand. She watered the thirsty violet on the windowsill, took Sam's and Callie's pictures down, and carefully laid them in her bag, zipping it closed. "Well, then, I guess I'll see you later."

He stood, and in a soft voice, more like a minister than a doctor, told her, "When you want something for the pain, don't be too proud to call me. I can phone the prescriptions into Monroe's pharmacy in Conner for you."

She felt her face flush. "How soon will that be?"

He shook his head. "Should have happened already, but in any event, don't hesitate to call. One more thing, if you like, later, I mean, we can arrange hospice care for you at your house. They can be a big help, and your insurance will cover it."

Dr. Stein walked to the window, picked up the violet, and handed it to her.

"Take it home. It'll die here."

She took the plant and wondered if he'd heard his own words.

Chapter Nineteen

S am laughed. "Awesome, huh? That's a good word. Don't hear it too often out here, but it's a good word."

Barbara kept Cactus in stride with Bullet as they rode along the north side of the mustang herd. "Do you think I did okay today? I mean, do you think I found my legs? Morgan and me, heck, we were flying." She bent forward and gave Cactus a few good pats on his sweaty neck.

"Young lady, you rode like you were born in a saddle."

"Really? Wow! You know what?"

Sam gave her his finest grin. "What's that?"

"Me and Cactus, we could have passed Morgan, but I didn't want to embarrass him. Plus, I didn't know what to do, with the wild horses, I mean."

"I see. Well, you did a fine job today, and by golly, you can be proud of yourself."

"Mr. Holt, is Cactus faster than Ruth?"

"You like speed, don't you?"

"I guess I do. You know what else? I don't think it's all that hard to learn to ride a horse. That picture you drew in the dirt last night, for running barrels? I think I'm ready." She moved Cactus closer to Bullet and pointed to a lone mesquite about fifty yards ahead. "I'm gonna run Cactus around that bush."

Sam grabbed her rein. "Maybe you should let Morgan give you a few lessons first."

She waved off his concern. "About what?" With a hard tug, Barbara jerked her rein from Sam's grip, then kicked Cactus hard and shot away. In three strides, the fiery roan was in a flat-out run.

"Slow down, girl, you won't make the turn!" Sam yelled after her.

She kicked for more speed.

Morgan pulled Ruth up alongside Sam. "Where's she going?"

He shook his head. "Into the dust." He raced after her at Bullet's fastest gallop. "Barbara, don't try to turn. Slow her down, girl!"

She ignored Sam. In fact, she kicked and whipped and yelled for more speed, right until she reached the mesquite bush. Then she pulled her inside rein hard, forcing Cactus to turn.

Too sharp.

Barbara flew straight through the air, heels overhead, hit the dirt hard, and rolled over a cactus bush. Sitting where she'd landed and staring blankly into space, she brushed the dust from her sleeves. "Ow, ow, ow."

Morgan rode after the runaway Cactus. Sam jumped down and ran to Barbara.

"What the crap happened?" she demanded.

"Are you hurt? Did you break any important bones?" He needn't have asked, The spit was already returning to her eyes.

"I got an armful of thorns, but I didn't break anything. What the crap did she do?"

"What you told her to." He reached down and pulled her to her feet.

She backed up a step and studied her arm. "What's that supposed to mean?"

"You asked for a hard turn. She gave you one. The problem was, you kept going straight."

"Well, crap, she didn't even slow down." She gestured toward the mesquite bush, then with a hiss of pain, let her arm fall abruptly to her side.

Holding her by the wrist and shoulder, Sam reined in a chuckle and examined the damage. "Better let me pull these thorns." He dug his pocket knife out of his jeans.

Barbara jerked free. "You're not gonna cut them out?"

"No, but I'll need my blade to hang on to 'em."

Morgan rode up, leading Cactus. "She all right? That sure was a pretty spill. Cleared Cactus' head by two feet."

Barbara's mouth tightened. "Yes, I'm all right," she snapped. Then, in a softer tone, "I have some thorns in my arm, but Mr. Holt is going to pull them out."

Sam grinned at Morgan. "You bet I will. Morgan, go slow the herd. Give us a little time."

"You got it." Morgan gave Sam a nod, tipped his hat to Barbara, touched heels to Ruth, and trotted away.

Once Morgan had ridden away, Sam turned Barbara's arm upside down. "Now, let's have a go at those ol' thorns." He slid the sharp edge of the blade under the first thorn.

"This'll burn like the dickens, young lady."

Her arm jerked. "Ow! Ow! Ow! That hurt."

He chuckled, then painted a concerned look on his face.

"Yeah, they smart comin' out a bit. But you're tough." He yanked another. "Aside from the fact that the ground can come up to meet ya in a hurry, what do you think you learned from all this?" He yanked another.

"Ouch! Cactus thorns burn like crap!"

"What else?" He yanked another.

"Huh? I don't know. Horses aren't safe."

He yanked another. "You're partly right. Do you think this was Cactus' fault?" He yanked another.

"Ouch. Crap! Well, she didn't even slow down. She should've slowed down."

Sam pulled a smaller thorn. "Did you ask her to?" He locked eyes with hers, plucking out the final thorn, and released her arm.

"That one didn't hurt." She rubbed her arm. "I guess I didn't ask her to."

Sam handed her Cactus' reins. "Can you ride?"

She grinned. "In a slow, straight line."

"Well, then, let's ride a slow straight line to the herd and finish this drive. Be time for lunch in a couple of hours."

After riding in comfortable silence for a few minutes, Barbara asked, "Will Morgan still teach me to bend poles? I mean, will he think I'm stupid now because I fell off?"

"Young lady, the only thing guaranteed about riding horses is coming off once in a while."

"Did you ever?"

"A time or two. 'Course if you tossed in the buckin' broncs of my youth, that number would climb a might higher. It's good to get your first dustin' out of the way, as long as you learn from it."

"Dusting?"

"That's what we call it when you hit the dust."

Rusty met them just outside the herd. He tipped his hat to Barbara. "Sure was a pretty flyin' job you did there, young lady."

"Thank you. I had my first *dusting*." There was noticeable pride in her voice.

Rusty pulled off his hat, scratching his balding head. "Yeah, you sure did. Boss, you wanna take a break, or walk 'em right along? We still got a good ten miles to go."

Sam studied the riders. As far as he could tell, each of the guests seemed comfortable enough on their horses and were doing a fine job moving the herd peacefully along. "I reckon we can all make it. Let's keep 'em moving. If some of the guests get sore backsides, we have liniment in camp."

Shocked, Barbara turned on Sam. "You can be mean." She rubbed her sore arm.

Rusty laughed. "Meaner than a cat with a stomped tail!"

Sam wiped his brow, staring at the sun. "Rusty, go fetch Philip Cunningham. Tell Morgan to take the folks and walk the herd in. You, me, and Mr. Cunningham are gonna drop back and look for strays."

"Strays?" he questioned.

"Yeah. Strays. Ride in with him, Barbara. I'll drift back awhile."

"Thank you, Mr. Holt, for pulling the thorns out."

"We're lucky it was only thorns. Sure was a high flyin' dustin', all right."

Barbara grinned, "It sure was, wasn't it?" She followed Rusty toward the herd.

Sam used this interval to re-saddle Bullet, with the dry side down on the saddle blanket. Then he pulled the cork from his canteen, poured a little in his hand and let the horse slurp a few handfuls.

He sat in the shade of his horse and thought about Mary. He shouldn't have listened to her. He should have fought harder. Then he'd be with her now. She hated hospitals and all that went with them. She shouldn't have been there without him.

Could be those tests wouldn't find anything, anyway. Could be they'd give her a clean bill. She'd come riding out to camp tomorrow, waving a doctor's report, shouting it was all over. Then life could get on like it was supposed to.

When Rusty and Philip came over the rise, he stepped into the saddle and set his jaw. "I hope you forgive me for what I'm gonna do, Mary. Some things just need doin'."

Philip stopped his horse near Sam, pulled off his hat, spit on the ground, and then looked at him with a look that told Sam he was worried. "Rusty says we're going after strays. I'm getting a little tired. Don't you think you two can find them without me?"

Sam smiled and started Bullet walking. "Come on now, you're tougher than all that. We'll ride west, check those gullies and valleys yonder, gather whoever we missed, and join up with the herd in about an hour. You have that much left, don't you?"

"I suppose, but why did you choose me? I think Paul would have been a better choice."

"I figured you'd get a kick out of this. I know I will. Let's step it up a little." Before Philip could protest, Sam pushed Bullet into a trot. Rusty and Philip followed along over the scrubby ground, riding carefully between cactus and mesquite.

"You're in the education business, I hear," Sam said.

"Yes, I'm a physical education teacher. This is my tenth year. Keeps me in pretty good shape, too."

"That's a good thing, I reckon. You like teaching?"

"Yes, yes, I do. It feels good when you can help a student learn something. I suppose that's what I like best, the feeling you get when you know you've made a difference in a young person's life."

Sam quietly picked up the pace to a faster trot, making sure Philip kept up with him. They had already put a mile between them and the herd. "I get the same sort of feeling when I school a horse or one of the guests here at the ranch. Take your stepdaughter. She's coming along just fine. Still has a sharp tongue, but she's coming along all right."

Philip gave Sam a look that told him the fellow couldn't care less about Barbara.

When they reached the bottom of a deep arroyo, Sam pulled up. "Philip, step down and have a look at the ditch there. Looks to me like there might be some tracks in the sand."

Rusty stopped his horse alongside Sam and shot a confused look at his boss.

Philip slid from the saddle, passed his reins to Rusty, and bent low to examine the dirt. "I don't see any tracks. Nope, not a thing, except ... hey," he picked up a small stone and tossed it to Sam. "Is this an arrowhead?"

Turning the sharp-edged stone over in his hand, Sam broke into a grin. "Yes, sir, I reckon it is." He pitched it back to Philip. "Stick it in your pocket. It might help you remember today's lesson."

Philip straightened. "Lesson? Oh, Barbara's dusting. We could all see the show." Perhaps hearing the annoyance in his voice, he pasted a look of concern on his face. "She had me worried for a minute there. Thanks for taking care of her."

Sam lifted his hat, pushing his gloved hand through his hair, crossed a leg over the saddle horn, and got real comfortable. "Naw, I was referring to the lesson you're gonna learn today." He settled his hat on his head and smiled wide.

"My lesson?"

"Yes, sir. I figure I'm about to make a difference. Now, Philip, take a look at the bare knob on the mountain ridge yonder."

Philip turned and studied the treeless nose on the side of the mountain, some five miles distant. "Yeah?"

"Look real hard. See the tiny white dot?"

"I do." He shrugged. "What about it?"

"That would be Anaba's hut. He'll turn ninety-one this summer. His name means *returns from war*. He was a Navajo code talker in World War Two."

He glanced at Sam over his shoulder. "You're going to teach me Navajo? We could do that around the fire tonight."

"Hang on, you're gettin' ahead of me." Sam scratched his chin, grinned at Rusty, and turned back to Philip, without the grin. "You know, he's been living in that mud hut since before Mary and I bought the ranch. I ride out to ol' Anaba from time to time. He likes to tell me stories about the old times, about his ancestors. I suppose I know more about Navajo customs than just about any white man in these parts." He took a breath. "Last night, you got me to thinkin' about one of ol' Anaba's stories."

"I did?" Philip turned to squint toward the mountain again. "How?"

Sam reached over and quietly picked up the reins to Philip's horse. "You helped me remember a story he told me once, a long time ago." He rubbed his gloved hand across his face, then leaned forward and spoke in a voice that chilled even Rusty. "Philip did you know it took your wife an hour to quit crying last night? I held her, right there on the chuck wagon's tailgate, for an hour while she cried. She told me she's afraid of you."

Philip charged toward Bullet. At a look from Sam, Rusty ran his horse right into the man, slamming him to the dirt.

Philip staggered to his feet. "You piece of hick crap!"

Sam lifted his eyebrows, grinning at Rusty, but talked to Philip. "They sure talk rough in the east. You teach Barbara those words?" He used a calm, quiet voice modified with a sarcastic chuckle.

"Drop dead!" Philip repeated the sentiment with his finger.

Sam wasn't impressed. "You ever hear what the Navajo did to braves who beat their wives?"

"You rednecked hillbilly! You'd better leave my wife alone."

"How about that? We're both aiming for the same thing here. Let me finish my story. It's a good one. If a Navajo brave was found to be slapping his wife around, the chief would order him lashed to a pole. Then all the women in the village would take turns clubbing him with sticks. Sometimes they'd get carried away and stab him a few licks with an arrow."

Philip tried to back away. Rusty cut him off, bumping him again with his horse.

"You're nuts, you clod!"

"Probably a little, but I never hit a woman. Ever!"

"Yeah, well, big man. You going to tie me to a pole, you *wonderful* gentleman?"

Sam smiled warmly, rubbed his face, and then shook his head. "You're making this too easy. I warned you once. I don't know what your problem is, but you'd better figure it out on the walk back to camp."

"Walk back to camp? It's miles to camp." Philip's bravado vanished in the face of his fear.

"About twelve, I'd figure. See, I have this trick I use on an ornery horse. I back off some, give 'im a little time to think on it, and let 'im figure it out on his own." Sam pointed a hard stare at Philip. "Seems to me you could benefit from a little thinking time. If you stay at it, and you were bragging about being in great shape, you can cover about four miles an hour. You should be in camp in time for supper." Sam gave a chuckle, shrugging his shoulders. "Of course, if you'd rather, heck, I reckon we can find a pole, let the girls have a go at you." He put his foot in the stirrup and turned Bullet away. "Ready to head in, Rusty?"

"Sure, boss."

Philip ran up to Rusty and clutched his leg. "No, wait. I'll die out here. I'll get lost and die. I don't have any food or water. Come on, guys! You've made your point. You were fooling around, right? A stunt you pull on greenhorns. I get it."

Sam tossed Philip his canteen. "It's about half full, which should be plenty. If you lose it, I'll have to charge you. You can't get lost. Just follow our tracks to camp. Couldn't be easier." He squinted toward the sun. "You're in luck. I'll bet it won't even hit a hundred today."

Philip threw the canteen at Sam. "Charge me? I'll sue you stupid hick! I'll own this broken down ranch!"

"Now see, for a minute there I thought we were making progress. Now you're all ornery again. Sue me?" Sam flashed a cold grin. "Remember the big, bold, black sentence in your contract? The one clearly stating you willingly choose to participate in a variety of ranch activities and events, even though there may be risk of bodily harm, or even death, and you hold the ranch, the owners, and its employees and guests harmless? I checked. You signed it ... and Paul and Lucy Keaton witnessed it.

"As far as me and Rusty know, you said you wanted to walk back. You wanted to think and look for arrowheads. We tried to talk you out of it, but you were plumb determined. Wouldn't even allow us to keep you company. Isn't that about right, Rusty?"

"We tried our best, boss."

"There you have it. If you don't get started, you'll be late for beans."

Philip let go a snarl that sounded like an enraged dog and charged at them. Sam spun Bullet toward him, pushing him over with his foot. "Walk that temper off, fella. I'd have sent you packing, except for the fact Linda and Barbara are enjoying themselves. I don't need to mess with a loudmouth bully like you."

Philip crawled to his feet, his face pale, eyes bulging. "You can't be serious. I get the picture, now come on, give me my horse."

Sam shook his head. "I tried that already. I really think a short walk will do you a world of good." He and Rusty turned their horses and trotted away.

Philip picked up the canteen and ran after them. "This isn't over, *cowboy*!"

Sam whirled Bullet around, galloped right up to Philip's face, and leaned down. "I think it is over ... *Mr. Cunningham*. Now take your medicine and show this cowboy you can be a man. I'd like to put this behind us and move on." He held out his hand. "See you at supper." After a moment, Philip finally shook his hand, but kept his eyes downcast.

"Pace yourself, but keep moving, and watch those cacti." Sam turned Bullet away and trotted to Rusty.

They rode in silence to the crest of the first ridge, then Sam motioned for Rusty to hold up. "He's doin' all right, don't you think?"

Rusty laughed. "Good strong walker. If we don't keep a move on, he's likely to catch us. You figure he's gonna let this go?"

"Like to think so, but I don't get a real good feeling about the man."

"I don't reckon even a good old-fashioned butt kickin' would change that one." Rusty turned to Sam. "Best watch your back."

Sam touched heels to Bullet and rode on. "I reckon it was a dang fool thing to do, but I just can't abide a man who lays a hand on a woman."

Rusty nodded. "Should've hanged 'im."

By the time they made camp, the wild herd was grazing in the big corrals and the guests were relaxing in the shade of the pavilion. Morgan noticed the rider-less horse first and came running to meet them. "What happened to Mr. Cunningham?"

Sam looked back over his shoulder. "Fella insisted on walkin' in. Said he wanted to look for arrowheads."

Chapter Twenty

"What a beautiful morning." Mary passed the coffeepot to Susan and looked up into the massive branches of the live oak. "Sam claims this tree was here before the first white man crossed the Mississippi. I'm glad whoever selected this spot to build the house didn't cut it down for lumber."

Comanche marched to the table, sniffed, and snorted at the remaining muffin on the plate.

Mary laughed. "He's more of a biscuit fan."

Susan reached for the muffin, cut it in half, slathered each piece with soft butter, and handed half to Mary. "He had his chance."

"I'm so grateful I didn't need to spend last night in Conner General. I'm taking Comanche for a short ride this morning, and I'm running barrels with Chester, too. I want to surprise Sam on the Fourth."

"Here's where I should tell you not to overdo, but as your closest friend, next to Sam, Comanche, and Chester, I'll just pretend I told you." Susan sipped her coffee. "As that friend, however, I'd like to point out that you have yet to tell me why Dr. Stein decided not to keep you overnight."

Mary walked to Comanche, slipped her hand under his forelock, and scratched. "Would you make a new costume for me?"

"I'd love to! What do you have in mind?"

"Something with lots of flash, long fringes on the arms and leggings." Mary's face lit up with excitement. "Silver fringes and red blouse and leggings. I wore those colors when I first met Sam. I don't know why I ever switched to blue. Callie always wore red and silver, too. She loved those outfits you made for her. Do you remember the first costume you made her? She was so proud. She slept in it for a week." *We buried her in the last one.*

Susan stretched her hands apart slowly, as if holding a tape measure. "When do we start?"

"If we start right now, what are the chances of being done by the time everyone returns from the wild horse range? Wouldn't it be fun to surprise Sam?"

"If, and that's a big *if,* we can find what we need in Conner, no problem." Susan jumped up, stuffing the last tiny piece of her half of the muffin in her mouth. "Let's get your measurements."

The entire process of measuring arms, legs, and waist took less than half an hour. Electing to trust Susan's ability to select the perfect fabric, as long as the red was the brightest of bright reds and the silver rivaled the shimmer of light on water, Mary sent her to town alone. She had decided the time had come to saddle Comanche and ride him for the first time in four years. Well, she'd decided she didn't want to wait anymore, anyway. Besides, shopping for fabric had never been her thing.

Mary led Comanche to the tack room, thinking they might enjoy a quiet ride to the stream where she'd find a cool spot to dangle her feet in the water and discuss her plans with him for their freestyle routine.

She brushed him a little longer than was necessary, lost in her thoughts of what a magnificently beautiful horse he'd been when she'd sold him to the Hardens. She knew he didn't blame her. But, she knew she should, and did, blame herself for the neglect he'd been forced to suffer. He managed to make her smile as he stomped his foot impatiently, as if to say, "Come on, Mary. Let's get this show on the road!"

Thin as he was, saddling up required a thicker saddle pad than normal. She lowered his saddle gently onto his back. It settled into place as if it had been used the day before. She backed away to admire it. "Boy, that looks good on you!"

She'd been tempted to sell his saddle with him but hadn't been able to go that far. For three years the handsome saddle had waited patiently in the tack room, resting, hiding on its stand, protected under layers of blankets. This morning had been the first time in those four years it had seen light, and the well-made show saddle had endured the passage of time remarkably well. An hour of lovingly applied saddle soap and silver polish had done a terrific job of restoring the fine saddle's luster.

Mary beamed. "Yes, sir, Comanche, you look like a million bucks. Of course, with a few more pounds on you and a few more hours of shining leather and polishing silver, you'll look like a billion bucks!"

The ride down the trail to the water was easier than she'd expected. Comanche walked quietly, with enough confidence and security for them both. What an exhilarating feeling to be riding him again. He was by far the most fabulous horse she'd ever ridden. And there had been some great horses in her life. She closed her eyes and remembered all the fine horses she'd known. Like a slide show, they flashed through her mind. She folded her arms on Comanche's neck, bent forward, and rested her head on her arms while he walked along a trail they'd traveled so many times before. He needed no guidance. But she needed a moment to travel down memory lane.

ॐ∼ॐ∼ॐ∼ॐ

Lucy Keaton was the first to spot Philip trudging, head lowered, toward the camp. "Hey, look who made it in time for hot beans." Jumping up from her seat on an overturned bucket, she threw an *aren't-you-coming* look to Linda and sprinted his way.

Linda decided to let Lucy have him. She wasn't sure what it meant to be so uninterested, but she wasn't about to change her mind. If ever she'd gotten a clear signal someone wasn't worth the effort, she was receiving one now as she watched Philip. This nowhere-land air had some powerful medicine in it.

"He doesn't look real happy to be here, Mom," Barbara muttered.

Deciding it might be better, for everybody, to feel him out away from the crowd, Linda reluctantly approached him. "Find any interesting arrowheads?"

The halfhearted smile he bestowed on Lucy morphed into a narrow-eyed, bitter glare as he turned to his wife. "You can stay if you want, but I'm leaving."

She pursed her lips, searched his face, and glanced at Lucy. "Really?"

He kicked the dirt. "You can have your cowboys and Indians or you can come home with me. I couldn't care less, either way. I'm out of here."

Embarrassed, Lucy managed a polite, if timid, smile. "I wasn't prepared for this."

"Yeah? Well, I had all afternoon in the sun to prepare for it."

He marched to the pavilion, with Lucy and Linda following a few paces behind, and confronted Sam with enough volume for all to hear. "I've had enough of your Wild West. I'm leaving. My family can do whatever they want. I don't care the least little bit. I want transportation out of here. *Now!*"

Linda studied the faces of the guests grouped around the tables in the pavilion. She didn't see shock on their faces, or even interest. One expression did sweep over every member of the group, *good riddance*. She could almost hear a collective sigh of relief descend on the camp.

God, how stupid must she have been?

Barbara glared at him then yelled, "I'm staying. Mother, tell him I can stay." She raced to Linda. "I want to win a ribbon. I want to learn how to ... Mom, I just want to stay!"

Embracing her daughter, Linda spoke to her husband's stiff back. "I'll be staying here with Barbara. Perhaps a few months apart will be good for all of us."

"Suits me." Philip moved fast, spinning around, and striking Linda in the face before anyone could react. She fell back, pulling Barbara to the ground with her.

"What's wrong with you?" Sam grabbed him by the collar and punched him full in the face. Philip swayed, dropped to his knees, and wiped his bloodied lip. "Thanks, cowboy. My lawyer'll be in touch. Like I said, I'll own this ranch."

"Do your best, tough guy. You put on your little show here in front of an audience. Do yourself a favor. Go on home. Forget about all this." Sam nodded to Rusty. "Saddle a couple of fresh horses, take him in."

The guests sat in stunned silence as Sam, Linda, and Barbara moved into the pavilion.

Linda spoke first, her eyes wet, her hand quivering over her newest ugly. "I'm sorry that happened, I ..." Her face crumpled as she twisted toward Barbara and collapsed, sobbing, against her. The child stroked her mother's hair with infinite tenderness. Her eyes hardened with the coldness of stone. "It's okay. He's gone. He can't hurt us now."

෨෨෨෨෨෨

The morning and afternoon had slipped away for Mary. After her ride, she'd waded awhile in the stream, picked some wild daises, and fallen asleep in the shade. She might have slept through to morning were it not for Comanche's nose in her ear. "Oh my, Comanche, we've certainly made a day of it. I suppose you're right, we should get back." She sat up and stretched her arms overhead. "Come to think of it, I *am* getting hungry."

She picked up her bouquet of wild daises then climbed on Comanche, noticing how much easier it seemed to go, even without her mounting block. Refreshed and exhilarated, she gave the softest cluck, and Comanche broke into that spectacular long striding trot of his. He was still far from fit, but so eager to play. Surely a short run could do him no harm. She touched heels to Comanche's belly.

The willing mustang broke into a canter. Smooth and even. Will he remember? She slowed the pace, adjusted her posture, and asked for a lead change. Like magic, she felt the subtle shift, the smoothest transition. She signaled again. Comanche responded instantly with the grace of a ballroom dancer. Mary couldn't resist. One more time she asked. One more flying lead change was perfectly executed.

Giddy with excitement, she threw her arms around the proud horse's neck and screamed with joy. Poor Comanche, hearing the scream and fearing certain peril, broke into a flat-out run. Up the trail he raced, with his neck stretched and ears flat, moving as fast as she ever remembered. She knew he was in no condition to maintain this demanding pace, but boy, it felt great!

Reluctantly, she signaled for Comanche to come down to a walk. As responsive as if they'd been training every day, he slowed gently with each stride. Mary counted. He'd required only four strides to shift from a flat-out run to a dog-walk, and he'd done it so smoothly. If the wind hadn't quit whistling in her ears, she may not have even noticed.

She gave him plenty of congratulatory pats on the neck as they walked along. "I'm so proud of you! That was truly amazing! I'm digging the tape out of the trunk as soon as we're back at the barn. I think we'll do Callie's routine!"

When the barn came into view, Mary hopped off Comanche. A newfound energy was running through her, demanding that she walk.

Chester raced to the fence. With squeals and bucks, he announced his displeasure at being left behind. "Tomorrow, I promise." Mary reached over the top rail and scratched his face. "I need to tend to Comanche, but I'll bring you an apple as soon as I'm finished."

Turning to walk away, she saw the Cunninghams' Chevy, or one like it, driving away. She noticed it didn't slow down or pull aside for Susan as her jeep passed by, coming in the lane.

Susan reached the barn just as Mary led Comanche around the corner. "I found it all!" She bounced from the car. "Miller's Five-and-Dime had everything we needed. I'll start making patterns tonight. Maybe I'll sleep at your house, work late ... Were you riding this entire time?"

Mary had to laugh. "I had a pretty long nap by the stream." Her eyes opened wide, her face exploding into a grand smile. "That is wonderful news!" She danced around the car and leaned on the hood. "I have some good news, too. On the way back to the barn, I asked Comanche for some flying lead changes and transitions." She snapped straight, throwing her arms in the air. "He was perfect! Like we'd never missed a day's practice. This is so fantastic!" She leaned back against the car and gave Susan a serious look. "Do you think it's all some terrific sign? Comanche coming home, you finding all the fabric on one trip, and Comanche performing so well after all this time? Isn't it wonderful?"

Susan ran to hug her. "Best of all, you're smiling again. Oh, Mary, I've missed that!"

Mary beamed. Yes, it certainly felt good to smile again. She had been smiling more in recent days. Except for that miserable trip to the hospital yesterday, she'd been feeling darn good. "Oh yeah, this will be a summer to remember! Let's rub him down and start on those patterns."

After turning Comanche into the pasture with Chester, and treating them both to apples, Susan and Mary were walking through the barn, headed for the house. Rusty suddenly appeared in the wide aisle.

After an initial gasp of surprise, Susan gave a shriek of delight and sprinted to her man.

Mary remembered the Cunningham's car. "Something's wrong, isn't it? What happened to Sam?"

Susan stepped back. "What's happened? Why are you here?"

Rusty pulled off his hat and pushed at his thin hair.

"Sam's fine and everybody's all right, only ... Philip Cunningham decided he'd had enough ranchin'."

"I thought that was him I passed on my way in, but I was so excited to tell Mary what I'd found in town, I forgot all about it."

"I came in earlier to tell you all about it, but you two were having such a good time and all, I figured it could hold on a little. So I sat in the lodge and watched you carry on like a couple of school girls." He gave them both a friendly grin. Then a raised brow. "Sam thinks this here could be serious. Can't say as I disagree."

They sat together on straw bales while Rusty continued, "That Philip, he's a load of trouble, all right."

Mary nodded. "Barbara confided in me once. He must have a terrible temper."

"Well, Sam caught him roughin' Linda up last night after you two went on home. He broke 'em up. Tells me it took Linda an hour to catch her wind."

Mary drew a breath. "Poor girl."

198

Rusty went on, "Today after we had the herd all gathered, Sam tells Morgan to fetch him Philip. Says that me, him, and Philip are goin' to backtrack to look for strays. I knew right off Philip was about to get a little fetchin' up, but I figured Sam was taking him away to kick the tar outta him. You know what he does instead?" Rusty grinned and shook his head.

Mary took a guess, "Roped him and dragged him through the cactus."

Rusty chuckled. "Nope, ol' Sam, all he does is set Philip afoot ten, twelve miles from camp, right at noon. He says, "Have a nice walk and think about what ya done." Rusty shook his head, giving another chuckle. "Philip, he straggles into camp a couple of hours later, cussin' and yellin' he's gonna sue you folks." He sat up straight and cocked his head as if he were shocked. "Then, right there in front of us all, he slugs his wife. Sam runs over, flattens him, and sends 'im packin'. Linda and Barbara, they don't want to leave with him, so Sam sends me back with him so he can get his things and be on his way." Rusty's face telegraphed his concern. "Sam wants me to stay here till everybody gets back. Says he don't trust Philip not to come back and try something."

Mary gasped. "What kind of something?"

"No tellin', but don't you ladies worry any. I'm not lettin' you out of my sight. Not for one minute."

Chapter Twenty-One

L inda drafted Nicky Bartlett to help with the chuck wagon detail. Barbara had been her first choice, but she'd insisted on going with Morgan and Sam to help set up crowding gates in the working corral just outside the pavilion. Greasing a black skillet, she smiled to herself. That girl had fallen head over heels in love with ranch life and horses in three weeks. She watched as Barbara explained to the men just how to secure the gates. Sam nodded his head and praised her ingenuity, as if he'd never secured the gates before. Morgan, meanwhile, bounced a look of pure befuddlement from Sam to Barbara.

"Coffee's real good this morning, Linda." John saluted them with a half-empty tin cup and wrapped his arm around Nicky's waist.

Nicky smiled. "It's her secret mix of coffee and cinnamon."

"Wait'll you taste this morning's pancakes." Linda danced and twirled her spatula in a move that could easily make a baton twirler envious.

A loud banging outside had heads turning in time to see Dr. Adams drive over the ridge and pull up at the corrals. He flung open the truck door and jumped to the ground almost before the truck came to a stop a few yards from the pavilion. "I sure hope I didn't miss breakfast. I had my head out the window, trailing the scent of frying bacon for the last two miles." He pointed to the coffeepot and grinned at John.

Nicky laughed. "John, you can tell everybody we're ready to serve bacon and coffee."

Seconds later, Zack Collier led the assault on the pavilion. "Hope you made plenty. From the sound of things, we won't get much of a lunch break."

The tables nearly buckled under platters of steaks, bacon, and fried potatoes and trays filled with pancakes swimming in pure maple syrup and melted butter along with pots of steaming hot coffee. Satisfied she and Nicky had met the early morning onslaught and quelled it with ample supplies of calories and heart-stopping fat, Linda leaned comfortably on the chuck wagon's tailgate, sipped her coffee, and nibbled at a broken pancake. She'd watch from a safe distance this morning. Pleased as she was with her culinary skills, she could only lament her wifely talents … or lack thereof.

Barbara in the center of it all, asked as many questions as Sam and Morgan could field between mouthfuls. Then, just in that moment, Linda noticed a change in her daughter's eyes. A new look of genuine interest, excitement. A sparkle she'd never seen there before. She was so glad they'd stayed. It really was worth enduring the embarrassment, the unasked questions, and the almost annoying show of support, to see that look in her daughter's eyes.

I'll handle the legalities when we get home, but husband number three is officially tossed on the trash heap, or mountain, of stupid decisions I've made in my life. The rest of the summer was for Barbara. Period. She knew, though, it wasn't like Philip to forgive and forget. She also knew worrying would change nothing. What would be, would be. She smiled behind her cup and decided to look on the bright side. Maybe before they went home Philip would send a telegram asking for a divorce. She had to giggle a little. Maybe she could send hers first. Just to think about him screaming and cussing when he read it. She brushed her hand over her latest bruise. No, I'll tell him in person, that's a show I want front row seats for.

As the morning wore on, everyone adjusted to their new routine. Toss a rope on a horse, lead it to the working corral, stand it in the squeeze chute, wait for Doc to examine and Sam to check hooves, then give it an apple and lead it to the big corral in the trees. Rope the next one and do it all again. The older horses had been through the process often enough and cooperated so well, Linda thought they surely must have remembered the apple. The foals trotted along with their mares. The two-and three-year-olds were a little dicey, but the real challenges were the yearlings.

"Best time we ever made," Sam announced when they finally stopped for a break. "Likely finish by dark."

Zack dropped to the dirt. "You're one tough old bird."

Sam laughed. "Naw, just been doin' it a few years. I don't figure I'd keep up with you on the ice, young fella."

Morgan joined them. "Five good-looking three-year-olds to trail home in the morning."

Sam nodded. "As good a bunch as we ever had."

"Trail home?" Barbara questioned.

"Each year I pick a few three-year-olds who I think will make good saddle stock in the future. Since I like to hold the herd a day or two in the big grazing corral before we move 'em to the summer pasture to give 'em a chance to settle down after all this ruckus, we can use the extra days to trail the three-year-olds, back to the ranch."

"Can I help ... *trail 'em*?" Barbara shifted closer to Sam, focusing intently on his eyes.

He grinned. "Sure thing. It takes four or five of us. The others'll stay here with Morgan and keep an eye on the horses and camp." Sam tossed Barbara a not-too-subtle wink. "I could use a hand with skills like yours to trail this bunch of young 'uns."

"Mom, I'm going along with Sam in the morning to trail the three-year-olds home."

Linda smiled at Sam. "I gather that he can hardly do it without you."

❧❧❧❧❧❧

Mary felt odd brushing Comanche while Rusty watched over her. He didn't really have much to do, and it was obvious he'd rather be back with Sam working the wild horses than sitting on a straw bale in the barn, braiding yet another leather halter. She noticed he was still wearing the pistol he carried when on the range. Philip Cunningham might be good for one thing, she mused. He took her mind off the hospital visit and the new pain in her hip. Almost.

She'd slept very little last night while struggling with words, searching for the perfect ones to tell Sam of her decision. Try as she might, however, she'd never found the right thing to say. Or the best way to say it. She did set the scene in her mind, though. A romantic scene. By the time Sam and the guests returned, Comanche would be in shape to take a nice long trail ride. She'd pack a picnic basket and whisk Sam away to a special place, then fill him with biscuits, fried chicken, and his favorite pie, snuggle with him and kiss him under the trees by the swimming hole, and gently tell him ... That *telling him* part required more work, but she had the movie set all worked out. A weak smile forced its way onto her lips when she pondered how well a lemon meringue pie traveled in a saddle bag.

"He sure has come around already," Rusty observed. "Like Sam always says, you got a way with horses."

Mary stepped back to admire her work. "Thank you, Rusty. He is starting to shine, isn't he?"

"Never seen a horse dapple up so quick."

"I have never seen a horse dapple up so quickly," Susan corrected as she entered the barn.

"You neither? I'm tellin' you, Mary's got the touch."

Susan bent to kiss her husband's cheek and gently ruffle his hair, giving him a look that said she knew he was teasing her. "Would you like me to saddle Chester for you?" she asked Mary.

Mary considered the offer. "I'll do it. Meet me in the corral, and you can time me." She put Comanche in his box stall and tossed him a flake of hay, "Just for a little while," she told him absentmindedly, distracted by the annoying new twinge in her right hip.

In a few minutes, she had Chester saddled, and it was obvious to her that he was eager to play. All the exercise of the past weeks had put him back in shape, and his energy was palpable. Except for a few expected muscle aches, Mary felt fairly fit, too. She mounted Chester in the barn, giggled at his protests, and trotted to the corral. That thing in her hip, though ... that was a bother.

Susan and Rusty sat in the shade of the judge's booth while Mary trotted Chester around the corral for warm-up. She studied the barrels and tested her hip. If she took the right barrel first, opposite her normal run, she could shift her weight onto her left hip for two out of the three barrels.

Mary held Chester at the starting line. When Susan raised her hand, Mary cued Chester, and they raced toward the right barrel. He cooperated with the strange request but went wide and lost the pocket. At least a second too slow. The second barrel turn was as tight as ever, but as they ran to the last barrel, Chester tried to go outside. Mary turned him, but another second was lost. He recovered nicely and raced home.

"How'd we do?" she yelled to Susan from the finish line.

"Twenty-one point three. What was that all about? You never run the right barrel first. No wonder he went wide."

Mary took her time riding to the booth. What should she say? Rusty was studying her stirrups, looking for a clue. She had to say something. May as well come out with it. "My right hip has been bothering me." Here comes the lecture.

Susan jumped up, unable to mask the anxiety painted on her face. "Mary ... " She stopped abruptly, closing her eyes. "Did it help?" She asked in a voice that was both steady and worried.

Mary lied, "It did." She patted Chester's neck.

"Probably wasn't fair to him. We should've walked the course a few times first. Do you mind?"

"Just tell me when to hit the watch." Susan gave a quick smile but kept her eyes on the stopwatch in her hand.

She walked Chester around the course in the new direction three times, giving him clear signals along the way. Now that she thought about it, Callie always started with the right barrel. Maybe Chester remembered.

Satisfied they had reached an understanding, she went to the starting line, nodded at Susan, and gave Chester a tap with her heels. They launched for the right barrel. A much better turn. He stayed in the pocket. Second barrel felt good, third barrel was very fast, then the flat-out run for home.

"Twenty point two," Susan cheered.

Rusty jumped up and tossed his hat high. "That's how to run them barrels, lady!"

Mary laughed. "Seven seconds over last year's national champion, but I'll take it!"

Susan giggled. "Anything under half a minute'll get you some kind of ribbon at our homespun Fourth of July rodeo."

A loud rumble had them all looking toward the road. A familiar motorcycle was thundering in the lane. Mary shot a smile to Susan. "He's here!" She kicked Chester into a gallop and raced from the corral.

The motorcycle and horse met at the house, and both riders dismounted as quickly as possible.

"Oh, Robert! I've been so anxious to see you!"

He pulled her into a hug and lifted her from the ground. "Well Sis, here I am."

They strolled to the barn, Mary leading Chester, her brother pushing his Harley. Years before, the first box stall on the right had been remodeled to house Robert's Harley on his annual visit.

Rusty began to unsaddle Chester while Mary and Susan shared a straw bale seat in the aisle and Robert untied the ropes holding his pack on the motorcycle.

Comanche stuck his head over the stall guard, snorted, and fussed. Robert locked the stand in place on his bike and moseyed over to him to scratch his nose. "Hey, fella, don't you like bikers?"

Battling tears, Mary ran to Comanche's stall door. "That's Comanche. Sam found him a few weeks ago."

"Really?" He backed up and studied the intense horse. "I'll be danged if it isn't. What the world happened to him?"

Mary drew a deep breath. "Don't know. I thank God Sam was at the auction that day and recognized him." She squeezed between her brother and the door, flung her arms around Comanche's neck, and buried her face in his black and white mane. "We're competing in this year's freestyle musical routine at the state fair." She wiped her eyes before turning around, "And you, brother, are doing the finest fireworks display you've ever done in your twenty-five-year career."

Shocked, Robert turned to Susan. "What?"

Susan smiled, raising her eyebrows and cocking her head. "Better do what little sister says, Brother."

Rusty lifted the saddle from Chester. "That's what *we* do."

Robert ran a hand over his weathered face, "What about ..."

Mary threw up her arms. "Take a look at me." She arrowed a *shut-up* glare to Susan. "I haven't used that stupid golf cart in at least a week. I have color in my face. Not made by Avon. And I've been riding every day. I haven't felt so alive in years!"

Robert looked at her face and gave her a grin. "You want fireworks, I'll give you fireworks. What'd you have in mind?"

She knew that what she must do next would crush her. But she simply had no choice. She gave Comanche a quick kiss on the cheek, crawled under the stall guard and out into the barn aisle, and pointed to the tack room. "I have the tapes you made of Callie and me, the last ... time we ..." She looked at Susan and sucked a breath. "The last time we competed together. I packed them in the show trunk with ... with our old costumes and ribbons and such."

Letting herself slide down along the stall wall, she sat on the floor and struggled to breathe. Susan moved toward her, but Mary waved her away. "I haven't opened that trunk in four years. I touched it two weeks ago, but I couldn't open it."

His grip soft on her arm, Robert pulled her up. "Come on, Sis. We'll dig through that old trunk together. Don't know that I need the tapes to remember that year's show, though. Biggest flag I ever painted on the night sky, past or present." He turned to Susan and Rusty. "You two still remember how to grill a couple-a steaks?"

Susan nodded. "Yeah." Her eyes remained fixed on Mary.

"Got six pounds of T-bone in the left saddlebag. You and Rusty start the grill, Sis and me'll dig through that old trunk. Meet you in the lodge in ten. And, Rusty, set up the chess pieces."

Rusty laughed. "Hope you been practicin'."

Even though her brother held her hand there in the tack room doorway, Mary's heart pounded so loud he must have heard it. As her eyes adjusted to the dim light, she felt panic seize her. The red trunk Sam had made when Callie was seven sat innocently in the corner, patiently waiting to be needed again, like Comanche's saddle.

While Robert dragged it into the light, she glanced at Comanche's saddle, now covered with only one blanket. Her stomach tried its best to flip inside out. Maybe this was a stupid idea. If she couldn't even handle opening the trunk, how would she ever manage watching the tapes? Her husband's hands had made this beautiful trunk. He'd been the last one to close its lid. She ached for him to hold her. She could open it if he were here.

"Here goes." Robert flipped the clasps open and gently raised the lid.

"Oh," Mary gasped. "I'd forgotten that."

The contents of the trunk were neatly covered with a blanket made of the finest green-and-yellow wool and lettered boldly with the words *Callie's Comanche*. The final award they'd won together.

Robert held it up. "This is one classy blanket. Let's air it out, make it part of your show!"

Dear Robert, he knew how tough this was for her, but he could always be counted on to prop her up. She managed her crooked smile. "What a terrific idea! What's more, we'll enter him as *Callie's Comanche*."

"There you go, Sis." He returned his attention to the trunk's contents. "A lot of ribbons in here ... you should hang 'em on his stall. Let everybody know you're back in the game."

Mary eased a little closer to the trunk. "Well, a lot of them are Callie's."

"Well, yeah, but they're all Comanche's, aren't they?"

"Actually, she won more ribbons barrel-racing with Chester." The memory made her smile widen. "Callie always liked speed a lot more than finesse." They both laughed remembering Callie's love for speed.

Robert pulled the tapes from the trunk and closed the lid. "She was a pure hot dog, that girl. Always reminded me of you during your barrel days." His eyes suddenly flooded. "It was a good thing you did, Sis ... that last summer ... traveling the circuit with her."

Chapter Twenty-Two

The five three-year-olds were refusing to cooperate. Four times, Sam, Barbara, Zack, and John had started the small band of horses down the road for the ranch headquarters, only to have one or more of the young horses break free and race back to the herd in the grazing corral. Sam saw the morning slipping away. After the last breakout, he hollered for everyone to sit tight. "We'll need to cut out a few of the older mares to walk along. This bunch ain't goin' nowhere alone. You folks sit here and let 'em pick at the grass. Don't let 'em get any more worked up. We don't need 'em breakin' for the open range. Morgan and I'll rope two or three mares who don't have foals at their side to trail with us and nurse-maid these youngsters."

Barbara rode with Sam. "When you get the old mares, do the young horses just give up?"

"I don't know if I'd call it givin' up, but they'll trail along all right then. Most times, anyway. The mares give 'em confidence, you might say."

She gave him a puzzled look. "Why didn't you do that right away, then?"

"I'd rather let these old girls rest and eat, get ready for the move to summer pasture." He stopped at the gate. "Now they have a twelve mile walk in and a twelve mile walk back."

"What if we waited till tomorrow and tried again?"

Sam smiled. "You're catching on fast, young lady, and I figure that might work. But, well, I had my heart set on dining with Mrs. Holt tonight."

Barbara puffed out her chest. "Then I *figure* those old girls got some serious *walkin'* to do, boss."

As Sam had predicted, the three older mares they selected from the herd settled the three-year-olds like magic, and the drive got underway only an hour or so behind schedule. The sun made its daily trek higher and higher in the cloudless blue sky, tugging the temperatures along with it ever higher as it climbed. By late morning, it was one of the hottest days the guests had experienced.

The heat had an even greater effect on the young horses than the older mares, and their youthful cantankerousness gave way to sensible cooperation. Heads low, the tiny herd marched along at a slow, easy walk, following the well defined road, never testing the riders who circled them.

Every now and then, Sam rode around the bunch and checked on the guests and the horses. There was no need to worry. The sun was making everybody sleepy. As long as no coyotes came along to spook a horse, and that could be mighty bad, they'd be in by mid-afternoon. He wondered what Mary would be doing then. Working a horse, one way or another, he could count on that. Now that she was all fired up to compete at the state fair, she'd be practicing seven days a week. She was planning to run barrels on the Fourth, too. He was ready to see that again. He grinned at the thought. Nobody he'd ever known could wrap a horse around a barrel like his Mary. He laughed quietly to himself as he pictured poor Chester getting a full workout and then some. Comanche was lucky to still be recuperating. Of course, his day would come. Pretty soon, too, considering the way he'd been putting away groceries and packing on the weight.

The smile faded as he wondered what Dr. Stein had said. Couldn't be bad, could it? Wouldn't she have come out to be with him if she'd gotten bad news? No, that was no bet. She wouldn't want to upset him with any bad news while he was out with the guests. Squinting into the sun, he pushed his hat back. Did that mean it was bad news? Wouldn't she have come out and told him if there'd been good news?

What did it all mean?

What would anything mean without her?

"Hey, Mr. Holt, is that the lodge?" Barbara jolted him back.

He cleared his throat. "Yes, ma'am. You've finished your second trail drive." He forced a weak grin. "We should ride into camp in a half hour or so." He glanced around at John and Zack, who were bringing up the rear.

"Rounding up the wild herd was more fun."

Sam had to shake his head and chuckle. "You sure like your runnin'. I see you rode Leroy today. He's a good, solid, sure-footed horse. How'd he do for you?"

"Well, like you said, he's a good, solid horse, but I think I like Cactus better."

"Faster?"

"You bet!" She gave Leroy a gentle pat on the neck. "But Leroy would probably never *dust* me."

Sam thought a minute. "Let's see what kind of daylight we have left when we get these horses put away. Maybe we can get Mrs. Holt talked into a lesson running barrels with ol' slowpoke there."

Barbara beamed. "Really, would she? But," she wrinkled her nose, "Leroy?"

"Don't you worry about Leroy, he's got plenty of speed for you. Remember the cactus thorns."

She winced at the reminder. "Oh, yeah. You said I should learn poles first."

"I'm beginning to think you're more of a barrel kind of girl." Sam winked at Zack, who had moved alongside.

"I think I'll be satisfied watching," Zack said.

Susan and Rusty held the gates open wide while Sam and the riders guided the herd into the corral and directly to the big, round water tank. Sam spied Mary standing with her brother, waving her arms wide to get his attention. "You've got the outfit, Rusty." Sam pulled Bullet around, tapped heels, and ran to her. Jumping down before Bullet was even stopped, he snatched her up, held her close, and whispered in her ear, "Dang, Mary, these last few days were long ones."

"Howdy, brother-in-law." Robert tapped Sam's shoulder only slightly rougher than necessary.

He held on to Mary but freed one hand to offer a welcome. "Good to see you, Robert."

"You can put me down. I promise I won't run away." She pushed his hat back and fluffed his white hair. "From what I can see, you've brought in some good looking young horses. Let's go have a closer look."

They moved to the board fence to watch the horses mill around and drink their fill. "Only one paint this year." Mary studied the group. "I was planning to pick a favorite for you to help me start, but I'll need more time to decide."

"Mrs. Holt, everybody went to take showers and change, but Mr. Holt said you might show me how to run barrels with Leroy."

Surprised, Mary turned and found Barbara wearing an ear-to-ear grin and holding Leroy's reins. "He did?" She smiled at Sam. "You must have impressed him. He is usually quite stingy with my time."

"Oh well, I already had my first dusting. I fell off Cactus, and onto a cactus, but Mr. Holt pulled out all the thorns with his knife. My arm's sore, but I can probably learn barrels tonight. I mean, if you have a few minutes."

Sam and Robert exchanged an amused glance, happy to watch Mary explain to the eager girl that a few minutes might not be quite enough.

"Have you watered Leroy since you've been in?"

"Yeah, I watered him before I walked over here. Do you think we could start, at least? I mean, he's not tired or anything. I think he slept most of the way in."

❧ ❧ ❧ ❧ ❧ ❧

It was obvious to Mary that Barbara wasn't the least bit tired, either. "Why not? Let's go to the small corral. I have the barrels set up there." She turned to Sam. "You two can go catch up on guy news. We won't be too long."

"I think I'll watch." Sam led the way.

"I'll watch, too, at least until Susan has supper ready. That T-bone should've lasted longer." Robert rubbed his belly.

Sam cocked his head. "T-Bone?"

"Boy howdy! Susan knows just how to grill 'em." He smacked his lips.

Ignoring the men completely, Mary stopped at the gate and gestured to Barbara. "There are three barrels set up in a triangle. While this is a timed event, riding the pattern correctly is just as important as your speed."

The girl nodded. "Do you want me to gallop around them?"

"Not just yet. Lead Leroy around the course. I'll watch from there." She pointed to the judge's booth.

Barbara stopped, cocked her head and gave Mary a, you-gotta-be-kidding look. "Lead him? You mean, like, walk?"

"Leroy's like you. He's never run barrels, so you need to walk him through it. You can still see the starting line in the dust. Wait there until I go sit down."

Barbara led Leroy to the line and twirled the end of the reins impatiently while she waited for Mary to get comfortable.

"Okay. Now the three barrels are your cloverleaf. Walk to the first barrel on your right, circle it, going around the inside," Mary instructed.

The eager girl led her sleepy horse around the barrel and gave Mary a feeble smile as she headed for the next barrel.

"Good, now look at the second barrel, walk to it, and circle around the same way, inside first. Great, now the third. Look at it as you approach, circle it from the opposite side ... Excellent!"

Barbara finished circling the final barrel, walking a little faster. Leroy followed obediently.

"Now walk back in a straight line to the starting line."

Barbara stopped at the line and gave Mary a cocky look. "That's it? I can do that. Want me to get on?"

From the gate Sam laughed. "Remember the cactus."

"Oh yeah." Barbara shrugged and rubbed her arm gingerly.

"What gets confusing," Mary continued, "is holding the pattern. You'll be eliminated if you circle the wrong way. It's not enough to run the barrels. You've got to stay on course. Now walk it through again."

While Barbara led Leroy around the barrels, Sam and Robert joined Mary in the booth. Sam scooped his wife onto his lap and nuzzled her ear.

"Jeez, will you two ever get over it?" Robert feigned disgust.

They looked up, "No!" they declared together, wrapping their arms around each other and falling from the chair onto the floor, giggling and kissing.

"How was that, Mrs. Holt?" Barbara called from the line.

Laughter danced in her voice as she pushed Sam away. "Do it again, Barbara. I may have missed something."

Sam made a move, but Mary blocked him. "Behave," she giggled. "I've got to pay attention to the poor girl. It's hot out there."

Robert laughed. "It ain't exactly an ice chest in here."

Shaking her head with exasperation, she pretended to ignore the men. "That looked great, Barbara. If you think you've got the idea, go ahead and get on. Walk him over the course, slow and easy."

After two trips around the course, Barbara seemed anxious to give real time a try.

Mary held firm. "You can ask for a trot, but no more. All the speed in the world won't count if you knock over barrels or go off course." She knew she'd just frustrated the girl to no end, but she couldn't seem to quell her own elation. She was so happy sitting there with Sam and her brother, coaching a young, enthusiastic girl. All this made her miss her students. It had been too long since she'd schooled a student. How many young girls had she taught to run barrels and master musical freestyle right here in this ring? Forty, fifty? Those were happier times. It made her miss Callie, too. It felt good just the same. She studied Sam's face on the sly. Yeah, he was thinking about Callie. He was smiling, too.

After a while, their freshly-showered guests started lining up along the fence to watch the show. Barbara trotted Leroy as if she'd done it hundreds of times. Mary couldn't get over how quickly that girl picked things up.

When Barbara crossed the finish line again, Mary stood up. "I think that's enough for your first lesson, and I want you to know you were very impressive."

"Can't I try one more time, a little faster? Please?"

Mary looked at Sam, who offered a wink. "Hey, I think she can handle it." He walked out of the booth toward the starting line. "Just don't get too excited and go too fast. Leroy may feel slower than Cactus, but he's got plenty."

Barbara grinned victoriously, pulling the strings tight on her hat. "Okay, Mr. Holt." She sent Leroy on, and took the first barrel, wide but correct. The second barrel was a little easier for her to maneuver. On her way to the third, the folks watching started to cheer, so Barbara asked for more speed. Leroy obliged and ran faster. She lost her balance going into the turn, causing Leroy to take the barrel too tight and her knee knocked it down. Grabbing for the horn, she dropped her reins. Leroy kicked at the barrel, firing both hind legs at the treacherous rolling menace in a fashion that would make any self-respecting mule proud, but the tough quarter horse never lost a step, nor did his speed waver.

Those gathered at the fence let out a combined gasp as Barbara struggled to keep her seat.

"It's all right. Get your reins and bring him home," Sam yelled and waved her on from the finish line.

"Darn! Darn! Darn! I really goofed that up!" She shook her head when she stopped but gave Leroy a hug and a pat. Mary recorded the lack of more colorful language. Mary and Robert came out to join them. She put her hand on Barbara's leg. "You goofed up nothing. I'm so proud of you today. If I didn't know better, I'd think you'd been practicing for months." She shot pretend daggers at Sam, who backed up in defense. "The only goof here is hurry-up, *Cowboy Sam*. You weren't ready for that, but you handled it beautifully.

Take Leroy to the barn, walk him till he cools down, then rinse him off before you put him in the pasture."

"Yes, ma'am. Mrs. Holt?"

"Yes?"

"Thank you. Thank you, too, Mr. Holt. Come on, Leroy, I guess you get a shower before I do." She led the horse toward the barn, skipping, singing, and twirling the ends of the long leather reins.

࿇࿇࿇࿇࿇

Mary sat on the bed, listening to Sam sing "Swanee River" in the shower. She giggled softly when she realized she could also hear Robert snoring in the bedroom down the hall. She could hear Barbara puttering in the kitchen, too. She had asked to spend the night on the couch. Poor child, it must be terrible to watch her mother go through something like this. She was a tough kid all right, but Mary knew she wanted not to be quite so tough. She wanted what kids all over the world wanted. A loving, happy family. No one could predict how this thing with her stepfather would eventually play out, but Mary would do her best to take the child's mind off it.

The bathroom door swung open, and Sam stood washed in soft light from a single bulb shinning through its flowered shade. "I was beginnin' to think I'd never get you to myself."

Okay, new movie scene. He wasn't going to wait until she could schedule a picnic to tell him about the tests. If only life *were* a movie and she could fast forward past the part where she told him.

He lunged for the bed, plowed in beside her, and yanked the sheet over their heads.

"Sam! You're still wet!"

"Didn't have time to dry. I was in an awful big hurry to snuggle my gal." He rolled on top, held her gaze with those intense brown eyes, and lowered his lips to hers.

Oh my, this cowboy knows how to kiss. She pushed her face into his neck. I'm gonna miss this.

They held each other, like they had thousands of times. His arms, his chest, his cheek next to hers felt so safe. She wanted to be safe. What would it be like not to touch him, not to hear his voice?

He traced her ear with his finger. "Mary."

Oh God, he's going to ask now. Not now, Sam, please not now. Let's go to sleep holding each other. I don't want to talk now. I want to dream. I want you to hold me and let me dream, safe, here in our bed, in your arms.

He blew soft, warm breath in her ear then kissed it. "It's okay, Mary."

"It's not. Not really." She struggled for breath. "Sam, I'm afraid."

He lurched upright, grabbed her shoulders, and pulled her up to face him. "What?"

Without a word, she grabbed onto him and clung so tight, her fingernails dug into his back. Nothing could stop the tears now. She didn't even try. She could feel his tears running down her back. Felt him jerk with every sob. She *was* afraid. Afraid of leaving her cowboy. Afraid of never feeling his stubble scratch her neck again. Afraid of never hearing him call her *his gal* again. She was afraid for him, too. What would he do? How would he manage? For thirty-five years they'd shared every day. Looked across the table at each other every morning, slept next to each other every night. Built a life, a ranch. Buried a child together. They'd tackled each and every problem side by side. Droughts, fires, blizzards. Always with each other to lean on. To count on. God, he must be terrified. She squeezed harder. What could she do? What could she do?

She had to tell him. Now, in their bed. The telling would be the worst of it. Facing it wouldn't be so bad. They could hold each other all night. And face the new morning together.

She leaned him back, keeping firm hands on his shoulders. "Sam."

He looked up. His white face stunned her.

"Sam, they only did one test."

He choked, shook his head, and pushed her away. "No, Mary, no." He jumped out of bed and ran to the window. A tremor shivered through him. "Why?"

She pulled the sheet to her chin. "The cancer's in the bones now."

His head and shoulders sagged. He pounded the wall. Like a weary soldier crawling back into the trenches, Sam crawled back into bed and laid his head on her lap. "When do you start treatments?"

She knew he knew the answer. She hugged him tight ... and held her tongue.

"You're not doing treatments, are you? I tried not to think about it, but I knew ... I knew when you wouldn't let me take you to the hospital."

A single tear dripped onto his cheek. She dabbed it with a sheet corner.

"Your mind was made up at Callie's grave, before you went in for that test. How ..." His voice broke. "How long?"

She bent down, pressing her lips to his ear. "We'll have the summer."

Chapter Twenty-Three

Mary laced her fingers through Sam's and smiled quietly. She didn't lift her head off his chest, even though she could hear his tummy rumbling louder and louder the longer Susan rang the big dinner bell calling everyone to breakfast. Sweet Sam. He always woke up starving. She should let him up, and she would, in a minute.

"Mr. Holt, I think they're calling us for breakfast," Barbara yelled up the stairs.

Sam kissed Mary's head. "You go ahead. We're just gettin' around to kickin' off the sheets."

Mary tilted her head to look up at him. "We should get up. I heard Robert go down an hour ago."

"What if we never get up? What if we stay right here and hold each other for the next thirty-five years?"

She giggled. "I'd have a hard time sleeping with that freight train in your belly."

"Sorry. I reckon it's empty." His arms wrapped around her, and he held her tight against him. "I wanted to have something to say this morning. Something smart. I wanted to have a way to tell you not to be afraid anymore. To tell you it's okay ... That I'll be okay. But ..."

She tugged his ear and forced a smile. "You just did. Sam, I want a promise from you."

He sat up, dumping her to his lap. "A promise? Anything, just ask."

She touched his nose. "From this moment on, no more sad talk. Only happy talk. It's taken enough. We can't give it what we have left. We can't." She held onto her cowboy, wondering if she should have said that. But, she'd meant it. She was going to die soon enough. But she wasn't dead yet, and *No*, she wasn't going to live like she was. She'd done that for too long already. Wasted four years waiting to die. She wasn't doing that anymore. Not one more day! She watched his eyes cloud as he struggled with the new reality.

"I promise." Sam kissed her head one more time then slid out from under her. "Just give me a little time to make the adjustment." He hurried to the bathroom and closed the door.

Like a pair of love birds, they preened each other, getting ready to face the day, and one hour later they walked outside, hand in hand. Comanche greeted them at the bottom of the porch steps.

Sam studied him for a second. "Mary, I don't know what you've done to him, but by golly, he's beginning to look mighty fit."

She mixed his morning ration and sat the tub under the live oak. "He eats enough for three horses and has responded well to our daily rides. He'll be ready."

Watching the feisty horse bury his nose in his breakfast, Sam nodded. "I have no doubt."

A few minutes later, Mary was convinced Comanche could finish his rations without her guidance, so she grabbed Sam and led him through the gate. Happy voices from the lodge drifted down to them as they walked up the hill for breakfast.

"Well, look at the sleepyheads who finally rolled out of their blankets," Robert said as they strolled into the lodge and sat beside him. "Only thing is, we ate everything except an old pair of boiled moccasins."

"Don't listen to him." Susan poured coffee. "I have plenty. Sit. I'll be right back."

John Bartlett ambled over to them, sat next to Sam, and flipped open a tablet. "I've made a list of supplies: breaker panel, wires, and lights for the lodge. Wire and speakers for the small corral and rodeo arena." He slid the tablet to Sam. "Robert agreed to take this to town this morning, pick up what he can, and call my shop for the rest. We'll have everything we need by the time we're done moving the mustangs to summer grass."

Sam tightened his lips as he studied the five-page list. He glanced at Mary. "Thanks, but we can't come close to affording this." He slid the tablet back across the table. "Just fix the lodge and patch the speakers. I reckon we can get another year out of the old system."

Mary looked across the table and saw Barbara's face wilt. That girl had been counting on quite a show.

Robert spoke up. "No, we're doing it. You've got no say. You either, Sis. I'm going to town to order my own supplies for the show, and I'll be taking care of this." He waved the tablet, nodding to John. "He's giving you a hang of a break on supplies, and the labor's free. So, smile while you eat them eggs."

Susan slid heaping plates in front of Mary and Sam. "Yeah, like your brother said, smile while you eat them eggs."

"I reckon I will." Sam rocked forward and filled his fork.

Mary could only pick at her eggs. She wasn't really sad anymore ... a little melancholy maybe, but not out-and-out sad. She wasn't anxious to see Sam leave for the range again, but she *was* anxious to ride Comanche a little before it got too hot. Sam ate and listened to the chatter. She worried about the heat as she watched the sun climb.

As Sam was chasing the last of his hash browns around his plate with a tiny piece of biscuit, Rusty strolled into the lodge. "Got all the horses saddled, boss."

"Saddle one for yourself."

Rusty aimed a startled look at him.

"Robert'll be here now," Sam explained.

"Oh yeah, right." He started away, paused, then turned back. "You stayin' behind, too? 'Cause you can, you know. We'll get the horses moved to summer grass for you."

"I'll come out, get you under way, then come back in." Sam squeezed Mary's hand. "That is, if it's all right with you. It's a cinch they don't need my help to trail 'em to mountain pastures, but I'd like one more look at the young ones before they disappear into the high country. I'll be back by tomorrow night. Before sunset."

She knew very well what Sam wanted, needed. Whenever he'd been troubled over the years, he'd saddle up and go visit Anaba. How could she stand in his way now? "I'll be fine. Frankly, we have a lot to do. Susan has the material for our new outfits, and we want to get started sewing. Chester and Comanche need exercise and a little more rehearsal, and," she turned to Barbara, "there's a certain young lady among us who needs plenty of practice running barrels."

Barbara lit up. "Really? You mean I can stay home, or in, or ... here?"

"It's less than two weeks until the Fourth of July. Even though it isn't a sanctioned event, if you expect to represent Mar-Sa, you'll need to practice."

"But Cactus is out there, on the range." Panic flared in her eyes. "I only have Leroy here."

"Let's start with Leroy." She gave Sam a conspiratorial wink. "Maybe in a day or two, you can give it a go with Chester."

Barbara jumped up, gave Mary a long hug and Sam an even longer one. "You'll tell mother for me, won't you? Oh, and here are the clean jeans she asked me to bring her. Mrs. Holt, if I saddle Chester and Comanche, maybe we could take a ride to the stream."

Sam kissed Mary goodbye and stepped up on Bullet. "See you tomorrow evening." He nodded to Barbara and smiled at Mary. "Better keep a handful of rein on that one."

He swung Bullet around and dashed up the hill after the others.

The three older mares they'd trailed in to calm the young mustangs required no effort at all to control. In fact, they practically led the way. The sun was directly overhead when they rode into camp, and there was still plenty of daylight left when Sam finished his final inspection of the wild horses bound for summer grass in the high mountains on the northernmost border of the ranch.

Rusty and Morgan had things well in hand, and Sam had no second thoughts about handing the reins to them. The guests trusted Rusty and got a kick out of Morgan. Linda had enough supplies to feed them all, and she'd been so excited for Barbara. If she worried at all about her husband, she sure didn't let it show.

Sam rode Bullet toward the bare nose on the distant mountain. It would be dark by the time he scaled the final summit and broke into the clearing Anaba called home. Anaba would have a tiny fire burning outside the cabin's door. A greeting fire. He'd know Sam was coming. He always knew.

Even though it had been months since he'd made the trek, Bullet knew his way and carefully maneuvered the tight trail winding ever upward through the dark woods. An owl flew silently across their path and landed on a naked branch ahead of them. Again and again, the owl spread its great wings and flew silently along the path, only to settle on another naked branch, as if guiding their way.

Then, at last, the owl watched from its final perch as they passed beneath, into the clearing. Sam could see the form of a man huddled by a tiny fire in front of the mud-and-log cabin. The man tossed dust into the fire and bright silver sparks shot into the air as deep red flames lit his weathered face. Anaba.

"I have been sitting here thinking of you, my friend. We will smoke by the fire tonight and speak of these things you cannot understand and those that weigh heavy on your heart, until the sun burns the darkness away."

After removing Bullet's saddle and bridle, Sam turned him free to pick at the wiry grass. Then he simply folded his legs and squatted next to the fire, facing the old Navajo. He drew deeply on the pipe handed him, held the rank smoke long enough to burn his mouth, puckered his lips, and allowed it to drift out. Sam looked across the fire at his dear friend. He studied the faded shirt that covered shoulders made uneven by the passing of years, and the deeply furrowed skin sagging around Anaba's still keen eyes. Such a man was Anaba. You needed to study his worn-out body closely to notice the wear of it. The spirit living in those rich black eyes created a cloaking aura that prevented all but the most determined examiner from seeing the toll the years had taken on the mortal Navajo. But even quickest glance could not miss that vibrant spirit.

"I remember the times I would come here to listen to your tall tales and legends. Now, it seems I only come when ... " He sucked the pipe.

"We must try to understand, my friend. You are passing through a very difficult and important time. It will not be an easy journey, but like all journeys, it too will end."

Sam dropped the pipe and covered his face with his hands. "Like my daughter's journey ended? How much must one man bear?"

"That is not for us to know. No one of this world could help your daughter for she came into this world with an imperfect body. But she had a good life. Her memories rest in your heart, and her spirit surrounds you, and Mary. Do you not agree it is better for her spirit to have enjoyed the happy life she had with you, than to have had no life at all?"

"She was still a little girl. A sweet, innocent young girl who loved life and who was loved by everyone who ever knew her. Why should she have such a short life?"

"We do not know why some travel this world long and some only a short time. I have outlived all my children. And three wives. I have left two brothers in faraway lands, too far to even bring their bodies home for sacred burial. I do not know why I have been asked to live this long life. I do know it is right and natural to sometimes feel sorrow."

Sam pulled himself up and walked to the edge of the clearing, staring down the vertical wall to the desert floor some thousand feet below. He yelled Mary's name, fell to his knees and screamed out over the dessert, "I'm not ready to live without you." He sat very close to the edge, wrapped his arms around his knees, and wept. Then in a broken, sobbing voice, he told Anaba, "It's not sorrow I feel ... It's emptiness. Emptiness and *rage*."

The old Navajo grabbed him by the shirt and dragged him back from the edge, back to the fire. He sat hunch-shouldered and glared into Sam's eyes, yet his voice was calm. "Emptiness and anger are selfish feelings, and they do no good. They will make you bitter."

Sam glared back at him. "I am bitter. I have every stinking right to be bitter." He ground the heels of his hands in his eyes. Spit the ground.

Anaba gave him a soft, quiet look and handed Sam the pipe. "We will smoke now. We must not speak again until you have a question."

Sam lay back against his saddle and watched the moon walk across the sky. He sucked on the pipe selfishly, passing it to Anaba only when it needed refilling. He studied his old friend. Never before this night had Sam felt anger toward him. When he looked back to the moon, he saw it sinking into the horizon. He wanted to say goodnight to Mary but was afraid. What if it was the last time?

Sam pushed out of the saddle to sit upright. "Why won't Mary let the doctors treat her?"

Anaba didn't answer. He reached for the pipe, sucked deeply, and handed it back to Sam. He began humming, then chanting softly and rocking gently, side to side. He dipped his fingers into the wooden bowl at his side, held his hand over the tiny fire, and dribbled a fine powder on the flames. The flames swallowed his hand, but Anaba never flinched.

Sam noticed there was no wood on the fire. The flames sprang up from out of the ground. Yellow, red, and blue. He could see the powder slip from Anaba's hand, grain by grain. Each grain changed the fire's color.

Finally, Anaba stopped chanting. The fire shrank to a single tiny yellow flame no bigger than a candle's glow. Still the Navajo remained silent.

Sam wanted to shake the answer out of him. *Why wouldn't he say anything?*

Anaba sat rigid, eyes closed. Finally he folded his hands on his lap. "I do not believe Mary has faith that the medical doctors can be of help."

Jumping to his feet, Sam towered over his friend. "That's insane! They kept her alive for four years. You were supposed to have answers for me. I trusted you!" He kicked the ground. "I trusted you!"

Calmly, Anaba met Sam's furious gaze. "I have given you an answer, my friend. That it is not the answer you seek does not make it wrong."

Sam paced the fire ring, kicking at anything in his way. The glow on the horizon told him the sun was waking, and he'd solved nothing.

He fell to his knees. Through flooded eyes, he searched his friend's sad face. "What is it that makes her so sure? ... Why?"

In the next instant, Anaba was there, sitting beside him in the dirt. "Only she knows, my friend. Her body is very sick, but her heart and spirit are strong. She is not sad for herself. She is sad only for you. Her love for you is strong. I feel it surrounding you. It is a most powerful love. You should do as she asks and never speak sad words again. This ... is important to her."

Chapter Twenty-Four

Mary watched Barbara closely as they rode together in the morning sunshine. She noticed her cues to Chester were becoming lighter, more subtle. The girl was a natural born equestrian. A little too sure of herself, perhaps, but that was better than being timid. Especially considering the grand ideas this girl had.

After they returned to the barn and hosed down the horses, Mary surprised Barbara with a new plan. They were going to decorate Chester's and Comanche's stalls.

Barbara gave a puzzled look and nodded to the sign over the door of the first box stall. It read, *Chester*.

"I know. Comanche took Chester's stall, but that's because Robert took Comanche's old stall for his motorcycle. I thought we'd turn the box stall next to Comanche's new stall into Chester's official home."

"But they're almost always outside, anyway."

"Most of the time ... but they enjoy a home base, I always like to think. Sometimes it's just nice to have a few horses in the barn. Anyway," Mary felt girlish giggles bubbling up in her throat, "I just want to do it." She was fully aware of the challenge she faced opening the trunk again. Somehow, though, Barbara's recent enthusiasm fed her inner strength.

That inner strength started to wilt, however, when she reached the door to the tack room. Mary froze, steadying herself on the fire extinguisher mounted to the wall.

"Mrs. Holt, are you all right?"

Mary gave herself a mental shake. "You bet I am." She worked the latch and gave Barbara her crooked smile. "Let's get started."

Even as they stepped through the door, the red trunk frightened her. It took serious conviction, and a deep breath, but she conquered the fright. "What I had in mind," she forced her voice to sound cheery, "was to go through the old trunk there, take the ribbons out, and hang them on wires on the stall fronts. We have some pictures in there, too."

"Awesome! Let's do it!"

Together they dragged the trunk into the light. Mary sucked in another big breath for courage, flipped the latches, tightened her lips, and shoved open the lid. She stepped back unevenly and supported herself against the doorjamb, staring at the contents with eyes that seemed not to be her own.

Barbara rescued her. "Wow! Look at all those ribbons! You must be the best barrel racer in the world!"

Mary laughed freely. "I was pretty darn good in my day." She slid a framed picture out of the trunk and tapped the face of the cute blond girl smiling from behind the glass. "A lot of these are Callie's."

Barbara took the picture. "Boy, she's pretty. Hey, that's Chester ... Callie, that's your daughter, right? I'm sorry she died." At Mary's gasp of surprise, she cringed. "I'm sorry. Lucy told me about her. One night Mr. Holt told us how you guys got married, then when he went to bed, Lucy told us about your daughter ... I hope doing this doesn't make you sad." Barbara jumped up with the picture, ran across the aisle to Chester's stall, and held it against the wall. "We'll hang Callie's picture right here, so everybody can see her as soon as they come in the barn. She shouldn't be stuck in any old dark trunk!"

God bless Barbara. Mary pulled herself up, gave an impatient swipe across her eyes, and marched to the tool room where she found a hammer and nail.

She pounded the nail herself.

"That was a wonderful idea, Barbara. Thank you!" She met the girl's wide grin with a genuinely happy smile of her own.

For the next hour and a half, they pounded nails and stretched wires across the face of the two stall walls. Mary backed away to inspect the final result. "I think we're ready for ribbons."

Shoulder to shoulder, they dragged the trunk to the tack room doorway and started separating ribbons by horse, according to the labels on the back.

"Boy, Callie won a lot more ribbons than you did. She even won a lot on Comanche. Are you ever going to let me ride Comanche?"

"We'll see." She smiled. "Let's get you ready for the Fourth and barrel racing with Chester. Comanche has a ways to go yet. So do you, young lady."

Barbara squealed. "So you're gonna let me barrel race Chester?"

"Maybe. As I said, get the pattern down with Leroy, and then you can try Chester."

Barbara nodded (a nod of determination if ever Mary had seen one) and pulled two very large blue ribbons from the trunk. "Wow, they're beautiful." She stood up and admired them. "They're both for Comanche, but one's yours and one's Callie's. What's musical freestyle?"

Along came the tears. She'd been doing all right, thanks in large part to Barbara's exuberance, but this was a tough one. "I'm sorry." Her voice sounded as weak as she felt. "Those are from the last time we competed together. Callie, Comanche, and me." She cupped her face and started to sob. "Maybe this wasn't such a good idea after all."

Barbara dropped to her knees and held her tight. "You can cry on me, Mrs. Holt. I'll hold you like I hold my mom when she cries."

As they sat on the hard wooden tack room floor, Mary sensed the moment was as cleansing for the child as it was for her. Finally, after she'd cried herself empty, she pulled Barbara to her feet. "Let's hang these ribbons!"

They worked for an hour, pressing the wrinkles out of ribbons and creating a wall of blue, red, green, and white. So many ribbons hung on the wall that it shimmered like a satin sheet. They were sitting on a straw bale admiring their work while Mary explained musical freestyle. "My brother made tapes of some of our competitions, so if you like, we can watch them together."

Sam stopped abruptly in the doorway. "Well, holy cow! Look at those ribbons." His eyes rested on Callie's picture.

Barbara jumped up. "Did a good job, didn't we, Mr. Holt?"

He draped his arm around her shoulder, reached for Mary, and hugged them both. "You sure did. This place looks like a genuine, first rate, show barn. A winning show barn at that." Mary saw him wipe his eyes on the sly. "Gotta tell ya, I've missed seein' that."

Just then, Susan pulled up in the Gator. "I have lunch ready if anybody's hungry."

"You ladies take lunch up to the house." He dropped his arms and stepped back. "I've got a right tired horse on my hands who needs a hosing and some groceries." He smiled at Mary, "Might be fun to spend the afternoon watching those tapes and planning your new routine."

She flashed her crooked smile. "That, Cowboy, is a terrific idea." She knew there would be a rough patch or two, but if she was going to win at the state fair, she would need to choreograph a spectacular routine.

"You go on to the house. I'll run to the lodge and grab the sandwiches." As soon as Sam stepped into the Gator's bed, Susan revved the motor and sped away.

Mary laughed and yelled to Sam, "She drives like you!" Barbara and Mary had finished setting the dining room table and sat waiting on the porch. They watched the black clouds gather as Susan roared up with Sam standing in the rear of the Gator, holding his hat over her eyes. Barbara held the door wide, screaming for them to run. He grabbed the sack of sandwiches, Susan gathered a large paper bag, and they sprinted up the steps just ahead of the cloudburst. Sam turned back to look out the screen door. "Holy cow, that sure came outta nowhere."

Susan plopped the paper bag on a chair. "I have your costume all cut. If I can use your machine, I'll sew while we watch the movies." She opened the bag and pulled out the red and silver fabric.

Sam examined the brilliant fabric and aimed a man-sized grin at Mary. "Whew, Mary, goin' at it full gallop. Like the old days."

"You bet." She stood on tiptoes and gave him a peck on the cheek.

"Look at the rain! I can hardly see the barn!" Barbara yelled above the thunder.

They were still huddled on the porch enjoying the mist splashing through the screen when a single headlight caught Mary's eye. "Oh, no. Poor Robert. He's caught in this."

They stayed on the porch, getting wetter themselves as they watched Robert maneuver his Harley into the carport next to Mary's cart. He shot a soggy look their way and bounded up the steps. "Dang Arizona weather!" He stomped inside, shook his arms, and stamped his feet. "Why couldn't you guys buy a ranch in the desert, like normal cattle ranchers?"

෨෨෨෨෨෨෨

"This is beautiful." Mary turned every which way, examining herself in the mirror. "Oh, Susan, you did a fabulous job."

Robert and Sam had gone to bed hours earlier, and Barbara lay passed out on the sofa.

"It did turn out pretty darn good, and you look twenty years younger in it." Susan slapped her hand over her mouth. "I didn't mean ..."

Mary beamed. "I almost feel twenty years younger wearing it. I may never take it off. I'm so excited, I ..." She glanced at her closed bedroom door, listened to Sam snoring, and sighed. "Boy, I want to wake him but ... we shouldn't."

Susan cast her a devilish grin. "We *can* wake Barbara." Down the stairs to the living room they hurried, like two giddy school girls about to share a very special secret with an unsuspecting friend. Without hesitation, they pounced on her.

"What the ... ?" Barbara shot up and rubbed her eyes. Mary struck a pose, holding her arms high and grinning as if she'd won first prize in a beauty contest. "We're finished. What do you think?"

With a stretch and a yawn, Barbara stood and paced slowly around Mary, eyeing the sequin-laden blouse and silver-fringed slacks. "That looks exactly like the outfit Callie wore in the last tape. Wow, you guys did an awesome job!" She stopped abruptly and looked Susan right in the eye. "I want one just like it. Just like in the tape. Only the two of us will do a team routine ... If that's what you call it. I'm awake now, if you want to measure me." She thrust her arms wide and waited.

Mary took a shuddering breath then took Barbara's hands. "I'd be honored."

The next hour was spent measuring, marking, and cutting patterns. And giggling. Barbara proved to be quite helpful and skilled with a pencil, drawing thick black lines on the brown paper shopping bags they used for pattern material.

"I think I may have found an assistant." Susan examined the final pattern for Barbara's blouse.

Barbara gave Mary an uncertain smile. "This is fun, but I'll stick to the horses."

"Well, if we're going to do anything, be it horses or costume making," Mary pointed to the clock, "we'd better go to bed. It's one thirty."

"I got the couch." Barbara turned and dashed for the living room.

"I'll be going now, too. Goodnight, Mary." Susan started for the door.

Mary stopped her. "Why don't you spend the night? You won't have so far to come for breakfast."

"No, thanks. I want my own bed. If it's okay with you, I may skip breakfast. I have just enough fabric to finish a blouse for Barbara and wouldn't it be fun to surprise her?"

"We should be careful. I think we've already created an out-of-control monster." Mary glanced toward the couch. "I'll walk out with you and give Comanche his midnight snack."

Susan giggled, "A little late. You should tell him it's his early morning snack."

The storm, having passed some time ago, let the moon hang bright and beautiful in a sparkling sky. They stood together at the bottom of the porch steps, admiring the stars. Susan leaned on the gate. "This was fun tonight. I'm happy you decided to compete. You look better than ..." Her voice faltered. "I'm sorry." She turned to face Mary. "I worry so for you."

Mary sat on the step and pulled Susan down beside her. "Please, don't worry about me. Sam and I had our talk, and I'll ask you the same favor." She rubbed the goose bumps on Susan's arm. "We don't talk about sad anymore. Okay?" After Susan nodded agreement, she continued. "It is *very* important to me that I finish what I started with Comanche. He should never have suffered like that. It might be the last thing I do, but I want to see him bow for the applause again!"

Susan gave her a teary smile and another weak nod. Mary looked around. "Speaking of Comanche, where is he?"

"There." Susan pointed to the corner of the yard, where the paint horse stood hanging his head over the fence, staring at the barn and stomping his foot.

They followed his stare into the barn through the open double doors.

Mary saw it first. "What's that light in the far end of the barn?"

"Fire!"

They ran for the barn. Mary clung to Susan's hand and willed herself to keep up. The combination of fear and determination gave her unbelievable strength and vitality. She ran the distance, hardly losing her breath.

Inside the barn several small fires were beginning to take hold. The straw bales at the far end were the worst. Mary raced for the fire extinguisher, yanked it from the wall.

She turned in time to see a man knock Susan down and come at her. Moving on instinct she swung the extinguisher and landed a lucky blow to his head. The man fell back and lay sprawled on the ground. Mary lurched forward to hit him again then realized he was out cold. She glanced at Susan, who was beginning to stand, then ran from fire to fire and killed them all. By the time she sprayed the last one, the barn was thick with smoke and fogged in chemicals. But it was safe.

"Mary, you should come here."

She looked down the aisle and saw Susan standing over their attacker with a pitchfork aimed at his middle.

"It's Philip Cunningham!"

She felt the toll now and gasped for air as she staggered toward him. "Why?" She had a lot more to say but not the breath to say it.

He didn't say anything, just shrugged his shoulders. "Hey." Susan poked him. "She asked you a question."

Hatred flared in his eyes. "Screw you."

Susan whacked him over the head with the fork. "We're not your wife, buster. We hit back."

"You bitch."

"Got that right." She hit him again, re-aimed the fork, and grinned at Mary. "Slow learner this one. Go get the men. I'll hold him here."

Mary stumbled to the open doors, flipped the light switch on her way out, and fought with the stubborn latch on the old truck. She crawled across the seat and laid on the horn, keeping it up until the lights came on in the house. Finally the men charged out the door, but then they stopped on the steps, looking confused. She tried to yell for them but her breath was still coming in short gasps. She coughed and choked and leaned on the horn until Robert and Sam bolted down the steps and started running for the barn. Sam reached her first. "Mary, what's going on?"

She coughed and pointed. "He tried to burn the barn!" Robert ran by them. Barbara was two steps behind. Sam helped Mary to stand and supported her as they went inside the smoky barn. Susan still held Philip pinned to the floor, the tines of her pitchfork inches from his throat.

"Philip," Barbara yelped. "What did you do?"

Susan didn't flinch or raise her eyes. "He tried to set fire to the barn. We handled it."

241

Sam shook his head. "Reckon you picked a scuffle with the wrong women this time, fella."

Barbara goaded. "He can't handle nowhere-land pioneer women."

Sam grabbed a bale, gently settled Mary onto it, then sat next to her. "Mister, you should've gone home like you said you would. This here's gonna be a problem." He shook his head and raised his eyebrows.

Philip tried to get up.

Susan poked him. "Try again. I'm just waiting to draw blood."

Robert offered him advice. "Better lie still while we sort through this." He turned to Sam. "Call the sheriff?"

"Yeah, call the sheriff." Barbara sidled over and bent low in his face. "Maybe this time you'll get what you've got coming. I'll bet nowhere-land cops have guts, too."

Sam pulled Barbara back and steered her to his vacated seat. "Sounds to me like there's more to this than meets the eye. Wanna tell me anything?"

She aimed hard eyes at the pinned man. "No. Just call the sheriff."

After coaxing Susan to relinquish the pitchfork, Robert yanked Philip to his feet, marched him to Chester's stall, and shoved him in. "Sit tight while we arrange more suitable accommodations."

Barbara stared at him through the bars. "He'll go to jail for this, won't he?"

"Sheriff'll hold him for a while, I reckon. It'll take time to sort it all out, a day or two just to fetch your mother."

"Let's not do that." The words came out in a rush.

Mary knew the young girl held too much inside. "Barbara dear, we need to tell her."

"Not right now. Can't we just let her have fun cooking and stuff on the range?" Barbara paced back and forth in the aisle, then spun to face Sam. "What's it matter? Why upset her now? Can't the sheriff lock him up and let Mom deal with it when she gets back?"

Sam grinned and shook his head. "We can ask the sheriff."

“∼“∼“∼“∼“∼

Philip sat in the straw on the stall floor, picking his teeth with a stem. Meanwhile, Sheriff Whip Bannon walked through the barn, taking pictures and measurements, mumbling to himself from time to time. A careful, methodical man, he'd demanded that no one leave the barn. Now the sheriff snapped the lid on his camera case closed. "So you intend to press charges?"

Sam looked to Barbara, waiting for her nod. "Yeah, Whip, reckon I need to."

"All right, then. I might as well get your statements." He pulled a pad from his shirt pocket, clicked his pen, and sat on an overturned bucket. "Who wants to go first?"

Susan related in careful detail how they'd discovered the fires with Comanche's help. Mary admitted to slugging Philip with the fire extinguisher, in self-defense. Susan explained how she'd held him down with the pitch fork.

"Did either of you actually see him set the fires?"

Mary and Susan shared a glance.

"I was first through the doors. I saw him squatting right there." Susan pointed to a black smudge on the wall near the third box stall door. "I ran toward him, and he hit me."

"Then he came at me. That's when I hit him with the extinguisher." Mary lifted her eyebrows and cocked her head in challenge.

Sheriff Bannon slid the tablet back in his shirt pocket, stood up, and pulled Philip to his feet. "Come on, fella. I'm placing you under arrest for assault and arson."

Barbara watched through narrowed eyes as Sheriff Bannon cuffed him and stuffed him in the backseat of his cruiser. Philip didn't say a word. He was quiet and obedient. She continued to watch until the lights turned onto the hard road. Then she followed the others to the house and into the kitchen. She sat next to Mary but questioned Sam. "What will they do to him? He'll go to jail, right?"

"I think we can count on Sheriff Bannon to hold him long enough for your mother to get here and go into town to talk this all over with her husband."

"When she does, would you take her? I mean, would you go with her?"

Sam tapped his finger on the table. "I can. If she asks."

Barbara turned to Mary and pleaded with her eyes before turning back to Sam. "No. That's not good enough. Mr. Holt, you *must* go with her. If she goes alone, he'll twist this all around and convince her it's her fault. Please, tell me you'll go with her. Don't let him talk to her alone."

He hesitated, considering.

"Sam." The tone of Mary's voice said so much. The look in her eyes said the rest.

He gave Mary a nod, then reached across the table, took Barbara's hand, and patted it gently.

"I'll go with her."

Chapter Twenty-Five

Within a few days, Philip Cunningham was nearly forgotten. Robert had even gone to town and rented a sandblaster to blast all of the ugly black smudges from the walls. Sam and Robert had loaded the damaged straw in the manure spreader and spread it on the grassland, out of sight of the homestead. Robert had started stringing new speaker wire in the arena, and John Bartlett's supply house had delivered a note informing them the speakers and other supplies would arrive in two days. On the first day of July.

Thanks to the watchful eyes and encouraging words of Mary and Sam, Barbara had continued to increase her skills as an equestrian. For the past three days, she'd been taking Chester for a morning ride to the stream and back. Today would be her first chance to try barrels with Chester.

As on every other day, Sam sat with Mary in the judge's booth while Barbara practiced barrels.

"Okay now, Chester's a lot like Cactus. You remember her, right?" Sam teased.

"Don't listen to him." Mary gave her cowboy a playful shove. "You may be surprised when Chester takes a barrel. He leans low, almost pivots around them. So hold the horn, keep your center of gravity, and when you turn him, be soft. He knows what to do."

Barbara walked Chester to the starting line, nodded to Mary, and sent Chester. Mary could see his start was faster than she'd been ready for, even though they'd practiced the fast start on their morning rides. At twenty, Chester hadn't lost a step.

Mary watched Barbara's eyes. Good focus on the barrel. They rounded the first barrel beautifully. Barbara's eyes were perfect, leveled on the third barrel before Chester finished his pocket around the second one. Ears pinned, he raced toward it. Barbara's hand on the rein was as light as air when she turned him. Smooth. They exploded for home.

Mary nearly crushed Sam's hand. She hit the stopwatch. "Eighteen point five!"

Barbara hugged Chester's neck and threw her hat. "Holy cow! That is the most incredible thing I've ever done. Holy cow, he's fast. I think he's faster than Cactus."

Sam laughed. "That was a great ride, young lady."

"You gonna run?" Barbara dismounted in front of the booth.

Mary shook her head. "No. I think a time or two is all I'll need between now and the Fourth. We shouldn't press Chester."

Sam ran a hand down her arm, then suddenly jumped up. "Look there." He pointed across the corral to a dust cloud rising over the grassland. "Reckon our wranglers are comin' in."

Barbara swung up on Chester and backed away from the booth. "See ya! I'm going to tell my mom my awesome time. Eighteen point five seconds! Woo-ha!"

From the shade of the booth, they watched Barbara gallop Chester up the hill toward the dust cloud. Sam fussed with Mary's collar, then pulled her onto his lap. "That hip botherin' you today?"

She knew he knew. "It's not bad, really. I honestly thought poor Chester didn't need any more practice today."

"Would you tell me if it was bad?"

"No." She kissed him again and squirmed to get up. "I'm going to help Susan prepare lunch. Wanna help?"

Holding hands, they walked to the lodge, where they settled into the business of making lunch and watching the folks assemble in the large corral.

Rusty and Morgan set the guests to unsaddling and rubbing down their mounts. Of course, Morgan was a bit distracted by Barbara's retelling of her great run on the barrels. Mary and Sam exchanged glances and laughed quietly together as they watched the boy try to walk away from her, again and again. Horses snorting and laughter floating up to the lodge was all the proof they needed to know their guests had a great time. That was important, not just because the guests had paid good money, but because the purpose of any adventure should be to have a great time.

One by one the guests gathered in the lodge for a hot meal and lively conversation. Mary had relinquished all kitchen duties to Susan and Linda, having decided Sam's lap was much more inviting.

"I don't think I've ever seen a more beautiful place than the mountains of your summer horse range." Nicky Bartlett sat crossways on the picnic table bench, nestled between her husband's legs. She leaned back into his arms and let out a sensuous sigh. "It was hard to leave."

"Oh, yes, and that lake." Debby Collier shivered. "The water was so cold in that lake. It was amazing. You have it all here—desert, grass, mountains, rivers, and lakes. If I hadn't seen it, I wouldn't believe it."

Zack laughed. "Of course, you've got to ride for a few weeks to see it all."

"By golly, I'm sure glad you folks enjoyed yourselves. That's the whole purpose of the wild horse trail drive. It gives the guests a chance to get to see the beauty we have out here." Sam grinned. "Well, that and moving the horses to summer grass."

Mary snuggled deeper into Sam's lap to enjoy the chatter.

"What have you got planned for us next?" Zack asked.

Sam gave Zack a well-I'll-tell-ya grin and stood. "Folks, I'm sure you're all excited about the Fourth of July rodeo we hold here each year. I have a few announcements regarding that. First, as some of you know, it's also Morgan's seventeenth birthday."

Paul Keaton started a round of cheers that took Sam a second to quiet. Barbara snuck up behind Morgan and flipped his hat off his head, then caught it and smashed it onto her own head. Morgan sat like the gentleman he was and patiently waited for her to return it.

Sam shook his head and aimed a smile their way. "All right, then. What we have to look forward to is a great time. We talked a little about the shindig, but I'll wager that until you've lived it, it's a might hard to imagine."

"Here, here," Paul cheered. "Like seeing the mountains for the first time."

"The next couple of days will get pretty busy while we set things up. Pitch in as much as you like, but enjoy yourselves while you're at it."

"When do the people for the rodeo start arriving?" Debby asked.

"The livestock suppliers and equipment handlers roll in on the second. Friends, neighbors, and spectators start to appear on the third. We get a good amount of company for a few days."

ॐ∽ॐ∽ॐ∽ॐ

After a while, everybody's questions were answered, and the guests drifted to their cabins to relax, nap, or visit in the shade. Barbara, Morgan, Mary, and Susan were happily reviewing Mary's ideas for her routine. Sam figured it was time to bring Linda up to date.

He paused at the cabin door before he knocked. It was the first time he'd ever had the need to tell a woman that he'd had her husband tossed in jail, and he figured the no-good should stay there.

Linda opened the door. Her smile of welcome froze in an instant and then twisted into a mask of fear. "Oh, Sam. Is Barbara all right?"

He pulled off his hat. "She's fine, just fine. I'm sorry to bother you, but I need a word."

"Sure. Would you care to come in?"

Sam pondered a second. "Let's talk out here, if that's all right." He motioned to the table at the end of the porch. Linda sat across from him, her shoulders slumped. "We'll leave. I'm sorry we caused any trouble. I apologize for the bother Barbara has become. I know how demanding she can be."

Sam shook his head. "Oh no, *I'm* sorry if I gave you the wrong idea. Barbara is the best thing to happen for Mary in some time, next to Comanche coming home. By golly, that daughter of yours has Mary hoppin' for sure." He rolled his hat through his fingers and offered a grin. "No, ma'am, I may never give your daughter back." Then he paused. "We had a little incident with Philip while you were gone. I'm not comfortable with putting you through this, but we can't avoid dealing with it."

Linda breathed a sigh. "I'm so sorry. Did he cause you more trouble?"

Sam leaned forward. "He tried to. When I think about it now … it's a little funny. A few nights ago, he tried to set fire to our barn."

Linda gasped. "Oh no! Sam! Is everything all right? Was anyone hurt?"

He smiled. He shouldn't have maybe, but he had to. "He had a run-in with Mary and Susan. And Barbara. His plans didn't quite go the way he figured. He's in the county jail now, waiting to talk with you."

"In jail?" Linda collapsed back against her chair.

Sam nodded then smiled again. "Yeah. The girls roughed him up some. He's all right now. Not happy, but all right."

"How long can they keep him? I mean, what happens next?"

"Well, I promised Barbara I'd take you to see him. Promised her I'd sit with you. If that makes you uncomfortable, I'll wait outside. But I must take you. This mess he got himself into is mighty important business."

Linda tightened her lips and looked away. "You know, I'm dead beat ... but let's get it over with. Can we go now? The sooner it's behind me, the sooner I can look for number four."

෨෴෨෴෨෴෨

Sheriff Bannon didn't seem annoyed in the least when Sam asked him to stay late so Linda could see her husband. In fact, he had fresh coffee steaming when they arrived.

"Howdy, Sam, Mrs. Cunningham." Sheriff Bannon held the door open for them.

"Evenin', Whip." Sam nodded to the sheriff and made the introductions.

Linda shook the sheriff's hand. "I feel a bit awkward. I've never met my husband in jail before."

He just smiled. "That's all right, ma'am. Have a seat at the table, and I'll bring him out."

Linda tensed when Philip strolled out a minute later and slid into a chair across from her at the table. A few nights behind bars didn't seem to have done him any harm. Or any good for that matter.

He jabbed the air with his thumb. "I've got nothing to say in front of Cowboy Joe here."

Linda cocked her head. "Still Mr. Tough-guy, aren't you, Philip?" She gave him a hard look. "I don't know what I *should* do, but I've had plenty of time to think us over on the ride in here tonight, so I'll tell you what I'm *going* to do." She wasn't sure where the courage was coming from, maybe all the nowhere-land oxygen in the mountains, but as long as she had it, she'd use it. "This is the happiest I've seen Barbara in a long time, and I'm not letting you mess that up. It's odd, isn't it? This whole trip was your idea. I'm beginning to feel like it worked out fine. I intend to find a lawyer right here in town, and I'm filing for divorce. Immediately! You're going home and moving out of the house, immediately. Don't leave me any surprises, Mr. Tough-guy, or Cowboy Joe here will press charges, and," she leaned into Philip's face and lowered her voice to a barely audible whisper, "I'll talk to the superintendent of schools."

Linda leaned back in her chair. She'd never seen Philip speechless before. Or so pale.

Chapter Twenty-Six

Comanche was as attentive as he'd ever been. Mary stayed focused on his transitions and not her joint pain. Last night had been a little rough, but this morning her hip and back seemed to loosen up as Comanche moved. She leaned forward and gave him a good scratching under his mane.

"Boy that was beautiful, Mrs. Holt." Barbara sat with Chester in the center of the corral, waiting for her turn.

"Thank you. You do know, I have a first name. It's Mary."

She blushed. "Yeah, but it doesn't feel right to call you Mary. Morgan calls you Mrs. Holt and Mr. Holt." She moved over to Mary and rode beside her around the corral at a slow walk. "I still remember the first time I heard him call you Mrs. Holt. Seems a lot longer than a month ago. I don't even feel like the same person. That's weird, isn't it?"

"I'll answer to Mrs. Holt as long as you like, and you're not the same person." She stopped Comanche. "Over the years, I've taught many young people to ride. There is no doubt in my mind you are one of my finest pupils. You're eager. Sometimes a little too eager, perhaps. And you are very good with the horses. A lot of people simply can't connect the way you do. I hope when you leave here, you don't leave horses."

"I don't like to think about leaving here. Mrs. Holt, what do you think my mom's gonna do?"

Tough question. Mary walked Comanche on. They started to circle the corral side-by-side again while she thought of an appropriate answer. "First, I'd say it looks like she's getting a divorce."

"Can't happen too soon for me. Now, if she'd only stay divorced. How long before she hunts down number four, do you think?"

"You want her to stay single the rest of her life?" Mary gave her a silly grin.

"Better that than the choices she makes. She's picked some real jerks, but Philip was the worst. I hate him."

Mary reached for the girl's leg and gave it a pat. "I know, and I'm truly sorry for whatever he's done to you. You've got to deal with it and look to the future. Things happen in life. Some things we can change, others we must deal with, accept. Sometimes it isn't fair, but we must always go on, move forward." She stared boldly into Barbara's eyes. "Right now, we're getting back to the business at hand."

She clucked to Comanche and started him with a slow trot, then moved into a beautiful, slow canter, and finished with some flying lead changes.

Barbara caught up to Mary, tossing her arms in the air. "How do you do that? Chester and I can't seem to get it right."

Mary stopped in the center of the corral. "They're a little tougher to master than flying around the barrels, but I have no doubt you'll do fine. We'll start working on them after the Fourth, but if you want that blue ribbon for barrels, we need to stay focused." She stepped off Comanche. "Morgan can do marvelous lead changes with Ruth, although he'd rather race and rope steers. He's got talent he doesn't often let show. Now, let's see if you and Chester can shave off a half-second."

"Okay, but then I want to watch you and Comanche again." Barbara stopped at the start line and pointed to Comanche. "You talk about *me* changing. I wouldn't even recognize him now if I hadn't seen him with my own eyes. He's beautiful!"

Mary hugged his neck. "Yes, he is beautiful." Comanche dropped his head, always ready for all the loving he could get.

Mary and Susan had set up the laser timer a few days earlier. When working with tenths of a second, as Mary had explained, the old-fashioned stop watch just couldn't get the job done. Now, Mary stood by Comanche and enjoyed Barbara's run without scrutinizing a stopwatch.

She looked at the laser timer an instant after Chester flew over the finish line and yelled, "Nineteen and three-tenths! We'll take it a half-second at a time. Great run! I can see another blue ribbon on Chester's stall already!" She held out her hands as if awarding Barbara a magnificent blue ribbon.

"That felt fast!" She leaped from the saddle and plopped herself down in the canvas lawn chair in front of the judge's booth. "Now, I want to watch you."

"Happy to oblige." Testing her legs with a gentle bounce, Mary led Comanche to the mounting block and swung up. "Come on, fella, I feel a little showing-off coming on."

She did a single lap in a slow trot. At the far end of the corral, she looked up at the rodeo arena, trying to pick Sam out from among all the people working up there. No chance. All the guests, Rusty and Morgan, too, had gone there right after breakfast to hang the last of the lights and speakers. The place was a beehive of activity. Also, the first of the many motor homes that would arrive in the next few days had pulled in before breakfast and obstructed some of her view.

Comanche fell into his comfortable canter exactly on cue. She let him enjoy the easy gait for half a lap, then cut diagonally across the corral and turned in the corner to reverse directions. She cut the far corner off, steered him through the center again, then rounded the next corner and went on to complete a figure eight. Mary chanced a look at Barbara, who was jumping and squealing and cheering them on.

Time for a little more flash. *Never mind the hip*! She cued for a lead change. He responded perfectly. Every other stride, as they crisscrossed between the barrels, she cued him for another lead change. Comanche never missed.

Now she'd test him. As they circled out from the corner and aimed for the center of the corral, she asked for flying lead changes with each stride. Mary could feel the excitement swell in his body. He shifted his weight effortlessly. That old feeling she'd nearly forgotten overwhelmed her. That feeling of dancing on air. This magnificent, once wild, once starved and neglected horse hadn't lost an ounce of spirit. He was a performer, and he knew it. And he loved it.

They danced by Barbara, who was jumping and clapping and screaming. Mary turned him in the corner, sent him down the center, and asked for a flat-out run. Comanche exploded. He stretched his neck, pinned his ears, and shot toward the center like a rocket. Even though it must have been years since Comanche had performed, Mary knew he knew what was coming. Mary could sense his excitement, his heart racing. She shifted her weight back the tiniest bit, their old signal for a high energy ending.

Comanche threw on the brakes. He squatted his hind end and skidded to a dusty stop. Mary knew he wasn't done. She could read his mind.

He was back in the show!

And so was she!

Her legs were weak and unsteady, but her will iron.

She backed him three steps, pulled both legs from the stirrups, grabbed the horn, and stood up in the saddle. Mary pursed her lips, kissed a cue. Comanche took two more steps backward. She turned to face Barbara, who was screaming so loud they must have heard her at the arena. Then she held her arms high and wide, sucked in a breath, and jumped to the ground.

She fell face down. Curse her legs!

Mary pushed herself up, waved Barbara away, turned back to Comanche, and touched her toe to his knee. As if they'd practiced yesterday, he bent his leg and bowed low. Mary stood tall, held her arms high, and waved, urging applause. Barbara jumped and cheered and clapped and cheered some more. Exhausted, Mary slid her back down along Comanche's leg and settled in the dirt.

Racing to her, Barbara fell to the ground beside her and rolled onto her back. "Holy crap! Holy crap! That was like—like magic. I mean, we watched the tapes and all, but holy crap that was freaking incredible! How do you do that? I wanna do that. I wanna do that right now. You know what? I think my freaking heart is gonna explode."

Mary leaned in and gave the girl her crooked smile. "Can I assume you would consider us in the running for a blue ribbon, too?"

Barbara bolted to her feet. "In the running? Crap! I mean, who could beat that? You have got to show my mom that! Don't you even need to practice? I mean, I've been with you every day since you started really riding Comanche again, and crap, you never did that before. Holy cow, you're *great*!"

Mary pulled herself up to her feet, wrapped her arms around Comanche's neck, and squeezed. "He's the great one." She buried her nose in his mane. "And we've been practicing on the sly."

"You have?"

"Oh, yes. I guess you never noticed on our morning rides to the stream, but I'd fool around. Partly because I wanted to test him, and partly because I couldn't resist, but this was our first full-blown rehearsal, and I agree with you. I think he did outstanding. Now we need to pick our music."

Chester wandered out to them. Barbara gathered his dragging reins. "I think you should do a little exhibition on the Fourth."

"I'm tempted, believe me, but he's only had five weeks to get his strength back. I'm pushing it as it is. I couldn't resist today, though." Only God knew if she had the time to wait.

At the barn, with the saddles removed and blankets hanging on the fence to dry, Mary sat in the shade, watching Barbara hose the two horses. "Have you ever heard of a group named ABBA?"

Barbara spun toward her. "Heck yes. It's my mother's favorite group. I kinda like them, but I'm a little young, since I wasn't born till, like, *way* after they had their last hit."

"Well, you know from the tapes that the last time Callie and I performed, we used Lee Greenwood's 'God Bless the USA.' I'm not sure I want to use that. We chose it because of Nine-Eleven."

"Mom likes country a lot now. She says modern pop music isn't any good. Most of the time I agree with her. Yeah, I like that song too, 'God Bless the USA.' You could sure do that again, and the fireworks your brother did. Awesome!"

Mary moved to Comanche and tugged gently on his mane, deep in thought. "My very first musical freestyle was to 'Dancing Queen.' " She smiled wide and pointed to the sky. "You should have seen the disco ball! Robert's fireworks set the sky on fire with the biggest yellow glittering ball. People still talk about it. He won't tell anyone how he did it. Sam loved that yellow ball."

Barbara threw the hose in the air. "You *are* the dancing queen! Dancing is what you two do!"

Mary gave Comanche a kiss. "Yes, he can certainly dance." She tossed her head back, let out a sigh and pointed to her chest. "But you know what? I was born to ride! My whole life has been riding, ranching, competing. You've heard the music I like to play in the barn. MaryAnn Kennedy's songs. How about her song, 'Born To Ride'?"

"Yes!" Barbara squealed. "I love that song! And you *were* born to ride. Nobody rides like you do. Nobody!"

"So, I take it you approve my song choice?"

"Approve? Heck yes, I approve!"

Mary cocked her head, 'Born To Ride' it is!"

ॐॐॐॐॐ

This was the first time in a few weeks Mary had used her cart. It felt odd, but she was tired, and to walk from her house to Linda's cabin would have been just plain dumb. She'd snuck out of bed after Sam tucked her in. Then he'd gone to the growing RV Campground surrounding the rodeo arena. When the trailers hauling the rodeo livestock pulled in, he'd barely been able to finish supper. He'd been so anxious to visit his buddies he saw once a year. Robert's pestering and encouragement hadn't helped matters. Of course, she'd been invited along, but she had other plans.

She stood on the dark cabin porch with her fist positioned to knock, braced herself, then knocked. The door swung in. "Mary, is something wrong?" Linda stepped back and waved her inside.

"Not wrong really. Well, sort of … I wanted to ask for your help with a personal matter."

"Why sure, come in. We can sit on the couch. Would you like something to drink?'

"No, I'm fine." She sat down and looked around the cabin. "Barbara?"

Linda cocked her head. "She's out with Morgan, checking out all the trucks and campers and cowboys. She didn't do anything wrong, did she? If she's taking too much of your time, I can …"

"Barbara? No, of course not. I love working with her. She's one of the most naturally gifted young people I've ever had the pleasure to work with, and I'm proud to know her." Mary shifted to look Linda in the eye. Okay, she ordered herself, just spit it out. "I wanted to ask you about Reiki."

"Oh ... Of course." She joined Mary on the couch. "What can I tell you?"

"This is difficult," she heard herself say, but was surprised at how matter-of-factly she could talk about it now. "I suppose it's obvious to everyone I'm a little under the weather. I have cancer ... again. I suppose it never went away, but this time I've refused treatment, and before you ask, I'll just say that I have my reasons." She tightened her lips. "I want to know if you can help with the pain."

"Why ... Never mind." Linda folded her hands and looked deeply into Mary's eyes. Then she pulled the little lavender pouch from her shirt pocket and opened it to retrieve the crystal. She rolled the purple crystal between the fingers of one hand while wiping the tears from her face with the other. "Many times Reiki can help. It also has remarkable healing abilities. I ... Mary, you should consider following your doctor's recommendations."

"Could we try?" Mary locked her eyes on Linda's and reached for her hand.

"Of course. Right now?"

Mary simply nodded.

Linda stood. "Can you lie on your back on this couch?" Mary fidgeted until she was stretched out comfortably. Grasping the silver chain, Linda held the pendulum over Mary's heart. It began to spin clockwise in increasingly wide circles. "You see the widening of the circle? That tells us your heart is very open." She broke into a big smile. "That, we already knew.

"I like to start with my pendulum, holding it over the chakras. Chakras are located at different areas in our bodies and represent different things. From your head to the soles of your feet, Reiki works with the universal life-energy. That energy flows through us all, through everything in the universe. Our chakras are sort of like portals. They allow the energy to flow in and pass through and go out again." As she spoke, she moved from place to place, holding the pendulum above Mary's body, watching its pattern of movement. "When we experience sickness, pain, or even stress, the chakras can become blocked. This prevents the life-energy from flowing freely through our bodies. We become, well, out of whack."

Out of whack, Mary agreed silently. *That's how she felt. Definitely, out of whack.*

Linda laid the pendulum on the table behind her, gently placed her hands on Mary's belly, and stood quietly. "My hands act as collectors ... directors, if you will. They guide the energy to you, through me. This will open your blockage, allow healing, and allow you to use the universal life-energy to wash the pain from your body. I like to picture it as a stream of clear water flowing through me, carrying all the sickness and pain away with it."

For the next half hour, Linda placed her hands delicately on different parts of Mary's body.

Finally, she paused with her hands cupping Mary's head. "Where do you feel the most pain?"

"Right now I feel sleepy, maybe a little dizzy."

"That often happens. Try to take a deep, comfortable breath, and as you breathe it in, imagine it traveling through your body and softening where you hurt, carrying the pain out with it. Think about it entering as you breathe and flowing like a cleansing stream of water. Picture it leaving and taking your pain away with it."

Mary inhaled several long, easy, comfortable breaths, allowing each one to leave slowly, quietly. She could almost imagine each molecule of air carrying dirty contaminated pain away with it. "Linda, this really works. I feel lighter. Still dizzy but, I don't know, peaceful somehow."

"Do your hips feel any better?"

How had she known about her hips? "I think they do. This is so strange. I feel like … like I can do this." Mary opened her eyes and gazed up at Linda. "Do you think I can do this?"

Linda slipped her hands from under Mary's head. "I'm sure you can. I get the feeling that you're very intuitive and self-aware." She dragged a chair from the table and sat down at the head of the couch. "I can help you as often as you like, and you can do this on your own, too, in between sessions. Take your thoughts to the place where you feel safest and happiest. Think about the energy flowing through you. Inhale a breath, direct it to the pain, and imagine it flowing away."

"This feeling is remarkable. It happened so quickly. I'm amazed. You should bottle this stuff."

"Universal energy probably doesn't like bottles." Linda laughed softly, then turned serious. "Mary, Reiki is a wonderful thing, and I wouldn't want to minimize its possibilities, but if your pain … well, you can take pharmaceutical medications and use your Reiki, too. Okay?"

"I understand what you're saying. And I …"

A knock on the door interrupted her thought. Linda shot a look of surprise at Mary, opened the door a crack, glanced back at Mary and swung the door wide. "Sam, what a pleasant surprise. Come in."

He stepped through the door, pulled off his hat, and turned to Mary. "I saw your cart. Is everything okay?"

Stifling a sigh of exasperation, Mary signaled for him to sit with her. "Of course, it is." What should she tell him? An hour ago, she'd been tucked in bed with a good book. She'd turned down his invitation to visit their friends. Yet she'd thrown off the covers to drive her cart helter-skelter around the camp in the dark. There was an explanation. Just not one she wanted to share.

He sat beside her and gathered her hands in his. "Doggone, Mary, when I saw your cart … I don't know what to say."

What should she tell him? She hardly wanted to admit to the worsening pain, much less to the fact that she was seeking unconventional ways to deal with it. "I'm fine. Really. I woke up and was restless and thought I could catch Barbara here, but she's off with Morgan inspecting horses, campers, and trucks." She watched the relief put normal color back in his face, and it pleased her. She hated that lying to the most honest man in the world was becoming so easy for her. She hated worrying him more. There would undoubtedly come a time when even her lies couldn't protect him. *For now, she'd lie.*

He smiled. "She's sure enough draggin' him this way and that, talking to just about every cowboy up there." He shook his head. "Ol' Morgan isn't sure if he should protect her or run for his life."

Linda laughed. "Well, Barbara's a very determined girl."

"Yeah, that's sure enough what I'd call her. *Determined.*" Sam gave Mary an ear-to-ear grin. "I've been keeping my eyes on you two practicin'. And how about Chester? He thinks he's five years old again."

Before Mary could do more than nod her head in agreement, Barbara barged through the door, dragging Morgan by the arm. "Mom, Mom!" She stopped suddenly at the sight of company. "Oh! Hi, Mr. Holt. Hi, Mrs. Holt. Anyway, guess what?"

Linda, feigning breathlessness. "What should I guess?"

"Morgan picked the most awesome song for my musical routine. Oh yeah, by the way, I decided to compete at the state fair in the freestyle musical routine. I'll still run barrels on the Fourth, but at the state fair, I'm doing both. Anyway, guess which song." She shoved Morgan into the remaining chair at the small table.

Linda shook her head smiling and leaned against the wall. "Your musical routine?"

Barbara pointed to Mary. "Oh my God, Mom! You should have seen her today. It was freaking spectacular. Oh my God, I want to do that! You know, it's when you ride a routine to a song blaring over loud speakers. I was talking about it with Morgan tonight, and I have my song. Now, don't go all crazy on me or anything. We played it at least ten times on his truck's CD player to make sure, and my God, Mom, it's perfect. Are you ready?"

"Should I sit down?" She shot an exaggerated look of pretend worry to Mary and Sam. Morgan covered his face with his hat.

"No, I think you'll love it. How about ..." She paused for effect, " 'Independence Day'! You know, Martina McBride's big hit. Awesome, right?"

"I think I'll sit now." Linda slid down along the wall and sat cross-legged on the floor.

"Good choice, huh?" Barbara ran to her and dropped to her knees. "You can have the announcer dedicate the routine to somebody and all. I'm gonna have him dedicate it to you, because, you know, you're like, independent now." She plopped onto her mother's lap and pointed toward the couch. "Of course, Mrs. Holt will win the blue ribbon. Nobody can top her and Comanche. No freaking way. But I'll win second. That's red, for you."

Chapter Twenty-Seven

Everything was under control, so it was easy to enjoy an early morning stroll behind the pens, weaving around campers, trucks, and trailers. Just walking along holding her cowboy's hand. The smell of the animals, the clanging of gates, the excited banter of contestants and friends made her remember. "Sam, late notice aside, and forgiving the irrationality of it all ..." Mary pinched his cheek. "Do you think they might have a bull here gentle enough for you to ride?"

He raised his eyebrows and cocked his head. "So you're thinkin' I've reached the time of my career that I need a gentle bull?"

"Well, you haven't ridden one in four years." She flashed her crooked smile. "You don't need to draw one like Midnight Special again."

Sam rubbed his arm and grimaced. "Reckon I'd like to forget ol' Midnight." He grinned. "By golly, Mary, if you don't always know what I'm up to. I already kicked it around some with Smiley. He says his outfit brought in a bull who might just fill the ticket. What do ya say we take a look at a bull named Cherry Picker?"

Her face brightened. "Cherry Picker?" Her voice was laced with giggles.

He shrugged. "That's what they call 'im. Supposedly, he has a regular right hand spin you can count on. Doesn't hit the air till you're ten feet away from the chute."

"Sounds safe enough. Yeah, Cowboy, let's go have a look."

"Mrs. Holt!" Barbara ran up behind them. "Oh, hi, Mr. Holt. Anyway, they just announced they're about to play the National Anthem. I'm gonna ride Chester in the opening parade. I look all right, don't I? Susan finished my vest. I like silver, too." She spun in a circle, her arms wide.

"You look wonderful!" As if putting the final touch on a piece of art, Mary adjusted Barbara's hat. "Absolutely beautiful! Now, don't be nervous. Chester has done it before, and even though it's been awhile, he'll remember."

"Oh, I'm not nervous." Barbara turned to point a finger at Sam. "But you'd better be nervous, because I've been practicing with Cactus to win the two-mile race tonight. Me and Morgan ran the course last night. Man, Ruth's fast. But so is Cactus! I think I can beat him! Well, I gotta go get ready. See ya!"

All they could do was smile when Barbara turned and ran. They watched her dart between people, trucks, and animals, and then Sam told Mary, in a voice so laden with chuckles she was sure she hadn't heard all he said, "I reckon I'd better not let ol' Cherry Picker bust me up too bad. Sounds like I got a tough race ahead of me."

She looked up into his warm eyes, which made plain his amusement with the girl's enthusiasm. "I reckon you do." She took his hand and led the way to the cattle pens with a cheery spring in her step.

They walked around the bullpens and found Cherry Picker, a good-sized Angus-cross, picking at a pile of hay in the corner of his pen. "He's a big one." Mary squeezed Sam's hand. "Maybe we should find a smaller bull." She gave Sam a halfhearted smile and a look that showed her worry. Not genuine worry, but just a hint, to let him know she could let him off the hook. If she should.

"Them small ones tend to be a whole lot faster and meaner." He shook his head. "We'll see what ol' Cherry Picker's got. Gotta give my favorite gal a good show, after all."

"Ladies and gentleman, please rise for our National Anthem."

Mary recognized Fred Jones's voice over the loud speakers. As had become the tradition over the years, Fred was in the booth to add some sanity to Smiley Hudson's crazy way of calling the day's events. A long-time friend of Sam's from his early rodeo days, Smiley had built quite a name for himself, both as a quality livestock supplier and talented, though slightly zany, announcer. Smiley never missed a rodeo at Mar-Sa and had been instrumental in the event's growth, starting with the very first year Rusty had recruited him to surprise Sam.

She wrapped her arm around Sam's waist and steered him to a hole in the wall of people and animals so they could watch the opening ceremony. They'd already been walking for a while, and her hip and back were beginning to bother her, so she shifted her weight to lean tight against him. She'd just hang on a little heavier and lean against her cowboy, pretend she was only snuggling up to him, take the pressure off that hip. Maybe he wouldn't notice.

The look he gave her, when he removed his hat, told her he knew.

How much did he know? She looked around at all the people standing with their hands over their hearts, their hats in their hands. Across the arena, from where they stood, the one section of bleachers they'd constructed over the years held close to two hundred people. She had to confess she was a little jealous of them. She knew this would be her last rodeo here with her friends. Her eyes burned at the thought. *Her last rodeo* ... She looked up at Sam.

The explosions of fireworks saved her. Even in the early morning sunshine, dazzling streaks of smoke and spinning displays of shooting silver colored the sky. Her eyes bounced from Sam to the fireworks, to the contestants riding in formation around the arena. She smiled when she saw Barbara riding Chester. Of course, that girl had found a way to place herself ahead of Morgan and Ruth.

"Your brother sure knows how to light up the sky, even in the daylight." Sam pushed a hand through his hair and re-sat his hat.

Mary tilted her head. "Best fireworks guy in the country." She gave his hand a tug. "I suppose I should get ready to ride. Ladies' barrels are up first."

"Let's find a seat for a while and watch Barbara run barrels." Without waiting for an answer, he led the way though the pens, gates, trucks, and people, politely, if hurriedly, acknowledging friends along the way. Two rows up on the bleachers, directly under the announcer's booth, they found a good spot next to Linda, Debby, and Zack.

As they settled onto the bench, Smiley's voice rang out clear and sharp over the new speakers. "First up, a young lady new to the sport, but I understand from Morgan Jones that she's not to be taken lightly. Ladies and gentlemen, please give a big rodeo welcome to Miss Barbara Sherman riding Chester."

Mary jumped up and started the applause. "Good luck, Barbara!"

Chester stood ready, waiting for his cue to run, fifty feet behind the starting line. Mary, who could see that Barbara was as cool as ever, saw the girl give the cue. Chester charged, raced for the right barrel, took it clean and tight. In the background, Mary could hear Smiley complimenting Barbara as they rounded the second barrel and flew to the third.

"What a remarkable ride for this first-time contestant." Smiley's voice rose with excitement. "She's setting a tough pace for the day ... clean turn on barrel three! Now take her home, folks. Let her hear you!"

The crowd jumped to its feet, clapping, yelling, and waving hats. Chester raced, neck stretched, over the finish line. Barbara turned him easily and trotted around to face the announcer's booth.

Smiley's voice boomed, "Seventeen and one-tenth seconds! What a ride for a young lady who is sure to be making a name for herself here today."

Mary started down the bleachers and pushed her way through the crowd, Linda close behind. Susan intercepted them.

"She looked like a real professional," Linda squealed with excitement. She grabbed Mary, pulling her into a hug. "I could never thank you enough for what you've done for my daughter."

"Oh, Linda, she's done plenty for me, too. She keeps me going in ways I'm not certain I'd be able to do on my own." Mary shot a look to Susan. "She's a high-energy girl, and I love her."

Barbara ran to them, dragging Chester. "Mom! Did you hear my time? Seventeen and one-tenth." She handed the reins to Mary, lunged forward, and smothered her in a bear-hug. "You're the most *awesomest* teacher in the world!"

Sam held out his hand to Barbara. "That was a humdinger of a ride, young lady. I'm proud to know you." He shook her hand, then turned to Mary. "You're just one away, beautiful." Mary sucked in a breath, accepted Chester's reins from Barbara and winked at Sam. "Oh yes. Help me adjust the stirrups. This young hotshot here has longer legs than I do."

As she started lengthening the off-side stirrup, Barbara giggled out loud. "Gonna have a better time, too."

When she finished adjusting the stirrup on her side, Mary looked across the saddle at Barbara. "How about a leg up, *giggles*?" Mary smiled at Sam but waited for Barbara to boost her. Then she turned Chester toward him and leaned down for a good-luck kiss.

At the gate, well behind the starting line, she focused on taking long, deep breaths and sending them to her right hip and lower back. She jiggled her right foot to loosen the hip. Chester turned his head, questioningly, but stood firm, waiting for his cue to run.

Smiley boomed over the loud speakers, "Up next, folks, we have another surprise. Also riding that fine sorrel, Chester, our hostess, and many-times state champion ... Mary Holt." Over the shouting and applause he yelled, "Great to see you in the saddle again, Mary. When you're ready, the barrels are yours."

Fireworks exploded again. The cheering went insane. Mary sat a second and watched the display of colors. *Doggone you, Sam.* She found him standing on the bleachers, yelling and waving his hat. She blew him a kiss. He sent one back.

She backed Chester behind the line again, settled her seat, and grabbed the horn with her left hand. "Ready, Chester? You need to help me today, like we practiced." She patted his neck. And sent him.

Chester shot over the line like a cannonball. He circled the right barrel wide, just like they'd practiced, so Mary could keep some of the thrust off her bad hip. Vaguely she heard Smiley yell they'd made a big pocket, but stayed on course. Chester stretched out, circled the second barrel so close, she could feel it. She felt the stab in her hip, too, but turned for the last barrel. As he accelerated around the final barrel, Mary lost her balance. She grabbed for the horn with her free hand and dropped her reins. She didn't have the strength in her legs to kick for speed as they raced for home, but Chester knew what to do. He needed no encouragement from Mary as he took control and hit his top gear. The crowd roared so loud Mary barely heard Smiley shout, "Eighteen and two-tenths—our third-fastest time of the day. What a comeback!"

The crowd continued to holler and cheer as Mary rode out the gate, waving her hat toward the bleachers. Sam, Barbara, Linda, and Susan found her and surrounded Chester.

"That was one heck of a run!" Sam took hold of Chester's bridle and rubbed Mary's thigh.

"Sure was, Mrs. Holt. I thought you were gonna beat me. I guess you would've if you hadn't gone wide on the first barrel." Barbara stroked the sweaty horse's neck. "He's something, isn't he?"

Mary nodded. "He certainly is." She kissed his cheek.

Through the speakers, they heard Smiley announce, "That's all for ladies' barrels. Official times are: first place, Rachel Madison on Quicksilver, sixteen and nine-tenths. Second place, Barbara Sherman riding Chester, seventeen and one-tenth. And running third, Mary Holt, also riding Chester, eighteen and two-tenths Our fourth place rider, Norma-Jean Anderson riding Star, nineteen seconds flat. And fifth, Jessie Cassidy on Knight, with a great time, nineteen and three-tenths seconds. Ladies, please come to the center of the arena for your ribbons and hold on while we take a few pictures."

At Mary's gesture, Barbara hopped up behind her, and they rode into the ring together. Susan ran out to snap a picture as they accepted the red and green ribbons and rode a lap around the arena to wild cheers and applause. Mary heard Barbara giggling and talking in her ear, but her mind was years away. She reached forward and patted Chester's neck, told him what a good boy he was, and watched a tear splash on the saddle horn.

Calf roping was up next, and Barbara wanted to stay and root for Morgan. Sam had a dozen or more friends to say howdy to, but Mary wanted to rest before Sam tackled Cherry Picker, so she headed for the barn on Chester. On the way, she stopped at the lodge to brag a little to Paul and Lucy, who had signed up to help Susan run the kitchen all day and night selling hot dogs, beans, and burgers as fast as they could cook them.

At the barn, she hung the saddle blanket on the fence and enjoyed her time hosing and rubbing Chester down. "What a day so far, Chester. You've made a young girl prouder than she's ever been, and you've given me quite a thrill, too. You still have what it takes, my friend. That's a certainty." She led him to the pasture, turned him loose with Comanche, and sat on the ground to watch him roll in the dirt. She wondered if she'd ever run barrels again. It gave her a weird feeling to think she may have just made her final run. Just for a moment she wished it could have been on Comanche ... But boy, hadn't Chester done himself proud?

She had intended to go to the house and lie on the couch to do a little Reiki, but she found herself so comfortable on the sun-warmed ground that she rolled over on her back, put her hand on her hip socket and focused on her breathing. The sun began to get a little warm, but she was so comfortable she decided not to move. A little sweat was always good, anyway. She opened one eye to check on her horses. Chester had had enough rolling and was stretched out on his side in the shade. Comanche, however, noticed her looking at him, trotted over, and dropped his head to frisk her with his nose.

Mary laughed. "Got no apples on me this time, Comanche my friend." She sat up and hugged his neck. "We have one show left in us, too, don't we, fella?" She gave a soft cluck and held on as Comanche raised his head and pulled her to her feet.

It was easy to keep track of the goings-on at the rodeo arena. Smiley's voice bounced off the barn and house without losing a single decibel. She shook her head in sympathy when she heard Smiley announce Morgan's miss in calf roping. "Barbara's sure gonna be hard on him. For his sake, I hope he does better at bronc riding." Comanche's expression gave her no clue as to whether he cared or not.

When Smiley called for the bull riders to start getting ready, Mary decided to make her way back to the arena. She mounted her cart and swung by the lodge for a burger on her way. She hadn't eaten since breakfast, and that had only been half a bowl of oatmeal. As Sam would say, "Them oats was long gone."

She thought about the first summer she and Sam had rodeoed together, before he'd gone to Vietnam. It didn't seem all that long ago. She'd always hung on the fence to watch him ride then. And hip or no bothersome hip, she was going to hang on the fence today. Maneuvering her cart through the people, horses, and trucks proved easier than politely excusing herself from the impromptu congratulatory conversations that sprang up along the way. Finally, she parked against the fence just to the left of the chutes, where Sam would know to look.

"Folks, today we're sure plumb full of surprises," Smiley announced. "You all keep your eyes on chute number three, where Sam Holt and a frisky bull we call Cherry Picker are fixin' to give us a show. Now, folks, I got nothin' ta say about ol' Sam's age, and I'm sure he cleared this harebrained idea about comin' out of retirement with Mary ... but what Cherry Picker is about to talk about ... well that, I reckon, is up to the bull."

Sam stood on the rails above the chute and searched the crowd to his left. Once he found Mary's crooked smile, he gave her a wink and a grin, then slid down on Cherry Picker.

"What's that?" Smiley asked the clown who was rolling a tire-padded barrel into the arena in front of chute number three. "You say Sam didn't want to do it, but Mary made him?"

The clown waved his hands in the air then smacked his own backside.

"Mary told you she's gonna wup 'im if he don't win?"

The crowd hooted and hollered. Smiley broke in over the loudspeakers, "You say you reckon ol' Sam's gonna get a wuppin' no matter what?"

The clown jumped on the barrel and nodded his head. "If the bull don't get 'im, Mrs. Holt will?" Smiley asked. The clown jumped off the barrel, tossed his arms in the air, then walked in a circle, kicking the dirt, shaking his head, and waving his hat.

"You say that you'd rather take your chances with the bull, too?"

The crowd roared with laughter. Smiley broke in. "All right, boys, turn Cherry Picker loose."

Mary sucked in a breath when the gate swung open. Cherry Picker jumped out and, as Sam had predicted, spun to the right and worked his way away from the chute, spinning in fast, clockwise circles. Sam had never looked better, with his right arm waving high for balance, left hand on the rope, and legs pounding the spinning bull's sides. Cherry Picker started to buck, then dropped his head and suddenly spun to the left. Sam slipped to the side, almost fell off, but the bull suddenly spun to the right and bucked higher. Then he kicked out and spun to the left again. Sam went flying to the dust.

The buzzer sounded a half-second later.

"That had the makings of a great ride, but a half-second short," Smiley announced. "Let's pay Sam off with a hand, folks. Not a bad ride, old friend. Not a bad ride at all."

The crowd jumped to its feet and sent up a roar. Sam found his hat, swiped it over his dusty pants, and headed for Mary.

"I was sure you were going to make it to the buzzer." She helped him over the top rail.

"Close, but that last direction change got me. Not bad for being so far out of practice, though." He gave her his most flirtatious smile. "Gonna wup up on me?"

"Soon as we get back to the house, Cowboy." Laughing, she flexed her muscles, then kissed his cheek. "Don't forget you have a race to win, and I know two hard-riding kids after that trophy."

"I reckon I ain't so busted up that I can't outrun a coupla hotshot kids."

They strolled among the commotion that is a rodeo, chatted with long-time friends, said howdy to some new ones, and then found a comfortable spot in the shade away from most of the activity to watch the youth calf-roping. Sam spread a blanket, and Mary fell asleep with her head nestled in his lap.

Too soon, Barbara ran up to them, out of breath. "They're going to start the race in fifteen minutes. I'm gonna race Cactus. Morgan's already warming up on Ruth." She started for the barn, then yelled back over her shoulder, "Better get with it, Mr. Holt."

Mary opened one eye and smiled. "Well, Mr. Holt, I suppose you'd better do as your young challenger advises."

He stroked her hair, then touched his finger to her lips. "Reckon I'd rather stay put and snuggle my gal. I've run plenty of races in my day."

"I could cuddle here all day myself, but we'd have a very disappointed young girl on our hands ... What a delightful young lady she's turning out to be. Keeps me stepping to stay ahead of her."

Sam pulled her tight, "I love you, Mary. You've always been my special gift from God. You make my life ..."

She put her lips to his ear. "I guess God knew what I needed, too."

Morgan stopped Ruth next to them, holding the reins of a saddled Bullet. "Figured you'd need an hour to rest up after your run-in with Cherry Picker. So I saddled your horse. Dad's gonna start the race in about ten minutes." He tossed Bullet's reins to Sam, kicked Ruth into a run, and sped away.

Sam caught the reins, then turned back to Mary and hummed a few bars from a song in their favorite movie, *Casablanca*.

They held on tight to each other, rocking gently until Fred Jones announced, "Ladies and gentlemen, our annual, *Run for the Cactus Thorns*, is about to begin. Riders up."

Mary pushed Sam gently away. "I'll be watching for a ...wild finish."

One more kiss, then Sam swung up on Bullet, tipped his hat, and trotted away.

She could see the entire course from her blanket. Or at least the finish line. So she settled down on the blanket and watched the riders trotting their horses to warm up. She couldn't help but hum that silly song over and over. It was a good song to reminisce to, though, "As Time Goes By." Her mind drifted, playing in black and white, memories of the years she and Sam had loved together. She hardly noticed Fred calling the race.

Chapter Twenty-Eight

After the activity of the past few days, Mary had decided to spend the morning alone on the porch with her violets. She'd been neglecting them too much lately, but that was the wonderful thing about violets, they didn't hold it against you. As long as you didn't let them die, they'd bloom and bloom and bloom. She supposed that was why they were her favorites. Not many plants bloomed like violets. Even the poor, uncared-for one she'd brought home from the hospital was full of buds now. It would be bursting with flowers in another day or two. Deep blue flowers, from the look of its buds.

Done with her watering and pruning, she settled down on the swing to watch the RVs, pick-ups, and livestock trailers drive down the ranch road. Almost every driver tooted the horn as they drove by the house. The line of vehicles extended from the arena to the hard-top road a mile and a quarter away.

Comanche paced the yard's fence line as if he wanted to chase the trucks. She studied him as he pawed the dirt. She couldn't see his ribs or backbone anymore. His black and white coat glistened in the midmorning sun. Mary knew he needed more time and attention to be back in full condition, but the recovery he'd made so far was truly amazing. She planned on allowing him a few more weeks of light duty work, and by then, she was certain he'd be ready to practice a full schedule. They had a very important ribbon to win, after all.

Susan weaved the Gator in and around the departing vehicles and parked in front of the porch. "Good morning. I brought you an egg sandwich." She ran up the steps and wiggled into the swing beside Mary. "It always seems so strange right after they leave, doesn't it?"

Mary took a bite of her sandwich and nodded. "This was quite a year. Smiley told Sam we had one hundred eleven contestants altogether. I was tempted to give in to Barbara and put on a bit of a show with Comanche."

"I wish you had. That was quite a show you *did* put on with Chester. I thought you looked spectacular." She paused to offer a tender smile. "I think you've done a wonderful thing for Barbara, too."

"Poor girl. It's far too obvious she's had plenty of rough patches in her life. With her stepfather gone, I hope she can relax and be a kid. Enjoy herself. Somehow ..." She took another bite of her sandwich as she searched for the right words. "I feel a definite connection with her. I don't know if I'm being silly ... you know, with the cancer, Comanche, and Callie. I feel as if I've known her a lot longer than a few weeks. I feel as if she's reaching out to me, looking for ... I know what she's looking for." Mary tightened her lips. "She's looking for solid footing."

"I've seen a remarkable change in her already. We all have. Not that she was so terrible or anything, but she sure has brightened. She's enthusiastic about the horses. She's determined to compete at the state fair. She's been talking all about it with her mother, Morgan, me, and anybody she can pin down."

Mary smiled. "After the race last night, she announced she's through with barrels and wants to learn her musical routine. I was able to hold her off until yesterday, but she'll be relentless now." She rubbed her hip. "The fair's only six weeks away, you know. There's a lot for her to learn in a few weeks' time."

Susan shook her head. "She won't be satisfied with the same results as yesterday. Finishing tenth in the race wasn't in her plans at all. If anyone in the world can have her ready, it's you."

"I just hope I can keep up with her. I doubt her enthusiasm will be a problem." She gave a soft giggle. "Speaking of enthusiasm, Morgan's pretty tickled with his win. Sam's pretending to be all torn up about coming in second."

"Poor guy. I'm sure he was happy for Morgan, though." She dragged her hands back and forth over her thighs. "The Keatons are heading for home today."

Mary nodded. "Sam told me this morning. Paul has some important committee meeting. He said Paul tried to talk Lucy into waiting here, said he'd be back in two weeks, but she wanted to go home, too."

"She'd had an affair with Philip Cunningham, you know. Even before the trouble started here, that guy gave me the creeps. He's a good-looking guy all right, but creepy. Wonder what someone like Lucy Keaton would see in a guy like that?" Susan arched a brow as she suddenly wondered out loud, "You don't think she's going to ..."

"I hope we never find out." Mary's voice was flat.

Susan turned to look toward the lodge. "I should get back up there. Sam gave everybody the day off to recover, and they're straggling in for breakfast and coffee. Linda has things under control, but I shouldn't abandon her for too long. Are you going to come up later?"

"My plans are to finish my coffee, then take Comanche to the barn and braid his mane."

"Well, maybe I'll check in with you later." Susan kissed Mary's cheek and bounced down the steps. Before hopping into the Gator, she turned back. "You take care of yourself. You've been overdoing it lately."

Mary sipped her coffee and watched Susan weave her way to the lodge. Got a lot to do in whatever time's left, she thought.

The line of departing vehicles was beginning to thin to a trickle now. Up at the arena only Smiley and his crew remained. She laughed quietly to herself when she thought of Sam and Smiley sitting on a tailgate retelling old stories, bragging bigger and bigger with each telling. No doubt Morgan had barely had a chance to brag on his accomplishment of the day before. She wondered how many times he'd described the finish to Barbara, and how many times she'd told him to shut up.

Tilting her head back, she closed her eyes, picturing the fireworks display her brother had created yesterday. He was an absolute magician. She clapped her hands together, sat upright, and said out loud, "Robert, for my freestyle routine, I want a disco ball again. Bigger and brighter than anyone has ever seen!"

She tied Comanche to the cart and drove to the barn. She maneuvered straight into the aisle and stopped in the center, where the shade and the constant breeze flowing down the aisle allowed her to work on his mane in relative comfort. Not that his mane needed work. Several-times-a- day brushings for the past few weeks had made it tangle-free and shiny with natural oils. But she really wanted to braid it and play with it. Maybe put ribbons in the braids. Yeah, today she was playing dress up. Or rather Comanche was.

She started combing his mane and looked over his neck at the two new ribbons hanging on the stall walls. They stood out all bright and fresh compared to the faded ones she and Barbara had re-hung a few weeks ago. Sam had already framed the two new pictures of her and Barbara. They flanked the gold frame that held a smiling Callie sitting tall on Comanche. Callie proudly showing off her blue ribbon, won that day, not so long ago. But too long ago.

Looking at that picture and holding a handful of mane didn't make her as sad as it had in the past. Made her remember, for sure. She realized she felt more pride than sorrow. Some folks would probably call that progress. She was still a little mad, though. At herself. She shouldn't have kept those memories locked away in a trunk for so long.

Memories ... That's what this summer was for her. A special time to make super-special memories for her long- legged cowboy. Memories of his favorite gal rehabbing a special horse, winning ribbons, and helping a young to girl get excited about life. She tied a ribbon on the end of Comanche's braid and smiled. Of course there was another batch of special memories, too. The kind that only lovers could make. The kind that could wash away any sad with a big bucket of happy.

Chapter Twenty-Nine

B arbara had mastered alternate stride lead changes with the grace of a pro. She responded to instruction as well as any student Mary'd ever taught. No longer interested in anything else, she hung around every day while Mary practiced with Comanche.

They'd been working with Chester for more than a week now. Every day they played the songs for their routines over the loud speakers. Every evening Mary fine-tuned the choreography. Every night Barbara slept on the couch in the Holt's house, since she could hardly tear herself away from Mary.

Sam would sit with Mary in the judge's booth, or make himself look busy fussing with horses in the big corral. He'd always be close enough to see Mary, whether he was trimming hooves or working with one of the three-year-olds they'd trailed home from the wild horse range.

Rusty and Morgan had set out two days ago, taking the guests on a week-long trail ride to explore parts of the mountains that couldn't be traveled any way but on foot or horseback. Robert decided to stay the summer and wait for the state fair, since he'd been informed of Mary's crazy scheme to explode another disco ball over the arena for her routine. He'd gone along on the trail ride because, as he'd explained, "no man could ever get his fill of those mountain views!" Before they'd started on their way, he'd told Mary he had his part of the show pretty near figured out and had even ordered the supplies. They knew Sam would be tickled. He loved that yellow ball.

Barbara finished going through her number, without music, and trotted to the judge's booth where Mary sat on Sam's lap. She jumped from Chester, sat on the floor next to them, and asked Mary for her tablet. She studied the page with Mary's diagrams of her and Comanche's routine, then pointed to Comanche, who watched their every move while impatiently pacing the fence line in the yard. "He looks ready, Mrs. Holt. If I beg, will you go through your entire number? You can go slow if you want, but come on, do it ... Pleeeease."

Mary leaned back, put her hands on her knees and smiled. "You tempt me, I'll give you that."

Sam slipped a sly grin to Barbara. "Hey, I'll start the music."

"Come on, Mrs. Holt. You already said Chester's had enough practice for today, and it's only ten. It's not even all that hot yet."

She knew she wanted to. She knew Comanche was up to it, but she hadn't felt all that great this morning. A little more stiffness and a lot more queasy. Barbara sure could turn on those begging eyes of hers, though. And Sam ... he looked worried. Maybe she could settle her own stomach, placate Barbara and erase Sam's worry all at the same time. One good show would do the trick.

"We don't have fireworks. How can I perform without Robert's disco ball?"

Barbara squealed. "That means you'll do it, right?"

She tilted her head. "For my cowboy and my prize student, I'll do it."

"Awesome! You rock, Mrs. Holt! Want me to help you saddle Comanche?"

"I think I'd like to do it alone. Show-prep, you understand, and you still have a horse to cool down." She turned to Sam. "Stick in the CD. Let it play all the songs, full volume. It'll pump me up." She used his arm to pull herself up, then tossed a wink. "Back in a flash, groupies."

She drove the cart to the house, as had become her habit over the past week. Riding wasn't too bad, but walking sure riled her bad hip, and lately, the hurt ran down her leg, too. As soon as she pulled up to the house, Comanche snorted and ran to the gate. He always could read her mind. She started to slip on his halter then had a thought.

They wanted a full show?

They'd get a full show.

She snuck inside the house and stuffed her new costume under her blouse.

By the time Mary had tied Comanche to the cart and started for the barn, the entire homestead pulsated to the rhythm of booming music. Vibrations swam through the air, bounced off walls and fired souls of all living matter. Mary felt she rode the music's energy with a power she'd not felt in days.

She set Comanche's saddle on his back, her foot tapping to the beat, and wished Callie could ride with her today. She looked out the barn doors and up the long hill behind the house. "You be sure and watch this." Mary turned to Callie's picture. "I put in a few of your moves."

Comanche looked like the star he was, all tacked in his show saddle with his fancy, silver-studded breast collar, lavishly jeweled bridle, and showy stirrups. Sam had worked tirelessly, softening leather and shining silver. The entire rig looked better than new. Including the spotted champion wearing it.

She left him tied to the cart and went to the tack room to slip into her costume. Susan was an excellent seamstress, and it fit perfectly. Red blouse and slacks, silver fringe on the arms and legs, and the newly finished silver vest. Mary admired herself in the full-length mirror, shot a glance to Callie's picture, and then positioned her red sequined hat to the exact tilt Callie preferred. When she stepped out from behind the door and into the aisle, Comanche nickered.

Using the cart as her mounting block, Mary settled into the saddle and marched him through the barn doors with all the swagger of a returning hero.

Today would be the first time she'd ask Comanche to go through the entire routine. She sat at the open gate, nodded to Sam, and laughed at Barbara, who was already jumping and screaming.

The first guitar notes of "Born To Ride" flooded the air.

Comanche knew the opening sequence flat. He bolted into the ring without the slightest hesitation. Mary dropped the reins and stood in the stirrups, her arms held high and wide. She rode one grand lap around the ring in a fast lope, standing tall and holding her hat above her head. She slowed Comanche as the lyrics began and listened for her cues. *"Visions of galloping in my head."* They cut across the ring's center in an easy lope.

"I knew that I was born to ride." She cued Comanche to slow for alternate lead changes. They moved along the rail, skipping beautifully.

"Like a bird was born to fly." Change direction, increase speed. Smooth figure eights, side passing and dancing all the way.

"Love me love my horse." Increase to a gallop, dash across the ring, turn into a figure eight and slower now, *"The world looks better from the back of a horse."* Flying lead changes with each stride. Comanche was perfect, on cue and light as air. Mary's leg pounded, but she almost giggled when she imagined it pounding to the song's beat.

The tempo picked up, *"That's the way I'm gonna spend my life ... Cause I was born to ride."* Mary cued for a spin to the right, then a second's pause, and then a flat-out gallop, shifting for a sliding stop. Followed instantly with a faster spin to the left. Her leg gave out under the force of the tremendous whirlwind spin, but she grabbed the horn and signaled Comanche to run. He delivered another fantastic, dust-kicking slide.

Comanche stood tall at the finish of the slide. " *'Cause I was born to ride.*"

Mary struggled to stand in the saddle. She prayed she'd have a better dismount than last time. She held her arms high as, to the fading of the guitar notes floating around them, Comanche backed up three steps. Her leg went numb again, and instead of hopping down gracefully, she crumpled to the dirt.

Sam raced to her, but she waved him away and managed to touch her toe to Comanche's knee ... As the final guitar note drifted into the atmosphere, Comanche took his bow.

Sam scooped her up. Weak and giddy with joy and excitement they tumbled to the dirt, hugging and kissing. "That was unbelievable ... But I think ..."

Fighting for breath she whispered, "Don't say it. I'll change the ending." She looked up at him. "This is the second time I've had a slight problem with my dismount."

Barbara ran to them and let herself fall to the dirt. "Holy cow, Mrs. Holt! I can't believe you! And Comanche! He is the most tremendous horse. How do you do that? I'll never be that good." She laid her head on Mary's lap, let out a loud, exaggerated sigh, and flopped her arms wide to let them fall in the dirt. "What a team! What a horse!" She rolled over to face Mary. "Could I ride him now?"

Caught off guard as she was, Mary couldn't deny those eager eyes, so with a smile, she nodded okay.

Barbara jumped up so fast Comanche lunged back. "Sorry, boy." She caught his rein and stepped up into the saddle. "Stirrups are a little short, but I'll be all right. Can I take him to the stream?"

Feeling very comfortable in her cowboy's arms, Mary had little concern at the moment. Not for Barbara, not for Comanche, not for herself. "Don't get his saddle wet, and no more than a trot."

A few moments after Barbara rode away singing "Born to Ride," Sam pulled Mary to her feet. "Are you steady now?"

She shot a disappointed eye his way. "I am."

Sam had to grin. "I reckon you're gonna have your hands full tryin' to get ol' Comanche back from that girl."

Chapter Thirty

Mary sat Comanche and waited while Sam tied the saddlebags to Bullet's saddle. She hadn't ridden for three days, not since the run-through of her routine, but by golly when she said she wanted a picnic he was more than ready. He knew how she loved their picnics under the trees by the swimming hole. Besides, he wanted his gal all to himself for a little while. He sensed she wanted him all to herself today, too.

"Been a while since our last picnic." Sam tied the final rawhide string on the saddlebag.

"We'll make up for it. I feel an all-afternoon picnic coming on. Not just an hour getaway. I'm keeping you till the moon comes up. Maybe longer."

He swung up on Bullet. "Sounds a whole lot like what I had in mind."

They rode down the trail by the barn and were soon in the cool shade of the old trees. Mary was chatting about the wildflowers, but Sam didn't feel much like talking. He was admiring his gal, how beautiful she was and how she sat a horse. No one he'd ever met sat a horse more gracefully than his Mary. Truth was, whatever Mary did, she did with a certain air. A certain poise. She was one of a kind, his Mary. Today, though, he noticed her tilting to the left as she rode along. He knew she was shifting her weight away from that bothersome right hip.

"Look there," she pointed. "A whole patch of wild asters. August is certainly their month. There seem to be more of them this year, don't you think? Sam, swing down and pick a few for our picnic-blanket centerpiece."

He stepped down from Bullet and used his pocket knife to harvest a sizable bouquet, tucking all but one gently inside his shirt. The one, he carried to Mary. She bent low, and he slipped it behind her ear, careful to adjust her hat so it wouldn't bend the flower petals too much. He drew another flower from his shirt and slid its stem under Comanche's bridle, behind his ear.

After remounting, he moved Bullet close to Comanche. As they had done so many times over the years, they rode happily down the trail, hand in hand. Before too long, they were at the water's edge where the trail flattened out and turned west. The sun was directly overhead, and its long rays sliced through the trees and danced on the water.

Soon the trail opened to the familiar meadow by the still pond they called the swimming hole.

While Mary prepared the blanket and the picnic lunch, Sam unsaddled the horses and threw together a rope corral under the trees. By the time he returned to the blanket, Mary had sandwiches ready and was sitting comfortably propped against a tree, fussing over the asters.

"What a lovely afternoon. I guess I wouldn't be the first wishing to save time in a bottle." She pulled him down beside her. "I wonder if there's another place in the whole world as lovely as this."

Sam laid his head in her lap. "I'm thinkin' most likely not, but a close second is on our ranch. The meadow by the lake in the mountain. The summer grass for the wild horses."

Mary nodded. "It is beautiful there, isn't it? It's been so long since I've been there I'd nearly forgotten how beautiful it is. You know what that place always reminded me of?"

"What?" He shifted to look in her eyes.

"Our first summer together. The lake we camped by in Wyoming. Remember? You proposed to me there." She pushed her fingers gently through his hair, then tapped the tip of his nose. "You proposed and ... I never wanted to tell you, but I always got lonely up there. I suppose it had something to do with you leaving for Vietnam. Silly, I guess, but I'll always remember that."

He jerked up. "Oh, Mary! I'm sorry!"

She pushed him down. "No, don't be sorry. There was nothing you could do. Then, when you came home and we got married right away ... Sam ..."

He sat up again. "What is it?" Tears slid from the corners of his eyes.

"We had a wonderful time of it all, didn't we?"

"We did! And we ain't done yet!" He threw his arms around her and pulled her tight.

"I need to ask a giant favor." She pushed him back— gently, but firmly—enough to see his eyes. "When I'm gone ..."

His gasp was loud and rough as he stared hard into her soft, wet eyes. "Mary! Can't we at least have a picnic without ..."

She waited for him to settle, then wiped his eyes. "It's not fair of me, I know. But ... I need to know ... I need to know that you'll be all right." She paused. "I can't die, thinking you won't be all right. I haven't been feeling too good these last days."

He wanted to jump up. He wanted to yell at her. Yell at God. He should yell at someone, shouldn't he? He fought it. He tried to fight the tears, too. But, he could only fight so many battles at a time. Of course, he wouldn't be all right. How could he possibly be all right?

How could he sit there, holding her frail body, and be so angry at her for asking that?

"I've made some plans, Cowboy." She tugged on his ear and scratched his stubble. "I've spoken with Fred Jones. He'll buy eight thousand acres and pay exactly enough to cover the mortgage and hospital bills."

This time he did jump up. "What? Why?"

She answered him calmly. "You know he's been after that grassland for five years. You hurt his feelings last year when you turned him down." She held her arms out and motioned for him to sit again. "It's not so hard for me to talk about dying now."

"Well it's mighty hard for me. Mighty hard!" He looked away. "I'm sorry ... I shouldn't have said that."

"I'll talk for both of us, then." She hugged him so tightly he could barely breathe. "When I close my eyes for the last time, I need to know our ranch is safe. I need to know you're safe. I need to know that what we've spent our lives building won't go to pay some awful, awful, overpriced, useless medical bills." She let go of him, searched his eyes. "Promise me, Sam. Promise me you'll take Fred's money." The sternness in her voice belied the softness.

He slammed his face into her chest and stayed there until he could breathe. "I promise." Sobs chocked him to silence.

Chapter Thirty-One

With the state fair less than three weeks away, Comanche looked as fit as any horse Mary had ever ridden. He loved being fussed over and stood perfectly still while Mary redid his braids and replaced the red ribbons on the ends. Sam had his hooves in picture-perfect shape. His coat shimmered in the sunbeams streaming in through the open barn doors. A close examination of the once clouded blue eye revealed no damage, and it sparkled like a jewel.

Chester was also in a state of euphoria, enjoying all the attention being lavished on him by Barbara. As on most mornings, Mary and Barbara were grooming their horses side by side. Barbara had copied Mary's color scheme, placing red ribbons in Chester's mane.

Although Barbara did more actual practicing in the saddle than Mary, they spent time together each morning. If Mary chose not to ride, as she'd begun to do more frequently of late, she coached from the judge's booth. She happily marveled at Barbara's increasing ability to dazzle any one of the guests who might be sitting on the fence watching.

Today just the two of them were in the small corral. Even Sam had gone along on the short ride with the guests to take hay to the mamma cows and calves. The grass had already begun to grow thin on most of the drier ranges, and hauling hay had become almost a daily job. At least until fall rains gave the grass a new growth spurt. Only Linda and Susan had stayed behind to prepare a good meal for everyone's return.

"You gonna ride today?" Barbara tightened the girth on Chester's saddle.

Mary stroked Comanche's neck. "I thought I'd just ride bareback for a little while. It's not very hot this morning, and I don't feel like sitting in the booth."

"Comanche's really beautiful. I think he likes when you ride bareback. You should do your routine bareback. That would be so cool!"

Mary tested her legs. Sitting bareback for a little while would be okay, but she feared she wouldn't be able to keep her balance through their entire number. The last few mornings she'd had enough trouble keeping her balance while walking. Yesterday, when no one was watching, she'd even used her cane.

"Barbara, a leg up, please." Once she was seated comfortably on Comanche, she announced with a girlish glee, "Let's play hooky today! You know that old routine inside and out. How about a ride to the stream?"

Barbara let out a squeal, leaped onto Chester, and galloped toward Mary and Comanche.

Fully aware of the foolishness of it all, Mary decided, against the advice of her gut, it was time for a race. She and Barbara had never raced together. While she knew Comanche had much greater speed than Chester, especially now that he was so fit, she also knew that if Barbara let him, Chester would give her one heck of a ride. The girl deserved that after all the hard work she'd put in these past few weeks.

"To the hard road and back," Mary yelled and turned Comanche loose.

He shot off and, in three strides, was in a flat-out run. Mary could hear Chester coming on behind. She gave Comanche her heels, and he found his next gear.

"Man, he's fast," Barbara yelled. "Yeehah! Go get 'em, Chester!"

Out of the corner of her eye, Mary could see Chester's nose. Nostrils flared, he wasn't going to make it an easy win for his stable mate. She felt the wind rush past her cheeks and heard it whistle in her ears. She held her arms high and let go a scream of delight. She felt like a teenager again, young and indestructible. Grabbing his mane with one hand, waving her hat with the other, she turned Comanche a few yards from the end of the lane and started for home.

Barbara took the turn a little wide and lost some ground.

Comanche must have felt Mary slip. He slowed just enough for her to re-grip his mane. Just enough for Chester to pull even.

Nose to nose, eyeball to eyeball, they thundered down the dusty lane to the barn. Mary lost her balance, but Comanche stayed under her and ran straight and smooth. Again, she re-gripped his mane and found her balance. Again, Chester gained.

A mere half-length ahead of Comanche, Chester stormed across the drive to the house. Barbara pulled up and jumped to the ground.

"Holy crap! I mean, wow, Mrs. Holt. Chester beat Comanche! I mean, we beat you! Bet you never woulda thought that in a million years!"

Mary let her head fall to Comanche's neck as her arms wrapped around him. "You won, fair and square. It's a good thing for a student to best her teacher sometimes." Her voice was soft and uneven.

ॐ≈ॐ≈ॐ≈ॐ

What Barbara saw in Mary's face sucked the wind from her chest. She ran to Comanche's side, gently putting her hand on Mary's leg. "Hey, you don't look so good. Want me to help you down or something?"

Mary stayed still, hugging Comanche's neck. "Not yet, but could you walk us to the barn? Inside. In the shade?"

Barbara backed up. "Are you sure? Wanna go in the house? You should probably go in the house. I think I should take you in the house."

Mary lifted a shaky hand and pointed to the barn.

"Okay, okay." Barbara led the two horses inside and stopped in the center aisle.

Mary raised her head. "Go into Morgan's room and drag his cot out here. Slide it into Comanche's stall and set it up against the wall."

She could see the weariness on Mary's face. Her eyes burned, her throat tightened. "I should call the hospital. I should get help. Or something. What, what do you want with a cot?"

"Barbara. Just. Do. It."

Sobbing, choking, she ran to Morgan's room, yanked open the door, grabbed the cot, and dumped the clothes stacked on it to the floor. "I'm coming, I'm coming. Hold onto his neck. I'll be right there." Her voice broke between sobs.

She glanced at Mary as she dragged the cot into the stall. Even in the shadows she could see how white her face had become. Barbara slammed the cot against the wall, then ran back to her. Mary's eyes were closed. Carefully, she led Comanche into his stall and eased him alongside the cot. "Mrs. Holt? Can you hear me? Please, say something. Mrs. Holt. Crap, say something!"

Mary opened one eye. "Young girls shouldn't swear. *Especially* ... not one of my students."

"I'm sorry. But ... are you all right now?"

"Help me slide down to the cot. I'll rest there awhile." Hugging Mary's legs, Barbara guided her down and helped her stretch out on the cot. She moved Comanche a step away. He came right back and nuzzled Mary's face.

"It's all right. I like his kisses. Could you fetch a blanket?"

Barbara raced to Morgan's room and ran back with a blanket, tucked Mary in, hugged her, and collapsed sobbing into the straw.

"Barbara." Mary's voice was so soft Barbara couldn't recognize it.

Barbara jumped up. "What ... What?"

"Can you find Sam? They're out with the mamma cows. Could you fetch him?"

"You want me to call the doctor? ... I know where he is. I've been there. What's wrong?" Barbara wiped her tears before they could fall. "You want me to call the doctor? Shouldn't I call the doctor? I really should call your doctor!"

"Take Chester ... cut across the range ... follow the ridge. It's only about three miles that way."

Barbara stamped her feet, then dropped down to her. "I should call the doctor."

"Tell your mother ... Then go get Sam. Please." She started for the stall door.

"Barbara," Mary whispered.

"Oh, my God!"

"No matter what anybody says ... *anybody* ... don't let them move me."

Falling to her knees, Barbara took her hand. "What do you mean?"

"Promise me."

For the first time, she kissed her. "I promise. But ..."

"Hurry, child," she whispered. "Please, find Sam."

She kicked Chester into a gallop and raced up the hill to the lodge. "Mom, Mommy! ... Mommy! Where are you?"

Susan and Linda ran from the lodge kitchen. "Barbara! What is—"

"Call the ambulance! Mrs. Holt's on a cot in the barn. In Comanche's stall. I'm going for Mr. Holt." She started to gallop away, then spun around and raced back to her mother. "She made me promise ..." She dragged her arm across her eyes. "She made me promise that no one would move her. Don't let them move her! Don't let them move her!" She kicked the willing sorrel hard and raced up the hill.

Across the ridge they flew. Barbara knew exactly where to go. She'd been there a week ago with Morgan. She knew why Mrs. Holt had told her to take Chester. The shortcut across the ridge was much faster, even on horseback, than the roundabout wagon road.

In five minutes of hard, fast riding, she'd covered half the distance. She could already see the cows, the wagon, and the horses. She kept at Chester and arrowed in a straight line for them. Down, away from the ridge, they raced across the flat. Why didn't they see her? They had to see her!

Finally, Sam started racing toward her, pushing Bullet hard. He reached her a half mile outside of camp.

His questioning eyes terrified her. She choked, "Mrs. Holt ..."

ನ∞ನ∞ನ∞ನ

The look on the girl's face was enough. He sent Bullet, demanding all the stallion had. His mind raced with fear, faster even than Bullet's flying hooves. He'd read Barbara's face. He'd read his own gut, too. Why had he let her talk him into going out today? The only day in the past three weeks he'd left her side. "Come on, Bullet. Run!"

Finally, they crested the hill above the lodge. He saw the ambulance. He beat Bullet mercilessly with his reins and galloped recklessly down the steep hill. They jumped the corral fence. Sam leaped from Bullet before the big horse's feet hit the ground. He pushed past the first EMT and ran into the barn.

Linda and Susan were holding each other and crying as they stared into Comanche's stall.

"Mary!" He shoved past them. His eyes flooded when he saw her on the cot. Her face was too white. He'd known what to expect. His gut had warned him. But ... he wasn't ready.

He didn't see the frail woman on the cot. His eyes could not, would not register that sight. His beautiful young bride lay before him on a red blanket, in the grass under the live oak.

Sam knelt by the cot and gently, with quivering fingers, pushed a straggling white hair from her eye. "Mary, how ..."

She brushed his wet cheek with a hand that felt too cold. "I don't wanna talk ... It'll make us feel sad ..."

I do, he kept inside. Mary, I do. Please, God, not yet. I'm not ready yet.

Even as he crawled onto the cot and felt her breath grow weaker, he pleaded with God. *Not yet, please, not yet.*

I want to talk. Mary, I want to talk with you. I want to laugh with you. Mary, remember when Callie caught us kissing in the ... Mary, I thought ... Mary. I can't say goodbye, not today. Please God, one more day. I'll be ready then, I promise.

She moved her lips.

He pushed his ear close to her mouth. "Sam, I love you ... I'll miss you, Cowboy. Goodbye ..."

Chapter Thirty-Two

Sam lay on the cot sobbing into Mary's neck, even as the EMTs tried to revive her. He never noticed them give up. After a while, he simply realized they were gone. Susan sat next to him in the straw. Comanche pushed his nose against Mary, time and time again.

Barbara had become inconsolable. Finally, Linda led her outside.

Robert came in and squatted at the foot of the cot. He put his hand on Sam's leg. "You gotta let 'em take her, Sam."

He shoved the hand away and smoothed Mary's hair. "She, uh, was gonna color it for the fair. Did she tell you? She told me. Dark brown. Like it was before." He lifted her hand, straightened her rings, and touched the tiny diamond. "I wanted to get her a bigger one for our twentieth anniversary." He cradled her hand in his palms and stroked his thumb over her knuckles. "She, uh, wouldn't hear it. Said this one ..." Sam turned red, begging eyes to Robert. "Do I keep it now, or leave it on her finger when we bury her? I don't know what you're supposed to do. Mary always told me. When I didn't know what to do, Mary always helped me."

Robert shook his head. "I don't know. I suppose you should do what you want." His voice was a weak whisper.

Sam held Mary's hand to his cheek, kissed it, and caressed it softly, as if it would melt away at any second. "She has the most beautiful hands, don't you think? Tiny hands, like a little girl. No matter what we were doing, she always kept her nails painted red. She knew I

301

loved that." He studied her face. Even now her crooked smile spoke to him.

With a shaky finger, he traced those fine, sweet lips. "Give us ten minutes. Just ten minutes, all right? Have them wait ten minutes. They can wait ten minutes, can't they? That'll be all right, won't it?"

"I'll tell 'em." Robert backed away, cleared the doorway, and closed the stall door.

Sam snuggled tight against his wife.

Comanche pushed his nose against Sam's cheek. Sam hung his arm over the paint's neck and ruffled his stubble against Mary's cheek. She'd always pretended to hate that. It made her laugh every time, though.

Suddenly he heard Anaba's voice, soft but clear. "No sad thoughts, my friend. This is important to her." Sam jerked up and looked around the stall. Seeing only Comanche, he laid his head back on Mary's neck.

He forced himself to remember happy, silly things. Their first summer rodeoing together, how she'd latched on to ol' Topper and never gave him up. Him sitting on the rails, watching her teach three-year-old Callie to ride. What a little hotshot Callie had been. Christmas, Mary's favorite time of year. The three of them walking hand in hand through the barn on Christmas Eve. While they listened to the horses chewing hay, Mary would tell the same story, every Christmas, about how all animals could talk on Christmas Eve.

He struggled to stand, then moved to Comanche and touched the pretty red ribbons in his braids. The last thing she'd done had been to tie those ribbons and run her horse. If only ... If only he could race her, one more time. Sam pulled Comanche's nose to his and kissed it. "Thanks, fella. Thanks for giving our gal one last run."

Turning to Mary, he leaned down, kissed her crooked smile, and scooped her up. He carried her to the door and kicked against it.

Robert swung it open, revealing a sea of sad faces. Everyone had come to the barn. Everyone was looking at him. Everyone was crying. He bit down hard on his lip to keep his legs from buckling and trudged to the ambulance door.

They cleared a path to the open doors. Sam looked away helping hands and carried his wife into the ambulance. He laid her down gently, covered her carefully, and gave her one more soft kiss.

He couldn't meet anyone's eyes as he stepped out of the back. Unable to speak, he smacked the closed door on the ambulance and nodded them away.

No one spoke as they watched it drive down the long lane. They circled around Sam. All at once Sam pushed his way through them and ran for the corral. Without a solid thought in his head, he swung up on Bullet and raced after the ambulance. They caught up to it halfway to the hard road and then slowed to a walk. At the end of the lane, he sat Bullet and watched until the ambulance was gone from sight. Then he turned and rode at a slow walk back to the house.

What now?

Everybody was still gathered at the barn when he rode in. Rusty approached Sam, hat in hand, unsteady eyes searching Sam's face. "You, uh, that is, Susan and I figured you and Robert should spend the night with us."

Sam leaned down and spoke quietly. "Take care of the guests, Rusty."

"Sure, boss but you should ..."

Sam swung down from his horse, pulled off his hat, and bowed his head. "Thank you all for being so kind. I'll bury Mary day after tomorrow. You're all welcome." He put his hat back on. "If it's all the same, I don't feel much like visitin' right now." His eyes focused briefly on Linda. "Thank you for all you've done for Mary."

Sam walked Bullet to the rail and tied him. He stood with his hands draped over the saddle and waited alone as the guests drifted up the hill to the lodge and cabins. When he could breathe again, he went to the tack room, gathered a fresh bedroll, and tied it to Bullet's saddle. Then he returned to the barn and headed toward the tool room. Muffled sobbing from Comanche's stall stopped him.

Turning, he saw Barbara lying on the cot, curled up on her side. "Here now, young lady, you should be with your mother. She'll be lookin' for you." He moved Comanche aside and squatted next to the cot.

Flush-faced and red-eyed, Barbara sat up, staring at him, and between gulps for air told him, "I was afraid of her at first. Did you know that?"

He patted her hand. "No. I figured you just didn't want to be here. Figured you had better things to do in the summer than hang around a bunch of grown-ups and horses."

She wiped her eyes and smiled a little. "Well, that too. But it wasn't like I thought. You guys ... I love her, Mr. Holt." She crumbled into his arms.

"Here, here." He held her close and fought as hard as he had ever fought to sound brave. "Mary is sure enough easy to fall in love with. Now she wants us to think of happy things. She made me promise not to think sad thoughts. Can you do that for her?"

She pulled back from him. "That's a stupid promise! How can you not think sad things when someone you love dies like this? I mean ... I thought she was getting okay ... Why did she die?" Barbara pounded on his chest. Over and over she pounded on him.

Wrapping his arms tight around Barbara, Sam drew her close and held her steady until she quit struggling and settled into an uneven sobbing. To himself he whispered, "I don't know why she had to die."

"She woulda won that ribbon, you know." She wiped her face on Sam's sleeve. "No way anybody could have ever beat her. No freaking way. She'd have won first place, for sure."

"I reckon that's a sure bet." He fought back some new tears of his own, reached behind, and stroked Comanche's leg. "You go on and keep up your practicing. You got a ribbon to chase yourself. Morgan and Susan can get you there." He saw the puzzled look. "I, uh, I might ..." He shook his head at her expression. "After the funeral, I'm ... well, I'm gonna disappear for a few days, and I wouldn't want you to miss any practice time." He stood and pulled Barbara to her feet. "We, Mary and I, expect you to do us proud at the state fair. Barbara, I've watched enough of your rehearsals to know, it's gonna be doggone hard for anybody to beat you, too."

"Where are you going?" She moved closer to Comanche. "He's gonna miss her, too, don't you think?"

Dang-it, girl. Sam tugged gently on a braid. "Yeah, young lady, I reckon he's bound to miss her, too." He gave Comanche a tender scratching on his neck, then a light pat. "You could do him a favor. Brush him good and turn him in the yard. Put Chester in with him for the day. Give 'em a few apples. While I'm gone, I'll thank you to give these two special attention, for Mary."

She hugged him hard. "You can count on me."

She went to the tack room for a brush. Sam scratched Comanche's special spot on his withers. "Yeah, I reckon we all got a pile of missin' coming up."

Sam went to the tool room and grabbed a pick and shovel.

Barbara stood in the aisle, brushing Comanche. "Hey, what are you going to do?"

Not sure how to answer, he simply stated the fact. "I'm going to dig Mary's grave."

Her response stunned him. "I think it's a pretty place up there."

He backed into the wall with a thud. "What?"

"I saw it. One day when we were riding, Mrs. Holt took me to your daughter's grave. We put some flowers there. Asters, I think she called them. We picked them for Callie. It's a real pretty place ... I could help you."

He shook his head. "I don't think so, but thanks. I ... I need to do this alone." Sam grabbed Bullet's reins and walked to the house. He choked a little at the bottom of the steps, then tied Bullet to the fence and reached to touch the steering wheel of her cart.

Intending to get a few supplies, enough for the night, anyway, he started up the steps. The porch froze him. Their swing, her violets, her cane by the door. Hanging onto the door for support, he forced himself to breathe, to think. It required all the effort he could manage to focus his thoughts. Finally, Sam pushed himself forward and went to the kitchen, thought about supplies, then ran to the living room, grabbed the top photo album, and bounded back outside.

On the way to the cemetery, he stopped at Callie's Summit, then rode on without another break until he reached the black iron fence. His plan had been to start right away, but as he stood over the spot, pick in hand, he simply couldn't swing it. The pick fell from his hands, and he collapsed onto Callie's bench. He held his head in his hands as the sun dropped lower in the sky.

At Bullet's snort, Sam looked up. The sun was a bright red spot in a fading horizon. He'd been sitting there for hours, unaware of the world around him. He unsaddled Bullet and turned him loose, spread out his bed roll, and began slowly leafing through the photo album. The evening shadows grew long, and soon it became impossible to see the images. He closed the book, got comfortable on his bedroll, pulled the blanket up to his chin, and found the moon. A silver sliver peeking up over the mountain. "Goodnight, Mary."

The sun had been working its way over the horizon for an hour already, but Sam hadn't wanted to start the day. Not this day. Not the first day he'd face without Mary. He pulled the blanket over his head to block the light. They'd done that sometimes when they'd played hide and seek with Callie. He almost had to laugh when he remembered how mad their spirited girl could get when they expected her to pretend she couldn't find them. Were they together now? Were they giggling at him, playing hide and seek from him? He imagined them huddling together under a blanket, giggling at each other, thinking they were so clever to hide out on him.

A loud rumbling made Sam sit up and throw back the blanket. He searched the rolling grassland and then saw the source. Coming slowly up the long hill toward him was Robert on his Harley. At first his heart jumped with gladness. Then his fist pounded his thigh. He resented the intrusion, even if it was made by Mary's brother. He stayed sitting and watched as Robert leaned his motorcycle against the black iron fence.

"We missed you at breakfast."

"Yeah, well. I wasn't hungry."

Robert looked around and saw the tools. "I thought I'd come give you a hand."

Sam pushed himself to his feet. "I reckon I'll dig my wife's grave. I meant to. I had always planned to, but ... I couldn't start. Couldn't take that first swing."

Robert put his hand on Sam's shoulder. "She's my baby sister." He grabbed the pick and swung open the gate.

Chapter Thirty-Three

Comanche and Chester stood harnessed to the flatbed wagon. Susan had taken charge of the flowers, and all the guests had pitched in. The wagon was draped in waves of asters, roses, and tiny red and purple violets. Morgan and Barbara had worked all day, shining the well-worn harness and altering the fit for Comanche and Chester. Even though Sam had wished for a private, quiet funeral, word had spread and the long lane was lined with cars from the barn all the way to the hard road. To his surprise, Sam found himself glad for the support, the well-wishers, and the expressions of condolence. After all, these folks all loved Mary, too. He'd have the rest of his life to grieve alone.

The hearse backed up to the wagon, and Robert, Rusty, Morgan, Fred, and Smiley slid Mary's coffin onto the wagon bed. Barbara sat with Sam on the wagon seat. After the hearse pulled away, Sam walked Comanche and Chester forward.

They started up the dirt trail that wound around the house, past the live oak that Mary loved so, and up the steep hill toward Callie's Summit. The guests, visitors, and friends all fell in behind them for the walk to the little family cemetery.

As they drove along, Sam admired the sky. She had a beautiful day. Not even a wisp of a cloud in a shiny blue sky. Just the touch of a breeze and a bright yellow sun. He smiled. She'd approve of the weather.

Riding beside them, single file, was a line of fifteen riders dressed in their finest show apparel. Susan had managed, in one night, to gather almost half of Mary's students.

Reverend Marshall led the group in song while Rusty and the other pall bearers placed Mary's coffin on the planks that straddled the grave. Sam sat on Callie's bench. He didn't feel like singing. He didn't really even hear the songs. When he thought of it, he noticed their mouths moving. He knew they were singing, but he didn't hear the songs. His mind was busy thinking about Mary, smelling her, kissing her, building the barn with her, raising dear little Callie with her, rodeoing with her. He couldn't think about burying her.

The singing stopped. Reverend Marshall started talking. Sam wanted to listen, but he couldn't hear him. He just sat and watched. Watched the Reverend, watched all the folks wipe their eyes. Watched Robert cry.

Sam wanted it over. He needed it to be over. He needed it to be over so he could stop thinking of her being dead and start remembering his Mary alive.

They started singing again while Rusty, Robert, Morgan, and Fred lowered her into the grave. He had made arrangements with Reverend Marshall to lead everyone away. He would stay behind, alone. He would shovel the dirt alone. It was hard to shake everyone's hand as they filed past him, but he forced himself through it. It helped that Robert, Rusty, and Susan stood with him. Finally, Rusty and Susan led everyone away. Robert stayed with him and they watched the people start the trek back to the house. He knew most of them were going to gather at the lodge. That was fine with him. Most of them would be gone by the time he finished here.

Sam turned to Robert. "I was plannin' on doin' this part alone."

Robert met his gaze. "She's my baby sister."

They took turns shoveling. Nothing more was said. When they finished, they gathered the flowers from the wagon and laid them across Mary's grave. Sam picked out a few and fashioned a bouquet for Callie's grave, too.

Chapter Thirty-Four

J ust as he had every other morning for the past week and a half, Sam stood at the edge of the sheer wall and gazed out over the vast desert floor below. The time spent here with Anaba had helped heal his heart some, but he knew it could never be whole again. He woke this morning to find himself alone in the old Navajo's camp. Anaba had told him he was going for a walk, maybe a week-long walk. He needed to gather things before the weather changed.

Even though Susan and Rusty had assured him they'd take care of the ranch, Sam had never intended to stay away this long. But each day, as he'd stood and looked toward the ranch, he hadn't been able to imagine going to bed, to their bed, without Mary. So he'd stayed another day with his old friend, and those days had begun to add up.

This morning a rider was coming toward the camp. Since he had no coffee to make, really had few provisions at all, and none that were worth offering, Sam stood and watched the rider approach. After a while he was fairly certain the rider was Rusty. He rubbed his hand across his face and pondered his beard. He took another look across the flatland to judge the distance of the rider. There would be time enough time to shave. He'd need to start a fire and boil water, but even so, there would be enough time.

"Yo the camp," Rusty called out as he rode into Anaba's clearing a half hour later.

Sam was putting the final touches on a new, smooth-faced look. "I'd offer a cup, but I have none to offer."

Rusty rode to the center of camp and swung down. "That's all right, boss. Didn't come for a visit. Came to trail you home."

"Trail me home?"

"Sure enough. It's time to come home. I reckon you lost track of time. It's been two days more 'an three weeks now."

Sam swore as the blade sank into his cheek. "Three weeks? Can't be." He wiped his face dry with the dirty shirt he'd been using as a towel.

Rusty settled into the lone wooden chair and watched his horse pick at the few short blades of brown grass. "Yes, sir, and I'll tell you more. They all left yesterday for the state fair, and if you don't get there, I predict there'll be one mighty disappointed young lady."

"Barbara. What about the others?"

"Everybody's gone home now, except Barbara, her momma, and Robert."

"Robert stayed on?" Sam dumped his wash basin on the fire, then stomped it out.

"Sure did. He was a mighty big help, too. Took close to a week to get Barbara back on Chester. All she wanted to do was sit with Comanche and cry. She didn't eat for two days. Susan, Morgan, and her mamma tried to help her, ya know. She was powerful put out by the way you rode off and left her. Says if it wasn't for you, she'd have never got on a horse in the first place."

Sam dropped his face into his hands and shook his head. "Blast it. I talked to her some. Told her to keep up the practicing." He looked up. "I thought she understood. I told her I'd, we'd, Mary and me, be countin' on her to put on a good show. I'm sure sorry, Rusty. Shouldn't have left you with all that."

"Ah, well. You just be sure to make it up to her at the fair. She's got a real show in store for you, boss. Robert snapped her out of it all right. Claims he was practicing for her routine, setting off fireworks, ya know. Dang fool had a bunch misfire. Set the barn roof on fire. You should'a seen that young girl tear into him.

Poor Robert, he run away so fast I thought he'd get clean to Mexico before he quit. That put her back on the right road, though. She's been rehearsin' every day, most of the day, ever since. Funny thing about Robert, though."

"What's that?"

Rusty shook his head. "In all the years he's been settin' off those fireworks, I never once heard of him makin' a mistake like that."

Sam tightened Bullet's girth, swung into his saddle, and shot Rusty an ear-to-ear grin. "Me neither, Rusty. Me neither." He looked up at the sun. "Let's ride! We have a fair to get to!"

🦋🦋🦋🦋🦋🦋

It had been four years since Sam had driven through the main gates at the state fair grounds. It sure seemed bigger than he remembered. Louder, too. It didn't take long to find their rig. Parked with all the new big duallys and goosenecks, his old green Chevy and rusty two-horse trailer stood out like a flea-bit hound at a high class dog show. He smiled when he looked at it. It might not be the ugliest rig on the grounds, but it would sure enough put up a good fight for second place in the ugly division.

Chester and Comanche were happily munching hay in the rope corral set up next to the trailer. Sam was glad they'd brought Comanche. He knew that paint mustang loved a good fair, and even if he wasn't competing, well, he'd get a kick out of being there all the same.

Barbara ran to the jeep and swung the door open before Rusty had it fully stopped. "Mr. Holt! Rusty found you!" She grabbed his arm and dragged him from the jeep. "Hurry up! Come here, look at Chester and Comanche. See? I've put new ribbons in their braids.

315

Well, Susan helped me ... and Mom, too. Aren't they beautiful? See? Look, I did Chester's in green, 'cause my costume is green, well, except for the vest and other silver stuff. Look at Comanche. I did his ribbons in red, like Mrs. Holt likes. And look at his hooves. I painted them red, too. She'd like that, I'll bet. Cool huh?"

He grabbed a fence post for support. "He ... you bet, Barbara. They look all set for a show." He stopped for a second and thought about apologizing for his long absence but reasoned it was better left alone. She was all excited and charged up to go, just the way she should be. "Yes, ma'am, you've done a mighty fine job with these two. I'm proud as I could ever be about anything or anybody, young lady."

Susan walked out from behind the trailer. "How about a sandwich? That's about all we have time for." She pointed to the setting sun. "Musical freestyle starts in half an hour. You won't get to see Robert until after the show. The fair committee asked him to do all the fireworks this year. I heard Smiley had something to do with it."

Barbara stood on her tiptoes and kissed Sam's cheek. "I'm so glad Rusty found you. I was gonna win you a ribbon anyhow, but I'm real glad you're here." She winked at Susan. "Me and Morgan have a very special surprise for you. Well, I gotta go get ready. Oh yeah, we have a special seat reserved for you, too." She pointed to her mother, who had just walked over from the bleachers. "You see he gets to it!"

Five minutes, and a half-eaten sandwich later, Susan and Linda each took a hand and guided Sam through the crowd to seats roped off with red ribbon in the center of the bleachers. He had tried to stop and say howdy to his friends as he'd passed them along the way, but those women just shoved him along.

The announcer was a new fella. Sam didn't recognize his voice, but the man did a good enough job of finishing the calf-roping and entertaining the audience with silly stories while the tractors drove back and forth preparing the ring for the musical routines that were about to start.

"Ladies and gentlemen, my favorite moment of our state fair is about to begin. There's always plenty to do here at the fair, and there's always plenty of excitement here at the rodeo grounds, but what these ladies do each year with their musical routines is simply magic. This year we have seven contestants, and I'm sure it'll be a night to remember. First up, traveling all the way from Maricopa County is last year's champion, Sally Barton, riding her beautiful quarter horse, Rose, to Toby Keith's, "American Soldier." She dedicates this ride to her son, David, who left for Afghanistan three weeks ago. May God keep him safe."

The speakers blared, the darkening sky exploded into colors with the first volley of fireworks, and Sally galloped Rose around the arena. Sam's heart pounded as hard as the opening booms of Robert's heavens-lighting display. The sky settled back into darkness, and the arena lights took over. Sally performed flawlessly to the music, as spectacularly as Sam remembered she always had. Her routine ended in perfect time with the final notes of the song. She took a bow and led Rose to the exit as the crowd cheered.

"What a ride, folks," the announcer broke in. "I guess it's not hard to see why she's the reigning state champ, but hold on to your hats! Up next is a tough competitor from Dolan Springs, Frankie Tyler and her mustang, Belle. You might remember them running barrels yesterday. She dedicates this ride to her husband."

Sam watched but found himself searching behind the gates, trying to get a glimpse of Barbara. The fireworks gave enough light at the start of each ride to see behind the chutes where she would be waiting, but so far he'd had no luck. Linda had told him that she'd be the last to ride, so while he watched each performance leading up to hers, his eyes were leveled as much behind the arena as in it. He hadn't been this excited to watch a ride in ... too long.

"All right, ladies and gents. We've come to our final contestant. I'm told she has quite a show in store for us tonight. Please welcome Barbara Sherman riding Chester to Martina McBride's hit, "Independence Day." She dedicates this ride to her mom because Barbara says, 'She's like, independent now!' "

Linda covered her face to hide her embarrassed laughter. The thunderous roar from Robert's display made her, and everyone else, look up.

Chester pranced into the arena on cue as the music started. Sam had not seen Barbara's new green costume. He smiled and nodded approval to Linda and Susan. He knew the routine because he'd been on hand when she'd learned all the basic moves from Mary. Sam turned his eyes skyward for an instant and found the rising moon. "You watchin' this, Mary?"

Barbara guided Chester around the arena to the music, hitting every lead change, every direction change, never missing a single choreographed step. She finished with a terrific spin that ended exactly on the song's final note. She jumped from Chester, took her bow, and with the audience yelling, ran out of the arena leading Chester through the gate.

Sam threw his hat, squeezed Linda and Susan in a group hug, and started down the bleachers. Susan grabbed his arm and stopped him. "Hold on."

He turned and shrugged. "What? By golly, there's a young lady down there who needs a great big pat on the back."

Rusty met Sam's questioning gaze. "Hold on a second, boss."

Smiley's voice broke over the loudspeaker. "Ladies and gentleman, this is Smiley Hudson takin' over the microphone for a bit. Now what you all just saw was a remarkable performance by a young lady, who up until a few months ago had never sat a horse. I think she deserves another round of applause. Let her hear it, folks!"

The crowd obliged and sent up a roar that took Smiley a full minute to quiet. "A lot of you folks know Mary and Sam Holt. Heck, some of you and your kids learned how to perform from Mary." His voice broke. "Barbara ... Barbara was Mary's final student. Mary passed on a few weeks ago." He choked. "Folks, she wanted real bad to be here today." Smiley cleared his throat. "So, here is Barbara Sherman one more time, on Mary's horse, Callie's Comanche, dancing to MaryAnn Kennedy's, 'Born To Ride.' Sam, Barbara says this is for you and Mary."

Sam fell to his knees.

Rusty grabbed Sam's shirt and pulled him up as a massive glittering yellow ball shot up in the air. Barbara galloped Comanche through the yellow glare. She was wearing Mary's red and silver costume. She stopped and faced Sam, held her hat high in a salute to him, then reached with her toe and tapped Comanche on his leg. He bowed. The crowd jumped to their feet. The speakers boomed.

Sam collapsed.

"Come on, boss." Rusty steadied him. "She's gonna ask you how she did, so you'd better watch." Rusty leaned into Sam's ear. "She practiced all day, every day, while you were gone. Almost killed Morgan. I think he's afraid of her now."

Sam jammed the heels of his hands into his eyes, smeared away the tears, and stood on his seat to watch. He stretched tall to see over the man in front of him, who was standing on his own seat, waving his hat and yelling at the top of his voice.

The speakers blasted the tune. *"Manes flowin', tails held high—I knew I was born to ride."* On cue Barbara changed direction and increased speed. Then she slowed for the figure eights, side passing, and gliding all the way across the arena as smooth as any ballroom dancer.

"I was born to ride—like a bird was born to fly." Comanche broke into a gallop, dashed across the ring, turned a figure eight, and eased into a breathtaking extended trot. *"The way they move is poetry."* Flying lead changes with each stride. Comanche was perfect. On cue and light as air.

The tempo picked up again. *"The world looks better from the back of a horse."* Barbara cued for a spin, a second's pause, a flat-out gallop the length of the arena, and finally a tremendous sliding stop.

Comanche stood tall. *"That's the way I'm gonna spend my life— 'cause I was born to ride."* The music faded.

Barbara stood in the saddle, held her arms high and wide, waved the crowd into a frenzied applause, then jumped to the ground and touched her toe to Comanche's knee. He bowed. They took their bows in all four directions. Then she tapped Comanche on the chest and led him skipping out of the arena.

Sam fell into his seat. He heard Smiley trying to quiet the crowd, but Barbara controlled the moment. She galloped back into the ring and ran Comanche flat-out around the arena before backing out the gate again.

Linda pushed past Susan and Rusty, jumped on Sam, and smothered him in hugs and kisses. "Oh thank you, Sam. Thank you, thank you, thank you!"

"I sure feel like I should be thanking you for lending us that spunky girl of yours." He used his sleeve to wipe his eyes again, then turned to Susan and Rusty. "Excuse us. I reckon we got a young lady to congratulate."

Sam dragged Linda along as they pushed their way through the crowd, out of the arena, and around the back to where Sam's old green Chevy and rusty two-horse trailer were home base for a spirited young girl and a couple of very special horses.

She saw them coming and broke into a full-steam-ahead run. She charged yelling and screaming headlong into Sam, knocking him to the ground. Then she sat on his chest while her mother demanded she stop acting insane.

"Oh, Mom, I am insane. Insane with excitement and happiness and … I don't know what." She remained firmly planted on Sam's chest and grabbed his hat and plopped it on her own head. "Oh, wow, Mr. Holt. I was so worried. But Comanche, he freaking knows everything! Chester's good, too, of course. But Comanche! Wow, he is way, way awesome! You know what?"

Sam had to laugh. "What?"

"I don't even care if I get a ribbon. Not one little bit." She looked at her mother, then back to Sam. "Were you surprised? Did I make you and Mary proud? I know she was watching. She told me she would."

He pulled her down and hugged her tight. "Oh, yeah. You made us *very* proud."

When Sam caught his breath, he rolled out from under her and pulled her to her feet. "And I'm pretty sure you can count on a ribbon for your top-notch performance."

Barbara searched his face. "Really? You think I'll win a ribbon? That would be awesome. I mean, even fifth. I don't need like first or anything … So you really are proud of me? Freaking awesome!"

Smiley's voice rang out over the speakers. "The judges have made their decisions. First place, Bonnie Ritter riding Dallas. Second place, Barbara Sherman riding Callie's Comanche. Third place, Barbara Sherman riding Chester. Fourth place, Sally Barton riding Rose. And the fifth place ribbon goes to Jane Shelby, riding Skye-Blue. Ladies, please ride your horses to the center and accept your ribbons."

Barbara tackled her mother. "Holy Cow, Mom! Did you hear that? Two ribbons!" She jumped up to swing on Sam's arm. "I never even thought about that! I was competing Chester for myself and all. I only did Comanche for Mrs. Holt and you. Holy Cow, two ribbons. I think my head is gonna explode!"

Sam tugged her along. "You'd better hold on to it. You need to ride out there and get your ribbons."

"Yeah. Oh yeah! Who do I ride? What do you do when this happens?"

Sam shook his head and winked at Linda. "Not sure. I never had this happen to anybody I know."

"Oh, I don't know." She turned to her mother. "Mom, you ride Chester for me. I'll ride Comanche." She looked Sam dead in the eye. "You get on behind me on Comanche."

He smiled and shook his head. "No, you go on, young lady. This is your moment. You and your mother's. You earned it. I want to tell you, Barbara, that was one humdinger of a show you just put on. I'm as proud and grateful as any man could ever be. And young lady, I know Mary's bustin' out with pride right now, too."

Barbara poked a stiff finger in Sam's chest and kept jabbing as he backed away. "You are riding with me, Mr. Holt! I wouldn't have a ribbon at all if it wasn't for you!"

Chapter Thirty-Five

Noon, Christmas Eve that same year.

It had been snowing for more than a day, but Sam was making the trip anyway. He saddled Comanche in the barn. On bad days like this, he and Mary had always liked to keep the stalls full. Older horses first, then whoever it took to fill the barn. The horses didn't really mind being outside, but it kept the barn warm. Besides, how would he do his Christmas Eve walk through the barn if there were no horses in there talking to each other?

As he led Comanche out to mount up, he took another look at the ribbons on Comanche's and Chester's stalls. The two new big ones stood out. He'd sent them home with Barbara. She'd won them, after all. She'd sent them back with his Christmas package. Said she'd showed them to everybody who mattered, and she wanted the horses to have them. Darn kid had baked him three dozen chocolate chip cookies, too. "Good for dunking in coffee," her note said.

Just before he slid the barn door closed on his way out, Sam turned back. "You horses keep it warm in here and don't start talkin' till we get back. Wouldn't want Comanche to miss any good gossip."

The snow was nearly as deep as Comanche's chest, but if he kept to the wind-blown areas, he could walk mostly on bare ground. It did appear to be a whole lot colder than he'd planned on. He kept on up the hill, over the ridge, and past Callie's Summit, on down the other side, and finally up the last hill toward the little cemetery. The half-hour ride took him over an hour today in the wind and blowing snow.

Finally, Sam saw the naked dogwood tree and the old black iron fence.

He swung down alongside the fence, tied Comanche so he wouldn't wander away in the blowing snow, and tossed a blanket over his rump. He kicked the snow away from the gate, forced it open, then sat down in the snow on Callie's bench and stared at Mary's grave.

"Don't feel too much like Christmas without my gal. Figured I'd come visit awhile. Been missin' you somethin' awful. Wasn't countin' on this blasted storm, though. I brought Comanche. He misses you about as much as I do, I reckon.

"Got a bunch of home-baked chocolate chip cookies from that little hotshot Barbara in the mail yesterday. She sent along her ribbons, said they belong here with Chester and Comanche. I already hung 'em with the others. She sent the cutest dang card, too. She says she wants to come work here next summer. Wants to help wrangle ... I was wonderin' ... do you reckon I should warn Morgan?"

About the Author

Dutch Henry lives with his wife of 40 plus years on their small farm in Appomattox Va. He has written columns for several equine magazines, published hundreds of articles and authored seven books. He enjoys trail riding in the deep woods near his home, exploring and enjoying God's beauty from horseback.

Horses have been part of Dutch's life, most of his life. As a foster child growing up on a farm, he became attached to the horses. After acquiring horses of his own, he worked with trainer Diane Sept to rehabilitate Tennessee Walking horses from show ring to trail. He also competed in long- distance endurance and competitive riding.

A lifelong birdwatcher, Dutch volunteered 20 years for the Parks Department, leading bird walks, and installing and teaching to maintain bluebird trails. He has worked with horses, helping at-risk youth discover their inner beauty and strength, and teaches equine posture exercises to horse owners. Dutch loves God, horses, dogs, cats, wild birds and wildflowers, and the joy and wonderment they give so many.

You can reach Dutch Henry at dutchhenry@hughes.net

He loves to hear from folks.

More Books by Dutch Henry

The Tom Books

Tom Named by Horse

From the Banks of Little Bear Creek

The Saturday Books

A Dog Named Saturday

A Dog Named Saturday Coloring Book

Saturday Loved Christmas

Coming Soon

Saturday Goes to Chincoteague

A friend, Ron Secoy, was so moved by Mary and Sam's story he wrote the following poems. Ron is a cowboy poet who lives in Central High OK. He has written three books of cowboy poetry:

COWBOY PSALMS
THE COWBOY, THE CREATION AND THE CREATOR
COWBOY AT HEART

He can be found on Facebook. Requests for his books should be sent to rsecoy@wildblue.net

WE'LL HAVE THE SUMMER

We'll have the summer
The fun and tears, sorrow and laughter
Like no other summer
Like none that will come ever after

We'll have each other
The cowboy and his cowgirl
One more chance to ride
And give our hearts a whirl

We'll have the horses
That challenge us to be great
Comanche and Chester, Bullet and Ruth
Companions that really rate

We'll have the land
Arizona, the ranch, the range
Tough and wild like us
But beautiful still the same

We'll have our friends
They'll be here to see us through
Both the good and bad
To strengthen and comfort me and you

We'll have our neighbors
To help us carry the load
To ease the burden a little
Of the things that have to be sold

We'll have our guests
To give us things to do
Showing them a type of life
That's always pulled us through

We'll have the roundup
Bring them mustangs in
Cut out a few noble ones
Then let them go again

We'll have the rodeo
Kinda like it all begun
Even if it was our last
This summer our best run

We'll have the picnic
Unlike any we've ever had
One more time together
Facing the things to make us sad

We will have the summer
And you know that when it's through
Remember our time together

And how much I love you

MARY

Mary never half did anything
Limited only by herself
She was a lady through and through
Not a doll to be placed on the shelf

Her first love was always her horses
But she never cared for a pony ride
She demanded much out of her mounts
Reflected by trust, relationship and pride

She had patience and a gentle hand
But believed in excellence and progress
Guided, directed and fine tuned
But wouldn't let them slide or regress

She could pick the special horse
Even from a group of the best
Looked for spirit and smarts
The stand out among all the rest

That's how she picked Sam
Though he thought he picked her
She liked spunk and devotion
And someone not easy to deter

Her life was about balance
Work, play and love real hard
Treasure friends and be one

Give an inch and she'd give you a yard

The balance was broken by cancer
Though she went at it head on
Just another competition
She'd finish and do it strong

The battle took all her stamina
Fought until she had little to give
There was only time left to die
Not so much time left to live

But Mary figured she'd give
The things she had inside
Until the summer was over
And she could no longer ride

To her friends she gave bravery
The kind that accepts the score
She'd win through unselfishness
Give until she couldn't give no more

To Sam she gave one more season
And a chance to live their life
Keep his pride and the ranch
He'd built with his wonderful wife

To Barbara she gave a prize
Of learning to push beyond pain
Leaving the personal suffering behind
Giving it all for a much better gain

Fired that teenager with confidence
And the desire to just compete
Put all herself into a pursuit
Making life rewarding and complete

To herself she gave the summer
Just to be shared despite the grief
Not allowing her own departing
To be stolen by the cancerous thief

SAM

Bull riding or bronc busting
Never caused him to be scared
Nor rounding up the wild mustang herd
Fearlessly he did most anything he dare

Sam Holt never knew any fear
But just maybe a time or two
And for months during the war
But that was eventually through

His fear wasn't of the action
In that place so far away
He was afraid it would rob him
Of that special wedding day

Sam loved Mary from day one
When he saw her on that horse
Followed her shamelessly
Without regret or remorse

Then there was another time
With fear he was beset upon
A day of both pride and fear
When baby Callie was born

Barely used to being a husband
When given a brand new role
How would he be as a father?
Good hopefully, but he didn't know

Sam had ranched and rodeod some
Knew the hardship of cowboy life
Made downright enjoyable
By his precious daughter and wife

When hard times came calling
They weren't without alarm
They'd just hang on to each other
Weathering every storm

Now there was something
That just hit too close to home
Threatening to rob him
Of everything he owned

Yep, he loved the ranch
All the hands, the horses, too
Cherished his way of life
And all the things he could do

Callie had been such a blessing
A younger Mary in a lot of ways
Pleasure and joy she brought them

Until the end of her short days

They laid Callie to rest
In a shady and peaceful place
With a bench nearby
As they envisioned her sweet face

Time went on for Sam and Mary
Bravely for just the two
They battled her cancer
Courageously seeing it through

Sam then faced the awful prospect
Didn't know how to make it go away
This was a time to cowboy up
Toughing it out day by day

He'd have to be strong for Mary
'Cause her grit was draining away
Couldn't face the prospect of her demise
Wouldn't know how to live on that day

The war waged within him
One that ends with a broken heart
One he could not change or win
Tearing him all apart

He visited the old Indian
To try to make sense of it all
The sage couldn't calm his fear
Sam didn't believe what he saw

Mary gave life all its meaning
Promised the summer was there to give

Sam would have to face the truth
Mary just had the summer left to live

It was her dying strength
Upon which Sam would rely
Promised to do as she wanted
Live for him and Comanche, and then die

So Sam faced that last fear
The way he had lived his life
Cowboy strong and steady
Loving Mary, his true and brave wife

CPSIA information can be obtained
at www.ICGtesting.com
Printed in the USA
LVHW080717110922
728091LV00024B/485

9 781734 968309